PENGUIN BOOKS

A Sea of Flames

Walter Lucius was the writer's pseudonym for TV director and documentary maker Walter Goverde. His striking thriller debut, the Heartland Trilogy, received fantastic responses from both readers and critics with rights for the trilogy sold to eight countries. The first part, *Butterfly on the Storm*, was awarded the Schaduw Prize for the best thriller debut and was nominated for the Prix du Polar Européen. Walter Lucius passed away in July 2021.

WALTER LUCIUS

A Sea of Flames

The Heartland Trilogy
Book 3

Translated from the Dutch by
Lorraine T. Miller and Laura Vroomen

PENGUIN BOOKS

PENGUIN BOOKS

UK | USA | Canada | Ireland | Australia
India | New Zealand | South Africa

Penguin Books is part of the Penguin Random House group of companies
whose addresses can be found at global.penguinrandomhouse.com.

First published 2021
001

Set in 9.25/12.5pt Sabon LT Std
Typeset by Jouve (UK), Milton Keynes
Printed and bound in Great Britain by Clays Ltd, Elcograf S.p.A.

The authorized representative in the EEA is Penguin Random House Ireland,
Morrison Chambers, 32 Nassau Street, Dublin D02 YH68

A CIP catalogue record for this book is available from the British Library

ISBN: 978-1-405-92145-9

www.greenpenguin.co.uk

For Jan

Far away
So close

The traveller recognizes the little that is his,
discovering the much he has not had
and will never have.

Italo Calvino, *Invisible Cities*

Central characters

Raylan Chapelle, war correspondent with *The New York Times*

Farah Hafez, journalist with *Algemeen Nederlands Dagblad (AND)*

Paul Chapelle, foreign correspondent with *Algemeen Nederlands Dagblad (AND)*

Other characters

Isobel Vallent, artist

Aadel Gailani, attorney general of the Department for the Organization and Defence of the Interests of Afghanistan and later interior affairs minister

Helai Durani, Afghan public prosecutor

Grigori Michailov, director of the Russian Cultural Centre in Kabul

Parwaiz Ahmad, director of the National Museum of Kabul; old friend of Farah's family

Askan Vaziri, editor of the newspaper of the youth wing of the People's Democratic Party of Afghanistan (PDPA)

Mason Williams, American gunnery sergeant

Patrick Goldwater, commander of the International Security Assistance Force (ISAF)

Sam Harcourt and *Wagner Mendosa,* operatives of the US Central Intelligence Agency (CIA)

Ashraf Hafami, commander of the Afghan National Guard

Ahmad Shakoor, Afghan secretary-general of the interior

Edward Vallent, editor-in-chief *Algemeen Nederlands Dagblad (AND)*

Nehal, female taxi driver

Sekandar, bacha bazi victim

Anya Kozlova, journalist with *Moskva Gazeta*

Roman Jankovski, editor-in-chief *Moskva Gazeta*

Alexander Arlazarov, director of the Counter-Terror Unit of the Federal Security Service of the Russian Federation (FSB)

Sergey Kombromovich, press director of Moscow State University

Valentin Lavrov, CEO of AtlasNet

PART ONE
A Sea of Flames

I
Farah

2009

Her right index finger rested on a mountain top. A shred of mist slid past and broke the illusion. Since the Ariana Afghan Airlines plane had begun its descent, she hadn't stopped staring out of the window. Sometimes with one eye closed and the other trained on the foothills of the Himalayas, from behind which she saw the sun rise.

She felt as excited as a child.

She'd made her decision on impulse. Guided solely by her intuition. Without verifying whether the man who'd phoned her in the dead of night really was who he claimed to be, the Afghan ambassador to the Netherlands. Yes, it was late, but it was important, he'd said. It was about an issue dating back decades. A matter that had never been resolved. His voice sounded as diplomatic as the language he used.

She thought of the first words on the note that had been added to the bundle of yellowed love letters written to her mother long ago: *The past sneaks up on us like a shadow.*

That shadow had now caught up with her.

It had taken thirty years. Starting from the moment she'd stood in the garden of the presidential palace, with butterflies fluttering all around her. A little girl, doggedly waiting for her father. She'd looked up in surprise: how could there be thunder in a clear blue sky? That's when she saw the three black dots in the distance. They approached buzzing like wasps, and growling they grew into fighter jets poised to strike.

I'm talking about the Saur Revolution of 1978. Prominent victims, including the then president, his entire family and ministerial team, have not been located until now ...

The man's voice at the other end of the line had become all but inaudible to her. The noise of explosions and shots inside her head drowned everything else out. Once again, she became that little girl running into the palace, dashing through the corridors, faster than her legs could carry her, so fast she appeared to be lifting off from the ground. Through a cloud of dust she flew across the carpets of immense rooms, through marble hallways where shots rang out, where fleeing men and women fell down and lay motionless. She raced past them, ducking into a corner, taking cover behind pillars, fleeing towards the light. Like in a dream.

And that dream had haunted her. For more than thirty years.

'A mass grave has been discovered a few kilometres outside Kabul.'

She searched for words in the long silence that followed.

'You found my father,' she eventually stammered.

'Dental records have shown that the person in question must be former Interior Affairs Minister Aadel Gailani. It took some effort, but we've finally managed to find you, his daughter.'

At that moment she hadn't asked herself how the authorities could have made the connection between her and her father. In fact, she hadn't asked herself any questions. All she knew was that there were only five days between the phone call and the ceremonial reburial of the former president, his family and her own father in Kabul.

Five days to bridge thirty years.

That same evening, her friend and colleague Paul Chapelle had been furiously pacing around her flat on Nieuwmarkt. 'It's too dangerous there. Two female journalists were killed last week. After Jakarta you shouldn't be putting your life on the line again!'

Paul was not the only one who'd tried to stop her. She could see the enormous figure of her mentor, Editor-in-chief Edward Vallent, looming before her again, his voice chillingly calm, full of unspoken concern, not to mention fear. 'What you went through in Jakarta and Moscow takes a normal human being years to deal with. You're not going!'

4

Her intuition told her to go. She'd made up her mind as soon as the phone call with the ambassador had come to an end.

The plane bored through an ash-grey cloud cover. The sound of the engines changed. The speed decreased. She heard the landing gear being lowered. A valley full of minuscule buildings, winding roads and miniature cars appeared below her. It was enough to bring tears to her eyes.

She was home again.

The wheels hit the runway with a dull thud. The braking force produced a low, loud roar. The aircraft took a left turn off the runway and taxied towards the terminal. Passengers were getting up to open the overhead lockers. Over the intercom the pilot urged everyone to stay seated with their seat belts fastened. A few passengers ignored the request. Two flight attendants strode into the aisle and told them to sit down. They did so nervously, revealing this wasn't the normal routine. Especially when one of them closed the curtain again to separate business from economy class.

She looked outside and saw that the stair car heading towards the plane was followed by a black armoured four-wheel drive with flashing lights. The stairs were placed against the aircraft, and the four-wheel drive parked at the bottom of it. There had to be an important passenger in business class, who would be escorted out first. That seemed like a plausible explanation, but it didn't explain why the flight attendants kept peering nervously down the economy-class aisle. Farah stared at them. One of the attendants averted her gaze a bit too quickly.

The pilot's voice came over the intercom: 'Cabin crew, doors to manual.'

Outside, two men in civilian attire got out of the four-wheel drive. Black shades, blue suits. They clearly meant business as they strode up the stairs.

She loosened her black headscarf a little and kept her eyes on the four-wheel drive when from the corner of her eyes she noticed the curtain in the aisle being pulled aside. The men appeared in economy class. The one in front, with closely cropped grey hair, took off his shades. He was followed by his colleague, who was olive-skinned with dark, slicked-back hair.

She was sitting three-quarters down the aisle, in a window seat, at least twenty rows from the men. She stared outside again. Cargo platforms were approaching the aircraft.

The man with the grey crewcut was only ten rows away now. When this was reduced to five it looked as if he had his eye on *her*. Her heart started racing. She kept staring out of the window. The man slowed down and came to a halt beside her row.

'Ms Hafez?' He sounded friendly enough, but the question still made her feel uncomfortable.

She turned to face him. 'Yes?'

He held his ID pass in his outstretched hand.

'My name is Agent Sam Harcourt. This is my colleague Wagner Mendosa. On behalf of the local authorities we'd like to ask you a few things. You have the right to remain silent and you are entitled to consult a lawyer prior to this questioning. If you prefer not to conduct the conversation in English, a Dutch-speaking interpreter will be provided. Would you please come with us?'

That final sentence was formulated like a question, but she realized it was an order. She remained seated, incredulous. 'What's going on?'

'We advise you to cooperate and come with us.'

Reluctantly she rose to her feet. The young husband and wife beside her anxiously pulled up their legs and pressed their backs into the seats. In the aisle she was hemmed in by Harcourt and his colleague.

'My hand luggage.'

Mendosa opened the overhead locker she indicated.

'The black shoulder bag. My laptop's in it.'

With a sturdy swing of his arm, he removed the leather laptop bag and held on to it.

'Please follow my colleague,' Harcourt said.

The flight attendants had gathered in the small space outside the cockpit. They did their best to give her and the two men a friendly smile but couldn't manage much more than a grimace.

Outside, she paused at the top of the stairs, tightened her scarf around her head and looked at the façade of the old terminal, which she remembered from her childhood. On an enormous billboard a man in front of a vast green valley extended his arms to her.

She read his words: 'Welcome to Afghanistan, the land of the brave.'

2
Raylan

1968

Raylan Chapelle was standing on Saigon's Lam Son Square, where young monks were chanting plaintively and burning incense. An old monk sat down on the stone in the lotus position. The sun shone on his bald head, which shimmered with the gasoline poured over him. The monks' singing sounded mythic and serene but took on a sinister character when the old man pulled a matchbox from under his orange robe. Raylan wanted to run towards him, but three young monks physically blocked his way.

The lit match dropped into the old monk's lap. Unwavering, without a single cry of pain, he was consumed by a sea of flames.

Raylan felt a hand gently nudge his shoulder.

'Sir, please.'

The heat of the fire forced the monk's body backwards against the asphalt. The monks who were circled around him sang louder to drown out the sound of the flickering blaze.

'Wake up, sir.'

The monotonous hum of aircraft engines filled his ears. Confused, Raylan opened his eyes. A flight attendant was bent over him. 'Are you okay, sir?'

Raylan hadn't been okay for a while. The minute he closed his eyes again that image of the old monk would surely return. With that serene, dogged look. But Raylan's tortured soul wasn't anyone else's business. Not even the stewardess with her compelling dark eyes. She offered him a glass of water.

He shook his head. 'I'm fine, thanks.'

She removed her hand from his shoulder and smiled reassuringly. He kept his eyes on her as she elegantly navigated the narrow aisle. Despite the turbulence, she had no trouble keeping her balance.

He pulled a second pint-size bottle from his bag. He'd bought them during the stopover in Frankfurt, given that Islamic law was observed on Ariana Afghan Airlines: during the flight no alcohol was served. He downed a few Anafranil tablets with a last swig of Jack Daniels.

From the pocket of the seat in front of him, he removed a copy of *The Kabul Times,* which he'd picked up at the last stopover in Istanbul. On the front page was the photo of a balcony at the Lorraine Motel in Memphis, Tennessee. A man was lying on the ground with others gathered around him. Alarmed, they were pointing at an indeterminate spot in the distance, where the fatal shot fired at Martin Luther King must have come from.

On the international page there was a report about a large-scale offensive that the US army had launched in Vietnam under the name Operation Toan Thang 1: Complete Victory number one. The names they thought up . . . Names that radiated glory, so the home front continued to wholeheartedly believe that droves of American boys weren't dying there for nothing.

Four years earlier, the first troops had arrived in Vietnam, sent to assist the South Vietnamese government against the advancing North Vietnamese communists. Supposedly, it wouldn't take long for Ho Chi Minh's communist army to be expelled from South Vietnam's rice fields, jungles and mountains. As a war correspondent, Raylan wanted to see it with his own eyes, so he'd linked up with troops on the ground. Initially, the GIs couldn't believe he'd volunteered to do this: 'Man, you must be out of your fuckin' mind!' At the first sign of a skirmish, they'd expected him to bail out, which he damn well refused to do. Though he did almost piss his pants from fear. Bullets didn't discriminate between journalists and front-line soldiers. The only difference was that GIs carried rifles while he only had a leather bag holding a notepad and pencil slung across his shoulder.

For three years he'd run the same risks as those young Marines, whose respect he'd ultimately garnered. And with that respect came their stories. About fallen or injured buddies. About their families. Their sweethearts anxiously waiting for them to return. The next day, one of them was certain to be fatally wounded in a swamp, or step on a land-mine, or be pierced by bamboo spikes laid as a booby-trap – thousands of miles away from home fighting a war nobody really understood.

In Vietnam's heartlands, Raylan came to understand what the American government hoped to keep from the rest of the world: namely that after two thousand years of fighting Chinese emperors, Mongolian dictators, French colonizers and Japanese executioners, the Viet Cong would before long also expel the Americans from their land.

Meanwhile, twenty thousand young American draftees sent to Vietnam had been zippered into army body bags. In coffins draped with American flags, they arrived – under cover of dark – at military airports in the states they called home, where they would be buried by family, wives and children.

Last January he'd lifted off by helicopter from the smoking ruins of the Imperial City of Hué, now laid waste after the overwhelming Viet Cong Tet Offensive earlier that year. They'd attacked no fewer than eighty locations at the same time.

The very next day he'd left Vietnam. But Vietnam had never left him.

Hardly a night went by without that monk appearing to him, again in a sea of flames. And if it wasn't the monk, then it was that boy desperately searching for his missing parents in a shallow mass grave. Plagued by nightmares, anxiety attacks and sudden outbursts, he'd spent weeks travelling across America. Ridden with anxiety, drinking and struggling with the inexplicable urge he had to return, despite everything that had happened there.

'Don't run from what you've undergone, write about it,' was the advice of a close friend and editor at *The New York Times*.

Raylan had then flown to Europe, hoping to find a place in Paris where his soul could find some peace. But he actually wanted to vanish into thin air, so nobody could find him, go somewhere he could stop time and come to terms with himself. At London-Gatwick airport, he boarded a Boeing 727 from Ariana Afghan Airlines. After two stops – Frankfurt and Atatürk airport in Istanbul – he was now on his way to Kabul, where the pilot announced they would be landing in a few hours. Inshallah: if God wills it.

Though Raylan Chapelle didn't give a damn any more about God's wishes. In the rice paddies of Vietnam, he'd forever lost his faith in Him.

An endless, desolate, rocky landscape passed below him, as Raylan listened to the monotonous throbbing of the jet engines. In the middle of a mountainous valley a mosaic of mud-coloured houses and dusty plateaus appeared. A river wound its way through pale-green strips of land. The plane made a sharp turn and descended towards the short runway at Khwaja Rawash airport.

A powerful gust of warm, dry air hit him head on as he exited the plane at the top of the flight of stairs. He looked out over the rust-coloured mountains of the Hindu Kush, which surrounded Kabul in such a rugged yet majestic way. To stop any sudden bleeding brought on by the high altitude, he firmly pressed a tissue the stewardess had given him against his nose. He was the last of the passengers to go down the metal steps towards the terminal, a brand-new three-storey building.

Flags fluttered everywhere, as if it were a national holiday. The covered roof terrace was full of curious people. Apparently, they were all eager to get a glimpse of the passengers arriving off the only international flight scheduled for that week.

As he entered the building, he picked up the raspy sound of the language spoken here by Pathans, Tajiks and other ethnic groups for centuries, which he couldn't yet understand. It was the same language they'd used to expel Alexander the Great and Genghis Khan, and to drive British colonial rulers back across the border. It was the language of a country now caught between the spheres of influence of two superpowers: the United States and the Soviet Union. For the time being, both countries were peacefully competing in Afghanistan for as much strategic influence as possible. This was done with lots of development money and prestigious construction projects. The Russians had built this modern airport and an Olympic swimming pool on top of the highest hill and they'd constructed numerous new housing estates on the outskirts of Kabul. The Americans built dams and schools and set up large-scale agricultural projects. Young Afghans could travel to America on Fulbright scholarships to get master's degrees at the best universities. And within this rivalry, two covert organizations, the KGB and the CIA, kept a close watch on each other.

Raylan handed his passport to the stocky official who flipped through it, irritated, looking for a page where he could stamp his visa. With a dull thud, the man finally placed it on a half-empty page, next to that of Vietnam. At customs Raylan had to open the suitcase containing his Remington Travel-Riter. The typewriter was a 1950s model, and despite what the name suggested it was actually much too heavy to take on a trip, but the thing was indestructible. He silently slid a handful of dollars into the outstretched hand of a sullen customs officer, who motioned for him to move ahead. In the arrivals hall, he made his way through the inquisitive crowd towards the exit.

Outside, a local bus and a long line of passenger cars were waiting for an array of visitors and Kabulis who were headed back to the city. About fifty metres away he saw a man in a faded grey suit polishing his yellow Toyota taxi as if it were going to be displayed in a showroom. The man spotted him, and Raylan could only imagine what he must be thinking: what kind of a strange fellow is this, with his bright blue eyes, scruffy beard and tousled blond hair? Why is he wearing a leather jacket and boots in this heat, and why is he carrying a camouflage rucksack and a hard-leather typewriter case instead of a suitcase?

'Hotel Serena, please.'

A polite nod with wary eyes. 'I know where. I bring you.'

Before the man had even opened the trunk, Raylan had already jumped into the back of the taxi with his rucksack and typewriter.

'America?' The driver asked, glancing in his rear-view mirror as they pulled away.

Raylan nodded.

The man stared at him with his eyes gleaming. His expression was a cross between compassion and contempt. 'Welcome to Afghanistan, American.'

3
Farah

She felt Harcourt's hand on her shoulder as she started walking down the stairway. Fear held her in its grip. Edward's warning echoed in her head. *It's too soon after Moscow! Interpol, MI5, MIVD, they've all removed you from their lists. But the Americans haven't!*

On the bottom step she felt the impulse to run away, just like she'd wanted to do in Kiev while checking in for her flight to Jakarta. She knew that it would be equally pointless here; a closed trap doesn't open of its own accord.

Mendosa put her bag on the front seat, opened his jacket and pulled a detector out of his hip holster.

'This must be a misunderstanding,' she ventured.

'Stand still, please.'

The scanner whizzed up and down her body.

'Do I get to make my one phone call?'

'For the time being you don't get to do anything.'

Next, Harcourt searched her bag. Mendosa held open the rear door for her. With the flat of his hand against her back, he manoeuvred her on to the dark-brown leather, behind the passenger seat. 'Fasten your seat belt.'

She did as she was told. Harcourt walked around the car, got in beside her and slammed the left door shut, almost at the same time as Mendosa sat down behind the wheel. The click of the central locking system sounded like a muffled shot from a fully automatic weapon.

Mendosa started the engine and spoke into his radio. 'Detainee secured. Coming in for interrogation. Over.'

They slowly drove past a row of three parked international airliners towards a concrete wall topped with razor wire. She saw a military helicopter take off behind it. They stopped in front of a barrier guarded by two military policemen, who emerged from a timber watchhouse and positioned themselves on either side of the four-wheel drive. Their English betrayed a European accent. The emblem on their uniforms sported the red-black-and-yellow of the Belgian flag. While one policeman slid a round mirror on a pole under the car, the other checked Mendosa's papers. She swallowed her fear when the red-and-white barrier was raised for them.

After little more than ten metres they stopped beside two low barrels filled with gravel; protruding from it were a PVC tube and a yellow sign with the text UNLOAD WEAPONS HERE. Mendosa got out, unloaded his weapon and got back behind the wheel. Then it was Harcourt's turn to get out and unload his Glock. The entire operation was extremely fast and choreographed to perfection; this was clearly not the first time they'd done this.

They drove across a football-pitch-sized expanse of concrete slabs lined with MI-17 helicopters in camouflage colours. Tanks came rolling out of two grey transport planes parked in front of the hangars. Via a roundabout, where the flags of all the ISAF nations with a presence in Afghanistan were fluttering, they arrived at a red-brick, windowless building.

A steel staircase led to a door, which opened with a heavy click after Harcourt keyed in a code. As they walked down the dimly lit corridor, she thought of what Mendosa had said into his radio. *Interrogation.*

Her heart was thumping against her ribs like a fist, she felt sick to her stomach, and every muscle in her body was tense. She thought of her jihad statement in Moscow: *I, Farah Hafez . . .*

In an empty room she was met by a young Afghan policewoman. Feet slightly apart. Hands behind her back. The sharply tailored blue-grey

14

police uniform, with the Afghan flag on her left sleeve, seemed custom-made for her. A black hijab was tightly wrapped around her head. She had carefully plucked eyebrows and dark eyeliner combined with thick black mascara created the illusion of enormous false eyelashes. Her dark-brown eyes fixed themselves on Farah, who didn't feel intimidated. On the contrary, it was actually reassuring to be facing a woman instead of the two broad-shouldered Americans, who'd left the room without a word.

Knowing how much courage it took for an Afghan woman to join the army or the police, Farah smiled at the officer.

This wasn't acknowledged in any way. The woman's English was poor. 'I search you.'

'You can speak to me in Dari,' Farah tried. 'I speak the language.' She thought she saw the slightest flicker of surprise.

The policewoman pulled on latex gloves and continued in Dari, but remained aloof. 'Would you please take off the hijab?'

Farah unwrapped her headscarf.

'Your shoes need to come off too.'

The concrete floor felt freezing cold. The policewoman pointed. 'Place your hands against the wall.'

Farah looked at the wall, saw an image indicating where she had to place her hands and did as she was told.

'Your feet here.' The policeman pointed to the floor.

She stared down at the markings where she had to place her feet. So far apart that she had to spread her legs. She let her hands slide off the wall, and looked as calmly as possible at the police officer, whose face hardened at her refusal.

'I am authorized to use force in the event of any resistance.'

A phrase she must have learned during training. This young woman, barely twenty, was literally rigid with tension. One wrong move, one difficult question or a refusal and she would no doubt reveal what she was capable of. And that was bound to be much more than parroting memorized orders. There was no room for negotia-tion. Farah cast aside her aversion, put her feet on the designated spots and placed her hands back on the wall.

'Are you wearing anything I could stab or cut myself on?'

'No.'

'Then I'm going to search you now.'

The latex-covered hands passed over the top of her head. Slowly and deliberately, they touched her cropped hair, neck, shoulders, armpits and the curve of her breasts underneath her *salwar kameez*, the tunic reaching down to her thighs. They mechanically patted down her back, hips and buttocks, slid over the delicate fabric of the wide trousers, arrived between her legs where they slowed, pressing deeper and thus crossing an obvious boundary. They roused a repressed rage in her body, then slipped further down her thighs until they reached her ankles, tapping her heels to signal that she had to show the soles of her feet. Then came the voice, betraying rapid breathing. 'Stay where you are.'

The sound of latex gloves being taken off and tossed into a metal bin. The voice now softer than before, as if her mind had been set at rest, although the words remained impersonal and cold. 'Come with me.'

'My shoes.'

'Shoes stay here!'

They walked down the corridor, past closed cell doors. With each door the light grew dimmer, until it was all but dark at the end. The policewoman opened the cell. Farah felt her fear of small spaces rear its head. She might have avoided this had she requested a lawyer, but she hadn't really deemed it necessary. If she were to ask for one now, it would be both an admission of weakness and a partial confession.

'Wait here.'

'What for?'

'The next stage of the procedure.'

'What's going to happen?'

'You must do as I say.'

She had to get the better of her claustrophobia as well as the rising anger born of her powerlessness. And all that in a matter of seconds. If the anger or the fear got the upper hand, she would lose control. And then she'd lose herself. She took a step, walked into the cell as calmly as possible and heard the steel door close behind her; with a metallic clang the mechanical lock cut her off from the outside world.

She'd had her first panic attacks as a child, during sleepless nights when, staring into the darkness, she'd tried to get her head around the meaning of 'eternity'. The Koran spoke of a life in which there would be no more time and nothing was finite because everything would be infinite. It always made her think that if she fell asleep there was a chance she would end up burying herself in the dark for all eternity. She remembered jumping out of bed, opening the window and gasping for breath. She didn't want to get back into bed. Sleeping equalled dying. Longing for a faraway place where death didn't exist, she felt compelled to climb into the apple tree and gaze up at the stars.

Lower that heartrate now. Inhale through the nose. Exhale through the mouth. Breathe in for four seconds, out for six. Somewhere deep inside she found a sanctuary for her fear and anger.

In her memory.

She was standing in front of the open window of her bedroom on the first floor of her parents' house, looking out into the garden. The branches of the apple tree were almost close enough for her to touch if she leaned forwards. From this vantage point she secretly observed her father's movements each morning – every step he took, every arm movement, every punch or kick. She'd practised the sequence in front of the mirror for months until she could do it in her sleep.

It was early in the morning. She knew he'd be there again shortly. Always at exactly the same time. She snuck down the stairs and walked across the garden tiles until she was standing under the tree. With her heart thumping, she waited for him to appear.

The surprise on his face when he saw her and she executed her first bow. The thrill of excitement at her first move. Followed by the second, the third. Down to the very last one. The silence in which he responded to her closing bow, his admiring glance when he took a step in her direction.

The sensation of his right hand on her head.

His calm voice, *My little Malalai.*

The cell door lock clicked open. Her father's silhouette merged with that of the policewoman in the doorway. 'Follow me.'

She walked down the corridor again, from dark to dusk, from

dusk to light this time, and entered a bare, windowless room. There was a metal table in the middle, riveted to the floor. Even the three chairs around it had been fixed in place. She sat down on the chair that the policewoman indicated, peered round and started counting.

A total of five cameras.

Underneath the table she discovered a sixth. That same moment Harcourt walked into the room with a laptop under his arm. Mendosa followed him with a voice recorder.

'May I have something to drink, please?' she asked the policewoman, who ignored her and left the room. Harcourt sat down opposite her without a word and flipped open the laptop. Mendosa took a seat beside him, positioned the voice recorder on the table and likewise pretended not to have heard her.

'I'd like to remind you again, Ms Hafez, that you have the right to remain silent and that you are entitled to a lawyer. Should you desire one, now is the time to say so. It won't change the procedure, only prolong it unnecessarily. It's up to you.' Harcourt delivered his monologue on automatic pilot, after which he continued to tap on his keyboard without waiting for her response.

'Why am I here? What do you want from me?' She heard the weakness in her voice.

'Lawyer or no lawyer?'

'No lawyer.'

Harcourt looked at her with what seemed to be a faint smile. Obviously a sarcastic one. The wilful perversity of someone pulling the strings. He let the silence last agonizingly long. 'You're a journalist,' he finally said.

'I work for the *AND*, the *Algemeen Nederlands Dagblad*. My editor-in-chief is Edward Vallent. If you phone him, he'll . . .'

'Why have you come to Afghanistan?'

Monotonous voice. Piercing brown eyes in a pockmarked face. The cloying scent of Old Spice aftershave mixed with stale sweat, which had stained the collar of his white shirt. She put him in his mid-fifties. Divorced. Or single anyway – what woman could put up with a guy like this?

'Why have you come to Afghanistan, Ms Hafez?'

'To bury my father.'

'And who is your father?'

'Aadel Gailani. He died on 28 April 1978.'

An intense silence ensued. The men looked at each other. She couldn't help but smile.

'Why are you smiling?'

'Sorry, nerves.'

'Your father has been dead for thirty years.'

'That's correct. His body was recently discovered in an anonymous mass grave. The then-president, Daoud Khan, his wife, children and a few other ministers were buried there too. All shot dead during the Saur Revolution. They'll be given a ceremonial reburial. The Afghan ambassador to The Hague invited me to attend.'

It felt good to talk: it gave her the impression that she could convince them of her honourable intentions, of her innocence. But talking could come at a price as well. If she let one wrong word slip in an emotional tone, they would pick up on it. That's what these men were like: trained to find a lie in anything. To them you were guilty until proven innocent. Any action, any sentence, any movement that went too far in their eyes was suspect.

'You decided not to accept the Afghan government's official invitation.'

'How do you know ...' She checked herself, realizing that they were bound to know everything. The truth, she thought. Nothing but the truth. 'Is that why I'm here? Am I a suspect because I refused to come over as an official guest with all the obligations that entails? I want to be able to write freely about my country.'

Harcourt regarded her impassively. 'You're a Dutch national.'

'Yes, and ... ?'

'You're talking about "my country". Sounds a bit overdramatic.'

'I was born here.'

Mendosa's voice: 'Your last name is Hafez. Are you married?'

'Does it say so in my passport?'

'Answer the question.'

'No.'

'Do you refuse to answer the question?'

'I mean, no, I'm not married.'

'Your name is Hafez. Your father's name was Gailani.'

'Hafez was an alias I assumed.'

'An alias?'

'A year after my father's death, the Russians invaded my country. I fled, together with my mother. When I arrived in the Netherlands . . .'

'Is your mother still alive?'

Suddenly it was as if a gust of wind had swept snow into her face again. She was hanging over the shoulder of the man who'd smuggled them across the border. Screaming. He was carrying her away, away from the place where her mother lay. A place she could no longer see because the snow had draped a white curtain over everything.

'She died during our escape. Somewhere . . .'

'Somewhere?'

'. . . in the mountains of Turkey.'

Harcourt carried on typing, unperturbed. Mendosa looked at her coldly.

'You arrived in the Netherlands. Without parents. You were granted asylum. Why the alias?'

'I was afraid they'd discover my true identity and that they'd find me.'

'Who do you mean by "they"?'

'The same people who murdered my father.'

Farah had never been able to look into the future. But ten years later, when the Russians were driven out of Afghanistan by the Mujahideen warlords, it was the turn of thousands of communist sympathizers to make a mad dash to leave the country. Some of them ended up in the Netherlands, perhaps even her father's murderer.

Harcourt abruptly stopped typing. Mendosa leaned towards her.

'Ms Hafez, can you explain to me how the Afghan government was able to figure out that a woman living under an assumed name in another country was actually the daughter of a minister who lost his life here thirty years ago?'

'I wondered about that too. Apparently the hawk-eyed Afghan ambassador in the Netherlands read about me in the newspaper and put two and two together. He was the one who phoned me to say that . . .' She felt the tears stinging her eyes but didn't want to give them the pleasure of seeing her sorrow. She took a deep breath and then continued. 'What I just told you . . . about my father.'

'When did the ambassador phone you?'

She thought about it. It felt like ages. Days, weeks even. 'The day before yesterday.'

In the silence that ensued, Harcourt and Mendosa exchanged glances. She spotted Mendosa's brief nod. At his signal Harcourt very slowly turned the laptop screen towards her and pressed *play*.

Her breath caught in her throat. She saw herself. Eyes like daggers, smudged mascara, her voice breaking. *I, Farah Hafez, support the jihad against President Potanin's criminal regime . . .*

Harcourt pressed *pause*.

Mendosa fixed his eyes on her. 'So, what's this all about?'

Her thoughts raced back to a few weeks ago. She pictured him lying on the stretcher in the Emergency Department. Made up like a doll, heavy kohl around his eyes, his lips painted bright red. Cut-up rags covering a tiny trembling body. Tin bracelets with small bells around his ankles and wrists.

Sekandar.

She'd known next to nothing about child trafficking. She paused, thinking. The whole truth. Nothing but. Memories and images of the recent past came tumbling into her mind. Her trip to Moscow, where she'd walked a tightrope, having been forced to play a game that wasn't hers. An inexperienced investigative journalist with a secret agenda, she'd gone after a Russian oligarch: Valentin Lavrov. He'd immediately seen through her. In his sleek, postmodern country retreat with the huge windows on Lake Glubokoe he'd lured her into a trap. She remembered the calmness of his threat as he coldly stared across the lake: *I'm throwing you a lifeline, Farah, do you understand?*

She barely looked at Harcourt and Mendosa as she told her story. She was determined to stick to the deal she'd made with herself: the truth, and nothing but the truth.

'When I refused to work for Lavrov, he had me taken to a building at Moscow State University where a hostage situation was playing out. It was . . . I was put in front of a camera and forced to recite the text you just . . . I did as I was told. If I didn't do it, they were going to execute one of the student hostages. From that moment on I was wanted. As a terrorist. I had to get out of Russia somehow. I travelled from Kiev to Jakarta on a fake passport. If you're well-informed, and I have no reason to doubt that you are, you'll know that Lavrov has been arrested in Jakarta, and that . . .' She swallowed and managed to maintain her self-control.

'That what, Ms Hafez?'

'. . . that my colleague, Paul Chapelle, has handed over sufficient evidence to the authorities to prove that Lavrov set me up in Moscow. The Dutch public prosecutor has confirmed that the evidence is authentic and watertight. Interpol, Scotland Yard and even the FBI have removed me from their lists. So why haven't you? What more do you want from me?' She could barely contain her anger. 'Do I need to confess who I do it with, how often and in what positions?'

A poker-faced Harcourt moved the cursor to a folder with images, double-clicked and turned the screen back towards her.

The photo was in black-and-white. Just as it had been published in the paper.

She and Detective Joshua Calvino on the deck of his houseboat on a canal in Amsterdam. A tight embrace. His hands cupping her buttocks.

Her blood was boiling. The voice of the old Indonesian woman resonated in her head: *Be as elusive as water.* Breathe in for four seconds. Out for six.

Harcourt crossed his arms, leaned back and looked at her impassively. 'Within a short space of time your . . . actions have made you notorious the world over. And didn't it occur to you that not accepting an official invitation might mean jeopardizing your safety?'

She nodded.

'Then surely you must realize that somebody with your reputation is an attractive target for the Taliban.'

Paul's voice: *Two female journalists were killed last week.*

'It's an occupational hazard.'

'If you say so, Ms Hafez, but it's our job to give you some sound advice.'

'And that is?'

'Watch your step and stay out of trouble.'

'I'll take your warning to heart.'

'All right, then.' With a sigh Harcourt closed the laptop.

Along with a sense of relief she felt a smile steal over her face. But it froze the moment Mendosa took two sheets from a folder. He placed them in front of her. He drummed his fingers on the paper. She looked at the whimsical shapes, which remained a mystery to her. A slender structure jutting up into the sky, above a few angular shapes. It could be a tower rising above roofs. A large dark smudge to the left – a mountain maybe? Something hovered in the air in the middle of the page. A bird, or perhaps a plane.

'What's this supposed to be?' Mendosa asked.

'They're drawings by the boy.'

In her mind, she pictured Sekandar wandering around Isobel's studio. He'd been wide-eyed as he looked at the old streets of Kabul depicted in her immense paintings. They were so lifelike that you felt you could step inside them. Isobel had given him crayons and a few sheets of drawing paper when she saw how fascinated he was.

'What's it supposed to be, I asked.'

Farah stared first at the drawings, then at Mendosa. 'The boy doesn't talk much. This is currently his only way of communicating. We're trying to find his family. It could be a lead. A location. A landmark. Perhaps I'll be able to find out in the next few days.'

Mendosa's smile was downright condescending. 'In that case we'd better not keep you much longer.'

'What do you mean?'

'You're free to go.'

She looked at him in surprise and was about to get up when he spoke again, in a voice dripping with sarcasm.

'After you've given us a statement.'

'I just did.'

He slid a notepad and a pen towards her. 'Written and signed pleased.'

She began to write down everything they'd talked about, in the style she used to take notes for her articles: brief and to the point. The truth, and nothing but the truth. After putting her signature under the final sentence, she slid the notepad back to Mendosa, who skimmed over the text and then nodded to Harcourt. The latter got to his feet, swung open the door and asked her to follow him to the adjacent room.

Farah followed him in silence. She thought that was it.

She was wrong.

Stunned, she looked at everything on the two metal tables. Her large Eastpak Tranverz suitcase had been brought in and emptied. Everything she'd packed for this trip had been neatly laid out in the yellowish white light of a fluorescent tube. Shirts, trousers, knickers, bras, scarves and shoes. Ditto the contents of her shoulder bag: laptop, satellite phone, prepaid mobile, press card, credit card, cash, notepad, pens, sunglasses and make-up. Even her tampons had been taken out of their box and lined up.

'Please check carefully whether anything is missing and then repack it all.'

With as much restraint as she could muster she retrieved her suitcase and put all her clothes back in. Then she filled her laptop bag. She slipped on her shoes and finally wrapped the hijab around her head. At the door Harcourt gave her back her passport. As he did he made a point of holding it open at the page with the visa stamp.

Outside, at the bottom of the steel staircase, an idling jeep was waiting for her. It took her to the main gate of the military airfield. There she had to walk down a twenty-metre-long narrow pedestrian corridor created by towering fences topped with razor wire. At the checkpoint her passport was inspected, and then she was allowed out.

There she was. On the edge of a large, muddy plain, at the side of a road full of cracks and potholes, with roadblocks in every direction. She was left with the same numbing sense of powerlessness and felt just as lost as that time when she'd reached the Dutch border as a child.

The large puddles told her it had rained. The sky had been clear blue when she arrived, but now dark clouds were drifting overhead. A convoy of military trucks thundered past. She felt a tugging at her sleeve. A little girl, barely ten, in ragged clothes and splattered with mud, looked up at her. Her long hair was caked with dirt. Where a left eye would normally be, there was now a dark, inflamed cavity full of clotted blood. The boy beside her had no fingers on his left hand.

The girl's plea was drowned out by an irate male voice, '*Boro gom-sho!* Get lost!'

He was lanky, with black curly hair, and he was wearing a faded striped turtleneck sweater. His sudden grin, baring yellowed teeth with a few missing here and there, was in sharp contrast to the snarl he'd shown the children. He gestured invitingly to a canary-yellow Corolla, which was covered in dust. Farah nodded once she spotted the taxi sign on the car roof. When he reached for her luggage, she instinctively blocked his hand. The man shrank back. The beggar children's laughter sounded flat and shrill.

With her suitcase beside her, she sat in the back, on the right, behind the passenger seat and rolled down the window to give each of the children fifty afghanis.

'Where to?'

She gave the driver the address of her hotel. He accelerated so fast that the children disappeared in a cloud of dust, exhaust fumes and spraying gravel.

'Every morning they're dropped here in a minivan and collected again in the evening. They're deliberately mutilated for the purpose of begging. Your cash goes to their bosses, not to them!'

She saw him eyeing her up in the rear-view mirror and instantly realized that because she'd forgotten to negotiate a price before getting in, she'd become his goldmine for the day. Then came the second realization: amidst the chaos of loudly honking Land Rovers, lorries, vans, clapped-out taxis and decrepit passenger cars on the road to the city clearly this man was the king of the road. In his canary-yellow Toyota he swerved in and among the other road users, all the while yammering on his phone and pounding his horn.

4
Raylan

1968

It felt like they were taking the scenic route through the Old Testament. The low houses along the often unpaved roads were all made of the same rust-coloured earth as the surrounding hills. Horses pulled wooden carts filled with threshed wheat, donkeys carried large blocks of ice wrapped in jute on their backs, and a caravan of camels emerged from a cloud of gravelly dust.

Closer to the heart of the 3,000-year-old city were a few modern high-rise buildings, a branch of Marks & Spencer and the brand-new Ministry of Finance building with a futuristic-looking restaurant and a fountain. They sat alongside century-old bazaars and narrow shops with open fronts.

In the past three years, Raylan had grown accustomed to Saigon, where every major building was surrounded by sandbags and razor wire; where military patrols permanently controlled crowded streets; and where hordes of beggars, homeless children and prostitutes were permanent fixtures at the intersections. In recent years, Saigon had lost its dignity. But the city through which he now rode had retained its age-old grandeur as a former crossroads of the ancient Silk Road.

Everywhere he looked there was the lively trading of embroidery, lapis lazuli, silk, antiques, meat and vegetables. Men in traditionally wide Aladdin trousers, with long shawls draped over their shoulders, wearing grubby white turbans, dominated the streets and the boulevards. Women were in the minority by far, and most were dressed in the *chadari*. Between them meandered young, self-assured Afghans in tailored Western-style suits, unveiled women in dresses and high-heels, and young Westerners in billowing peasant shirts and trousers with psychedelic patterns. They were hippies, who with little luggage and even less money had crossed the Bosphorus near Istanbul in their Volkswagen vans to drive through Eastern Turkey via Tehran to reach Kabul. Free spirits who'd embraced Eastern philosophy but in fact were barely interested in the country's culture, because they were mainly in search of 'their true selves'. Apart from their desire for adventure, Raylan had nothing in common with them. He even found their lack of interest in what was happening to the less privileged of their generation who were serving in Vietnam utterly disgraceful.

A sudden, forceful braking movement hurled him against the back of the front seat. A few metres in front of the taxi, policemen were busy cordoning off an intersection. From the distance came the shouts of an approaching crowd. He instantly recognized the threat that hung in the air. He shoved a handful of dollars at the driver, opened the door and with his rucksack and typewriter case squeezed out of the taxi to get in front of the procession of demonstrators streaming by.

They were young, these men and women with their fists raised in the air, chanting slogans, holding up banners and carrying large photos of a young man with dark eyes and long curly hair. Ryan didn't understand what they were saying, but he understood the fanaticism of these protesting boys in their corduroy trousers and girls in skirts decently covering their knees. As the procession moved further into town and the police opened the intersection again, he felt a hand on his shoulder. Behind him stood his driver, who raised his arms to the heavens as if he'd been overcome by despair.

'Hotel Serena not here. Come. I bring you.'

Raylan shook his head, threw his rucksack over his shoulder, grabbed the typewriter case from the pavement and walked into the old city.

In the shimmering heat, he wandered along the busy banks of the River Kabul. Men washed their faces, hands and feet and then bowed their heads in the direction of Mecca for afternoon prayers.

Irritated by the honking behind him, he turned around. The taxi driver had followed him every step of the way. To rid himself of the man, he ducked into the first alleyway he saw and ended up in a jumble of narrow streets, where century-old houses with carved window frames blocked out almost all the sunlight. In a courtyard, men with bloody aprons were slaughtering sheep. Grimacing children were prancing around him and roaring with laughter, '*Harami, harami!*' Raylan suspected it was a swear word, like the word the Vietnamese used to refer to the American GIs: *dumas* or motherfuckers. He couldn't help but smile. Chaos was familiar territory for him. For the first time since Vietnam, he felt at ease somewhere.

He stopped at an old gate that opened on to a crowded courtyard. He stared in fascination at the geometric patterns and incomprehensible inscriptions in the cement of the arched passageway and observed the hustle and bustle of the market. This must have once been a caravanserai, a safe place for traders to spend the night with their goods and pack animals when they travelled the Silk Road and arrived in Kabul. The buildings around the courtyard were equipped with niches and rooms where weary travellers could sleep. A small mosque in a corner offered the possibility to pray.

He entered the courtyard, which was crammed with wooden stalls and covered by tent canvas and old tarpaulins. Men with faces bronzed by the sun loudly praised their wares: nuts, spices, dried fruits, tea, dishes of raw meat, ornamental birds in bamboo cages, blankets, strands of lapis lazuli beads, silver bracelets, antique daggers and onyx chess pieces. Sparks leaped from the screeching wheels of the knife sharpeners; pieces of beef sizzled in large pans of sesame oil. For hundreds of years, time had stood still here.

At most it was a flash, a glint a few metres away.

Yet it was enough to make him instantly seek cover. A reflex of his muscle memory that he obeyed – thanks to three years in Vietnam – even before his brain had registered it: he ducked for cover, awaiting the impact.

But nothing happened, the pandemonium of daily life on the marketplace continued undisturbed: the merchants kept shouting over each other, and the birds in their bamboo cages chirped just as shrilly.

When he stood up again, he found himself staring directly into a pair of astonished eyes. They were sea-blue and encircled by a face with countless freckles. Her long, sun-bleached hair was tied in a ponytail. She couldn't have been much older than twenty. With a combination of alarm and disbelief, she held the camera in her hands. He realized what had happened. She'd pointed her lens at him, and it had reflected the sunlight.

He heard the laughter in her voice.

'This is a first: a man who's afraid of me.'

'Afraid of you? No . . .'

Her smile was dazzling. 'That's very reassuring.'

'Of how I look in your photo.'

She gave him a serious gaze. 'At best, tired.'

'I flew for almost ten hours and just landed. That said, I think I left my mind hovering somewhere above the Hindu Kush.'

'Then I wish your soul an easy landing.'

She said it with a wink, and there was a hint of mockery in the tilt of her head, but he couldn't take his eyes off her. She was so defiant, so sensual, without even trying. He always had this with hippie girls: he thought they were too beautiful for this world. But here was a girl who was so vivacious, she seemed able to take on the world with little or no effort.

He glanced at her camera, noting that it was a Leica.

'I borrowed it,' she said. 'My brother's a journalist in Amsterdam. He collects them.'

'Are you Dutch?' he asked, perhaps a bit too surprised.

Her amused gaze turned playfully suspicious, 'What do you think?'

'Uh . . . Swedish.'

She held up her blond ponytail. 'Because of this and my blue eyes?'

'Your accent.'

'I didn't know there were Dutch people who speak English with a Swedish accent.'

Her laugh rippled like a waterfall. It seemed like she was impervious to all the chaos, stink and shouting around them. Lewis Carroll could have had her in mind when he was writing *Alice in Wonderland*, but this Alice would soon step back through her looking glass into her own world. One of peace, flowers, psychedelic drugs and free love; a world in which there was no napalm, no bodies of dead children floating in rice fields, no American soldiers being zipped into body bags, no monks setting themselves ablaze. He felt the impulse to walk through that mirror with her, let his rucksack drop to the ground and extended his hand.

'Raylan.'

Her hand felt unexpectedly cool and strong.

'Hi, Raylan. I'm Isobel. My friends call me Ise.'

'Where are you headed, Ise?'

'To Goa, India.'

'Why?'

'To see the world. Get to know myself.'

'Do you have to go all the way to India to do that?'

She gave him a surprisingly serious look, held up her camera, pointed it at him and clicked.

It wasn't her action that suddenly made him feel uneasy. It was something else. Something out there. He could always depend on his intuition. He was constantly on the alert, registering sounds and movements before he consciously picked them up.

He could hear trouble fast approaching from the distance: the stomping of feet and gruff shouting. The sound of a scampering crowd, which reached the courtyard as an incarnate wave of fear. Young men and women with panic in their eyes, clutching crumpled banners in their hands, chased by an overpowering military force.

Isobel froze beside him, Leica in hand, now a fragile figure.

He put his arm around her. His eyes searched for a way out other than the gate, but, like the protesters, they were completely surrounded by a cordon of police that moved across the courtyard with raised batons, wrecking everything in their path.

A stall right in front of them was smashed to the ground. The old merchant who'd been displaying his beads lay motionless among his glittering goods. The line was headed straight for them. Raylan assessed the situation, grabbed Isobel and pressed her to him. With one hand, he swung the typewriter case over his shoulder to shield his back.

He managed to ward off the first blows. The one to the back of his head, he barely felt.

Only when the outline of the crowd began to tilt around him and the bright-blue sky appeared in his field of vision did he realize he was falling backwards. He was also conscious of letting go of the typewriter case and both his arms, searching for something to grab on to, helplessly flailing in the air as the screams around him seemed to die down and his body went numb. Even before his head hit the ground, the blue sky had been snuffed out.

5
Farah

POLICE – RING OF STEEL. The big blue sign marked the first of a series of checkpoints blocking the access roads to the centre. Kabul was and remained a city on the frontline where all official buildings, ministries, embassies and NGO offices were entrenched behind high walls of reinforced concrete. But it was common knowledge that no ring of steel, concrete wall or checkpoint could withstand a Taliban attack.

Police officers in grey-blue uniforms with AK-47s slung casually over their shoulders waved through cars as if they were doing personal favours. The taxi driver waved back at them, but the officers seemed fixated on the young woman in the back seat who'd put on her sunglasses and kept staring straight ahead.

The realization, when it finally came, was painful. Buildings razed to the ground, half-finished concrete complexes, roadblocks, razor wire, sandbags, checkpoints with armed police and junctions where beggar women in burqas charged at cars stopped for traffic lights – this couldn't be her city.

This wasn't Kabul. Even the trees had disappeared.

And yet. After an intersection it appeared. Protected by a new extension, like some sort of shell. Somewhere in there, in one of the rooms of Bibi Mahro Hospital, she had been born.

They ended up in the maelstrom of Kabul's biggest roundabout, Massoud Square, with its enormous obelisk in the middle. A large white Mercedes without plates cut them off. At the same time she tasted something warm on her lips. Something metallic. She rubbed her hand across her mouth. She'd been warned. Kabul was located at an altitude of 1,800 metres above sea level. Anyone who wasn't used to this could expect symptoms: dizziness, headache, a nosebleed. She pressed a tissue to her face.

The taxi turned on to Shir Ali Khan Road. It took her only a split second to recognize the place they were now approaching. 'Pull over.'

'This is not hotel.'

'I want you to stop here.'

She gathered her luggage, pressed the afghanis he requested into his hand and got out.

Mesmerized, she looked at the dusty display window right in front of her. The façade had once been bright blue, but the paint was now faded and peeling. Yet the door still made that familiar squeaky noise when she pushed it open.

Hardly anything seemed to have changed in thirty years. As a child, whenever she felt lost in a reality she didn't understand, she came here, to this wondrous world full of books, to discover the secrets that lay hidden on these shelves.

She counted five customers. All foreigners. Diplomats, journalists, NGO workers. Quiet. Their heads down, absorbed, temporarily deaf and blind to the world around them. Books everywhere: along the walls, on shelves, in stacks on the ground, occupying every inch from floor to ceiling. Collections of poetry, travel books, art tomes and novels: a world made of words, the whisperings of poets, prophets and historians long gone. In this world she'd travelled with Marco Polo to the court of the Chinese emperor, learned the life lessons of the major Sufi poets Hafez, Rumi and Inayat Khan and lived through the Spanish Civil War with Ernest Hemingway.

On one of the top shelves in the WAR DOCUMENTATION section she found what she was looking for. She gazed at the photo on the back cover. The stubbly chin, the tousled hair, the piercing blue eyes.

Is it hard? she'd once asked him in this very place. *Writing a book?* The American journalist had regarded her inscrutably. Not the way adults usually look at children, but more intently, as if he genuinely wanted to connect with her. She remembered the effect it'd had on her.

'This was a bestseller, back in the day,' said the shop owner at the till when he saw the cover. 'A signed copy that's been here for years. As if it were waiting for you, ma'am.'

On the front landing of the Golden Star Hotel the uniformed hotel guard toting a Kalashnikov glanced at her passport then stared back at her in surprise. 'If you're Dutch then so is my mother.' With a sceptical grin, he opened the bullet-proof glass door leading to the lobby for her.

All she heard when the door shut behind her was a vague murmur of the traffic chaos and yelling of street vendors. Right at the heart of the old centre was a world within a world, a cool enclave of tranquillity. But even within the walls of a tightly guarded hotel you were never completely safe. Earlier that year, Taliban suicide bombers disguised as police officers had forced their way into a hotel lobby. They'd shot dozens of guests and staff before the Quick Reaction Force had managed to eliminate them.

A small group of men, clearly Americans despite their curious choice of apparel – loose-fitting long Afghan shirts and baggy trousers – were making a nuisance of themselves in the lobby. Just about every wall sported a sign saying FIREARMS PROHIBITED, but they all carried a Glock in a shoulder holster.

'Welcome to the Golden Star Hotel. How may I be of service?'

Behind the mahogany counter with inlaid silver plate, which resembled tarnished mirrors, an older receptionist flashed her a friendly smile. White starched shirt, black tie, burgundy-red suit, shiny silver buttons and a grey beard. His smile became wider when she told him in Dari who she was. A reservation for seven nights. Needless to say, she'd be given the hotel's best room, with a view of the main road. The one thing she did *not* want for security reasons.

In the end, a spotty adolescent, who appeared to be outgrowing his bellhop uniform by the minute, took her to the top floor, at the back, which had a fire escape she could flee down if need be. In the room he offered to unpack her luggage and exchange her money at the best rate going and then suggested his services as her permanent guide.

She slipped him a handful of afghanis and pushed him out the door.

*

Farah stood alone in her room and undressed. After a while the tepid shower grew warmer. The latex hands all over her body, the impassive gazes of the two Americans, their arrogant tone as they asked their questions, issued their orders – she was keen to wash it all away. Even with the water at its hottest and strongest, the hands kept touching her, the questions kept coming, the cell door kept closing with an ever-louder thud.

She shut her eyes and heard the voice of the man who taught her to be hard. Like a rock. Her father. *Take up your position.*

They practised together under the apple tree, every single morning. She blocked his kicks and punches. She wanted to be a rock. Like him. She wanted to hold back the tears that stung her eyes. She wanted to learn to tolerate the pain. Do anything to earn his respect. But the tears wouldn't be held back. That disappointment she always saw flickering in his eyes. She wanted so badly to please him, to give him what he was entitled to. Because he was her hero. And she, his own little Malalai. She had to learn to tolerate the pain. Become numb to be his pride and joy.

She'd taught herself to wake up in the middle of the night. To go barefoot into the garden, a scarf tied around her mouth so she could sink her teeth into it to smother the cries of pain. As hard as she could she'd kick the trees with the soles of her feet. Shred her fists as she pounded the trunks. After washing the blood off her hands and feet, she would wait in bed, trembling, for the sleep born of pain and exhaustion to take her. She longed for the day when she could counter her father's every kick, every punch without flinching when they practised.

That day had come, thirty years ago. The day she'd stood in the butterfly garden of the presidential palace, as the planes arrived.

She walked out of the bathroom, soaking wet.

Through the window she could see the sun serenely suspended over the mountains. Below her, the city was bathed in rust-brown smog. She sat down on the bed and ran her hand over the book's title: *The Great Lie.*

She thought of the bundle of love letters which she'd left largely unread in Moscow. 'Uncle' Parwaiz had given them to her, shortly before he'd collapsed and died on the square in The Hague. She hadn't had a chance to ask him: why had her mother given him those letters for safekeeping? Why had he been tasked with giving them to her when he considered the time ripe? Why, after all those years, did her mother want her to know who she'd been in love with?

Raylan Chapelle. She thought of the opening words of his first letter. *The good fortune that I got to know you and the good fortune that you allow me to love you.*

She opened the book at a random page; her eyes skimmed the lines.

The role of fortune in life ... In a war there are no bombs, no bullets with your name on them. You may accidentally walk into the path of a bullet or a sniper who happens to catch sight of you. There's no plan, there's no specific time, no designated place where you'll take your last breath. But one thing is certain – it will happen. It's like Russian roulette. Believing in good fortune is all you can do to keep it at bay for as long as possible.

She put her hand on the page, lay down on her side and closed her eyes.

6
Raylan

1968

Two slender hands with long bony fingers slid from his temples to his crown. The doctor at Bibi Mahro Hospital touched Raylan's head like a jeweller would examine an 800-carat gemstone: devotedly and from every possible angle. In carefully formulated English, he whispered his remarkable findings.

'Your head is so symmetrical it might have been sculpted by a Bactrian Buddhist.'

'Thanks for the compliment, doc, but besides that how's it doing?'

'No external injuries. It was quite a blow, and that's causing a painful swelling you might feel in your neck and the right side of your face. I'll give you something for the pain.'

The doctor held up an oblong box that he'd removed from a glass medicine cabinet. The irregular Dari lettering had something menacing about it.

'Don't get behind the wheel for the next few days, because of the opiates and rest your head on a soft pillow, or' – a naughty grin appeared on the doctor's face – 'a woman's loving lap.'

Raylan sat up on the treatment table. He felt dizzy and grabbed the edge of the table. 'Where's my stuff? So I can get out of here.'

The smile on the doctor's face froze. He looked questioningly at Raylan.

'Your stuff?'

'My rucksack and my typewriter.'

'Ah! Just a moment.'

The doctor went to the door, opened it and called a few words Raylan didn't understand into the corridor. Before he realized it, two unknown men were standing before him. In their dark blue suits with wide lapels, they reminded him of poorly dressed gangsters from an American B-movie. Neither of them appeared to speak English.

'These gentlemen will take you to your belongings,' the doctor said.

Raylan surveyed the two clean-shaven faces strained with tension.

The doctor leaned towards him and whispered, 'You'd do well to follow them.'

'Am I under arrest?'

'Not that I know.'

'Well then. Give me my stuff, damn it. Arrange a taxi to Hotel Serena, and we'll all live happily ever after.'

One of the men spoke in a commanding tone to the doctor, who translated it with a slight tremor in his voice.

'First, you must go to the department.'

'What "department", damn it?'

Raylan felt a stabbing pain in his head and another wave of dizziness coming on.

The doctor grabbed him by the shoulders with both hands and spoke as if he were begging him. 'Listen to me. Just go with them, please.'

One of the men gave Raylan a formal nod with a faint smile, as if to say it was all right, but the problem was it didn't feel that way, it didn't feel that way at all. As the doctor helped him from the treatment table, he heard one of the men ask something in a snappy tone.

'They want to know if you need help walking,' the doctor translated.

Raylan gestured he didn't need their help and staggered down the corridor, while the two men positioned themselves on either side of him to escort him outside. A Borgward was parked in front of the main entrance of the large grey building. While one of the men started the engine, the other held the rear door open for Raylan. The car pulled away from the hospital grounds headed towards the city, which seemed to be getting less predictable by the minute.

*

The sombre grey façade of a three-storey building loomed behind towering iron gates. A guard who saluted like a rusty robot opened the gate. As soon as the car came to a stop in front of the building, a man in a pale-blue uniform pulled the car doors open to let Raylan and the two men get out, after which he went to park the Borgward.

The duo led him up the wide steps to the front landing, into a large, tiled space that was a mix between a mess hall and a hotel lobby. It was teeming with men wearing identical suits.

In the corridors panelled with dark, traditionally carved wood there was a restless atmosphere caused by loudly ringing telephones, men busily talking at the same time and the rattling of typewriters. If Raylan didn't know better, he would have thought he'd entered the editorial offices of a huge newspaper abuzz with deadline stress.

They turned a corner and ended up in another wing of the building. Their footsteps on the marble floor echoed against plastered walls and the vaulted ceiling. At the end of the corridor the men stopped in front of a massive door. They straightened their backs, brushed imaginary specks off their shoulders and sleeves – as if it were a reflex – after which one of them firmly knocked on the door. After a few seconds, a muffled deep male voice coming from the room indicated they should enter.

Through two high windows, beams of ochre-yellow daylight filled the large room panelled in dark wood. Behind a huge desk, files piled high on either side, a man with a virile face and a well-groomed moustache looked up from his writing with a furrowed brow. He had a cigarette between his lips. He screwed on the cap of his fountain pen, which he carefully placed next to him, after which he pressed the cigarette into a marble ashtray and pushed back his office chair.

Despite his robust build, the man approached Raylan from behind his desk with an unexpected suppleness and elegance. His dark-blue suit with subtle pinstripes was an excellent cut, clearly tailor-made. The dignity with which he extended his hand was heightened by his fluent English.

'Aadel Gailani, Attorney General of the Department for the Organization and Defence of the Interests of Afghanistan. Thank you for coming, Mr Chapelle.'

*

39

Gailani looked older than he probably was. Raylan estimated him in his early thirties. He had a high forehead and a receding hairline, and his slicked-back hair was jet black.

'Given you didn't come here entirely of your own free will,' Gailani said almost solemnly, 'I will do my best to make your visit as pleasant as possible.'

Gailani's cordial smile momentarily vanished when he told the two men in Dari that their presence was no longer needed. Raylan saw a man who was courteous to those he considered his equal, but who would be impolite and condescending to anyone he thought was of lesser status. Silently, like ghosts, the two disappeared from sight and closed the door as quietly as they'd opened it.

Gailani gestured to an armchair. 'Please, sit down.'

It took a few seconds for Gailani to actually realize that Raylan wasn't about to sit down, and then an almost sardonic expression appeared on his face. 'They already told me that, uh ... how shall I put it, you're an unconventional fellow.'

'And who might "they" be?'

'The American embassy. While you were at the hospital being treated for your injuries, we gathered information indicating ...' Gailani paused and gave Raylan a scrutinizing look. 'Why don't you sit down? Makes talking so much easier.'

'I would like my passport and stuff returned, and then I want to go to my hotel without delay.'

'If my only intention was for you to pick up your papers and belongings, I could have saved you the trip and myself this regrettably uncomfortable encounter.'

'Seems like a win-win situation.'

There was a respectful knock at the door. Gailani muttered something in Dari, after which a servant entered carrying a large silver tray with a steaming pot, a tea service and a plate of sweets. Gailani gave the servant a quick formal nod in the direction of a side table. After the man had set down the heavy tray – which caused a worrisome rattle of teacups – sweating profusely, he disappeared behind the door again.

Aadel Gailani gallantly pointed to the seating area again. 'Mr Chapelle, please.'

Raylan sighed and slumped down in one of the armchairs. The chair on which Gailani himself sat was somewhat elevated; a detail, Raylan realized, which had been well thought out. He was now obliged to literally look up at his shorter host, who picked up the silver pot with a gracious movement and looked at Raylan.

'Some tea?'

Raylan grinned flatly. 'What's the chance of getting a whiskey here?'

Gailani refrained from any kind of reaction. With a powerful arc, he poured some tea into both porcelain cups.

Raylan looked around the room. The tall bookcases full of bound reference works and files were undoubtedly there to impress visitors. The massive globe on the wooden stand next to his desk was turned so you could see that Afghanistan was surrounded by a whole range of countries. Pakistan to the east and south, in the west Iran and to the north Turkmenistan, Uzbekistan and Tajikistan. And then there was also a small piece bordering China. Jagged grey mountain peaks, some over 7,000 metres high, cut across green valleys and plains in the north of the country. In the south, there were areas of white, indicating the enormous desert of the Helmand basin. A portrait of King Mohammed Zahir Shah hung on the wall behind the desk. Raylan didn't recognize the portrait hanging next to the king.

'Daoud Khan, the king's cousin,' Gailani said, handing his guest a steaming cup of tea. 'We call him the silent power behind the throne. Almost all the nation's reforms in the past ten years were initiated by him. Milk?'

Raylan shook his head and gave Gailani an irritated look. 'Mr Attorney General. Now that you've persuaded me to sit here and drink a cup of tea with you, why don't you tell me what the hell I'm doing here.'

Gailani cleared his throat. It was more than obvious that he wasn't used to being spoken to like this and would normally never tolerate it. Yet, until now he'd played the role of perfect host in every respect, and for the time being it didn't seem like he was going to exchange this role for that of offended public official. He leaned back, looked at Raylan with a cordial smile and took his time choosing his words.

'Coincidentally enough, I wanted to ask you the same thing. Of course, without the colourful expletive you just used. You're a journalist, your articles about the Vietnam War regularly appear in *The New York Times*. Afghanistan is neither at war nor exactly an obvious travel destination, given you're clearly not a hippie, I wonder why you've chosen to honour us with your presence?'

'Well put: this country is not at war, and that's precisely why I'm here. I've got three years of war behind me. I need distance so I can write something worth reading about it.'

'And you think Kabul can offer you that distance?'

'I certainly hope so.'

Gailani thoughtfully sipped his tea. 'Let's put that hope into effect right away.' He put down the cup, went to his desk, took a manila envelope from behind a stack of file folders and handed it to Raylan. 'Your passport and your *taskort*, a visa that allows you to stay in our country for as long as you want. Take advantage of what we call *Pashtunwali* here, an ancient code that offers travellers hospitality, even when you discover your guest is your worst enemy.'

'Have I given you any reason to think that?'

Gailani pursed his lips in a smile. His tone remained business-like, yet a hint of friendliness was beginning to emerge.

'On the contrary, Mr Chapelle, on the contrary.'

Gailani removed a narrow silver cigarette case from the inside pocket of his jacket. Raylan caught a glimpse of an exotic nude woman engraved in relief. He flipped open the case with one hand.

'Indonesian,' said Gailani, holding the case in front of Raylan. 'Kreteks. The name is derived from the crackling sound they make when lit, because of the clove oil extract. Just listen.'

He conjured a flame from a silver-plated Zippo Sterling. Raylan inhaled, and as he tasted the flavour of cloves, he felt like he'd stuck a firecracker between his lips.

'*Kretek-kretek*, can you hear it?' Gailani grinned and lit one himself. 'My nanny used to smoke them. The smell always reminds me of my childhood. Forgive my reminiscing.'

'Consider yourself forgiven.' Raylan replied. 'But can we get back to the point?'

'You Americans … Always in such a hurry. Well, this afternoon, you were – as they so beautifully say in your language – in the wrong place at the wrong time, wouldn't you agree?'

'If this is an attempt to put a positive spin on police brutality, you might consider running for office, Mr Attorney General.'

'I'm told you attacked a policeman.'

'I don't know where you get your information and, to be honest, I don't really care, but it's nonsense. I saw officers chasing protesters into a courtyard, as if they were driving cattle into a corral. Then they started randomly hitting people with their batons, apparently with no regard for whether they were clubbing demonstrators, market vendors or visitors. There was a young woman with me, a Dutch woman. I was simply trying to protect her.'

'Well, chivalry mistaken for resistance, I understand. Anyway, this shouldn't have happened to you. On behalf of the Afghan government, let me offer you our official apologies.'

Raylan closely examined his long-stay visa, making use of the time to collect his thoughts. He couldn't figure out what Gailani's endgame was, but he realized that behind his proper, friendly yet distant gaze was a man you'd better have as a friend. He took a last puff of his cigarette and stamped it out on the metal swivel-plate of the standing ashtray next to him. 'Apology accepted.'

'Thank you, Mr Chapelle. I greatly appreciate that.'

With an energetic movement, Gailani rose from his armchair again, walked back to his desk and pulled a folder from one of the drawers, which he attentively began to browse through. 'The young woman you just mentioned, what's her name?' He asked without looking up.

'Isobel,' Raylan replied. 'That's all I know about her. I just happened to meet her in the courtyard.'

Gailani looked up, silently stared at Raylan for a few seconds, then glanced down again to peruse a list of names. 'I only have you here,' he said hesitantly, his eyes following his finger to the bottom of the page, 'no other foreign names among the detainees.' He looked up with a calm sort of resignation. 'But I will check whether a foreign woman has been admitted to one of our hospitals. However, it's probably safe to assume that isn't the case, given how much foreigners in Kabul usually stick out.'

'I understand,' Raylan replied, 'and I appreciate you making the effort for me.'

'But of course,' Gailani said, placing the folder back in his desk drawer and sitting down opposite Raylan again. 'You talk of a chance encounter, but in our faith scarcely anything is happenstance. Encounters are like road markers to a future that has long been mapped out.'

'Predestination?'

'The will of Allah. Kismet.'

'In your opinion, was it the will of Allah that so many innocent people were beaten up?'

Gailani let out a long sigh. 'If you're willing to listen, I'd like to try to explain the broader context of this incident to you.'

'By all means.'

Gailani sat up as straight as possible and solemnly intertwined his fingers. 'You know we have a ruler with a pro-Western orientation, and that Prince Daoud . . .'

'The cousin . . .' Raylan said, gazing at the portrait on the right.

'Correct. Prince Daoud in particular is doing everything possible to stimulate democratic reform in the country. Thanks to him, Afghanistan has grown from a third-world country into a modernized and technically well-developed nation. Until a few years ago, the Afghan Parliament, the Shura, was only a formal and very bureaucratic entity. The authorities determined who could sit on it. Now for the first time in our history we have a democratically elected Parliament. We have a constitution that gives men and women equal rights, a secular judicial system that is above Islamic Law, freedom of religion, the right to free expression and the possibility for citizens to form organizations and new political parties.'

Gailani picked up the plate of sweets and offered it to Raylan. '*Kulche khatai*: flour mixed with ground cardamom, corn oil, sugar and pistachios. A taste explosion, in my opinion.'

'No, thank you,' Raylan replied, watching as his host popped a whole biscuit into his mouth and chomped away with a heavenly expression on his face.

'However,' Gailani continued, after washing down the crumbs with a sip of tea and carefully wiping his fingers on a white handkerchief, 'if a society has barely any experience with democratic principles, as is the case in Afghanistan, you quickly see that there is a very real risk of radicalization, both on the left and the right. The Jamiat-e Islami, the Islamic Society, claims that our country is being corrupted because Muslim norms are not being followed. The Khalq faction socialists are convinced beyond all reasoning that the government only serves the aristocracy. In the recent elections, the PDPA, the People's Democratic Party of Afghanistan, got five seats in the Lower House. A dubious matter, because much like Hitler's National Socialists, who had little to do with "socialism" at the time, the concept of "democracy" has little to do with what the People's Democratic Party is after.'

'And that is?'

'A communist dictatorship along the lines of the Soviet Union. Especially the party's youth wing, the People's Youth Organization of Afghanistan, is strongly in favour of this.'

It was oppressively warm in the room, but at least Gailani was a good talker. He had the gruff voice of someone who smokes too much, but still sounded warm-hearted. Whatever else you might think of him, you couldn't deny he was charming and charismatic.

'Recently, my department received reliable information that more was happening at the newspaper of the party's youth wing than collating sheets of paper. After a raid on their office, my men found evidence that suggested they were preparing to overthrow the king. The plan was to attack the king's convoy with Molotov cocktails and grenades. The newspaper's entire editorial staff is now on trial for preparing a violent coup. The PDPA claims there is a government conspiracy to silence the party and has organized student strikes and demonstrations.'

'During the demonstration, students were carrying a photo of a young man. Who is he?'

'The editor of their newspaper, Askan Vaziri. He's the personification of the red danger and the face of the anti-democratic forces.'

By now a bluish cloud of smoke filled the space between them. Gailani stamped out his kretek. He had a concerned look in his eyes.

'Our country, Mr Chapelle, has unlimited possibilities. But it also requires an unbelievable amount of willpower, guidance and authority to definitively transform it into a modern democracy. We will rigorously combat any action aimed at preventing that.'

'As rigorously as those officers this afternoon?'

'I understand where you're going with this. The right to freedom of expression.'

'Demonstrating is part of that.'

'Permission was granted for today's demonstration. The police only intervened when a small group of radicals started hurling stones. One of which seriously injured an officer. I admit that the reaction of his colleagues was unprofessional and excessive, but again: you must see the incident in a larger context.'

'I get it,' Raylan said, intrigued by the whole issue. 'What kind of penalty are the suspects facing?'

Gailani straightened his jacket, then his back and leaned slightly forward.

'Do you know what they did to the student who killed the former king in 1933? The executioner severed his body parts one by one: in the order he'd used them to kill the king. First, he put out his right eye, which the perpetrator used to aim his weapon at the king. Then he cut off the finger with which he'd pulled the trigger. Then the hand in which he'd held the gun. And lastly the head in which the idea for the murder had taken shape . . .' Gailani then leaned back and let out a sigh of relief. 'Fortunately, we now live in different times. But the death penalty, as it were, seems a given.'

'When will the verdict be pronounced by the judge?'

'We expect it within a few days. Tomorrow the public prosecutor and the defence will make their final arguments. If you're interested, I can arrange for you to be admitted to the courtroom and that you get an interpreter.'

A short silence ensued. Raylan frowned. This entire visit appeared to be for the sole purpose of positive news coverage. He was most likely the only foreign journalist in town, the only one who also regularly wrote for *The New York Times*. The brutal attack on the protesters in Murad Khane would undoubtedly result in bad publicity abroad for the government. The background story would offer a broader perspective. A planned murder attempt on the king's life had put a young and fragile democracy to the test. Moreover, it was an interesting story, certainly in the context of the Cold War. Communist forces were emerging everywhere in Asia.

'You know by now that I'm not the type of journalist who says what government officials want to hear,' he said to Gailani, who scrutinized him with folded arms.

'You can express your independent opinion, exactly as you have done in recent years. We won't stand in your way.'

'And if I report on this matter, I'll want to speak to all those involved.'

'In any case, I can arrange for you to speak to the public prosecutor tomorrow. Permission to put you in touch with the main suspect Askan Vaziri will require a little more doing, but I don't expect many problems making that happen.' Gailani stood up to indicate the meeting was over. 'I will personally make sure that you have full cooperation tomorrow in the courthouse. And if you need me to do anything else for you, please contact me immediately. My men will now escort you to the room where your personal belongings have been safely stored. Then they will take you to your hotel.'

As they shook hands, Aadel Gailani unexpectedly placed his left hand on Raylan's shoulder and gave him a friendly pat.

If there was anything besides God that Raylan Chapelle truly didn't believe in, then it was coincidence. For him events had a cause and a logical effect. It was therefore unthinkable that he would ever exchange his worldview full of causative links for a world in which coincidences determined events. The idea alone could make him feel completely helpless.

Yet, moments later he stood with that incapacitated feeling in front of the table where all his things were lying, and he realized that the Leica lying there wasn't a coincidence. During the chaos on the square in Murad Khane, Isobel had dropped the camera and left it there when she fled. Given Paul's profession as a journalist, Gailani's men must have thought it belonged to him.

Raylan picked up the camera and touched the dented front. In his mind he heard the panic and the shouting in the courtyard again, but those noises in his head were silenced by the whistle of an approaching bullet. He purposefully placed the Leica back on the table, started packing his rucksack, swung it over his shoulder, grabbed the typewriter case and strode to the door.

One of his escorts gestured at the Leica, which he'd left behind on the table. 'Take.'

'No. Not mine.'

When he exited the building, the Borgward was waiting for him with the engine running. One of the officers held the rear door open. Raylan stepped in and put his rucksack and the Remington case beside him on the back seat. Even before he could close the door, the second officer leaned in and placed the Leica beside the typewriter case. He then slammed the door, after which the Borgward pulled away and exited via the main gate.

In one of the side mirrors, he saw the officers lingering by the gate, possibly instructed to keep an eye on him for as long as possible.

7
Farah

2009

Farah did what she always did when she stared at herself in the mirror: she caressed the many small scars on her arms, her breasts and her belly, the result of cutting into her skin when she was quite a bit younger. So much sorrow, so much loneliness, so much fear. The self-inflicted pain had allowed her to forget it all for a brief moment.

She ran a hand through her hair, which had been hacked short in Moscow, and checked her watch. Another half hour before she was due to be collected. She reached for her phone and keyed in a number that was so important to her. The voice she heard, more than 3,400 kilometres away, felt reassuringly close.

'Farah?'

'Paul . . . I'm here.'

'Where?'

'In Kabul, at the hotel. I . . .'

'What happened?' She heard the concern in his voice.

'They picked me out. While still on the plane. They locked me up and interrogated me.'

'Who did?'

'Two operatives. Americans. I'm not sure which agency. But they knew everything.'

His muffled curse. He'd warned her. And he'd been right. Still, he remained calm and patient as he offered an explanation. 'They deploy a system that creates a risk profile for each passenger. It's called ATS-P and collects data from more than thirty different sources. As soon as

49

the Russians earmarked you as a terrorist, it was automatically passed on to ATS-P. The European intelligence agencies may have removed you from their lists, but it looks like you're still considered a significant risk to the Americans.'

In the silence that followed she could hear how rapid her breathing was. Paul must have heard it too, because he asked, 'Are you okay?'

'I took a nap.'

'That doesn't answer my question.'

'I know. Yes . . . I'm okay. All things considered. But more importantly, how's Anya?'

The long silence at the other end sounded as distressing as her own breathing.

'They're keeping her in a coma,' he finally said.

'When will they wake her?'

'In a couple of days, perhaps. They won't be able to say anything until the swelling goes down.'

She could feel her heartbeat accelerate even further. 'If only I'd been stronger . . .'

She was back in the underground vault of the compound in Jakarta, where she'd been subjected to waterboarding, not once but twice. She would never give in, because death by suffocation was nowhere near as bad as betraying Paul and Anya. But she couldn't let Aninda die. the young Indonesian woman who'd been such a great support to her. Through her tears Farah had hurled Dari curse words at the man who was torturing her. Valentin Lavrov had just stood there smiling. He'd waited until she was done ranting and raving and then repeated his question: 'Anya Kozlova. What's her role in all this?'

'Farah?' Paul's voice sounded tender and worried. 'You have to put it out of your mind.'

'I can't. I'm to blame for what happened to Anya . . .'

'Stop it. All three of us knew the risks. We have to move on.'

'Is that the solution: move on?'

'Do you have a better one?'

'No.'

'Me neither, damn it.'

She sensed the beginnings of a faint smile. That's the effect he had on her. He could defuse any situation with his irony.

'You've missed your vocation,' she said.

'What do you mean?'

'You should have become an evangelist, or one of those TV preachers, you know . . . Someone who tells people we're all sinners, but that God is all-forgiving.'

'I'd rather die.'

'I'd never forgive you for that.'

'You've got nothing to forgive, you're not God.'

She felt lighter and thought of the unexpected visit to the bookshop during her drive through the city. 'Do you remember that old bookshop on Shir Ali Khan Road? It's still there. I . . .' Emotion got the better of her. 'They had one copy left. Of Raylan's book, I mean. I bought it right away, of course.'

She heard him chuckle. 'How many do you have now?'

'One in every language. Twenty-six in total.'

'You really know how to exaggerate.'

She swallowed. 'Paul . . . I wanted to ask you something. That bundle of old letters I put in storage, along with my passport . . .'

'The ones in the station locker?'

'Yes, those. I'd like you to read them. They're . . .'

'. . . personal, right?'

'That's why I want you to read them.'

'I don't get it.'

She took a deep breath. 'They're his, Paul.'

'Whose?'

She fell silent. She caught the disbelief in his question.

'Raylan's . . . ?'

'My mother once gave them to her best friend for safekeeping. The evening before she was due to flee the country with me, thirty years ago. His name was Parwaiz Ahmad and he was the director of the National Museum. He kept them all this time. Shortly before his death he gave them to me. I only read the first letter.'

'Why would I want to read my father's love letters?'

'Because he wrote them to my mother.'

There was a long silence. In the background she heard the sound of the pump administering oxygen to Anya.

'Paul, I don't want anything to come between us ... half-truths, secrets. You said so yourself: we have to keep going. And we can only do that when we know absolutely everything about each other. I want to be there for you. You understand? Whatever happens. That's why I want you to read those letters. It concerns us both.'

'It's embarrassing. He was my father.'

'I know. But ... it happened. It's the truth. And we shouldn't hide from it.'

'Okay. I'll go and pick them up. And read them.'

'Thank you. And call me if you need me?'

'I know where to find you.'

She heard him chuckle. Then there was a long silence. They listened to each other's breathing.

'Fah?'

She swallowed again. He'd never called her that before. It sounded intimate, close, almost frightfully familiar.

'Yes?'

'Be careful.'

She stared into space, absentmindedly listening to the noise on the disconnected line.

8
Paul

2009

The dreary weather shrouded Moscow in a stifling haze. Once Paul Chapelle had ended his call with Farah, he absentmindedly listened to the insistent drumming of raindrops against the window on the top floor of Pirogorov Hospital. They drowned out the rhythmic lament of the pump supplying Anya's lungs with oxygen. A cocktail of muscle relaxers, painkillers and sleeping pills flowed into her body through transparent infusion tubes. It was scary to think how unbearable her pain might be if she woke up.

The attack had resulted in a fractured skull, a severe concussion, a shattered collarbone and a double jaw fracture. Anya's hands were broken; three fingers were crushed. Given the chance of brain swelling, the doctors had inserted a drain in her head.

It was tropically warm in the ICU. Despite the rain that might be blown inside, Paul cracked open a window. A cacophony of sirens, car traffic and the dull drone of crowded trams reached the room. Paul stared into the distance, beyond the Baroque outline of the Novodevichy Convent, where ash-grey clouds blocked out the sky. That morning on the steps of the building where Moskva Gazeta's editorial office was located – facing a crowd of photographers, journalists and camera crews – he'd called on the Russian authorities to guarantee that an in-depth investigation into the attack on one of Russia's leading journalists would be undertaken.

He strongly suspected his plea would fall on deaf ears.

Memories flashed through his mind, leaving images behind like quickly developing Polaroids: Anya and he working deep into the night at the office of the *Moskva Gazeta*, Anya and he drunk in her bed, making love, Anya and he the next morning hurling the contents of her kitchen at each other. After their first night together, she had his number: 'You're a bastard. Unfortunately, a fucking sexy one. And I have a weak spot for bastards. And the bigger the bastard, the better. How does that strike you?'

'Problematic,' he'd replied.

A few days later he moved in with her. No woman had ever given herself to him so unconditionally. No woman had ever provoked him like she had. He thought of that morning when he'd closed the door of her apartment behind him as quietly as possible, with hardly any luggage in his hand and a one-way ticket to Johannesburg. With his departure he was certain he could leave the desire for her behind. He'd never been more mistaken. Anya Kozlova had become an indelible part of his life.

He hid his longing for her behind a façade of new loves, doomed in every respect to failure. What remained was emotional emptiness and the realization that he was constantly burning bridges behind him to be able to move on again, without ever arriving anywhere.

He'd recently returned to Moscow to help Farah investigate one of Russia's most powerful oligarchs, Valentin Lavrov. Anya had immediately sensed the special connection between him and Farah. But the way she'd taken care of Farah after the hostage-taking in the Seven Sisters had shown him just how much she actually admired her Dutch colleague. An admiration that even exceeded the obvious jealousy.

It was perhaps the respect that fighters have for each other; just like Farah, Anya was a fighter. But unlike Farah, Anya had the habit of keeping people at a distance instead of letting them in. That was the tragedy of it all: she was a lone fighter, in her work, in her few friendships and in her scarce loves.

'I still miss you.'

She'd sat across from him in the Chekhovskaya Bar and had spoken those words as if announcing she'd quit smoking. But they were damn well words he should have also said if he'd been braver and honest with himself.

It was evening when they'd last spoken. A mist hung over the river, and they'd walked towards each other through that mist. He'd stood opposite her. Among the ancient oaks, birches and linden trees, beside the old graveyard in Kolomenskoye Park, by that small watermill on a tributary of the Moskva. Her hands were shaking when he took them in his. He spoke to her as gently as possible, hoping in this way to convince her how necessary his departure was. *They know we're in this together. I don't know how, but they do.*

The certainty of her expression had confused him. *I've been on their radar for years, Paul. They know about us. About us back then, I mean. Lavrov will come after you. And then it won't matter whether you're in Amsterdam or in Tokyo. He'll find you.*

Sure, but then he'll find me. *And me only. You . . . You'll be able to carry on here.*

In parting, she'd taken his face between her hands. She'd never looked at him with such sadness. And when she kissed him, it was not with the lust she'd exhibited previously. The kiss was vulnerable; her lips tasted of salt. Then she let go of him and vanished into the fog.

The unrelenting sound of the oxygen pump interrupted his thoughts again. He bent over her motionless body and pressed a kiss to her forehead. 'I should have stayed with you,' he whispered. 'Then this wouldn't have happened, you would have . . .'

His phone vibrated. When he answered he heard Lesha's raspy voice. It sounded like he was in a hurry. 'Paul, I know who it is.'

'Who?'

'The man who . . . to Anya. Damn, how soon can you get here?'

The clouds hovering above the ring road around the centre of Moscow crept closer together, gathering into an ashen mass behind which thunder and lightning erupted. Wherever he looked he saw her face. As if every Muscovite had been cloned from her and adopted her kamikaze way of driving. Anya was behind the wheel of a dark-grey Lada Samara and slalomed across the wide boulevard passing Hyundais, Kias, Dacia Dusters and Zhigulis. In a black Mercedes with flashing lights, she shot past Pushkin Square over the lane that was reserved for party officials. In a RAV4 she overtook Paul on the right, glancing at him with that familiar mischievous look, her upper lip curled in an Elvis-like smile.

But she should be here. Where he was now sitting. Behind the wheel of her yellow Škoda, on her way to the former Hammer and Sickle steel factory. Somewhere on the east side of the centre of Moscow, where Lesha, a chain-smoking hacker, who'd surrounded himself with a bunker of computers, was staring at a monitor showing the face of a man who'd tried to kill her.

Paul quickly lit a cigarette. Not his first one of the day. He'd stopped counting hours ago. He went through an average of two or three packets a day. His heart was beating like a drill about to give out.

On the security camera footage from Anya's apartment complex, which Lesha had hacked into, he watched her briskly walk from the stairwell into the lobby, which the lift also opened on to. The man behind her seemed to come out of nowhere. He was wearing sunglasses, a baseball cap and a leather jacket. Normal posture. Only his nose was strikingly broad, fractured in a fight once, like you see with boxers. He had cauliflower ears. The bunch of flowers in his right hand seemed out of place. When Anya slowed her pace and turned around, he jerked the bouquet into the air. Freeze-frame.

Without thinking, Lesha brushed away the cigarette ash in front of his keyboard and typed a command. The digital time display on the left screen of the computer set-up – on the workstation full of dirty coffee mugs and ashtrays teeming with butts – was almost impossible to make out as it quickly rewound. As if she'd landed in a 1920s silent movie, Anya hurried backwards through the large lobby into the stairwell and then disappeared from the screen. The unknown man behind her was hidden in the shadows. Several people walking backwards entered and exited through the lobby at a slapstick pace.

Lesha paused the image at the time display 6.15 a.m. The moment when the unknown man with the flowers appeared backwards out of the darkness, and then exited the lobby backwards.

'So, he waited almost half an hour for her,' muttered Lesha, whose face and the large bald spot on the right side of his head were covered in white make-up. With his long, pitch-black dyed hair, he looked like an over-the-hill geisha; an appearance that contrasted sharply with the nonchalance with which he let cigarettes burn down to ashes between his lips. He fast-forwarded the security camera's silent images to the moment when Anya came down the stairs.

They could have her walk backwards, Paul thought, but it wasn't possible to have her do anything after that. Once again, when the time display hit 6.40 a.m. – the moment she emerged from the stairwell again at her normal brisk speed – she was confronted by what fate had in store for her.

Again, the man behind her appeared from the shadows.

Anya slowed down. Turned around. He swung the bouquet upwards with a forceful blow. Petals, pollen and pieces of stem flew through the air as the bouquet hit her right shoulder. She screamed; Paul could tell from her wide-open mouth. The lead pipe hidden in the flowers must have broken her collarbone with the first hit.

She slumped halfway to the ground, her arms protecting her face.

Her fingers, long and slender – when she typed it always looked like she was playing piano – were shattered when the man started bashing her hands. Head and hands: the symbolic weapons of writers and journalists. If you wanted to take them out, you first needed to deprive them of the powerful tools of their trade.

The moment Anya turned away from her assailant and staggered backwards, Lesha froze the image again. His finger pointed to the man's neck. He enlarged the frame until the pixels turned into small squares. 'I can't zoom in any closer. The resolution is too low. But here we have the first clue. A trail of ink, to be precise.' He pointed to the man's neck tattoo. 'Tattoos of Russian criminals reveal their status. You can tell from this tattoo whether we're dealing with a crook, a murderer or someone who calls the shots. And this goon is certainly not in charge.'

On the screen, using a white paint marker, Lesha traced the contours of the tattoo, which was visible on the man's neck. Then he let the monitor go to black. Paul watched white lines appear on the screen. Lines in the shape of a knife.

'This thug only follows orders. He's a hired killer. Hence the knife.'

He erased the marker lines with a tissue and clicked *play*. The silent horror in the lobby continued. Under a rain of blows, Anya collapsed against the wall. A heap of bloody anguish, her arms help-lessly raised halfway, still trying to protect her head. The man came and stood right in front of her and raised the lead pipe as high as pos-sible. Just before he was about to split her skull in two with a final blow, Lesha froze the image. Paul knew what came next. The man would pull Anya towards him by her hair and smash her in the face with his knee. Her head would then slam against a wall, and she'd collapse motionless again. Afterwards, he'd slowly turn around and demonstratively give the surveillance camera the middle finger, then he'd calmly walk off screen.

'Look at his hand,' Lesha muttered, zooming in. Paul saw the man's wrist on the screen come closer. What he previously thought was a black braided armband turned out to be a razor wire tattoo.

'Our second clue,' said Lesha, whose white make-up had bled on to the edges of his mouth, making it look like he was constantly puck-ering his lips. 'You can tell from his tattoo how long this guy was inside. The total number of wires suggests fourteen years. And while not a boss, he's someone with a reputation that precedes him. That means we have to go back at least fourteen years and check the regis-ter of prisoners in the Moscow area.' Lesha's fingers flew over the keys. 'You can say what you want about Russia's criminal justice sys-tem, but the prisons have their records in order.'

On the middle screen, a list of names appeared followed by per-sonal information, dates and the reason behind the detention.

'A list of men who have served prison sentences from twelve to sixteen years.' Lesha opened a file with photos and corresponding data. Men with bare torsos staring into the lens with empty eyes. Their shoulders, arms, chest and bellies covered in tattoos. He scrolled through the images, stopped at a man with a boxer's nose and cauli-flower ears and pointed to the tattooed knife on his neck.

'He's our man. Mikhail Kavtaskin, thirty-nine years old. Been out for a year and a half. He works as a night watchman at a steel factory. Suffers from tuberculosis. Member of the Hell Wolves, the most feared bike gang in the country. These fellows see themselves as defenders of traditional Russian values and consider Joseph Stalin their hero. Everywhere they go they sing the praises of the "Motherland", the

Slavic brotherhood and the Orthodox Church. There's a total of five thousand members, only men. The gang runs a number of rock venues and organizes heavy metal concerts by bands such as Genocide or Prescription, Epidemia and Pseudogod.'

Paul could feel an old familiar rage rising to the surface. It was an anger that truly frightened him. It often made him do things his conscious mind could barely grasp. He'd been engulfed by this anger at an early age. Paul went over to one of the arched windows of the large space, which offered a panoramic view of Moscow. Kavtaskin was out there somewhere, free as a bird: the man with a knife tattoo on his neck. With a lead pipe hidden in a bouquet, he'd turned the life of a seasoned journalist into a miserable hell.

9
Farah

From behind the window on the top floor of the Golden Star Hotel Farah looked out over the swarm of afternoon activity in the city's dusty streets. At this height, behind double glazing, the noise was all but inaudible. In the distance, built against a hill, she could see the heavily damaged Darul Aman Palace. In the 1920s, it had been the residence of King Amanullah and the epicentre of power. During the war of the 1990s, the rival warlords had bombed it to smithereens. Now, many years later, it remained a desolate ruin with a collapsed roof and walls peppered with bullet holes, in the middle of a no man's land riddled with landmines. Vague plans to restore it to its original state had been abandoned long ago. The palace seemed symptomatic of the country as a whole.

She thought of her familiar view of Nieuwmarkt in Amsterdam. She'd only had the chance to spend one night in her flat, between arriving home from Jakarta and leaving for Kabul.

She started to unpack her luggage, got dressed and then inspected herself in the mirror. A formal looking black blouse with three-quarter-length sleeves and a high collar, light-grey trousers with a belt that had a buckle in the shape of an eagle. Black low-heeled shoes and a silvery-grey hijab draped loosely around her head. Earrings. No other jewellery. Subtle make-up.

The phone beside her bed rang. The receptionist's voice: 'Ms Hafez, your car has arrived.'

As soon as the hotel's glass entrance door opened for her, the sour-smelling smog crept up her nostrils. Air that claimed the lives of thousands of Kabulis each year: more than the number of civilians killed by NATO troops and the Taliban combined.

The hotel guard with his Kalashnikov was most gallant. He escorted her to the silver Mercedes, where a young man in a chauffeur's uniform waited for her beside the opened rear door. Once enveloped by the bullet-proof windows and the buzzing air-con, she hardly felt a part of the day-to-day chaos of this suffocating city of millions in a valley filled with smog and exhaust fumes.

Everything in the narrow streets, which couldn't handle so much traffic any more, was made of sand-coloured stone covered in a layer of dust that was swept into the city all summer long. But this time she saw things she'd failed to notice during her drive in from the airport: the flags hanging outside; the hand-painted, brightly coloured signs above shops; the trees and islands of pale-red roses in the midst of the asphalt; the razor wire and the concrete of the many security fences. The stone fountains hadn't spouted any water for a long time, but they were still there, like monuments from a forgotten era.

They drove on to Butcher Street, a public abattoir more than a kilometre long. There were no slaughterhouses in Afghanistan; animals were butchered in the street. Halal, without being stunned first. Their carcasses were hanging upside-down from iron hooks, like merchandise. Goat skins were spread like carpets on the ground. A live sheep stood as if in a trance beside the hunks of meat, awaiting its own end. A colossal bald man in a leather apron was chopping ribs in half. Sheep's heads and legs, local delicacies, were drying on a cloth in the sun. Even with the windows closed, she could smell the sickly aroma of spoiling meat and clotted blood.

Beside the congested junction of Butcher Street and Shir Ali Khan Road, which was practically an open sewer, a group of women in pale-blue burqas, filthy with mud and exhaust fumes, sat begging. They all had one arm raised with the palm of their hand turned up, as if expecting it to rain down money. They could be found at all the junctions, most of them with a child. Children brought in more money. Some motorists threw a few afghanis out of the window. When her driver rolled down the window to do the same, she heard the women shout '*Zan e bewah!*' That's when it dawned on her. *Zan e bewah* was a code of conduct. An appeal to the moral obligation of Muslims to help those who have lost everything. And these veiled women had indeed lost everything.

Street urchins were running in and among the cars to sell phone cards, chewing gum and newspapers. She rolled down the window and bought a copy of *The Afghan Press*. The front-page headline left little to the imagination: DEVASTATING TALIBAN ATTACK ON UN GUESTHOUSE.

Once past the junction, all of the city's motorists seemed to be taking the same exit at the same time. Her driver had to slam on the brakes three times to avoid a collision with the car in front. Pedestrians and cyclists appeared from nowhere and dashed across the street. Everybody honked their horns at everybody else and tried to squeeze into any available space just to get a few metres ahead.

As they approached a T-junction, a grey saloon popped up behind them, seemingly intent on boring straight through all the other vehicles. The Mercedes swerved left. When the car pulled up alongside them, Farah found herself looking into the distraught eyes of the driver. With his head stuck out of the window he was fiercely gesticulating with his left arm, shouting that he had to get through. She spotted the cause of his panic on the back seat: a woman in a long grey robe, her legs spasmodically pulled up and both hands on a belly as round as a pumpkin.

At the T-junction the saloon gathered speed and took a right turn, half-mounting the pavement as it did so. She saw a US military patrol approaching from the opposite direction. The driver of the lead car, a Humvee in camouflage colours and with tyres as big as the rear wheels of a tractor, stepped hard on the brakes. The angular behemoth came to a surprisingly rapid halt. But the saloon was going too fast and, forced to take the turn too wide, slammed into the side of the Humvee.

The screech of singeing brake discs. The tension of her own bated breath. The split-second silence that preceded the impact of tinny metal against reinforced steel. The armoured counterforce of the Humvee catapulted the passenger car into the air, where it rotated a half turn before landing hard on its roof and sliding towards the middle of the road.

Farah saw a man jump out of the front Humvee. He yelled orders at the soldiers, who jumped out of the other vehicles with their rifles ready and immediately formed a defensive cordon around the saloon. The man had olive skin, a broad jaw and piercing eyes. Like a pillar of strength in army fatigues he stood there, amidst a cacophony of noise, dust and chaos, as if he'd always stood there. As if he'd been sculpted on that spot before this part of the city was erected around him. His every move and every glance revealed that he'd instantly surveyed the situation. When he saw Farah jump out of the Mercedes – she *had* to do something – he raised his hand.

That gesture alone was enough to stop her.

Bystanders who'd come running out of shops, homes and alley-ways were kept at bay by the armed Marines. In a snarling American drawl, they reeled off lines in Dari they had memorized: 'Stand back!' 'No further or I'll shoot!'

Farah saw a female leg sticking out of the smouldering wreckage. A leg that jerked involuntarily. Screaming that turned into long-drawn-out, high-pitched keening. The patrol leader crouched down, turned his head sideways, peered into the overturned car and said something to the woman. When he rose to his feet a few seconds later, he shouted to his troops: 'I need an interpreter.'

Farah waved at him and yelled at the top of her lungs: 'I speak Dari. I can help!'

He turned towards her, looked her up and down before glancing at the government car and then, with a few measured hand gestures, motioned for her to approach.

'I have to do this, I'm sorry,' she said to her driver and ran over to the patrol leader. The closer she got to him, the more she was struck by the intensity of his gaze. He was fully focused on her, while at the same time keeping an eye on the protective cordon his men had formed around the cars.

'I'm Gunnery Sergeant Mason Williams. And you are?'

'Farah Hafez.'

'All right, Farah.' He pointed to the saloon. 'I need to communicate with this woman.'

She knelt down, leaned towards the woman lying amidst the broken glass beside the motionless body of the driver, reached for her hand and, when she found it, gave it a squeeze and felt the waning strength with which the woman returned her grasp.

'*Bachem* ... My child ...', she moaned. Her faint words were drowned out by the shouts of bystanders flocking around them. The soldiers with their automatic weapons were struggling to keep them at bay. The air was thick with menace. The crowd hurled torrents of abuse at them: '*Marg ba Amrika!* Death to the Americans!'

Mason squatted next to Farah and peered into the car. His face was beaded with sweat. A female soldier with a first-aid kit ran from the front Humvee towards them and knelt beside Farah.

'This is Gaby Davidson,' Mason said. 'Tell the woman that we've got a doctor for her.'

Farah nodded and translated, but there wasn't much of a reaction. Her face was covered in blood. The fluid that had saturated her robe smelled sickly sweet.

'Amniotic fluid,' Gaby said. 'She needs immediate attention.'

'We're taking her with us,' Mason said. He turned to Farah. 'Tell her that we're getting her out.'

'*Tora azad medem.* We're going to free you.'

Together with Gaby, Farah brushed away as much of the broken glass around the woman as she could. Then they carefully manoeuvred her leg back through the open window. Meanwhile Mason yanked open the rear door and began sliding the woman out of the car as carefully as possible – her legs first and then, after sinking down on to his knees, he put his arm under her buttocks and with Gaby supporting the woman's head he slid her further out of the vehicle.

'You'll be fine, they're going to help you,' Farah said. '*Rahat bash, baret komak mekonan.*'

Mason carried the woman in his arms. 'Tell her that we're taking her to the hospital.'

'And the husband?'

'We don't transport dead people.'

Farah walked alongside Mason, tightly gripping the woman's hand. A rock narrowly missed them. It bounced off the lead Humvee, whose broad-shouldered driver was transferring boxes of ammunition from the trunk into the support vehicle.

In the hail of stones that followed, soldiers fired warning shots. Bystanders broke through the cordon. They were fronted by a savage-looking man with a bull's neck. He charged straight at them, hurling abuse. He wasn't far now. Only a few metres away.

At that moment it was as if a second Farah took over. Without thinking she swapped her everyday self for another version: a woman trained to recognize when lives were at risk and to act accordingly.

On impulse she yanked off her belt and in one fluid motion took the loose end in her right hand. Then she whacked the metal clasp with the eagle motif against the charging man's head. Before he had a chance to lash out at her, she grabbed the belt with both hands, blocked his blow, wrapped the belt around his right fist, and by ducking underneath it dislocated his arm.

Now run.

Ten quick steps separated her from the Humvee. Behind her the man was howling with pain.

Six steps.

Mason and Gaby slid the woman into the car via the tailgate. More warning shots, more yelling, more stones flying through the air.

Two more. She was going to make it.

Mason caught her and grabbed her by the shoulder. 'You're coming with us.' He pushed her into the raised steel chassis; she had to stoop for the low entrance.

Inside, everything was large, coarse and dark. A space big enough for at least seven people now held just her, the injured woman on the seat and Gaby, who hurriedly unrolled a camouflage bag full of medical instruments.

Mason had leaped on to the front seat beside the driver, locked his door and now leaned over to Farah. 'No worries. Gaby is with Air Force Special Operations, Para Rescue.'

She looked at Gaby, who'd bared the woman's belly and breasts and was listening through a stethoscope. Para-jumpers like Gaby were part of an elite medical corps. They were trained to treat extremely serious injuries in combat environments and to keep victims stable for up to seventy-two hours. Not only were they highly adept at treating the serious trauma sustained by commando parachutists and divers, but they were also authorized to take and act on decisions that would normally be the reserve of doctors.

'Your name?' Gaby asked after she'd taken off her stethoscope.

'Farah.'

The turbo-charged engine roared. The wide tyres gripped the road.

'Okay, Farah. Ever assisted with a delivery?'

'No.'

The woman howled and retched as if she might vomit. She was close to pushing out the baby.

Gaby appraised Farah. It was the look of a woman who was used to keeping her cool under the most stressful circumstances and to doing what needs doing. 'In that case you're about to have a totally new experience, because you're going to help me with this one.'

A hail of stones hit the Humvee's aluminium plating and bullet-proof glass. The three-ton giant leaped forward. Gaby handed her a pair of latex gloves. 'Put these on. And ask her to pull up her knees. It will make things easier for us.'

Farah did as she was told. The woman had become all but inaudible. She sounded dazed.

'She says she can't move her legs.'

She could tell from Gaby's eyes that this wasn't good news. 'Dysfunction symptoms.'

Gaby turned to the front and called to Mason to notify the OR and to have the MRI operational. Then she spoke to Farah again. 'She may have a skull fracture, definitely a spinal injury.' She shone a bright light into the woman's eyes. 'The brain's not getting enough oxygen. Even just a short lapse could cause irreparable damage.'

Farah heard Mason talking loudly but with composure into his radio to make himself heard over the noise. She detected no trace of distress in his voice. 'Alpha Zero, this is Chainsaw One.'

A pinched, tinny response at the other end: 'Chainsaw One, this is Alpha Zero, over!'

Meanwhile Gaby continued to talk to Farah. 'I have to stabilize her. Hold her head, so she doesn't thrash about. I can't help her with the delivery. You're going to have to do that. You can do it. I'll talk you through it.'

The driver accelerated. Mason shouted his orders into his radio. 'Alpha Zero, we have an emergency medevac. One WIA-nonmil. Status female. Special, I repeat, special!'

The Humvee behind them passed and took over the lead. The third pulled up closely behind them. They were now protected on either side.

Gaby kneeled behind the woman on the back seat and placed her elbows on her knees to make herself as stable as possible. She placed one hand with outstretched fingers under the woman's neck, the other, also with outstretched fingers, under the back of the head. The woman's head was now stabilized as much as humanly possible between Gaby's arms.

The driver braked suddenly, sounded his horn and then stepped on the accelerator again. The unrest outside forced its way in, nestled in Farah's body and sent her breathing into overdrive.

The woman's contractions became more intense. Gaby sounded calm. Not a trace of panic. 'Tell her to breathe deeply in between the contractions.'

Farah saw something dark appear: the baby's head.

'Support the head,' Gaby shouted. 'The baby shouldn't come too quickly.'

Mason's voice from the front seat: 'Pregnant woman in labour. Life-threatening injuries. We're coming in hot. Prep ER. Chainsaw One out!'

When the next contraction came, the woman howled again. Gaby's hands pressed harder on either side of her head. 'Check if the umbilical cord is wrapped around the neck.'

Farah's trembling fingers moved all over the baby's head. 'I feel something . . . around the throat.'

She heard the vaguest hint of panic in Gaby's question. 'Is it very tight?'

Farah felt again. It was like holding a slippery and pulsating piece of rope. 'Yes.'

For a second it seemed dead quiet in the Humvee. They all knew what this might mean. The baby wasn't getting enough oxygen.

Gaby's urgent voice: 'The next contraction may bring out another piece of umbilical cord. Support the head and turn it a little, very, very slowly.'

Despite the heat, Farah was now shivering all over. She moved the head very slowly. After the next contraction the umbilical cord was clearly visible.

'Is it any looser now?' Gaby shouted

Farah wanted to respond, but no sound came out of her mouth. Tears were streaming down her face. She nodded to Gaby.

The car sped around an unexpected bend. At precisely that moment the woman shrieked. During that contraction Farah saw part of the shoulder appear. She gently held the head, which felt slippery. The next contraction brought the baby out in its entirety. She could hold the child. Hold it in her arms.

'It's a girl,' she stammered.

'Wipe the membrane off her face. Lift her up. Check if she's breathing.'

Farah listened, and shook her head in shock.

'Slap her on the buttocks.'

She slapped. The baby started crying.

'Hold her face down.'

She did as she was told and saw fluid and mucus come out of the child's mouth.

'Well done. Now wrap her in your scarf and cover her head.'

By now the car had come to a halt, and the doors were yanked open. She heard Gaby describe the woman's condition, saw hands appearing in her field of vision, but she clung to the child the entire time, even when Gaby reached for her. Everything around her appeared to slow down. All noises faded. She stared at the woman who was carried away on a stretcher. Then she felt two strong hands on her back. Mason spoke to her calmly.

'You've got to let go now, Farah.'

Her head started spinning. Carefully, she handed the infant to Gaby. In the background she faintly heard Mason's voice. 'It's all right. You did a great job.'

10
Raylan

1968

The blue mosaic tiles on the bottom of the swimming pool rapidly came closer. As he cleaved the clear water, Raylan left a long trail of air bubbles behind him. After taking a sharp angle downwards, he tapped the bottom with his fingertips, pushed himself off and let the momentum carry him diagonally upwards. Once he reached the surface, he began a high-tempo front crawl, finally touching the end wall after five or so laps, out of breath.

Hanging over the edge of the swimming pool, he looked across the atmospherically lit and luscious green inner courtyard of Hotel Serena, located in what was now considered the gently beating heart of a 3,000-year-old city. The Garden of Eden might have looked like this if both Adam and Eve had been blessed with green thumbs: symmetrical ponds, fountains, paths made of colourful old tiles, citrus trees, flowering shrubs and borders full of jasmine and fragrant herbs. In addition, the imposing and dark contours of the Hindu Kush towering in the hazy distance.

He listened to the singing of late birds, turned around, leaned back against the tile wall and watched the moving water in the pool reflect the rear of the hotel like a surrealistic mirror. The balcony of his third-floor room was bathed in inviting sunlight. He hoisted himself out of the water, took a refreshing shower beside the pool and put on his snow-white robe. Back in his room, he grabbed the dented camera and sat down on the edge of the bed.

It was a Leica M. The M stood for Messsucher, a German term for a combined rangefinder and viewfinder that enabled you to see not only the subject but the action going on around it. It was a compact, light device, virtually silent with a fast shutter speed. Ideal for documentary photography. Iconic photos had been taken with this type of camera: the falling soldier in the Spanish Civil War; the sailor passionately kissing a girl in New York's Times Square; and that monk's self-immolation on the square in Saigon, three years earlier.

He could still see the frail figure of that young woman stepping further away from the retreating crowd around the monk. She was slender, petite and agile. With her Leica in hand, she'd efficiently circled the erratic blazing flames and had not stopped shooting until the charred body of the monk had disappeared into a coffin. After that she had no idea what to do with herself. She stood there in the middle of the square, shaken to the core, and couldn't speak. It looked like she was about to faint. He rushed towards her and grabbed her tightly. 'It's okay,' he'd said. 'You did well.'

Her name was Fabienne Montand. Two days before the monk set himself on fire, she'd arrived at Tan Son Nhut airport in Saigon on a one-way ticket from Paris. At the Associated Press in Saigon they'd given her three black-and-white film rolls and a press card and told her to come back when she had something they could use. As the rows of monks in their orange robes were chanting on their way to the square, she'd initially thought they were going to hold a peaceful demonstration.

That day, clutching her trembling body, he realized that both of them had been initiated into the madness of war at exactly the same moment. They decided to jointly incorporate the monk's fiery sacrifice into an article: his reporting and her photos. Three days later, the monk's self-immolation was a worldwide press phenomenon that heralded the start of a collaboration that would last almost three years.

They boarded Huey military helicopters with the same ease as jumping into a taxi. Whenever they were on the road – in the heat, the drought, the rain, during long, cold nights in the field, on rocky plateaus, halfway between hills concealed by elephant grass, or with a patrol going through the jungle – they felt truly alive. Their stories appeared in best-selling magazines: *Life*, *Look* and *Paris Match*. They were an invincible team.

Raylan felt a migraine coming on, placed the Leica on the bed, took his packet of Lucky Strikes and lighter from the dresser and walked to the balcony. While sucking the nicotine into his lungs, he didn't see anything of the hotel garden he'd admired earlier. He was distracted by the shrieking sound of AF Skyraiders, which he now heard in his head. They flew low over the Imperial City of Huế dropping napalm. The bombs spun like tops, hit the ground and exploded into clouds of fire and black smoke, burning everything and everyone in the narrow streets and alleyways.

When Raylan and Fabienne, accompanied by a platoon of GIs, had crossed the River Perfume the next morning, they saw the incinerated bodies of men, women and children. The smoke was still rising. In search of remaining Viet Cong fighters, the GIs kicked in door after door, threw a grenade into each house, stormed in after the explosion and shot at everything and anything that still moved. Sometimes during those raids, they stumbled over a wire attached to an explosive and they were blown to smithereens. Others were wounded in the narrow streets by the sniper bullets fired by Viet Cong boys, who'd hidden like moles in tunnels.

He remembered when a medic was bent over one of the GIs trying to stop a bleed in his neck. When the young soldier raised his head, he was shot right through the eye. Fabienne captured that with her Leica. Raylan was no longer sure, but he thought he'd shouted for her to take cover. But that might have been in hindsight. Just like he'd thought in the middle of the chaos he'd heard the hissing of an approaching bullet.

The bullet that hit Fabienne in the chest.

She abruptly fell backwards, didn't move. He'd crawled over to her. Her face had a greyish-blue tint. 'It'll be okay,' he said. She stroked his arm. The hint of a smile started to appear. Halfway through, she stopped breathing.

On the balcony, as he placed another Lucky Strike between his lips, Raylan thought of what Fabienne had once said to him: *Taking pictures was much like dancing. You held the device and moved with it, with the flow of life.*

He turned around, leaned against the balcony's iron balustrade and stared at the Leica lying on his bed. It was the same kind of device Fabienne had used, complete with dented housing. He imagined her spirit retrieving it from the rubble of the Imperial City of Hué to secretly bestow it on a wandering hippie girl from the Netherlands, so that she could capture his image here in the middle of a crowded courtyard in Murad Khane.

Raylan was surprised by the doggedness with which the demons of war continued to haunt him, even as far as Kabul, and the curious ways in which the dead made themselves known to him.

11
Farah

2009

Evening settled in the Green Zone in the heart of Kabul and within the high walls of the military enclave of Camp Eggers. In the clear sky the half moon and the stars were plainly visible. Farah tried to make out the Dragon, an elongated string of stars somewhere between the Big and the Little Dipper. As a child she used to do that a lot, lying on a top branch of the apple tree, staring up at the night sky.

The leaves and branches of tall trees rustled up against the grand buildings where kings and presidents had once resided. Gaby held out an open packet of cigarettes. Farah shook her head. She surveyed the contours of those buildings for any trace of recognition. She once swam here, in one of the pools, and ran around the lush gardens and played hide and seek in the staff quarters. But the swimming pools and gardens from that era had disappeared under concrete slabs. They now supported containers that had been converted into living and working quarters in this military camp.

Gaby flipped open her Zippo, lit a cigarette and inhaled greedily. 'How are you feeling?'

'I don't know . . .'

'You delivered a child for the first time. That's got to feel kick-ass.'

A few dull thuds sounded from afar.

'I heard they stormed the US embassy,' Gaby said.

'They?'

'Civilians. Irate civilians. Whole hordes of them. The story goes that we crashed into the saloon, instead of the other way around.'

The sound of a rapidly approaching jeep. Two headlights illuminated them. The vehicle slowed and came to a halt. The driver kept the engine running. Farah recognized him as the buff driver of the Humvee. He grinned at her. 'Terrific work this afternoon.' He shook her outstretched hand. 'Duncan O'Leary.'

Meanwhile Mason Williams also got out and came around the front of the jeep towards them. 'Mother and child doing okay?'

'All things considered,' Gaby replied. 'What's up?'

'Debriefing with Goldwater, ASAP.' Mason held open the rear door and looked at Farah. 'Your presence has been requested.'

They drove along the main street, Gator Alley, which ran straight through the labyrinth of metal living and working blocks, to the central roundabout with flags, where Duncan brought the jeep to a standstill between two other vehicles with a single impressive spin of the wheel. A large sand-coloured container building loomed up in front of them. Military personnel in a range of different uniforms, most of them carrying dossiers, walked in and out with measured steps.

'The Ark,' Gaby said. 'The general's headquarters.'

Seeing all those motionless flags, Farah's thoughts immediately returned to the square with the flags in the military section of the airport, earlier that day.

On the second floor of the Ark, a young and nervous sergeant escorted them to the commander's office. The wall to the left sported a detailed topographic map of Afghanistan. Behind the desk hung two clocks, one indicating local time in Kabul, the other Washington time. Three black-and-white photos next to one another: Goldwater with Clinton, Goldwater with Bush, Goldwater with Obama. The heavy-set Goldwater himself was on the phone. Judging by his reaction, he wasn't at the receiving end of good news. 'How many dead? Damn it!' he bellowed into the receiver.

Some men look good when they're heavy-set. Goldwater was such a man. From under his thick eyebrows he sized her up with a quick glance. She shaped her mouth into a formal smile. He nodded in acknowledgement, but only just, slammed the receiver down and gave Mason, Duncan and Gaby a brief salute. In response to his 'at ease' they stood with their legs apart, folded their hands behind their backs, raised their chins and stared straight ahead like poker players used to bluffing.

Goldwater stepped from behind his desk. He looked imposing. His handshake lived up to expectations: it felt like a vice.

'Ms Hafez. This afternoon, you unexpectedly played an important role in the rescue of a civilian casualty. I would like to personally thank you for this.'

'I appreciate it, commander, but my role was negligible.'

He looked at her, frowning. She noticed the twitching just above his right eyebrow.

'Allow me to disagree with you.'

For a split second she averted her eyes. That's when she spotted the painting. A horde of Afghan men on neighing horses galloped into view.

'A gift from my predecessor,' Goldwater said. 'I was told that Buzkashi dates back to the time when men on horseback went out hunting for mountain goats.'

She must have been five. The first time she'd been allowed to dress as a boy – the only way to see a Buzkashi match. Women and girls were only allowed to watch from a great distance away. Now she got to be really close. With her father's large hand securely on her shoulder. The riders on their fierce stallions wore caps, quilted jackets and high boots. They stood around a large circle drawn in chalk paint. Inside it lay a decapitated calf whose legs had been cut off at the knees and its entrails removed. .

Goldwater sat down on the edge of his desk and crossed his arms. 'But I didn't summon you here to chew the fat about old paintings. Since killing no fewer than seventeen civilians during an attack on suspected Taliban insurgents last week, we seem to have really screwed up with the ordinary Afghans. Today's incident brought things to a head.'

His jowls moved in unison with his sonorous bass voice. The twitching above his right eyebrow was a nervous tic. She wanted to listen to what he had to say but was distracted by the horsemen jumping out of the frame, their whips between their teeth, as they bent as low as they could to grab the calf's carcass.

'Offices of foreign aid organizations . . . raided . . . set alight. Staff at the American embassy evacuated . . . personnel flown to Dubai . . .'

Goldwater's words totally escaped her. She'd become the little girl who watched in awe as one of the riders managed to extricate himself from the throng. He grabbed the calf and quickly galloped away from the rest, holding the animal with one hand. With the other he directed his horse to the pole positioned a hundred metres away. He had to go around it. And then back to the circle where the calf had to be chucked down again. The others galloped after him, rapidly catching up.

'Believe it or not . . .' she heard Goldwater say.

She forced herself to suppress her memories and to listen to him.

'While defending their premises, a private security company opened fire on the protesters. Recent reports say at least five people died. The president has declared a state of emergency. The Afghan National Guard is patrolling the city, and it's authorized to shoot at troublemakers and plunderers.'

He rubbed his nose and massaged his right eyebrow. His silence took her straight back to the rushing horses foaming at the mouth. She saw the man in front being penned in by the others. Riders groped for the calf, yanking at its legs. The man fell. His horse crashed on top of him, yet he held on tight. The pack surrounded him. Horses reared up and threatened to trample the man along with the calf. Yet he kept holding on to the beast. Tears of rage came to her eyes. The only thought in her head was that she had to go to the rescue of the man with the calf. She was about to squeeze through the crowd to run on to the pitch, when a strong hand grabbed her from behind.

With both arms Goldwater gently pushed himself off from the desk until he stood upright again. 'Gunnery Sergeant Williams.'

'Yes, sir.'

'I'm expecting a detailed report on my desk first thing tomorrow. Right now just quickly bring me up to speed.'

Mason shifted from one foot to the other as he told his story. 'Around sixteen-hundred hours, at the T-junction of Butcher Street and Shir Ali Khan Road, our patrol was unexpectedly confronted by a passenger car heading towards us at great speed . . .'

His words were lost in the jeering and cheering of the crowd around her. She saw how the man with the calf managed to get back into the saddle and escape the tangle of riders.

'O'Leary was unable to avoid the car. The vehicle, a saloon with two passengers, rammed our left, flipped over and came to a halt several metres away.'

She saw blood dripping from the wound on the rider's forehead. He was almost at the circle but slowly slipped from his saddle again. There he fell, together with the calf he was holding. His head hit the ground and he lay there motionless.

'The driver must have been killed instantly.'

She could hardly breathe and felt sick when she saw that some of the riders wouldn't be able to avoid the man.

'We were able to save the passenger in the back seat, a heavily pregnant woman. She and her baby are in the Emergency Department here in the hospital.'

The man disappeared behind a cloud of dust, together with the calf. That's when she threw up. Nobody noticed. Except one man. Feeling defeated, she looked into her father's eyes, in which she saw dismay, shame.

Goldwater was standing right there and must have been staring at her in silence for some time.

'Ms Hafez?'

'Sorry . . .'

'I asked you what your motives were to come to Sergeant Williams' assistance this afternoon.'

'I beg your pardon.' She didn't know what to think of this man. No doubt he was keen to impress her with his military authority. When she started talking she could hear how tense she really was. 'At the time I was being driven to the Interior Ministry.'

'I'm aware of that.'

She looked at him in surprise.

'Your driver followed you to the gate.'

'Ah . . . I . . . I didn't know that.'

'Please proceed.'

'The accident happened right before my eyes. The vehicle Sergeant Williams was talking about had overtaken me . . . us, I should say . . . the

Mercedes I was in, at great speed just before the T-junction. I'd spotted this heavily pregnant woman in the back seat.' She swallowed a few times and spotted a jumble of burst blood vessels in the whites of Goldwater's eyes. 'I ran over, to see if there was anything I could do. I speak Dari so when I saw that Sergeant Williams was having difficulty communicating with her I offered to interpret.'

'Clear. Thank you.'

Goldwater turned back to Mason.

'Sergeant, the moment you managed to get the civilian casualty safely into the Humvee you knew she'd receive more than adequate medical attention. And yet you chose to take Ms Hafez with you. Why?'

Mason answered calmly. 'Ms Hafez had given us invaluable assistance on the ground. Not only did she interpret and explain to the woman what was going to happen, but ...' He paused a moment. Much to Goldwater's displeasure, who gestured for him to speed things up.

'I'm listening, sergeant.'

'... she also neutralized a civilian who tried to stop us carrying the victim into the car. If we'd left Ms Hafez behind, her loyalty and help to us would no doubt have made her a target of the angry crowd. Besides, we also needed an interpreter during transport to the hospital because PJ Davidson had to communicate with the victim.'

Goldwater said nothing, but as he walked around his desk he nervously drummed on the tabletop with his left hand. He stopped as suddenly as he'd begun and looked at them intently.

'I've been in touch with the Afghan president and have promised him full transparency and cooperation with an inquest into the circumstances of the accident. Pending that investigation you're obviously forbidden to talk to the press.' He glanced up at the painting. 'But given the situation I might as well ask you to register for the national Buzkashi championships.'

In the ensuing silence he looked mockingly at the surprised faces of his three subordinates. That's when she realized: Goldwater knew. He'd known all along.

'I see that none of you are aware that this afternoon you called on the services of a well-known, or some might even say notorious, journalist?'

Of course Goldwater had read her dossier. A file he must have received directly from Harcourt and Mendosa. She felt a peculiar shame creep over her. As if that last remark had stripped her stark naked in front of Gaby, Mason and Duncan. Unmasked as a journalist. As if she'd deliberately withheld this information amidst the frenzy of the past hours.

'I beg your pardon, commander, but my assistance this afternoon had nothing to do with the fact that I'm a journalist,' she said. 'Lives were at stake. I got out of the car to help.'

For years and years, her editor-in-chief Edward Vallent had criticized her for having poor impulse control, urging her to let herself be guided by her journalistic qualities rather than her emotional whims. When, several weeks ago at Amsterdam's Waterland Medical Centre, she'd come to the aid of a little boy in girl's clothing who'd been left for dead on a deserted woodland road, he'd described her as a loose cannon. *You throw yourself into something without considering the consequences.* But Edward had been wrong. She'd come to recognize this in the past few weeks.

There was a deeper power inside her. A strength that sprang from a source she'd only recently discovered. It had happened underneath a waringin tree in Jakarta. With the help of an eighty-year-old woman she'd first become aware of her highly developed sixth sense, *idera keenam*. A universal awareness of justice and truth. All the *silat* fighting techniques she'd learned were anchored in this consciousness. The impulse that had prompted her to jump out of the Mercedes and run over to help this afternoon sprang from that same consciousness. If she were to face the same choice in a different situation tomorrow, she'd do exactly the same. Since her stay in Jakarta she'd learned to trust what people like Edward, who she respected immensely, considered to be her weakness.

Goldwater had turned towards her. For a man who was in charge of a powerful military organization and who'd just slammed down the phone like a god of thunder, he now sounded surprisingly mild. 'No matter how you got involved in this situation or whatever your motives may have been, the fact remains that you're a journalist. And that means that you're better placed than anyone to portray the consequences of what happened today in a different light.'

'Meaning?'

'We're here to save lives, not to take them.'

The jetlag, the events at the airport, the accident as well as its aftermath were beginning to take their toll. She felt dizzy. She'd had nothing to eat since her flight.

'So if I understand you correctly, commander, you're asking me to turn a fatal accident into a heroic story.'

'What I'm asking is for you to see the bigger picture. Not as an obligation towards me or the US army, but above all as a responsibility to your readers.'

'With all due respect, commander. My responsibility to my readers is my business, not yours. You want to use the media to benefit from a situation that's actually tragic. A man crashed into a US patrol because he panicked as he tried to get his wife to hospital as quickly as possible. This man's death can't be made good by a heroic epic about your people saving his wife and child in a military hospital. I'm a journalist, not a PR consultant to the army.'

She noticed that the twitching above his right eyebrow had intensified.

'You're a beautiful woman with a great deal of ambition. I appreciate that. You'd go far if you weren't such a damn nuisance.'

She regarded Goldwater calmly and smiled. 'Did you just call me a nuisance, commander?'

'I believe I did, yes.'

'I'll take that as a compliment, sir.'

Eight boots marching, on their way to the Ark's exit. Approaching military personnel saluted them. Without a word they walked past the forty-odd flagpoles outside. When they got to the jeep, she was keen to break the silence. She should have addressed this earlier. She did so now.

'The fact that I'm a journalist. That I . . .'

She looked at the two men and the woman standing there. She'd seen the conviction of their actions that afternoon; the calm with which Gaby had given her the confidence to deliver a child in a Humvee, which Duncan had steered so smoothly through the traffic chaos, while an unperturbed Mason continued to issue his orders via the radio. She'd worked with them, three strangers, but in that collaboration she'd tasted an intensity and an ease as if they'd known each other for years.

'I don't care if you're the queen of Kabul,' Gaby said. 'You offered your assistance, and we accepted it.'

Duncan slammed his clenched fist on the bonnet. 'If there's anyone who should apologize it's Baritone Bob up there.' He glanced up at Goldwater's window, where the blinds were drawn. 'What a shitty way to treat your guests.'

She'd smiled at Goldwater. He'd responded with a faint smirk, which was supposed to camouflage the fact that his intimidating performance had achieved the exact opposite of what he'd been after. His offer had no doubt been tactical. If you couldn't beat your opponent, best to keep them close. He'd suggested she spend the night in one of the guest rooms he'd already reserved for her. 'Given the curfew you'd put your life at risk by returning to your hotel now.' On her behalf he'd rescheduled the appointment at the Interior Ministry for the following morning at nine. He would have her escorted there. 'And I'm sure my people will want to show their appreciation for your help by treating you to a square meal. Right?'

She looked at all three of them, standing around her beside the jeep. 'You don't have to. I should probably get some sleep and you . . .'

'Hold on. You're talking about sleep when you've got the chance to taste Drew's mind-blowing Philly cheese steak? Do I understand that correctly?' With the elegance of a Neanderthal, Duncan held the door of the jeep open for her.

'We want to do this with you,' said Gaby, who linked arms with her. 'This afternoon we worked as a team. We finish the day as a team. So get in, you damn nuisance.'

As they drove through the dimly lit camp, Farah looked at Mason, who was in the passenger seat staring into space. Against the passing dim background, his profile seemed to be chiselled from mahogany wood. She realized why she'd initially thought he was an Afghan. But on closer inspection, she'd seen that his light-brown skin had that warm glow that the average Afghan lacked. It was the colour of the sun and the sea. The skin tone of a Pacific Islander. His eyes were sparkling brown. He had long, jet-black eyelashes that were the envy of any woman. His short hair was a few shades blacker than hers. Stiff and thick, almost bristly. If it were longer, it would be wavy with a bluish shine. He was more than a head taller than her and muscular all over, with just enough fat to keep him from looking like a body-builder. The kind of man she couldn't keep her eyes off if he were standing naked in front of her, like that time as a girl in the National Museum when she'd come face to face with the statue of the naked Greek soldier.

He hadn't said a word since the interview with Goldwater. She wondered why. Was it because she'd stood up to Goldwater? Was it because Goldwater had insinuated that it was irresponsible to bring a journalist into the camp in this way? Or was he bothered by the messy fallout of the accident? She wanted to know but didn't dare ask him. Not now anyway. Maybe never. After tomorrow their paths wouldn't cross again.

Duncan stopped the jeep outside a flamingo-pink, two-storey container block in the women's section. Farah read the sign: HOTEL CALIFORNIA.

'You can check out any time you like.' Gaby chuckled. 'But you can never leave.'

The tiny room with freezing-cold air-con accommodated a bunk bed, a cupboard and a chest with a helmet and a bullet-proof vest on it. On the bed lay a camel-coloured military outfit, along with underwear and socks. There was even a pair of combat boots at the foot of the bed. Her size. Arranged around the washbasin were all kinds of toiletries: toothpaste, toothbrush, deodorant, shower gel, skin care oil, a hairbrush, tampons and panty liners. In the afternoon Farah had stared with restrained anger at her own toiletries, which had been plucked from her washbag by unknown hands and lined up as anonymous objects. This time she found herself looking at strange things that had been arranged with great care to suggest they were hers.

She took off her dusty, bloodstained clothes and, on Gaby's instructions, put them in a plastic laundry bag, which she left by the door. Shivering with cold, she walked over to the shower cubicle. When the steam came off the narrow jet, she stepped under it, lathered herself with the gel and scrubbed any remaining blood from her body.

She'd just put on the khaki-coloured military fatigues when there was a knock on the door. Gaby stood in the doorway. She looked different. A softer, more beautiful woman had appeared from behind the dirt, dust and events of the day. Farah noticed that she was wearing a bit of make-up and she caught a whiff of men's aftershave.

Gaby looked her up and down and laughed. 'You could strut down the catwalk in that outfit. You're just as elegant as the Italians here. I don't know how those guys do it, but they always look better than anybody else.'

After they dropped the laundry bag off at the launderette and Gaby urged the young man behind the counter to have everything ready at seven o'clock sharp the next morning, they walked over to the square near the Green Bean Coffeehouse. There they sat down with Mason and Duncan, under a pomegranate tree decorated with a string of coloured fairy lights. In a cloud of greasy smoke, a huge African-American with a grubby apron was standing behind a grill trying to satisfy half a platoon of hungry Marines with great big hunks of roasted meat.

'Grill Grandmaster Drew,' Duncan said, laughing. 'Our saviour in times of need.'

They clinked their four ice-cold bottles of beer before sinking their teeth into the Philly cheese steaks, which tasted exactly as Duncan had predicted: divine. They grinned at one another, took a second bite and then devoured the steak as if they hadn't eaten in days.

Mason was the first to speak. His question sounded casual, but she had a hunch that there was more behind it.

'What brings you to Kabul, Farah?'

'My father's funeral. I mean, reburial.'

So for the second time that day she recounted the story of her father's death and the Afghan government's invitation to attend his ceremonial reburial. But this time she didn't just stick to the facts.

Between the lines, she expressed her immense sadness – for the loss of a father who'd been declared dead, but whose remains had never been found. Until two days ago.

At the end of her story, all three of them were staring at her open-mouthed. Gaby briefly touched her arm and gave her a sympathetic nod. Duncan took a swig of beer and choked on it. Mason wiped his hands on a paper napkin. He seemed unmoved by what she'd just shared with them.

'Do you hate the war as much as most journalists we meet here?' he asked.

Surprised by his cynical tone and the sudden change of topic, she looked at him.

'How can you *not* hate war?'

'Let me put it this way. Are you in favour of this war?'

'How can you be in favour of a war?'

A faint grin stole over his face. 'Is this your standard journalistic method?'

'What do you mean?'

'Answering every question with another question?'

She sensed his hostility and was caught off-guard for a moment.

'Let me put it this way,' he continued. 'Do you think this war is necessary?'

'Give it a rest, Mason,' Gaby said. 'She's our guest.'

Farah took the time to lick her fingers clean and met Mason's eyes.

'I remember the second plane,' she said softly. 'The second plane to fly into the WTC. I was at the editorial offices in Amsterdam. Someone had switched on the TV and I saw it happen. I couldn't believe it at first . . .'

'That's not what I'm asking.'

'No. You're asking if I think this war is necessary. You can find a war cruel, unnecessary, it can disgust you, but none of that matters in this case. The moment those planes flew into the Twin Towers, the brain behind the attacks was here, somewhere in my home country. He was given shelter and protection by a group of young men with beards who think that people with a different faith should be slaughtered like pigs. They were just as guilty of murdering all those thousands of men and women in New York City that day as the man they were hiding in a cave somewhere. Do I think a war is needed to expel both the Taliban and their guest Osama bin Laden?' She kept staring at him intently. 'Yes, I think so. But the war hasn't driven them out, Mason. The men with beards are still here. They appear at night, abduct politicians, journalists, plant roadside bombs, blow up hotels. And the Afghans who shouted "Death to America" today stopped seeing you as their liberators a long time ago. To them you've become the occupier.'

Duncan clapped his hands together, agonizingly slowly, and then again, and again, until the applause gathered momentum. He grinned and yelled: 'Hear, hear.'

Mason seemed to be loosening up and raised his beer bottle. 'To the eloquent daughter of a minister who died too young.'

Their bottles touched. Duncan let out his roaring laugh. He was a country boy, born on a ranch in Mansfield, Texas. A hunter, fisherman and horse breaker who'd joined the military at eighteen. It was a family tradition. His grandfather had landed in Normandy, his father had fought in Korea. His strength and natural ability had soon brought him to the Seal commandos.

Gaby's route had been a little different. She'd been a GP. Immediately after the 9/11 attacks, she decided to join the army. 'I wanted to do something for the men and women defending my country on the other side of the world.' She enrolled at the US Military Academy at West Point and graduated with distinction. But Farah sensed that she too had doubts about what they were doing here. And not just between the lines.

'When I hear all the talk at home, when I see politicians and the commentators on CNN, they're talking about a very different war from the one I'm experiencing. Our politicians who come here to see the war "with their own eyes" are driven around in air-conditioned buses like tourists. They get to visit a local market that has been completely cordoned off by armed forces and a shitload of security guards, and then they walk around for a bit and buy a souvenir while some general whispers that it's just as safe in the rest of the country. And back home they tell anyone who wants to hear that we're making such progress here. They never get to hear our side of the story.'

'It's like *Groundhog Day*.' Duncan grinned. 'You know, that film with Bill Murray and what's-her-name, who did those soap commercials.'

'Andie MacDowell,' Gaby said. 'But it wasn't soap, it was shampoo.'

'Same difference. Anyway, Murray wakes up one morning somewhere in a godforsaken town with Sonny and Cher on the clock radio: "I've got you babe!" And the next day he wakes up exactly the same way, again with Sonny and Cher, and nobody else in the entire village, not even Andie MacDowell, remembers anything about yesterday, he's the only one. And it's the same story day after day, day in day out, identical. That's how it feels here. We conquer a village, we kill a handful of Taliban, but somehow or other they always come back the next day, shoot some of us and disappear back into the mountains. And the following day we return with a patrol, we shoot some of them and send them scurrying for the mountains and the day after . . . Oh man, it's all just as crazy as in *Groundhog Day*.'

'With one big difference,' Gaby said with a grin.

'And that is?'

'No Andie MacDowell.'

Mason hadn't said anything for a while. Farah had tried to avoid his searching gaze for as long as she could, but when their eyes met, she saw his smile and heard the challenging tone in his question. 'I'm sure I'm not the only one who wants to know.'

She saw the conspiratorial grin on their tired faces.

'I mean, what I saw you doing to that man this afternoon, I haven't seen any civilian woman do,' Mason continued. 'It was wicked. So . . .'

'So?'

'Who the hell taught you that?'

She smiled awkwardly. 'My father.'

'But he's . . . You were young?'

'Very young.'

She talked about the childhood mornings under the apple tree but concealed the pain and the loneliness. 'When I arrived in the Netherlands, I really wanted to do something other than Pencak Silat. I wanted to take up football, boxing, gymnastics. There was a gym in the small town where I lived. It was run by an Indonesian man. He must have been two heads taller than me. Guess what he specialized in . . .'

'Pencak!' they exclaimed in unison.

'I trained with him for years, seven days a week. His philosophy was: hit first, talk later. As a girl, I wanted to hold my own with the boys. For months my arms and shins were covered in bruises. But in the end I was seen as "one of the guys".'

Mason regarded her gravely. 'Like you were one of us this afternoon.'

She looked at him in disbelief. 'You reckon?'

'Hell yeah, after what you showed us.'

At that moment something inside her broke. A wave of fatigue washed over her. Her thoughts drifted, miles away. To the beach near Jakarta where she'd stood only a few days ago and where Satria had held her farewell ritual. She'd placed fruit and other food on a little bamboo raft as an offer to Ratu Kidul, the Princess of the Pacific. The raft, overlaid with silk, had drifted off before it was eventually swallowed by the waves.

She tried to smile, took a final sip and stood up. 'I'm sorry . . . but I really need to get some sleep now. I'm shattered. Thanks for your hospitality.'

'Hang on,' Duncan said. 'This is when Mason and I are going to fight about who gets to walk you home.'

She smiled. 'I'm an Afghan girl.'

'And they won't be escorted home?'

'Unless you propose to them first.'

Before she knew what was going on, Duncan got down on one knee, both hands theatrically on his broad chest near his heart. She ran her hands through his bristly hair.

'No man has ever done this for me.'

'Is that a "yes"?'

'That's a "yes", all right,' Gaby said, grabbing Farah's arm while laughing. 'As in "yes, go fuck yourself".'

As they walked off, they could hear Duncan in the distance calling after them.

'Please don't go! You're breaking my heart.'

'Apologies,' Gaby said with an ironic smile, 'we're all a bit screwed up around here.'

'What's up with Mason?'

Gaby paused. 'If you can lead a combat unit, like he does, you can do anything. But lately he's had too much on his plate. I'm telling you this in confidence, but just before he was deployed on his mission here, he found out that his wife and his best friend had spent a weekend in a motel together. He has two kids, and they mean the world to him. Then barely three weeks ago a roadside bomb blew up his Humvee. The explosion left him with a severe concussion. He's had cluster headaches ever since. The examining doctor's report hasn't landed on Goldwater's desk yet. It could mean early retirement. To be honest, I don't know how much longer he can keep going like this.'

Gaby had walked her to the door. When Farah closed it behind her, she heard the soft buzzing of her mobile inside her bag and saw that she had three missed calls from Paul. She answered and could tell he was in a car. He sounded rushed, agitated and had to speak up to be heard over the engine.

'I've been trying to reach you for ages. Where are you?'

'Camp Eggers.'

'What?'

'Long story. I can't go into it now.'

'Are you safe?'

'Yes . . .'

'Okay. I'll keep it brief. We've got him.'

'Who?'

'The bastard who attacked Anya and left her for half dead. Don't ask me how, but Lesha has managed to retrieve his data. The man we're after is a member of a motorcycle gang. I'm on my way to an informant, a guy doing undercover investigations into the club.'

Although the content of his statement told her it was good news, something about his tone of voice gave her inexplicable chills all over her body. 'Don't go, Paul. Turn back,' she blurted out.

'What's got into you, for God's sake?'

'It doesn't feel right. I can't explain.'

'Listen. You and I both know who's behind this attack, right? The same prick who tried to drown you in Jakarta. Or have you already forgotten about that?'

'I don't want you taking unnecessary risks. Anya needs you.'

'Unnecessary risks? Look who's talking!' Now, he sounded downright hostile.

'Don't hold that against me.'

'I'm taking this risk, with or without your permission.'

'Paul, please . . .'

'Sorry, I have to hang up.'

Before she knew it, he'd put the phone down. There was no point in calling him back; he wouldn't answer anyway. And if he did, she'd only make things worse. Of course he wanted retribution. But that was precisely why she wanted to stop him. When you're consumed by revenge, as Paul was bound to be right now, the consequences of your actions tend to be a second thought. What choice did she have? She had to trust that it would all work out in the end. That he'd emerge unscathed. But her premonition, which was undeniably strong, told her something different. Something totally different.

12
Paul

2009

The centre of Moscow lay far behind him, the roads were almost empty, and the night sky sparked with lightning. He'd placed the mobile phone next to him on the passenger seat. The screen would light up again soon. Farah would call him back; he was certain of it. And if she did, he wouldn't answer. He knew what was next: another attempt to discourage him. A renewed plea to swing the Škoda around, at the very moment he was en route to check out a promising lead.

Roman Jankovski, editor-in-chief of the *Moskva Gazeta*, had put him in contact with an informant. A former Spetsnaz frogman, who went under the code name Lyov and for whom a life without risks was not worth living. You had to have a contempt for death or suicidal tendencies to infiltrate one of Russia's most notorious motorcycle gangs. Maybe that was why Farah said she had a bad feeling: the horrors that increasingly pointed in Lavrov's direction. But even so. She'd recently followed Lavrov to Moscow too, without first considering the consequences of her actions. And then barely back from Jakarta, she was already on a plane to some other godforsaken spot. Kabul, of all places. Talk about taking unnecessary risks.

But perhaps that was why she reminded him so much of himself. The same character trait: an odd combination of fearlessness and stubbornness with a hint of the naive. Once they'd set their minds on something, nobody could convince them otherwise, no matter how great the risk. They both recognized they were their own worst enemies, so they tried to protect each other against their reckless tendencies. A few days earlier, he'd scolded her when she told him she was leaving for Afghanistan. *It's too dangerous there. Two female journalists were killed last week.* As if there were no murder attempts on journalists in Russia.

There was no time to think about this further. A concrete colossus nine storeys high appeared in front of him: the Akvadroma Water Park, constructed for the World Youth Games in 1998, now just stood there, abandoned, a half-built soulless skeleton being corroded by the elements. It had become a favourite hangout for addicts, junkies, the homeless and dropouts of all shapes and sizes. The Moscow police had recently conducted another raid. The place was cleared out, the fencing around the site reinforced. A top layer of razor wire made it impossible to climb over. But he knew exactly where he had to be: on the other side of the road, where there was a concrete structure, a planned metro station. The line to the Akvadroma was never extended, but a pedestrian tunnel had been built under the road. The lock on the iron gating had been picked open, just like Lyov said it would be.

The tunnel was full of filthy mattresses, needles, trash and rotting food. The perfect territory for an army of rats, which had no intention of fleeing for a solitary intruder trying to navigate the rubbish and muck with a light cast by his mobile phone.

Gravel crunched under his boots as he climbed the first wide spiral staircase of the 40,000-square-metre concrete carcass. He stopped and listened to the wind, the clattering rain and his accelerated heartbeat. The thrashing he'd received at the Ponte City complex in Johannesburg was still fresh in his memory. He thought about Arseni Vakurov standing opposite him, his bald head gleaming with sweat. That old condor with his inhaler was just as cruel as he sounded. '*Pentimento, pentimento.* Repentance, repentance!' Those sinister words he'd hissed in Paul's ear before he gave the order to beat him to a pulp: 'Fascinating to see how sons follow in their fathers' footsteps. As if it's a biological imperative.'

The narrow beam of light from his mobile phone glided over the walls of the first level, which were covered with grim graffiti. There was a large empty pool in the middle of the space. Paul looked around, stood still, turned 90 degrees and shone his light in the direction where he thought he'd heard footsteps. He pricked up his ears, concentrating on ambient noises. The rain, the distant sound of city traffic, a jet flying over. He must have imagined it.

Though everything made him feel that he wasn't alone, he refused to obey his instinct, which urged him to flee. The arm came from behind and closed around his throat like a lever. The sharp tip of a knife pressed against his windpipe. A voice muttered in his ear, 'Why don't you announce to all of Moscow you're here?' The knife pressed deeper into his skin. 'Turn it off, now!'

He switched off the light. The grip around his throat loosened. 'Stand still. Don't turn around.' The tip of the knife withdrew.

'If anyone gets wind of this meeting, I'm royally fucked. I'm not prepared to look over my shoulder for the rest of my life because you're a moron. You get my drift?'

'Crystal clear.'

The knife disappeared, followed by the arm around his throat.

'Just don't move.'

'Okay.'

'So Kaytaskin landed your girl in the ICU?'

'I have the security camera footage to prove it.'

'That miserable piece of shit is dumber than a donkey's arse. A day after the attack, and he's suddenly driving a brand-new motorcycle. Attention and vodka. I gave him both, in spades. Spilled his guts. I hacked his laptop when he was sleeping it off.'

The hand in front of him opened, revealing a mini-USB stick. Paul took it and placed it in his jacket pocket.

'Follow the money. The Hell Wolves' treasure chest recently got a thirteen million rouble injection. Business transaction. My arse! It's blood money. From Atlas Industries Moscow, a daughter company owned by chief dirtbag Lavrov. You should be able to do something with that tip, right, my American friend? End it. Spare no effort. She's entitled to that, our Anya.' Lyov grinned meaningfully. 'I've had the pleasure like you. At least, I hope you've had the pleasure.'

From underneath them came the roar of rapidly approaching motorcycles. There was a clamour of metal fencing collapsing from the surge of motor-powered aggression. When Paul turned around, Lyov had already vanished. Paul ran down the concrete spiral stairwell, stumbled in the middle and bounced the rest of the way. The concrete floor slammed the air from his lungs and the world went dark.

The first thing Paul saw when he tried to get up was the menacing silhouette of the man in front of him. And an incoming kick. A booted foot came rushing towards him, hitting him between his neck and chin. Paul grabbed his throat, gurgled, looked up and saw a second silhouette appear behind the unknown man. He was briefly visible in the flash of a lightning bolt: a broad muscular giant in a black leather jacket with tattoos that twisted like a garland from his neck to the back of his bald head. Paul now saw what the knife that had poked his neck minutes earlier was capable of. It slashed open the throat of his assailant; the blood spurted in all directions like a fountain.

'Move!'

He recognized the voice of his rescuer. It was Lyov. And as the room filled with roaring engines racing towards them, he ran into a long dark hall with wide pillars on either side. Zigzagging through the pillars, he heard the roar of the engines advancing from behind. He looked over his shoulder, lost his balance and fell between the two pillars. A motorcycle raced past, braked, spun round and came back towards him. A second motorcycle approached from the other side. In the blink of an eye he saw a metres-long, heavy electrical cable hanging from the ceiling. Paul grabbed it and tugged as tightly as possible.

Both motorcycles barely had a chance to brake. The impact with which they collided with the cable from either side caused one motorcycle and its driver to smash into a wall. In a shower of sparks, the other motorcycle slid on the gravel floor for another ten metres and then came to a halt.

Paul ran over to one of the motorcycles. His mind was blank; he let instinct take over. Grab the handlebars, try to lift the vehicle. He didn't get any further than that. A grip from behind made him spin around.

When he recognized the face of his attacker, he lost control. From one second to the next he felt no pain. All sense of time and place disappeared. His fists struck the man with the cauliflower ears and the knife tattoo.

How long did it take? Seconds, minutes, perhaps even longer. Soon Kavtaskin's face was barely recognizable as that of the man who'd attacked Anya with a lead pipe. It was only when the concrete on the pillar just behind Paul shattered and the stone splinters hit his head that he regained his senses and found himself staring directly into approaching headlights.

He'd learned to protect himself. *Incoming! Take cover!* Standard military commands his father had taught him. Relying on instinct could save your life. He had ducked, seized the fallen motorcycle as intended, lifted it up, jumped on it and given it gas. Before the others could reach him, he drove out into the open air, along the enclosed rough terrain, until he found an opening in the fencing.

The continuous rain had made the asphalt slippery. The streets of the Moscow suburbs that he raced through were dimly illuminated. He was only wearing his leather jacket and boots. No helmet. He tried to control the 300-kilo BMW mechanical beast. Falling meant an ICU bed next to Anya.

They caught up with him.

Time to risk it all. Trust the machinery. Take a right, onto a woodland path. A soft surface unfit for such a motorcycle, especially when you're going faster than eighty kilometres per hour. He stayed off the front brake and kept both feet close to the ground. The roar of motorcycles now seemed to be coming from every direction. The loose surface turned into cobblestone. He let the rear wheel slip slightly, causing the motorcycle to slow down just enough to take him through three sharp turns.

He felt the ground get harder under the tyres. The path became wider. He could see the lights of a narrow bridge. He rode over it, and at the end took a sharp right, after which he found himself on a quay covered by concrete slabs.

He yanked the throttle. The thunderous steel beneath him shot forward. The wind blew full in his face. His eyes teared. He heard an ear-splitting bang. His rear tyre exploded into pieces. The force of a sixty-horsepower engine propelled him forward into jet-black water. He flew through the air, as if gravity didn't exist. Until he slammed the surface of the water and instantly sank into darkness.

PART TWO
A Thousand Souls

I

Raylan

1968

The Mughal Emperor Babur once described Kabul as a paradise of gardens and boulevards, surrounded by orchards, clattering fresh-water springs and mountains 'like rows of clovers'. For Raylan it was mainly a barren stronghold full of shouting market vendors, where the dust from the mountains penetrated your nostrils.

He'd returned to the sandy courtyard of Murad Khane, where every trace of the violent police charge seemed to have been erased entirely. The stalls had been rebuilt, fresh, undamaged merchandise was displayed on the wooden planks, and the tarps against the bright sun had been tightened again. Everything had been returned to a tableau that must have looked just like this for centuries.

Nobody seemed to want to be reminded of what had happened the day before. Everywhere he inquired about a young blonde woman who must have been walking around here – 'with this camera' – he received a negative answer. A helpful taxi driver took him to a simple photo shop in the Jeddha Maiwand district. The wooden sign above the door indicated RONA STUDIO. The distinguished owner in a tweed jacket stood behind a display case full of old cameras and spoke to him in German.

'*Woran danke ich die Ehre Ihres Besuches?*'

'Sorry,' Raylan said. 'I'm American.'

'My apologies,' the man replied in English. 'I thought: blue eyes, blond hair, your appearance . . . You must be German.'

'I assume you mean that as a compliment,' said Raylan with a sardonic grin.

'Well, of course. I greatly admire the Germans. I studied colour photography in Leverkusen. But it's also an honour to have an American visit my shop. How can I help you?'

Raylan took the Leica out of his rucksack and carefully placed it on the counter.

'A magical device,' the man remarked approvingly, as he looked up at Raylan with a twinkle in his eyes. 'The story goes that if you are in possession of a Leica, adventure automatically follows.'

It would take a few days to a week for the dented Leica to be good as new. Behind a wooden table of a *chaikhana*, a tea house, adjacent to the bird market in the old centre, Raylan looked at the first photo from the roll the man from Studio Rona had developed for him. A group of kids, barely twenty, in plaid shirts and worn jeans, with tangled hair falling far below their shoulders, uneasily posing on Dam Square in Amsterdam. They were about to embark on a journey of thousands of kilometres. Yet, for now, they were still smiling in front of the day-glo-painted Magic Bus at the young woman who'd immortalized them with her Leica.

He took a first sip of the traditional *chai shireen* and almost gagged because of how incredibly sweet it was. He heard the mocking laughter of some men who were seated cross-legged on a carpet near him dipping sugar cubes in their tea, after which they enjoyably popped them into their mouths. It was clear from their gazes that they didn't know what to make of him. For a hippie he looked like too much of a tough guy in his denim shirt, indigo blue jeans, leather jacket and motorcycle boots – which he often wore at night – because you never knew how quickly you'd need to flee from a surprise attack of the Viet Cong or the impact of a rocket-propelled grenade. You could almost hear them thinking: how could the eyes in that tawny, unshaven and sun-tanned face be so amazingly blue? They invitingly gestured to him. '*Biya!* Join us!'

Smiling, he shook his head and continued to look at the other photos.

He could follow the route Isobel and her fellow hippies had travelled almost chronologically. They departed the country their parents had rebuilt after the Second World War, on their way to a place where they hoped, together with other soulmates, to realize their ideals of free love and a non-materialistic lifestyle. Along the way they slept in shabby inns, cheap boarding houses or at times on the hard leather benches of the bus, which might be parked somewhere near a river or on an open field. As the long trip progressed, he saw fatigue begin to appear on their faces. It brought back memories of young GIs crammed into military lorries on their way to new trouble spots: faces of boys hardened by coming of age too quickly, turned inwards, struggling with the crippling fear of death. A greater or more painful contrast with the flower power children he was now holding in his hand was hard to imagine. These photographs were an ode to youth and their burning desire for a better and freer life. The adrenaline of constant discovery kept them going; the sensation of unexpected encounters with strangers who spoke an incomprehensible language; the drug culture and undoubtedly the perplexing nature of sex – often with no strings attached. And the more he looked at the photos and saw the story of their trip unfold, the more captivated he became.

Over the course of the journey, the focus of Isobel's photos shifted. Her bus companions appeared less and less. The unpredictable, changing landscape and its inhabitants demanded more and more of a place in her photographs. They posed relaxed and proudly in front of their houses, their shops and the landscape that marked their lives. They posed as if they were in front of the lens of an old friend who'd come to visit them. He realized that was the secret of this disarming young Dutch woman. Her heart opened at the same moment as the shutter of the Leica. In turn, those in front of the camera opened up to her. Exactly what had happened to him, when he met her.

As he looked at the photos, it seemed as if Isobel was sitting opposite him and, in her own nonchalant way, light-heartedly telling him about what she'd been through during the journey. The elderly woman she'd met at a well somewhere in Turkey with whom she'd had a long conversation, even without them being able to understand each other, after which the woman proudly posed in front of the lens to bid her goodbye. She talked about the young customs officer in Islam Qala at the Afghan border, who tried to sell her a piece of hashish, which she politely refused, after which he stared into the lens like a Romeo who'd been rejected by his Juliet. She told him the story of three Bedouin girls with whom she'd exchanged her jewellery along a desert road surrounded by the camels, after which they'd smiled radiantly at her lens with their arms wrapped around each other's shoulders.

Ise didn't take photographs, she captured life's stories in a single moment of stillness.

She looked at him now, with her soft, shy eyes. A photograph probably taken by one of her travelling companions. The only photo she appeared in herself. The person who'd shot this image had come closer to her than anyone else, Raylan realized. Perhaps they'd made love in a hotel room on the border of Turkey and Persia, or in a tent on the Herat plateau. He immediately threw off the unexpected jealousy he felt and smiled when he saw the next-to-last photo, in which a vague glimpse of him appeared between the market stalls in Murad Khane.

He picked up the last photo, which she'd taken right before the police stormed into the courtyard, and saw himself, as she saw him, as if he were looking through her eyes.

The owner of the *chaikhana* stood next to him with a teapot ready to be poured. '*Chai talkh*,' he said with a smile, 'no sugar.' Raylan quickly emptied his cup, turned it over according to custom, put the pictures into the inside pocket of his leather jacket and paid. On foot he went deeper into the maze of alleyways of the Mandayi bazaar, where the smell of baked naan wafted from clay ovens, millions of flies buzzed round the carcasses of skinned goats and laundry was hung out to dry. In Chicken Street, where young backpackers spent their time smoking hashish in tea houses, carpet shops and coffee houses, he showed people the photo of Ise looking into the lens. And every time he asked, *Do you know this girl?* they shook their heads with glassy eyes and gave him that perennial smile which made it so easy to ignore the real world.

He looked at his watch, realized he was in fact late for the final session of the trial against the young newspaper editor and hesitated about whether he should still go. But he'd promised Gailani. He hastily raised his hand to hail an approaching taxi.

A little later, when he got out at the old courthouse, he recognized some of the determined young people who'd positioned themselves by the stairs in front of the entrance. He'd seen them the day before, when they'd all marched past him at the intersection during the long, impassioned demonstration. The second time he'd seen them, they were running in a desperate panic across the courtyard of Murad Khane, fleeing the riot police with their raised batons. And now they stood with their fists in the air opposite a circle of nervous young policemen protecting the courthouse.

A girl with long black hair tried to engage a policeman in discussion. Raylan knew that this was futile. The policeman and the girl were the same age, but that's where the similarity ended. Like most students, the girl was undoubtedly from the upper middle class. The young policemen were all from the lower social strata. Now they literally and figuratively stood opposite each other, scarcely able to understand one another and – perhaps worst of all, in the light of what had happened the day before in Murad Khane – struggling to keep a lid on their emotions. The uncontrollable dynamics of clashing cultures here prevailed over common sense. Most of the demonstrators were chanting slogans, which sounded like declarations of war, and were succeeding in provoking the nervous police officers into an extreme reaction. It probably wouldn't be long before the order for a new baton charge would be.

Raylan looked around and saw that the only way to reach the main entrance was via the stairs. He started to squeeze his way through the crowd until he came face to face with a policeman, to whom he presented the document dropped off in the hotel lobby that morning by a messenger boy from the ministry. In addition to three bold lines in Dari, it contained all kinds of official-looking stamps and a bold signature, probably Gailani's. The officer turned around and gestured to his commander at the top of the stairs. After this man had also studied the document with some suspicion, he made it clear to Raylan that he needed to follow him into the building's lobby. There, a skinny man in his forties, wearing horn-rimmed glasses on his narrow face, introduced himself as 'the interpreter'. The sergeant ordered the doors of the courtroom to be opened, after which he led Raylan and the interpreter along the middle aisle to the front row. There he told two men to relinquish their seats, so that Raylan could follow the public prosecutor's concluding argument, which had already begun.

Although this woman in her lawyer's robes could have stepped out of one of Dominique Ingres' Orientalist paintings, she seemed untouchable. What struck him immediately about her was the concise way she constructed her argument to form a coherent indictment'of the main suspect. Suddenly, in the middle of a sentence, she remained silent and looked at him as if he'd just gate-crashed her party. When their glances met, Raylan realized that he was intrigued not only by her unfaltering performance, but also by her eyes; the left one was dark brown and the right greenish-blue. She took a sip of water. He noticed her hand was shaking slightly and wondered how this was possible given that she displayed so much self-confidence.

As soon as she resumed her arguments, the interpreter summarized the main points. The Public Prosecutor's Office had provided a wealth of forensic evidence. There were preparatory sketches of the attack and accompanying texts written by the principal suspect, Askan Vaziri. A lead article he'd written for publication in the controversial party newspaper clearly showed that Vaziri saw the monarchy as a symbol of oppression and inequality. He advocated a violent coup d'état that would presage the fall of the royal family and the present government, after which a utopian communist state could be established.

All in all, the attempts to undermine the constitutional monarchy, the proposed revolution and the plans to assassinate the king were reason enough to demand the death penalty as the only suitable sentence.

The arguments were watertight. If applause had been allowed in the courtroom, she surely would have received a standing ovation. The seven suspects in their dull-brown prison uniforms were sitting there as if the word guilty had already been tattooed on their foreheads. Only one of them looked directly at Raylan. It was the main suspect, Askan Vaziri.

The judge gave the floor to the defence lawyer. The man had barely begun his appeal when Vaziri suddenly stood up. There was a nervous murmur in the room. The lawyer gestured for Vaziri to sit down, but he remained standing. Even before the judge had called him to order, he launched into a solemn statement, which sounded like a prepared speech. Raylan glanced at his interpreter, who only went as far as saying, 'It's an ode to the revolution.' At that moment, uniformed guards stormed the dock.

Their problem was that Vaziri was right in the middle of the line-up of defendants. In addition, the dock was elevated. The guards had to remove the three on either side before they could reach Vaziri. Everyone in the room was now standing and hurling all manner of curses at the defendant. Vaziri continued to speak in a controlled manner, although nobody could understand him in the turmoil. Raylan was impressed by the calmness with which the young man finally allowed himself to be overpowered and removed from the courtroom by the guards.

In the meantime, the disorder in the courtroom turned into complete chaos. Banging his gavel and shouting an order for everyone to leave the room immediately, the judge tried in vain to control the crowd. While police officers who'd rushed to the scene began to push those present outside, Raylan hurried unnoticed in the direction of a side door about to fall shut, which he'd just seen the public prosecutor disappear behind.

In the dilapidated courthouse corridor, the woman wearing the robes froze in her tracks and turned around startled.

'I'm a journalist,' Raylan said. 'I need to talk to you about this case.'

She regained her composure, looked at him with a slightly anxious gaze and answered in fluent English. 'I was informed of your visit, Mr Chapelle. And even if I hadn't been, you were hard to miss, given your grand entrance into the courtroom.'

With a certain elegance she pointed to a wooden bench in the corridor. 'You can wait for me there.' She then disappeared into her office.

The wait seemed to take forever and was finally interrupted by the appearance of the interpreter with the horn-rimmed glasses. 'I'm no longer in need of your services,' Raylan said grinning sardonically. 'I now speak fluent Dari.'

At that moment the door to the public prosecutor's office opened again. 'Whenever you're ready, Mr Chapelle.'

She was wearing a suit and seemed taller, due to her high heels. Her curly long hair was hanging loose, and he noticed it had a bluish sheen. Her eyebrows were carefully plucked and she'd put on some make-up. Fascinated, he looked into her different-coloured eyes.

She held out her hand to him. 'Helai Durani, public prosecutor.'

'Apologies, Mrs Durani, for the intrusion. I'm glad you're prepared to talk to me.' He held her hand just a bit too long.

She pulled away and waved her other hand in front of her face. 'Would you mind putting that out before we proceed?' With obvious disgust she pointed to the freshly lit Lucky Strike he was holding between his fingers. Raylan turned halfway to the interpreter, handed him the cigarette and walked into her office, of which two of the four walls were completely covered in jam-packed bookcases. On the wall behind her desk, buried in paperwork, hung the king's official photo, and next to it Prince Daoud. An immense ceiling fan displaced muggy warm air through the high space.

'My compliments on your English,' Raylan said, looking around some more. The vase of flowers on her desk and the blue Persian carpet with a floral motif under the seating area gave the room a personal touch.

'I studied law in your country, on a Fulbright scholarship.'

'Where?'

'I received my degree from Columbia Law School.'

'Interesting . . .'

'And why, if I may ask?'

Her slightly mocking smile suited this aristocratic-looking woman, who apparently felt at ease in any situation, and even if she didn't, she could probably still hide it quite well. Only now did Raylan realize he was staring at her. It reminded him of the first time he'd approached a girl at a school party to ask her to dance but couldn't muster the courage once he was standing in front of her.

'New York. The capital of the world. That seems like enough of a reason to me.'

'I was thinking more about the high quality of education there,' replied Helai Durani, who didn't seem to be in the mood to spend more of her precious time chit-chatting and got straight to the point. 'I suspect that it isn't easy for you to understand what happened leading up to this trial and how our system works, so therefore my question: what kind of journalist are you?'

'I didn't realize journalists could be distinguished by species.'

'Let me be more specific. Are you a journalist who thinks it's important to portray reality by separating facts from opinion, or are you the kind that plays fast and loose with objectivity?'

'Objectivity can sometimes get in a journalist's way, but apart from that I don't really believe in separating facts from opinion.'

'What do you believe in?'

'I think it's important that both sides get a fair hearing in a conflict.'

'I understand you covered the Vietnam War in recent years.'

'That's right.'

'So tell me how you managed to give both sides a platform in that conflict?'

'I'm not sure. What are you getting at?'

'You have a reputation of sympathizing with the North Vietnamese.'

Raylan got the sudden feeling that his body had become heavier. His movements now felt plodding and ungainly. It was an unease that contrasted sharply with the refined way she'd played him. He found everything about her challenging in a sensual way, which made him even more aware of how brashly he spoke, how unwieldy his movements were and how clumsily he presented himself to her.

'The Vietnamese people were never asked if they agreed with their country being divided. Our president started a war for the wrong reasons. A war he can never win. But he's prepared to sacrifice more than a hundred thousand young boys to not lose face. Young men with a future, wives, children, family. Moreover, I don't see how my way of reporting, or rather your biased view of it, should have any bearing on this case.'

She seemed intimidated by his answer. 'My apologies.'

Raylan placed his hands in his side and sighed a few times. 'I explained everything to the attorney general. He told me . . .'

'. . . that I'd be willing to receive you, yes. But you see, Mr Chapelle, I'd like to know why I have to give information about an internal matter to an American journalist, of all people, just because the attorney general has asked me to do so. Frankly, I still haven't heard a good enough reason from you as to why I should grant his request.'

Raylan stared at the king's photograph and turned to Helai. 'You . . .'

'You?'

'You Afghans.'

'Any idea how condescending that sounds, Mr Chapelle?'

'I'm sorry, I don't mean to be condescending. But . . . This country is still living in the Stone Age as far as democracy is concerned. This case puts that system to the test. I think a story about freedom of speech is interesting.' He saw her left eye twitch slightly.

'So, I understand that you consider "us Afghans" to be a people living in the Stone Age?'

'I used the term figuratively.'

'Perhaps our democracy looks rudimentary to you Westerners at first sight. For us, it's an excellent opportunity to finally free ourselves from centuries of colonial yoke and leave years of dictatorship and foreign domination as far behind us as possible. In the long term, democracy is the most stable and sustainable form of government to bring security and prosperity to our country.'

'But isn't an important aspect of democracy that groups with differing opinions be allowed to express their dissatisfaction with the system?'

'Not by throwing grenades at the king.'

'An act that wasn't committed.'

'A well-planned crime that would have been committed if the security service hadn't intervened on time.' She pointed to the pile of paperwork on her desk. 'It's all here. Facts nobody can ignore.'

'Facts you presented so convincingly that Vaziri probably thought his action in the courtroom was his last chance to cause complete disruption. But it didn't work. Your arguments were far too strong for that.'

She gave him a long, penetratingly look and seemed to relax. 'Thank you.'

'I assume he wasn't talking about the birds and the bees.'

She smiled. 'It was a poem.'

'A poem?'

She came and stood in front of him. He smelled a hint of caramel.

'Order of the Revolution: heads that don't nod in agreement must be chopped off . . .'

'Wait . . . Did he really say that?'

'And this: "I pray that a thousand souls will be sacrificed a thousand times for the sake of the people and the revolution."'

Raylan whistled between his teeth. 'I really should ask that handsome fellow with his dreamy eyes to write something in my autograph book.'

Helai Durani's different-coloured eyes softened when she smiled. After she got hold of herself again, she sounded as resolute as she had in court.

'Askan Vaziri may look innocent, but he's prepared to eliminate anyone who disagrees with his revolutionary ideals. Surely you must understand, Mr Chapelle, if we don't take a stand now and make young people like Askan understand that their behaviour is unacceptable, we as a society can dig our own grave.'

'I understand. And it's Raylan.'

'Sorry?'

'Raylan. Not "Mr Chapelle".'

The confusion he saw on her face was surprising. Suddenly a vulnerable woman was standing in front of him, who had difficulty keeping up an attitude. Surely his attempt to break the conventional way of doing things couldn't be the only reason for this?

She gave him a curious glance. 'Raylan . . . What does that name mean?'

'I don't know exactly. It originates from French and stands for "adviser" and "protector", I believe.'

He looked at her lips, her warm smile. 'It's an . . . honourable name.'

'That's good to hear.'

In a comfortable silence, they looked at each other.

'I'm willing to give you more information about the case, Raylan.

But at another time. I have an urgent appointment now. She walked to the door, folded her fingers around the handle and stood there until he was closer to her. 'When will we see each other again?'

'Soon . . . If that's all right with you.'

'I'd like that.'

He wanted to give her a hand, but he changed his mind. Instead, he bowed to her, while placing his hand on his heart. '*Tashakor, wa to didan, Helai.*'

'*To didan, Raylan,*' she replied, surprising even herself.

He walked into the long corridor and thought he heard her closing the door. Yet with every step he felt her eyes burning in his back. He turned around. She was still in the doorway, one hand resting on the handle, her other arm dangling relaxed alongside her body. Standing there, motionless, she looked both self-assured and vulnerable.

2
Farah

2009

The dim container room at Camp Eggers where she now found herself wasn't much bigger than the cell she'd been locked in that afternoon. The air-con unit had no on/off button, only a slider to adjust the temperature. The rattle and hum quickly got on Farah's nerves. She was briefly tempted to take her mattress and bed down outside, in front of her door. As a child, there'd been so many times when she snuck out of her room at night, when she tiptoed barefoot down the wide staircase with a blanket in her hand, over the tiled path through the garden. Only to then climb the apple tree as high as she could. Feeling that same urge, she pushed down the door handle, sucked in the night air and gazed across the dimly lit camp.

She couldn't get the conversation with Paul out of her mind. The combination of words such as 'undercover', 'informant' and 'motorcycle gang' had been enough to throw both her body and mind into a state of alarm. She kept hearing the aggressive tone of his voice. *Unnecessary risks? Look who's talking!* Thinking back on it now, she became angry with him. While she only wanted to protect him from himself, he'd tried to make her feel guilty.

She pressed the call-back button, waited impatiently for the beep after his voicemail greeting and left a message. 'Please call me when you hear this, will you? I'm worried about you . . . Kiss, Fah.'

No sooner had she hung up than she felt embarrassed about those last two words. They made her sound as if she was playing a role in a soap opera. But she felt the need to bridge the chilliness and the distance between them. She closed her eyes and remembered that barely two weeks ago she'd stood in the same way, leaning against the railings of the *AND*, looking out over the River IJ, without really taking anything in because her head was too full of everything she'd discovered the night before. The absurd experience at that moment: feeling as if Raylan Chapelle had come and stood beside her, like a ghost from the past.

She knew she wouldn't be able to fall asleep just yet and considered her options. Under similar conditions in Amsterdam she'd go for a walk along the canals in the old city-centre. At Sterk, the late-night shop opposite Waterlooplein, she'd buy a large paper cup of freshly made cappuccino and drink it as she wandered further. There was no Sterk at Camp Eggers, but Gaby had shown her how to get to the Green Bean Coffeehouse.

She decided to chance it.

As she walked past the dimly lit, high concrete fences, she thought of the walls around what had once been her parental home. It was hard to think of a clearer boundary between her protected life inside and the reality outside. At that time, she couldn't have imagined a life other than the one she was leading. But those walls hadn't been able to protect her against the course of events. Likewise the walls of this military complex wouldn't be able to alter the course of history. Once the Americans and their coalition partners were gone, another reality would take shape. And she didn't know what to fear the most: that future reality or the shadow of the reality she'd fled thirty years ago.

She slowed down. While brooding she'd ended up in another part of the camp. It was darker here. And messier than the part where her sleeping quarters were and where she'd eaten. A bit sinister too.

She was about to turn around when a sound made her change her mind. She hadn't heard it in years. They were the strains of a *rabab*, a fifteen-stringed lute. As a child, she'd loved it. Now there it was again, the deep resonance of the melancholic chords. It came from one of the barracks opposite her, some thirty metres away. A harmonium struck up, followed by the rhythmic sounds of a *dayan* and a *bayan*, two Indian hand-played drums.

Curious, she walked towards the music.

The harmonious introduction developed into a slow rhythm that became more and more rousing. She heard men's voices, clapping hands. In the barracks opposite her a door opened. An Afghan soldier emerged. She recognized the emblem on his uniform right away. Green, red, black: service, sacrifice, martyrdom.

She stopped dead in her tracks. The man was dragging a girl along. She was young – far too young. She looked around timidly as the soldier ushered her to the other barracks. She was wearing a long, pleated skirt and had twinkling bells around her wrists and her ankles. Her eyes were heavily made up with black kohl and her cheeks were smeared pink with rouge. Her lips were painted blood-red.

But the short black hair, the way she walked and the angular face betrayed something else: this girl, who was being pushed along against her will, was a boy.

The moment the soldier opened the door of the other barracks, the music grew louder. Farah caught a glimpse of some twenty men sitting cross-legged in a semi-circle around the musicians. They began clapping their hands and whooping when the boy's slender figure appeared silhouetted in the doorway.

The soldier shoved the boy inside. The door slammed shut. The music blended with the growing sound of the bells on the boy's wrists and ankles.

Farah knew what he had to do now. Shake his hips seductively, spin round, make delicate hand gestures. He was supposed to wobble his head from side to side and bare his shiny teeth in a come-hither smile.

Sensual and sultry movements, *that's* what he was there for.

That's what he'd been taught.

And while he was spinning around, the men in the semi-circle would clap louder and start singing along, and his skirt would whirl up a little so they could see his slender, hairless legs. They would eagerly reach out their arms and urge him to come closer so they could touch him. And the thought that only one of them would get to take the boy home that night to do what you were allowed to do with these kinds of boys would undoubtedly make their blood boil with excitement.

'No women here.'

Startled, she turned and looked into the face of a tense Afghan guard who'd approached her from behind. His flashlight was blinding. She lifted her hand to shield her eyes. His order sounded harsher and louder than before.

'You go. Now!'

Her heart was racing, but her answer in Dari sounded calm. 'Do you know what's going on in there?'

He dropped his flashlight, took the rifle from his shoulder, aimed it at her and approached her threateningly. '*Ejaza nest inja bashi!* This is forbidden territory!'

She saw his confusion. She was wearing an American uniform with no distinguishing marks, but she also spoke Afghan and was clearly not a soldier. She raised her arms and moved back in step with his advancing moves. 'I got lost. It's okay, I'm going.'

She heard the sound of an approaching jeep. The headlights glided ominously along the walls of the barracks. The vehicle stopped right in front of them. The voice of the driver, who jumped out at once, was deep and firm. '*Chi gap ast inja, dagarman?* What's going on here, corporal?'

'This woman claims she's lost, major. A *Garichi* who speaks our language,' the guard answered.

'Afghan,' she corrected him as she tried to get her bearings. 'I just wanted to know what's going on in there.'

The major stepped into her field of vision. He took his time looking her up and down. 'An Afghan woman in an American uniform. Interesting.'

'I'm a guest of General Goldwater.' She felt the blood slowly drain from her arms and her hands began to tingle. 'May I lower my arms?'

He threw her a scornful smile. 'Don't move, young lady.'

Beside the jeep the major conferred with the passenger, who then got out and walked over to her. She saw the stars on his leather jacket. There were four of them. He had piercing brown eyes, a trimmed beard and short grey hair. 'So you want to know what's going on in there, Ms . . .'

'Hafez.'

His smile couldn't have been more arrogant. 'So, a descendant of the great poet?'

He completely undressed her with his piercing eyes. She swallowed. Inside the barracks the men were cheering and clapping to the rhythm of the music.

'As you can hear, my men are having a party. They're happy. They did a good job today.'

She made every effort not to be intimidated. 'The boy I just saw going in . . .'

He looked at her with a blank stare, but she could tell from his eyes it was just a pretence. 'Boy? What boy?'

'He was dressed like a girl. He's dancing now.'

Grinning, he unzipped his jacket, slapped his thighs and put his hands on his hips. He came so close to her that she could smell the aroma of roasted mutton, garlic and herbs on his breath.

'Pretty Hafez, you haven't answered my question. What's a woman claiming to be a guest of General Goldwater doing all by herself in a place where she has no business being? Surely that's asking for trouble?'

A hand making a move for her breasts or hips would be enough. She'd pull him towards her and keep him in a stranglehold so she could use him as a human shield against the armed guard. But it wouldn't solve anything. It would alert the men in the barracks. It would only add to her problems.

She also realized that mentioning her name had been a big mistake. She made a snap decision and forced a smile. 'I made a mistake. My apologies.'

He leaned towards her. 'That's right, you made a mistake. There are no boys here. Only men. Lonely men who'd love the company of a woman like you.' With a morbid grin, he gestured invitingly towards the barracks. 'Do us the honour, lovely, curvaceous Hafez.'

She looked at him and shook her head. 'I'm sorry, but I must decline your invitation.'

The guard was pointing his rifle at her head. At the same time she felt a hand clamp itself around her arm like a vice. The hand of the man in the leather jacket with the four stars.

'A true Afghan never declines an invitation.'

She heard the sound of a second vehicle in the distance. Before she knew it, they found themselves in the glare of its bright headlights. The man's grip on her arm relaxed. The guard lowered his gun. The jeep braked right in front of them. The engine kept running with the headlights trained on them. The driver jumped out.

She breathed a sigh of relief when she recognized his voice.

Mason stood beside the jeep and rigidly saluted the man who'd now removed his hand from her arm. 'Good evening, General Hafami. Is there a problem?'

'This woman is lost. In more ways than one, if you ask me.'

'Thank you. I'll take it from here, general.'

'That won't be necessary, sergeant, we . . .'

Mason cut Hafami short with a voice that could split a rock in half. 'Sir, I have my orders.' He gestured for her to get into the car. 'Ms Hafez, you are confined to your quarters on General Goldwater's orders.'

She walked over to him and whispered, 'Mason . . . We have to do something! They're forcing an underage boy to dance in there . . .'

He didn't look at her and kept his gaze fixed on Hafami. His reaction was as muted as hers, but it sounded a lot more decisive. 'Get in the car.'

'But you don't get it . . .'

'Get in the goddamn car.'

His voice, the aggression in it. This was the same man who'd instantly overseen the chaos that afternoon. The same man who, in a hail of rocks, had calmly carried the woman in his arms to the Humvee.

But everything was different now.

Everything about him suggested as much. She had no choice: he had come for her, and for her alone. Not for the boy.

Without a word, she got in.

Mason put the jeep in reverse and tapped his cap. 'Good evening, general.' He stepped on the gas, and with a yank at the wheel he took a sharp turn backwards, accelerated again and sped off.

In the rear-view mirror, she saw the two men fade into the darkness. When she spoke, her voice quivered. 'How did you find me?'

'I received word that you were missing.'

'How . . . ?'

'A security patrol saw that your door was wide open and your cabin empty.'

It was clear to her that he could barely control himself.

'Do you know who you were up against? God damn it! That was Ashraf Hafami, the commander of the Afghan National Guard. One of the key players around here.'

They were driving way too fast.

'Would you please stop, Mason?'

They were approaching the roundabout with the flags. He slowed down but kept driving.

'Mason, please.'

He braked and parked the car by the side of the road but left the engine running. Without a word, he kept staring straight ahead.

She took a deep breath before she spoke.

'Several weeks ago, in Amsterdam . . . I saw a boy. He was Afghan and . . . He looked exactly like the boy this evening. Girl's clothes, costume jewellery, heavy make-up, bells round his wrists and ankles . . . He'd been hit by a car and left for dead . . . But this was in the Netherlands. Can you imagine: in the Netherlands?'

She looked at him. He was still avoiding her gaze.

'"Playing with boys" is what it's called. Don't tell me you've never heard of it and don't tell me you think it doesn't exist. It does. And now I've seen it again . . . Here, of all places. I couldn't do anything, I was alone . . . with all those men. Until you turned up. Thank God. I thought . . . I saw you save a woman this afternoon . . . But now . . . Now we're abandoning a child . . . a little boy who's about to be raped!'

She was taken aback by the abrupt way he got out of the jeep, loudly slammed the door shut and howled as he rammed his fists into a tree.

Then he just stood there in complete silence.

She wanted to run to him and tell him how sorry she was, but she couldn't move or utter a word.

His deep sigh, and the composure with which he walked back to the jeep and sat down again. The bloody knuckles he carefully folded around the steering wheel. All the while she just sat there, quietly staring straight ahead. Until, that is, he started talking. His words were considered and confident. 'I'll report this incident. But promise me: don't go back to that place.' He turned to face her and for the first time really looked at her. The concern in his eyes confused her. 'Will you promise me that?'

She nodded and looked away, feeling embarrassed. She didn't want to cry but couldn't stop the tears from gliding silently down her cheeks. Still staring into space, she felt his hand pat her on the back. And so they sat for a while. Until she wiped the tears away and looked at him.

'I won't go back, Mason. I promise.'

The drive back to her container block passed without a word. Just before she got out, she turned to him.

'I'm sorry.'

He nodded and drove off. She kept her eyes on him, long after the jeep had disappeared from sight.

In the blue light of her freezing container room, Farah sat on the hard camp bed with her phone in hand, listening to the voicemail greeting telling her to leave a message. The same voice that had shouted at her from Moscow earlier that evening. *Unnecessary risks? Look who's talking!*

'Damn it, Paul. Call me when you get this.'

She waited in vain, hoping he'd call back right away, and stared at her laptop screen. The man who'd just grabbed her arm was now staring back at her. This time not with ice-cold cynicism in his eyes, but with a look that was supposed to radiate confidence and authority. She read the article beside his photo.

In the 1980s, Ashraf Hafami served as one of many thousands of Mujahideen fighters. For ten years he fought the Soviet army, which was eventually forced to withdraw from Afghanistan. As commander of his militia, he played a key role in the American-led invasion that ousted the Taliban regime. Now the 57-year-old general is the heroic face of a nation with a new future.

She keyed in Edward's number. Who cared what time it was? She had to tell him what had happened, here in this camp of all places. That she'd seen a boy who was the spitting image of Sekandar. And that she'd abandoned him in a barracks full of horny men. While she waited for him to answer, she pictured him in the pose she'd last seen him in. His colossal body dressed in baggy light-brown corduroy trousers and an oversized blue jumper, casually leaning against the glass wall of his office. The steel-blue eyes in his unshaven face fixed on her. *In Kabul you're going to behave like I taught you. You're a journalist, not a loose cannon.*

Beating around the bush, putting up a smokescreen – it all proved to be unnecessary the minute he answered and heard her voice.

'I'm sure it's not a good time, Ed, but . . .'

'You're in trouble again, aren't you?'

She paused, aware that it might only confirm his suspicions.

'I know you, Hafez. I can tell. Where are you?'

'Camp Eggers.'

She could hear from the tinkling sound that he was swirling ice cubes around in his whiskey glass. 'I didn't realize they're in the bed-and-breakfast business these days.'

She didn't find it funny.

'All right, then, spill the beans.' He said it in an encouraging, almost paternal tone. That was all she needed to launch straight in and tell him everything that had happened from the moment she'd landed. The arrest on the plane by the American duo, the interrogation, the accident, the delivery, the discovery of the boy on the military base and the puzzling role Mason had played.

Then all went quiet for a while at the other end of the line.

'Are you still there, Ed?'

'Yes . . . but give me a moment, will you?'

She pictured him lumbering around the room, taking the stopper from the bottle, considering more ice, changing his mind and pouring an inch of whiskey into the glass.

'Let's look at the facts. You saw a boy dressed as a girl entering a barracks where music was being played and where men sat waiting for him. Did the boy put up a fight?'

'No, but . . .'

'Did you see him dance?'

'No.'

'Heard witnesses say he did?'

'Where are you going with this, Ed?'

'To the fact of the matter. That's to say: your lack of evidence.'

'I know what I saw.'

'Enough to accuse a general of child abuse? Enough to enter into a conflict with an American commander? Enough to publish a story about it? Not in my newspaper, that's for sure.'

'If we can expose a Russian oligarch as a criminal, then we can certainly do the same with a puffed-up Afghan general who thinks he's above the law.'

'Are you planning to name and shame an Afghan general during what little time you have in Kabul? When you're there to rebury your father, while also wanting to work with the authorities to secure Sekandar's safe return? Do I have to keep reminding you of your priorities? You're a grown woman, Hafez!'

'Jesus, Ed. Are you telling me to give it a rest?'

'I'm telling you to be realistic. You've done what you could.'

'It wasn't enough. Mason knew perfectly well what was going on in that barracks, Ed, I'm sure of it. I saw him free that woman from the car this afternoon. He could have rushed into that barracks and taken the kid to safety. But he chose not to.'

She heard the muted tinkling of the ice cubes, the slurp of another sip and the static on the line as he pondered this.

'This Afghan general, this Hafami . . . he was with the Mujahideen, did you say?'

'That's right.'

'They were known as holy warriors. Because of their opposition to the Soviet army's invasion of Afghanistan in 1979. US President Jimmy Carter saw Russia's offensive as the greatest threat to world peace since the Second World War. He secretly gave the CIA permission to launch an indirect military campaign against the Russians.'

'Operation Cyclone.'

'Madam knows her classics, excellent. Every year more than

600 million dollars' worth of arms were diverted to the Mujahideen via Pakistan. Quite a few Russian army helicopters were shot down by anti-aircraft missiles of American origin. It's safe to say that the man in the White House was privately very happy with holy warriors such as Hafami. They eventually forced the Russians back to where they came from on his behalf.'

'Tell me something new, Ed.'

'The Mujahideen operated from Pakistan and from remote corners in Afghanistan. They were away from home – and from their wives – for years. They solved that problem by bringing in boys. Boys who cleaned for them, fed the horses, made tea, that kind of thing.'

'Boy prostitutes, you mean.'

'Exactly. The whole *bacha bazi* ritual was revived around that time. I'd bet that to this day it's still systemic within the ranks led by commanders such as Hafami. And the Americans have to live with that reality, whether they like it or not. Which brings us back to the behaviour of that gunnery sergeant of yours.'

'You mean he may have been instructed to *not* intervene in situations like this?'

'To turn a blind eye, as they say.'

'But if that's the case, Ed, it would imply that US army bases operate a policy of tolerance towards *bacha bazi*.'

'With Afghan militias stationed in a camp such as Eggers, there's every possibility that those at the top have reached some kind of understanding: Keep fighting for our cause, and we'll look the other way when you're partying with your tea boys.'

'It would be impossible to prove.'

'There's a good chance that's exactly what you stumbled upon tonight. But you're not going to act on it. Not now.'

Edward took a big gulp; she could hear an ice cube cracking between his teeth and the thud as he put down the glass.

'"He who has something to live for can endure almost anything." Nietzsche once said that. You think you can deal with almost anything right now. That gives me no choice but to protect you against yourself. Listen Hafez, you're going to solemnly rebury your father and ensure that Sekandar is safely returned home. That's your mission, as we agreed. And I'm going to get in touch with Paul. That's the last thing you should be doing now. Got it?'

'Got it.'

The second she broke the connection, she dialled the other number and listened to the voicemail greeting again.

'Hi, you've reached Paul Chapelle. Leave a message or shut the fuck up!'

3
Paul

2009

Somewhere between the rocky bottom and the water's surface, his arms and legs had moved convulsively against the current. When Paul finally surfaced, his stomach was full of water. He vomited and gasped for breath. Quayside, the motorcycles of his pursuers were racing off in different directions. A male voice shouted at Paul through a megaphone. In the cone of light that slid over the water he saw a long steel hook coming towards him. He grabbed hold of it and was pulled aboard a patrol boat. Two policemen pushed him face down against the deck and handcuffed him. The smell of oil penetrated his nostrils. He felt a stabbing pain in his ribs, and his battered face glowed as if he were struck with a fever.

As the water police patrol boat bounced across the Moskva to the closest police station, he'd sat soaking wet and shivering against the back wall of the wheelhouse. Foaming river water flowed over the bow and splashed against the window of the wheelhouse. When the boat moored, he puked up his guts. On the gangway a policeman pushed his back so hard he almost rolled head first into the river a second time.

Hanging on two policemen, he'd been dragged into a rundown station, where they shoved him against the wall. He had to raise his hands above his head while they kicked his feet apart. The search was carried out so crudely that they missed the USB stick in his inside pocket. They pushed him in the direction of a counter, behind which the station duty officer, who resembled Attila the Hun, looked at him with little or no interest. '*Imya?*'

'Paul Chapelle.'

'*Professiya?*'

He hesitated. Journalist versus underpaid Russian bureaucrat. It'd probably be better to be jailed as a paedophile in a prison full of hardened criminals than to admit to being a freelance foreign journalist with American blood. But sooner or later they were going to find out about his background.

When Paul related what he did for a living, the duty officer looked at him as if he were having a sudden, severe attack of heartburn.

Also what wasn't going to help this situation was the fact that he was clearly connected to a recently wanted terrorist, the colleague of Russia's most critical journalist and the mouthpiece of the international press, who was trying to blame the Kremlin for the attack on Anya. Once they pulled up that info, neither the Dutch ambassador, Edward Vallent nor Roman Jankovski would be able to help him.

His brain feverishly tried to come up with a backup plan, solutions, connections. Lights started to go on in his head, like neon letters flickering on one by one and forming a name.

Alexander Arlazarov.

Director of the FSB's Counter-Terror Unit. The man who'd recently had him picked up for an impromptu interrogation in the former KGB building. Although Arlazarov was on the other side of the political spectrum, they shared a common objective: both wanted to find out the extent of Valentin Lavrov's involvement in the Seven Sisters' hostage-taking.

And now he was in possession of new-found, incriminating information against Lavrov. Hidden in the inside pocket of his leather jacket. Perhaps that was valuable enough to get him released from this shithole police station unharmed. And perhaps even enough to avoid jail time. Of course, there were some cardinal rules as a journalist. The most important of these was to not share your intel with the highest boss of a foreign country's Counter-Terror Unit. But in his shoes now, with your back against the wall, you didn't have much of a choice.

He leaned over the counter slightly. To his own surprise, he spoke as calmly as ordering a beer at the bar, 'I have information I think Alexander Arlazarov will be very interested in.'

The duty officer, who was hammering his fingers on the keyboard like a blacksmith, looked at him again. His wary eyes said: now, why doesn't that surprise me?

Perhaps it was because of the brief silence that had fallen among the men lingering about the counter immediately after Arlazarov's name was mentioned. Or maybe it was because of the hesitation and somewhat prolonged stares of the duty officer. In any case, a sense of uncertainty hung in the air.

Paul gestured to the inside pocket of his leather jacket with his chin. 'You'll find the information right there. Probably a good idea to get it to Arlazarov as quickly as possible, if you want to keep your job, friend.'

On a sign from the duty officer, one of the policemen walked towards Paul, roughly spun him around, pushed him up against the counter, opened his soaked jacket and unzipped the inside pocket. The plastic USB stick dripped as he held it.

'Just don't plug it into a laptop right away,' Paul warned. 'Needs to dry out first. And then get it straight to Arlazarov.'

Paul didn't ask for a lawyer. He had taken advantage of his secret weapon and let himself be moved to a concrete cell, slightly larger than a broom closet, where two policemen in the doorway watched him undress. Everything he was wearing had to be deposited in a plastic bag.

'*Na koleni!*'

Paul obeyed and kneeled. The policeman who had his hands free stood in front of him, unzipped his fly and grinned. 'Best to be very careful if you want to keep your pearly whites.'

It didn't matter that the guy then laughed out loud and pulled up his zipper again. Paul still felt completely humiliated.

The cell door was locked. An hour later, when the adrenaline rush from the fight and the chase had worn off and his body throbbed with pain, they returned. Shooting water from a fire hose, they pummelled him against the wall. They laughed and shouted that he should stand still. He trembled, and his teeth chattered like a junkie having bad withdrawal symptoms. They threw him a towel. Then he put on the overalls they shoved into his hand, a shirt with sleeves that were much too long and rubber sandals that were as big as the slippers of a circus clown.

In the interrogation room he took a seat at a narrow table opposite a detective with a boxer's nose.

'Formally speaking, we consider you the prime suspect in a brawl with a criminal gang.' The man said it with a mad look in his eyes as if he were Ivan the Terrible himself. 'You're suspected of stealing and destroying a motorcycle, breaking a host of traffic regulations, resisting arrest and refusing to cooperate with the Moscow water police. How do you respond to these charges?'

'That I've never heard such a bunch of crap.'

An unexpected blow to his face from a flat hand, almost knocked Paul off his chair.

Ivan the Terrible said, 'I have little patience for this kind of lip from you. What's your connection to the Hell Wolves?'

In situations like these, there were two things you should never do as a journalist: divulge your sources and snitch on your informants. 'Apart from taking one of their motorcycles out for a spin, not much!'

Ivan chewed up his toothpick and spat it out. 'You're going to talk now, arse-fucker. Otherwise you're going to eat your own shit, and mine along with it.'

'I'm only prepared to talk to Alexander Arlazarov. He's the only person I'm accountable to.'

Ivan sighed long and hard. Then he stood up, walked to the door and opened it. When he turned around, the look on his face was almost mild. He made a surprisingly courteous gesture towards the doorway. 'Pardon me for any delay.'

Paul stood up hesitantly, slowly pushed his chair back and walked around the table in the direction of the doorway. When he was near it, the door was slammed shut again. The blows that he felt to his kidneys were like lightning. The pain sent him crashing to his knees. The punches came from all sides. All he could do was protect his head and pray that he'd survive. And that while he didn't even believe in God.

When he regained consciousness, he was lying under a flickering fluorescent tube between three blank walls and a metal door. For a while he remained still with his hands over his closed eyes. Then he pushed himself up grasping the edge of the metal bed and sat with his head in his hands on the thin mattress, which was covered with water stains. From the hole in the corner of the floor rose the nauseating smell of faeces and urine. The rusty water pipe along the ceiling leaked. The constant dripping worked on his nerves like Chinese water torture. When his gaze had gone round for more times than he could count, he felt the claustrophobia setting in.

He carefully sucked in some air. His bruised ribs made breathing a hell. He needed to let out a slight cough, causing him even more pain.

The fluorescent tube crackled as if it might spark a fire. A bunch of keys rattled. Two men dressed entirely in black stood in the open doorway and gestured that he needed to go with them.

For years he'd been wondering why Russian men are among the ugliest people on the planet. And not ugly in an endearing way like the Hunchback of Notre Dame, the Phantom of the Opera or Frankenstein's monster. No. Ugly as in seriously-disgusting-inbred-ugly. The ugliness of the two men beside him in their black uniforms who now escorted him down the corridor to the back of the police station and pushed him into a four-wheel-drive with darkly tinted windows. They could have been the modern-day version of the *oprichniki*, a corps of armed guards from the mid-1500s, who dressed completely in black, rode black horses and killed Tsar Ivan the Terrible's enemies in the most horrific ways. Paul suspected these men were from Russia's NAST Close Protection Academy, where they were thoroughly trained in Systema combat, the method used by the Russian Special Forces.

By the time he saw the first morning light hesitantly emerge from behind the contours of the flats on the outskirts of Moscow, he'd lost all hope of ever coming in contact with Alexander Arlazarov again. He panicked and turned his back to the man sitting beside him. His fingers grabbed for the locked door. Immediately he felt a hand grip his shoulder and forcefully push him back against the seat.

Not a word was said about his pathetic attempt to escape. On ever quieter roads they drove past rolling farmlands and forests. Again and again, he was surprised when he caught glimpses of the winding River Moskva. They were nearing Zvenigorod, an ancient village on the river some sixty kilometres west of Moscow. They took a sharp right into a dense forest. At a swampy piece of land they slowed down. Crooked tombstones stuck out of an undulating layer of morning mist. After a few more turns they headed straight for what appeared to be the ruins of a castle.

He was ordered out of the car and pushed up some crumbling steps to a landing. In an entrance hall, supported by a wide steel beam, they removed his handcuffs. A large frosted-glass door opened. A man in a cobalt-blue velvet suit made a grand entrance. His skin was pale, his eyes grey-blue and his dyed black hair shiny with brilliantine. With an effeminate sort of disdain he presented Paul with a grey suit jacket and a black tie that had already been knotted.

'Put these on and follow me.'

He said it like you'd command a dog, but compared to the treatment at the police station it sounded as if an angel was welcoming him to the pearly gates. Over dark, creaking parquet floors and through rooms where oriental carpets muffled their footsteps, the man in cobalt blue trod lightly in front of him, swaying his hips. Two ceiling-high doors opened on to a conservatory overlooking a lake where traces of mist were accentuated by the melancholy sound of a cello.

At a table covered in white damask, Alexander Arlazarov was feasting on pancakes. With an air of haughty amusement he looked up from the opened *Moscow Times*.

'My dear Mr Chapelle. Somehow you always manage to attract trouble. You look like Popov the Clown after a cage fight.'

With a routine gesture he folded the newspaper and casually indicated that his guest should take a seat diagonally across from him. The vision in cobalt blue put a plate in front of Paul, placed a knife and fork next to it with an excessively graceful move, looked at Arlazarov and after a nod of approval exited the conservatory with the same sway of his hips.

'After all your night-time adventures I thought you might like some *syrniki*, pancakes with cottage cheese. I made them myself.'

'I'm not hungry, thank you.'

'You're here for a *sdelka*, a deal, I assume? Something to make last night's kamikaze-like antics worthwhile. The best deals are sealed over a good meal.'

Paul sat down. 'I want the culprit and the person who ordered the attack on Anya to be brought to justice.'

'You seek revenge. Revenge is a poor motivation for a journalist. Tea, coffee?'

'Coffee, please. If you've already looked at my information, you know the facts.'

'The facts, you say. Interesting. Milk?'

'Black.'

Arlazarov poured coffee from a large mat-silver pot. 'And what do you hope to achieve with your facts?'

'An actual conviction of Valentin Lavrov. Not some political charade.'

Arlazarov gave him a confident grin. 'Journalists like you tend to play judge, jury and executioner. Lavrov's trial is a matter for the public prosecutor, his accusers and impartial judges.'

'Lavrov gets a show trial and probably walks free again due to lack of evidence. And he continues to enjoy the protection of the president.'

Paul took a few sips of his coffee. Even swallowing hurt.

Arlazarov looked at him the way a rider looks at his injured horse just before he puts him out of his misery. 'There's a degree of heroism in your struggle to get Lavrov convicted, a tinge of David versus Goliath, the little man going up against the giant.' He pulled out the USB stick that Paul had given to the police duty officer.

'Any idea how counterproductive it could be for you to link the director of a state-run company like AtlasNet to a terrorist hostage-taking and attempted murder?' Arlazarov said it with an enigmatic smile. 'Finish your coffee, then I want to show you something.'

They walked down a long corridor with floor panels that creaked louder and louder. Paul was riddled with pain. Arlazarov was casually serving up anecdotes as if strolling with journalists who'd been beaten bloody was an everyday occurrence.

'We'd just started the restoration of the place when one of the towers broke away from the building. Don't ask me why; I don't know anything about old structures. We've reinforced it with a metal frame. Temporarily of course. An emergency solution. Eventually that tower will be removed and replaced by a new one.

He slowed down and led Paul into a room crammed full of silverware, hand mirrors, cutlery, plates and crockery.

'I had to show you this. More than a thousand exquisite objects made of silver, wrapped in newspapers from January and February 1917. Immediately after the Bolshevik revolution, the original noble residents had everything concealed in the ceiling.'

Arlazarov removed a wafer-thin silver case from his inner pocket, opened it and presented Paul with one of his slender cigarettes neatly held together by a rubber strap.

'And your point is ... ?' Paul asked, coughing from his first inhalation.

'Because I adore metaphors,' Arlazarov continued. 'Sometimes a man can be so blinded by revenge that he fails to see what has been right in front of him the entire time. And of course I'm not talking about works of silver hidden between the ceiling beams for almost one hundred years. This is about something completely different. As a journalist, something you'd certainly find interesting.' Alexander Arlazarov smiled impishly. 'Are you still with me my dear Chapelle?'

'I was never one for riddles,' Paul replied.

'All right, then. You recently had contact with Sergey Kombromovich, press director of Moscow State University. You were looking for the student who was held at gunpoint off-screen, forcing your colleague Hafez to make her jihad-statement in front of the camera.'

'You promised to go easy on that student.'

'We did. And her testimony resulted in your colleague being taken off the terror list. But let's not go off on a tangent. I assume you're aware of the biography Kombromovich wrote about the very first Soviet hero, General Michailov?'

'No, I don't know anything about it.'

'Well then . . .' Alexander Arlazarov crossed his arms and frowned. 'I advise you to contact Kombromovich again. Ask him about the things he deliberately left out of the book. After that, let's be in touch again. By the way, how's your girlfriend?'

'She's still in a coma.'

'I'm talking about Hafez.'

'She's in Kabul. Burying her father. Why are you asking?'

Arlazarov picked up a manilla envelope from a silver bowl. Paul recognized the passport he removed from it.

'She managed to leave the country on a false passport, but this document will allow her to return. I also removed her from our most wanted list. And this . . .' He took a bundle of old letters from the envelope. 'Forgive me, but it was necessary to inspect these documents, which were so amateurishly stored in a station locker. After all, they belong to a woman whom we initially suspected of terrorist activities. These are letters from your father. It turns out he wasn't only a dedicated journalist, but also quite the romantic. And at that time, he was already investigating Michailov.' Arlazarov gave him a friendly smile as he handed the bundle to Paul. 'Like father, like son.'

The cobalt-blue errand-boy entered the room again as if he were going to belt out an aria from an opera. He was carrying a large transparent plastic bag containing Paul's dry-cleaned clothing in the manner you might transport a relic.

'This charade is over, my dear Chapelle,' Arlazarov said throwing Paul's prison outfit a contemptuous glance and patting the plastic bag holding Paul's clothing. 'Time to don your journalist's garb again and get back to work!'

4
Farah

2009

She'd climbed up to the highest branch again. There she'd laid down on her blanket to look at the stars. And with all those stars far above her, she'd stretched out her arms, like wings. Agonizingly slowly, she slid off the branch.

Her hands groped around in a futile attempt to find something to hold on to. She kept falling until she opened her eyes and, still confused, heard the banging.

When she opened the door of her container room, Mason stood before her, sharply silhouetted in a shaft of morning light that hurt her eyes. She wasn't sure what was more confusing: the dream, being startled awake or his distant expression.

Mason handed her the transparent laundry bag. 'Goldwater is expecting us. You've got ten minutes to get ready. Take all of your belongings. I'll wait in the jeep.'

Then, as abruptly as he'd interrupted her sleep, he walked away.

She removed her borrowed military-issue PJs, jumped into the shower and put on her own clothes. Her blouse, her trousers, even her knickers and bra smelled strongly of lavender detergent.

A handful of pigeons flew over the square with the flags hanging limply on their poles as she walked into the Ark by Mason's side. They were made to wait in a small space while Goldwater was in a staff meeting. Mason sat next to her, but painstakingly avoided her gaze. After fifteen minutes, which felt more like twenty-four hours, the sergeant announced that Goldwater was ready to see them.

As they walked in, Mason and Goldwater saluted each other.

'At ease, sergeant.'

This time Goldwater looked at Farah without feigning friendliness. The tremor above his right eyebrow was out in full force. 'I'm sure I'm mispronouncing it, Ms Hafez, but you probably know what this means: *yak team wahed*.

'I don't see what . . .'

'"One team united". I love that slogan, because it encapsulates everything we're doing over here: training the Afghans so they can handle their own security in the future.' Goldwater grabbed a piece of paper, leaned over his desk and handed it to her. 'And by that I mean your security too.'

She read the first two typed lines and looked at him in dismay. 'What's this?'

'An agreement in which you declare that from the moment you voluntarily accepted the full protection of the US army everything you intend to publish about your experiences inside this camp will be subject to Operational Security and will therefore be vetted by our press information officers.' He pulled in his chair, gestured for her to sit at the desk and handed her a pen. 'As long as you enjoy the protection of the US army you're bound by this media code of ethics.'

She remained standing and responded as calmly as possible. 'General, the Afghan government invited me to attend my father's ceremonial reburial. I regard this invitation as an honour, but I've come here under my own steam and I'm paying everything out of my own pocket. As an independent journalist, I think it's fundamentally wrong to be dependent on any party, be it the Afghan government or the US military. I am and remain an independent journalist. I follow my own rules.'

'Not here. Here you follow our rules.'

'Is this connected to last night's incident?'

Goldwater came and stood right in front of her, his hands on his back and his legs slightly apart. 'Protection and hospitality come with a price. I expect loyalty, discretion and respect from our guests.' He looked over at Mason. 'And by that I mean respect for those who saved you from a precarious situation on two occasions.'

His gaze was almost as intimidating as that of the Afghan general the previous night.

She had no intention of lowering her eyes. 'What if I refuse to sign, general?'

'Then we're done with you. Then the US army is done with you. The minute you walk out the gate you won't get to set foot inside this camp again. And you'll discover how difficult it will be to do your job as a journalist here in Kabul or indeed anywhere else in Afghanistan. And you'll thank your lucky stars when you're safely back on that plane home.'

'In that case, general, we're done here.' She said it calmly and she could tell from his eyes that this wasn't the answer he'd anticipated.

Still standing in front of her, impassive and business-like, he snatched the sheet of paper from her hand and turned to Mason.

'Show Ms Hafez out. Straight to the gate.'

Mason followed her in silence. Just as he was about to get in the car, she placed her hand on his arm. 'I simply can't sign something designed to silence me.' He made no attempt to remove her hand. She didn't look away. 'But that doesn't mean I'll publish a single word about what happened last night.'

His annoyance turned to astonishment. 'Are you a journalist or not?'

'That's no excuse to discredit you. Especially not after what you did for me last night.' She removed her hand from his arm, walked around the jeep and sat down beside him.

He was about to start the engine when he changed his mind and looked at her. 'So you're not going to do anything with it?'

'You almost sound disappointed.'

'Sorry, I don't follow.'

'I think I know why you only came to my assistance last night and not the boy's.'

'Really?'

She picked up on the cynicism with which he tried to arm himself. 'I think you had no choice, Mason. I think you have orders to look the other way.'

'Orders? And whose might those be?'

'To ask the question is to answer it.'

He leaned forward, started the car, shifted into gear and accelerated.

'I'd like to say goodbye to the mother and child,' she said. 'May I?'

He ignored her and drove on. She'd get out at the gate, walk away from this camp and then try her hardest to forget what had happened, just as she'd done the previous day when she'd left the military airport.

To her surprise, he took a turn that deviated from the route to the gate.

As quietly as she could, Farah tiptoed to the crib, where she bent over the rapidly breathing child. She gently caressed the little body, which was kept warm under a flannel. When her fingers approached the crumpled face, she felt the grip of the tiny hand. It was a firm grip. In keeping with an age-old tradition, she leaned close to the baby's right ear and whispered the ritual words of the *Azan*. 'Allah, I am eternally grateful for the blessing of this life. This beautiful little girl will be protected and cherished like a jewel.'

She saw the woman lying in her bed, the drips in her arm, a collar wrapped around her neck, staring at the ceiling. She slowly approached the edge of the bed. 'Allah has blessed your gift. The girl will be safe with you,' she whispered to her. She saw the tears in the woman's eyes, her vulnerability, her happiness despite all the pain.

Her answer came as a wafer-thin whisper. 'May Allah reward you with blessings and grant you the same favour.' She took hold of Farah's arm. '*Namet chist?* What's your name?'

'Farah.'

The woman sighed; she was barely audible now. 'Farah ... That will be her name.'

Mason came and stood next to her. 'We have to go.'

She looked at him and saw the emotion in his eyes. 'Her mother has named her Farah.'

He smiled. 'The effect you have on people. C'mon.'

She looked him in the eye. 'Do you trust me?'

'I wouldn't have accepted your help yesterday afternoon if I didn't.'

'Will you tell me what happened last night? Was it a one-off incident or a regular occurrence?'

'Is that why you wanted me to bring you here?'

'No . . . I'm sorry. Never mind.'

She left the room. Mason closed the door behind them as gently as possible.

They drove in silence to the square in front of the exit, where a convoy of armoured vehicles was ready to leave. On the other side of the gate, a group of angry men was trying to stop workers and tradesmen from entering. There was a lot of pushing and shoving and shouting. The heavily armed guards, who had to search every incoming employee, were on edge. Farah realized that this morning – after the previous day's accident and the riots that followed – she'd be very much the wrong woman in the wrong place outside the gate of this hated American base. In her sober yet fashionable clothing with the scarf loosely around her head, she'd be very conspicuous.

She wasn't the only one who realized this. Mason walked over to one of the guards, had a brief chat with him and beckoned her closer. The guard was on the phone, turned around and gave them the thumbs up.

'You'd better wait a few minutes.'

'Wait? What for?'

'I have orders not to escort you out of the camp. And I'll obey them,' Mason said.

They were standing right in front of the closed gate. General Goldwater's words echoed in her head: *And you'll thank your lucky stars when you're safely back on that plane home.* She scanned her surroundings. In the left lane, a queue of lorries and passenger cars, waiting bumper to bumper to be admitted to the base. Drivers leaning out of their windows and shouting that they had to be let in, that they had cargo to deliver.

Some fifty metres away a yellow Toyota Corolla swerved away from the line of waiting and honking cars. It drove as close to the gate as it could, did a U-turn in front of the wrangling group of men and flashed its rear lights.

'Your lift,' Mason said.

'Thank you . . .'

Mason looked at her gravely. 'It wasn't a one-off incident.'

'What?'

'What happened last night.'

'You mean . . . ?'

'It's happened before.'

For a split second she thought that his eyes revealed everything he could or wouldn't tell her. Then she quickly pulled a pen from her bag. She took his hand and wrote a series of figures on his palm. 'My phone number.'

'You never give up, do you?'

She looked at him intently. 'Never.'

He signalled to one of the guards, who opened a separate section of the gate a crack, so she could slip unnoticed into the corridor of concrete protection walls.

As calmly as possible, she walked away from the place where she'd never even wanted to be, from the night she'd never wanted to experience, from the confrontation she'd never have sought, not in a million years. It was over, but it would remain with her, with every step that took her away from the military base, while she felt Gunnery Sergeant Mason Williams' eyes bore through the gate's metal fence into her back.

The men demonstrating in front of the gate were too busy setting fire to a doll representing Uncle Sam to notice her. To get to the taxi she had to bridge a distance of some thirty metres. She heard the screams of the men behind her. She should be able to make it.

Another twenty metres.

A loud male voice left her gasping. 'What are you doing here? *Khenayat kare kasief!* Filthy traitor!'

She tried to stay calm and started walking faster without taking her eyes off the taxi.

Ten metres.

To her surprise, the taxi pulled away. She started running.

Eight.

The taxi gathered speed. She ran faster.

Six.

More shouting behind her: 'We'll get you! *Tora gir mekonem!*'

She wasn't imagining things: the taxi was now going at practically the same speed as she was running. She heard a shot, a loud scream and then a dull thud behind her. She turned around. One of the guards had shot her pursuer in the legs. The man lay groaning in the street. In the smoke of the burning effigy, the group of protesters turned on her like a pack of wolves.

She could almost grab the edge of the door. Something whizzed through the air. It bounced off the roof of the car. A rock. She grabbed the door, leaned on its top edge, jumped into the car, hit her head and felt the rubber seal against her left temple. Her head twisted to the right. She fell crossways on to the back seat with her head down and saw the street roll away underneath her. A woman's voice shrieked above the roar. '*Basta ko, basta ko!* Close it, close it!'

In a daze, she sat up. The car had accelerated with such speed that the rear door now came straight at her. She scooted to the left and heard it slam shut. The Toyota crossed a busy junction. She felt nauseous, her cheeks were flushed, and her heart was thumping in her chest. 'Thank you!' she whispered. '*Tashakor.*'

The female voice again. 'What I really want to do is turn around and punch them all out, those bastards. Each and every one of them. But that's against Allah's will.'

She looked into the inquisitive, slightly squinted eyes that observed her in the rear-view mirror, and heard a big hearty laugh.

A woman's laugh.

'Where are you going, sister?'

'The Ministry of the Interior.'

'Expat?'

'Journalist.'

'You don't look like a journalist.'

'And you don't look like a taxi driver.'

They drove away from the heavily guarded zone surrounding Camp Eggers. The driver with her round face and the body of a wrestler watched her in the rear-view mirror. 'Where are you from, *hamshera*?'

'What do you mean?'

'You don't look like you're from around here.'

It didn't sound hostile, more like a simple statement of fact. Farah might speak Dari, but any taxi driver could see that she 'wasn't from around here'. Just like she could pick out the tourists in Amsterdam by their posture and the extra alertness in their eyes.

'I was born here.'

'You must have been away a long time.'

'Thirty years.'

The driver whistled through her teeth. 'That's a long time, sister. A very long time. What's your name?'

'Farah. And yours?'

'Nehal.'

They turned on to the noisy riverbank. Lots of people were milling around the stone water pumps by the side of the road. Most of the houses in Kabul had no running water. Just like the residents of the illegal huts of clay, mud and adobe up against the mountainside, downtown Kabulis also had to fill their jerry cans and pans with water down here.

'Our American liberators are providing billions of dollars in aid,' Nehal sneered, 'but ordinary Afghans wouldn't know it. They see the foreigners driving around in their luxury land cruisers, they see the villas that are being built for the expats and the politicians, while they go without running water or electricity. And then the Yankees wonder where all this resentment against them comes from.' She roared with laughter, but it sounded cynical.

Without thinking Farah ran her tongue over her lips.

'And can I give you a piece of advice? Keep your lips dry while you're out here.'

'Why?'

'The open sewers are backed up, and the heat does the rest. A fifth of all the dust in the air comes from animal and human waste. *Mawade fazela*. Shit. Lick your lips and you ingest our excrement.' Nehal produced another roaring laugh.

Farah didn't know whether she was pulling her leg, but there was one thing she'd noticed: unlike practically all the other taxi drivers, Nehal rarely used her horn. She didn't gesticulate or hurl expletives at other cars, didn't constantly stop and start just to squeeze into any available gap. She manoeuvred through the chaos as if the route had been mapped out for her in advance.

Farah sought eye contact via the mirror again. 'What happened last night?'

'What's been happening here for years. Hatred and fear rule. The city is a barrel filled with explosives. A tiny spark is enough to set things off. Yesterday's accident was just such a spark. And yet the same people who are chanting 'Death to America' are trying to profit as much as they can from the dollars that the Amrikaya are pumping into the country. But they're only thinking about themselves and passing up the chance to rebuild their country with the same money.'

They turned on to Ebn-e-Sina Road. Dirt-poor hustlers had their pathetic wares laid out on the ground. A little girl was half-submerged in a bin, rummaging for something that might be valuable or edible.

'Are you the only one, or are there more?'

'More what?'

'Female taxi drivers.'

'The only one. The Prophet has forbidden it, you know. Women aren't allowed to drive. But tell me: back when there were only camels, how could the Prophet have known that one day we'd be driving around in cars?'

'Being all-knowing is part of the job description, I guess.'

Nehal didn't seem to hear her and kept ranting. 'The men all shouted that I was a disgrace to the faith. They called me a whore. Some spat in my face. They threatened to stone me if I didn't stop at once. And look at me now! Do I look as if I've been stoned?' Nehal's roaring laughter filled the car again.

Farah looked outside and in passing saw the dusty Toyota reflected in the large glass façade of a building which had WEDDING PARA-DISE splashed across it in large lettering.

'Wedding parties may be the only consolation in this desolate city,' Nehal muttered. She drummed her ringless fingers on the wheel. 'But I don't need consolation. There's an old Afghan saying: a woman's place is in her husband's house or in her grave.'

They'd covered little more than a kilometre or two and were

approaching Cinema Park when shots rang out. Automatic gunfire, somewhere around a corner, from an alleyway; it was unclear exactly where it was coming from. Nehal slammed on the brakes. They both ducked and held their breath.

Seconds passed, and during that time all the traffic came to a standstill, and the whole city seemed to be holding its breath too. Then suddenly the cacophony of honking and yelling erupted all around them again. The silence had been short and intense, but now life continued as raucously loud as ever.

The gate of the Ministry of the Interior in Shahr-e Naw was guarded by sentries dressed entirely in black. They were rigid with tension. Like so many others, this government building had also been turned into a fortress. Under no circumstances were taxis allowed on site.

'Ordinary citizens have no idea what's going on behind those walls,' Nehal said. 'I understand the reason for the security, but it's beginning to look as if our government is hiding from its own citizens. Let me ask you: what's a government for? If anything, to protect its citizens, right?'

'Will you wait for me here?' Farah asked. 'Just let the meter run.'

Nehal refused the pile of afghanis Farah thrust at her. 'Pay me for driving, not for standing still.'

A female security guard checked Farah's passport at the gate and subjected her to a thorough search in a separate wooden cubicle before escorting her to a marble entrance lobby. The man waiting for them there was tall, athletic and self-assured. He looked impeccable in his dark-blue pinstripe suit. She put him in his early forties. The way he conveyed to the guard that she was no longer needed radiated the inherent authority and confidence of an experienced diplomat. Ahmad Shakoor, secretary-general of the interior, greeted her with his right hand on his heart and a slight incline of his head. The gesture was accompanied by a winning smile.

'As-Salaam-Alaikum, peace be upon you, Ms Hafez.'

With her right hand close to her heart and a nod of the head, she answered his greeting. 'Wa-Alaikum-Salaam.' She looked into his almond-coloured eyes. He was handsome.

'The driver assigned to you yesterday told me about your courageous intervention after yesterday's accident. I must admit I was rather surprised when I heard you arrived in a taxi just now. I was expecting a military escort.'

'Under the present hostile conditions, an inconspicuous vehicle seemed wise.'

'You're a woman of unpredictable choices, Ms Hafez. Come further.'

Ahmad Shakoor made an inviting gesture and together they walked down a long corridor with high ceilings. The old building reminded her of the classic ambience of the presidential palace. Then it dawned on her. She stopped in her tracks. Shakoor looked at her in surprise.

'Has the Ministry always been housed here?' she asked.

'As far as I know, yes. Why do you ask?'

'As a child I used to regularly visit my father's office. It was never here. Always at the presidential palace.'

Shakoor smiled. 'It was a highly unusual situation at that time. The Ministry was always officially housed here, but your father had his unofficial office at the palace. I was told that this was at the behest of President Daoud himself. Your father was his main adviser.' Shakoor wanted to move on.

Farah remained where she was. 'Forgive me, but there's something else that bothers me.' She could tell from the hint of displeasure that crossed Shakoor's face that this wasn't an opportune moment, but after days of uncertainty she needed an answer. 'Why has it taken thirty years for my father's grave to be found?'

Shakoor was now a bit less aloof. He leaned forward. There was nobody else in the corridor and yet he talked in hushed tones, like you do in museums or in churches. 'Three reasons, Ms Hafez. The Russian occupation, the civil war and the Taliban. Our country has known decades of wars. Although we're still officially at war with the Taliban, the social situation has stabilized to the extent that our president thought the time was ripe for an official investigation into Daoud Khan's final resting place. So imagine our amazement when, a day after the fact-finding committee was set up, a retired general came forward. At the time of the Saur Revolution in 1978, he was a young lieutenant, and on the evening of the killing he was ordered to remove the bodies of the president, his family and his closest aides and bury them outside the city. Having sworn an oath of secrecy, he kept the world in the dark for thirty years, but in the end he disclosed his secret and revealed the location of the mass grave to the government committee.'

'Where was it?'

'In the Pul-e-Charkhi district, east of the city, not far from the camp where the 201st Corps of the Afghan National Guard is based.'

The look Shakoor gave her seemed to say that as far as he was concerned the matter was closed.

High double doors opened on to a spacious room that had most of its shutters closed. In the middle stood a table without chairs. An elderly man was standing next to it, leaning on a classic walking cane with a silver-studded knob. Curly, ash-grey hair, interspersed with small tufts of black, fringed his balding head.

Shakoor stood between them.

'Ms Hafez, may I introduce Professor Yusufzai, forensic specialist and head of the government committee investigating the final resting place of President Daoud and his staff?'

Yusufzai regarded her with friendly, somewhat rheumy eyes.

'*As-Salaam-Alaikum.*'

When he bowed his head, his dark horn-rimmed glasses slid a little too far down his nose. He pushed them back up with his index finger.

She greeted him back with a polite smile. '*Wa-Alaikum-Salaam.*'

Yusufzai glanced at Shakoor, who stood at an appropriate distance and nodded to him. The professor told his story in an extremely formal tone.

'As you may have gathered, Ms Hafez, we were able to identify President Daoud and the others we located in the mass grave with the help of dental records. In principle, dental identification provides a sufficient degree of certainty. Nonetheless, we welcome any other details that can put it beyond any doubt. For example, President Daoud carried a small Koran with a golden cover in his breast pocket, a gift from the King of Saudi Arabia. I hope to achieve such absolute certainty in the case of the former interior affairs minister Aadel Gailani, your father. I therefore very much appreciate your willingness to cooperate.'

He inclined his head slightly and gave her an amiable look.

'In the telephone conversation with our ambassador to the Netherlands you mentioned that you saw your father on the day he . . .'

'. . . was shot.'

She hated this kind of unnecessary circumspection and here too she tried to break the unwritten rule that said women were tender-hearted and ought to be spared. Yusufzai looked at her in shock. For a split second she thought she detected a hint of contempt in his eyes.

'According to witness statements, Ms Hafez. But without forensic evidence to back these up it is only speculation.'

'I understand.'

'After a detailed examination it was established that all those involved did indeed die as a result of gunshot wounds.'

'So they were shot.'

Yusufzai pushed back the glasses that had slipped down his nose again, exchanged a brief glance with Shakoor and then gave her another amiable look. 'Can you describe to me what your father was wearing on that particular day?'

It wasn't hard to picture the bright linen suit. All these years, whenever she thought of him, whenever she was upset about something, whenever she asked for his advice and help, he was wearing it. Every single time. Whether it was on the side of a rainy road near Amsterdam or in a quiet courtyard in Jakarta's old town. She remembered wanting to stroke that suit as a child; the fabric was soft yet felt strong at the same time.

'It was made of heavier than normal linen. My mother thought the beige didn't reflect the gravity of his profession. But my father always wore it.'

Yusufzai cleared his throat before he continued. 'The bodies we found had been covered with canvas. After all those years in the ground much of it had decayed, as had most of the victims' clothing. But your father's suit was preserved relatively well. Linen contains an antiseptic substance that kills bacteria. Fungi cannot live on linen either.' He bent down and lifted a briefcase off the floor, which he placed on the table. He opened it, rummaged around and pulled out a plastic folder.

The heavy feeling in the pit of her stomach spread to her legs and when he showed her the sealed piece of linen she felt the blood rush from her head.

She became dizzy and averted her eyes. 'Yes,' she whispered after a few deep breaths. 'My father's suit was made of that fabric.'

'Are you certain?'

'No doubt about it.'

Yusufzai put the plastic folder back in his briefcase. 'May I show you the second detail or would you prefer a short break?'

'Let's continue.'

He scrutinized her. His tone was almost solemn now. 'Your father wore a ring. Could you describe it for me?'

'It was chunky with a wide band ... made of yellow gold. With a green gem set in the middle, jade, a rectangle ... If you looked closely, you could see ... butterfly wings.'

Yusufzai raised his eyebrows above his horn-rimmed spectacles. 'Why butterfly wings?'

'Because it had all these little round specks ... As a child they reminded me of butterfly wings.'

Yusufzai took a small wooden box out of his briefcase, held it between them and opened it. She looked at the wide ring with the flat-cut, greenish-black gem and the butterfly wings. It looked exactly the same as the time she'd stood hand in hand with her father in front of the large painting of Malalai.

On that last day.

She heard his voice again, the calm, deep tone in which he talked about the young woman on the large canvas, depicted robed in white on a hilltop waving the Afghan flag, while a huge battle raged below her.

It was supposed to have been her wedding day, Farah jan. But fate decided otherwise. Because on this day, almost a hundred years ago, Malalai carries water to our soldiers fighting the British oppressors at Maiwand. Her fiancé is the army's standard bearer. He encourages the men by waving his flag. But the British army bullets are whizzing around them, and the soldiers are dropping like flies. Suddenly the flag is gone. Malalai runs over to where she last saw him. And there he lies. The man she was due to marry. Dead.

He pointed to the woman in white.

In tears, she picks up the flag, runs up the hill and starts waving it. And she's shouting and encouraging the horsemen, who charge at the British soldiers with their swords held aloft.

He bent down, looked deep into her eyes and squeezed her hand. She felt his ring press against her fingers.

That day we defeated the most powerful army on earth. That day . . .

He glanced at the painting again.

. . . we won a great victory.

He smiled at her, but she remembered clearly that she'd seen something else too, something that made her feel uncomfortable, a feeling she couldn't explain. He hadn't been home for days. There were riots in the city, large demonstrations against the government, and she wanted to be with him, feel safe. But that smile told her even he couldn't offer safety at this moment. That smile told her he had doubts.

Her father never had doubts.

Except that time.

On that last day.

When he let go of her hand.

'Ms Hafez . . . ?'

The concerned voice of the secretary-general, who'd come to stand beside her.

'I'd like to have it,' she stammered. 'The ring. I have nothing to remember him by.'

The small garden of the Ministry of the Interior was home to exotic flowers in varying colours as well as a babbling fountain. She was looking out over it from Ahmad Shakoor's office. Five minutes ago, Professor Yusufzai had closed the little box with the ring and put it back in his briefcase. He had bid her a very formal farewell and assured her that he would do everything in his power to make the necessary notarial and administrative arrangements to ensure that it would go to her, as she was the rightful heir to the ring. It was only when he left the room leaning on his cane that she noticed his limp.

Shakoor had escorted her to his office. They were standing in front of the window, drinking tea from porcelain cups that had been brought in on a silver tray together with Afghan almond biscuits.

'It was the turning point,' Shakoor sighed. 'The day President Daoud was murdered was the last day Afghanistan was truly independent.'

Outside the walls of the Ministry everyday life simply continued. She heard the distant echoes of a city in constant chaos.

'Then there's the other matter you wished to discuss with me.' When Shakoor spoke it was with the same reserve with which he sipped his tea.

She looked at him expectantly. 'I hope you received the documents from the Dutch embassy in good order.'

'The diplomatic post is extremely efficient, ma'am, even in Afghanistan. And it's with the same efficiency that I intend to study this case.'

She refused to be riled by his patronizing tone. Shakoor was the only man who could help her at this moment. Without him, her plan to track down Sekandar's family and return him safely to them was doomed to failure. She took out one of Sekandar's drawings, held it by the edges and showed it to him.

'This is the only clue we have for now. I'd hoped that you . . .'

Shakoor raised his hand. She wasn't sure if what she saw in his eyes was a form of condescension or of pity. Probably both.

'You have to believe me when I say that after all these years of war, the problem of street children is disproportionate. On a national scale. And it's estimated that there are more than thirty thousand of these children in Kabul alone. The orphanages where we try to provide for them are overcrowded. Within this context, tracking down the family of a traumatized boy we know next to nothing about is extremely challenging, and that's putting it mildly.'

'I'm well aware, Mr Shakoor, of the difficult circumstances of our country, but . . .'

He looked at her in surprise. '"Our" country?'

'I was born here. I still consider this my country.'

'Even though you haven't been back for thirty years?'

'Despite that, yes . . .'

'How noble of you.'

His tone was now unmistakably patronizing. And somewhere deep inside she knew that he wasn't being all that unreasonable. It was inappropriate to lay claim to a country simply because it's the place where you were born and spent a part of your childhood. She knew she was kidding herself but she wanted to believe it so badly. This had been her home once, her reality. Why couldn't she capture that feeling again?

She folded the drawing and put it back in her bag. Her mouth was dry, but she wasn't interested in drinking anything. She wanted to talk, persuade him, win him over to her cause. She walked to the desk, returned the cup of tea to the tray untouched, next to the sweet biscuits, and turned to Shakoor again.

'You were talking about the street children of Kabul, the orphans all across the country. But Sekandar's case is different. A young boy who was found half dead, not here in the streets of Kabul, not somewhere in this country, but thousands of miles away. In the Netherlands. A Dutch minister is involved in the case. People have died during the investigation. We're still gathering all the evidence, but it's all connected to the Russian oligarch Valentin Lavrov. What I mean to say is that Sekandar is more of an international issue.'

'An issue that now has our attention too, my dear lady. But unfortunately we don't really have the necessary resources to facilitate an operation like the one you have in mind.'

She wanted to use everything in her arsenal to make him see and feel that she was serious about this.

'I think we have similar interests in the matter, Mr Shakoor.'

'Is that right?'

'You invited me on behalf of the government to attend the ceremonial reburial. I think that's an honour. But as always the knife cuts both ways. The ambassador who called me in the Netherlands told me that my presence at the ceremony would generate a degree of publicity for the government.'

Shakoor now looked at her with a faint smile.

'Yes, I must say you've garnered rather an illustrious reputation in a relatively short span of time.'

'Imagine the value of giving a face to all those anonymous countrymen and women who've fled in recent years, but who want nothing more than to return home. Sekandar can be that face. Especially now with the ceremonial reburial. Do you see what I'm saying?'

'My dear Ms Hafez, we're under permanent threat of war, and the country's racked by chronic poverty. Even if we were able to locate his family in such an impossibly short timeframe, who says that what happened to your boy won't happen again, that he won't be sold again?'

'My dear Mr Shakoor, whatever role his parents may have played in the matter, they're still his parents. A child without parents is a person without a soul. Trust me, I know.'

She looked him straight in the eye, in the hope of having hit a nerve, somewhere in a place he kept shielded from the outside world.

He averted his gaze. A member of his staff had appeared in the doorway. Shakoor shook his head, but the man didn't budge.

'It's urgent, sir.'

Following a brief whispered exchange with the assistant, Shakoor turned to her. I beg your pardon. I'll be back in a few minutes.'

Then he left the room.

She slowly walked around the room and examined the photos in their silver frames that were neatly arranged on the desktop. On the right, the private photos: Shakoor with his pretty wife, Shakoor with his model family – two smart-looking children, a boy and a girl. One by one she picked up the framed photos, looked at them closely and carefully put them down again. Not a speck of dust anywhere. Everything was kept meticulously clean around here.

On the left side of the desk were three photos that reflected her host's function. A formal portrait of Shakoor with the minister of the interior. A group photo of Shakoor with about eight colleagues. But it was the third portrait that really caught her attention. It showed the minister of the interior flanked by members of the Afghan National Guard. Her eyes skimmed over the unfamiliar faces. The pendulum in the room seemed to be ticking louder. But it wasn't the clock, she realized. It was her own heart. It was pounding at the recognition of the man beside Shakoor. The man who'd clasped her arm like a vice last night.

Her hand was shaking when she put down the frame. She turned nervously when she heard Shakoor enter the room. She saw the tense expression on his face.

'You told me that you took a taxi for safety reasons.'

'That's right.'

'I just heard a different version. General Goldwater has informed me of your stay at Camp Eggers.'

She sighed and warily shook her head.

'Let me keep it simple, my dear lady. Should you want to start a journalistic crusade against a general who, in his position as head of the National Guard, comes under the direct jurisdiction of this ministry, I can't stop you. I may be willing to help you track down the boy's family. But then you must make it possible for me to help you. The choice is yours.'

She looked at him and was momentarily dumbstruck.

Shakoor flashed a condescending smile.

'Everything in this life has a price, Ms Hafez.'

5
Raylan

1968

The first thing he always noticed in the large entry hall of the National Museum was the figure in the chainmail armour. He was completely made of marble and very imposing on his pedestal. One hand lay on the hilt of a large sword, reaching almost from chest height to the ground; his other hand was raised, like in a proud greeting.

'Mr Chapelle?'

Raylan turned to the slender man in a tailored suit who'd come and stood in front of him and, with his right hand on his heart, offered a modest bow.

'*As-Salaam-Alaikum*. My name is Parwaiz Ahmad, director of this museum.'

'*Wa-Alaikum-Salaam*, Mr Ahmad.'

'I'm in good company with King Kanishka to greet you here,' Parwaiz Ahmad said, pointing to the man in the coat of mail. If you allow me, I will accompany you to your appointment.

He gestured with his right arm in the direction of a large room and escorted him on a tour of an overwhelming number of exotic statues, murals and archaeological finds.

'Afghanistan was located at the heart of the Silk Road. Traders and travellers from Persia, Central Asia, India and China have traversed our country for centuries. Great powers from all over the world have imposed their cultures and religions on us, thus influencing our history. Here you find all the evidence,' said Parwaiz, stopping in front of a solid piece of slate. 'Greek-Buddhist art, excavated from a monastery in Eastern Afghanistan.'

As Raylan examined the carved group of worshipers adoringly kneeling before the Buddha, Parwaiz's attention had shifted to a glass vase depicting a tower with a large flame. 'This is a Roman heirloom. The first lighthouse in the world: the Pharos of Alexandria.'

Raylan's eye then fell on an ivory statue of a graceful woman in a transparent robe that hardly concealed her full breasts and curvaceous hips.

'Ah! The River Goddess from Begram,' said Parwaiz. 'Although she still looks lifelike, she dates from the first century AD. The myth goes that whenever she appeared in the River Amu-Darya, she drove men crazy and let them drown, drunk with desire.'

'That's what love and war have in common,' Raylan said.

Parwaiz looked at him, not understanding what he was saying.

'Both make people do crazy things.'

'I heard that you spent years in Vietnam. I admire your courage.'

'My country is doing the same there as the great powers that once left their culture behind here. The only differences: we gave the Vietnamese napalm, cluster bombs and Coca-Cola.

'The words of a true pessimist, Mr Chapelle,' Parwaiz replied, who obviously didn't know how to deal with Raylan's cynicism.

'What you call pessimism, I call realism.'

'Everyone is entitled to their opinion,' Parwaiz replied formally. 'But one thing I know for sure: no matter the war, art and love will always overcome. They are . . .'

'Invincible?'

'Eternal, if you ask me.'

Raylan followed Parwaiz down a spiral staircase that led to the museum's basement vaults. A heavy door gave access to a large, dimly lit space.

'The heart of the museum,' Parwaiz whispered. Our treasure chamber. Here we keep manuscripts, paintings and objects that are the heart of our society. This art is . . .'

'Eternal?'

'Our identity.'

They were both silent when a woman who'd been waiting for them in the shadows appeared.

Helai Durani was wearing a long-sleeved black dress that flared slightly at the waist and reached to well over the knee. The black fabric was speckled with white dots that looked like scattered snowflakes. She sounded calm, but Raylan heard the nervous undertone in the few words she exchanged with Parwaiz before he left them alone with a solemn nod.

The awkwardness between them was almost palpable when the door closed.

'I thought it best not to meet you in the courthouse,' she said with a voice that was lower than he remembered and a look that was significantly softer than the first time.

'Why not?'

'Your presence in the courtroom yesterday, of course, did not go unnoticed ... And even in the most progressive of circles, it isn't so wise for a woman here to appear in the company of men, certainly not men of your stature ...'

'My stature?'

'American, journalist ... If people see us together on more than one occasion, it could not only undermine my position as a public prosecutor, but it could also damage your reputation as a journalist.'

'Do you think that interests me in the slightest?'

Damn it. He'd meant to put it differently, but the words just popped out of his mouth.

Helai gave him a despairing look.

'Don't you care what encounters like this might mean for me?'

'Yes, sorry ... That's not what I meant to say.'

'I'm not supposed to meet you, not anywhere.'

'Yet, here you are.'

She sighed.

'Yes ... yesterday was a chaotic day ... I wasn't quite myself ... The way I spoke to you was ... inappropriate.'

'We all have our bad days.'

'Could you perhaps drop the sarcasm?'

'Okay ...'

'Sorry.'

'What for?'

'For yesterday.'

'You don't have to apologize. You weren't yourself.'

The silence between them lasted far too long. Staring into her different-coloured eyes for more than a second clouded his thoughts.

She tried to smile. 'Today, I am, I hope.'

'Sorry?'

'Today, I am myself. And you don't have to apologize either.'

She lifted up a book she'd had in her hand all along. In colourful Eastern patterns he saw a budding flower on the front and the English title: *The Selected Poems of Hafez*.

'If you want to understand us a bit better, this is a must-read.'

'"Us"? You mean . . .'

'Our culture, our history . . . Us.'

She pressed the book into his hands.

'There are people who think that reading means turning your back on reality to seek your salvation in an imaginary world. But books do more than that. They make you a better person. The poems of Hafez have that effect. He's the voice of millions of Afghans.'

He carefully opened the book. He saw the inscription in her handwriting: *For Raylan Chapelle, a truth-seeker*. Without actually reading a single word, he began to thumb through it. 'Thank you,' he finally stammered.

The way she was standing now reminded him of yesterday in the doorway as she watched him walk away. She radiated a vulnerability that made him want to put his arm around her shoulder and reassure her that it was okay for her to be here with him. However, he couldn't manage more than closing the book and staring silently at the cover.

'During my first six months in America I was very homesick,' he heard her hesitantly admit. 'I could hardly concentrate on my studies. I wasn't a big fan of the food . . . I was somewhere I didn't want to be, but where I had to be in order to achieve my goal.'

She put her hand on the cover of the book and touched his fingers. 'I read this every night. I put it under my pillow in the hope that Hafez would whisper to me in my sleep: *Helai, when you wake up in the morning, things will be better.*'

'And . . . ?'

'I remember a morning when I saw dawn breaking through a crack in the curtains and I got out of bed . . . and pulled the curtains open so hard that they fell on top of me, rod and all.'

He found her laughter utterly disarming. There she stood, with her arms stretched wide and her eyes closed. That young woman who'd tried in vain to catch the curtain rails and was now standing in the bright sunlight. She opened her eyes, lowered her arms and looked at him, relaxed.

'Do you know what I thought at that moment? I'm not leaving this place until I've achieved my goal. It was almost a . . . religious experience.'

'Don't let the Prophet hear you say that.'

'Anyway, Hafez is still my chief adviser, as well as my source of inspiration. He gives me peace and direction. I hope he can do the same for you.'

He rubbed the cover with the palm of his hand.

'I think it's very . . . thoughtful of you, but . . .'

'But . . . ?'

'I'm not exactly waiting for the help of a dead poet. What I need is the help of a public prosecutor.'

She tapped the book with her long, dark, lacquered nails.

'Check the flyleaf.'

He opened the book again and now saw that a document was hidden behind the flyleaf. He was about to remove it when he felt her hand on his.

'Not here,' she whispered. 'Later.'

She pulled her hand away and gestured with her head that he should follow her. She stopped in front of a large painting depicting a medieval battlefield.

'Maiwand, 1880. The Second Anglo-Afghan War. The British had occupied our country. In this battle the Afghan army of Ayub Khan retaliated.' She pointed to a young woman waving the Afghan flag on a hilltop. 'A seventeen-year-old water-bearer who'd picked up the flag after she'd seen the standard-bearer fall in battle. Her name was Malalai. She's never mentioned by the British. After all, she was a woman, and also an Afghan. But she was the one who, at the moment the Afghan troops lost all hope, singlehandedly led an entire army to victory . . .'

She gave him a piercing look.

'The strength with which a girl waves her country's flag can be as great as the single-mindedness of a young poet who wants to destroy the monarchy.'

'I see where you're going with this . . . but I'm a journalist, Helai. I mean, I can't be the spokesman for a public prosecutor.'

She silently took a document out of her handbag, folded it open and showed it to him. He recognized the stamps of the department and the signature of Aadel Gailani.

'Official permission for your conversation with Askan Vaziri.'

He looked at her in amazement.

'You have to write your own story,' she said. 'But will you promise me one thing?'

'What?'

'That you stop mistrusting me. I just want to help you.'

'Why?'

She gave him a look that made him feel like he'd jumped into a river and was drowning.

'Because . . .' she said, thoughtfully shaking her head. 'Somehow, you make me say things that a woman would be better off keeping to herself . . .'

At the moment she touched his arm, he heard a door open. The silhouette of Parwaiz was visible.

'When you want to see me again, contact him,' Helai softly said.

Then she turned around and vanished as quickly as she'd appeared.

Sometimes the memories in Raylan's head would slide over each other, like tectonic plates right before an earthquake. Like now. He was back in the large French colonial house with its high ceilings, where the creaking wooden floors were scattered with sleeping Marines. Once more, he couldn't shake off the relentless sound of firefights, airstrikes, whizzing bullets, the thud of exploding Viet Cong B-40 rocket shells and the constant screaming of the wounded. He'd cautiously slipped past the M-16s, the ammunition boxes and the stacked cans of C-rations to a window that had been shot to pieces. On the opposite riverbank, flares showered the ramparts of the citadel in bright white light. The North Vietnamese Liberation Army's red flag with its yellow star flapped on the watchtower.

'Enjoying the view? Room service okay?'

He turned around only to be confronted by the ashen face of Platoon Commander Thompson. The sunken, dark circles under his eyes were visible even in the dim glow of the kerosene lamp.

'How long have you been tramping around in the jungle with us, Chapelle?'

'Three years, sir.'

'Three years ... And in all that time we've arranged your transport, protected you, provided you with food and shelter. And yet I'm damn sure you'll report to the home front that we're fucking with two thousand years of culture here.'

They silently stared at the structures on the other side of the river. The centuries-old citadel was a labyrinth enclosed by canals and metre-thick walls. Inside was Hoang Thanh, the Imperial City of Hué, the imperial residence, guarded by cannons that the emperor once had cast from the war scraps of victorious battles.

'I hope you'll also mention that these so-called liberators from the North have chosen this very city because they want us to obliterate it. Because that's the only choice they're giving us. To liberate the city we have to destroy it. They're counting on it. Just like they're counting on you to provide front-page headlines about our barbaric behaviour here. They're reckoning on you being here, pal, so you can show the world us shooting this city to pieces. I swear: Ho Chi fuckin' Minh's boys who are dug in across the river aren't my worst enemies.' He glared at Raylan with exhausted, bloodshot eyes. 'My worst enemy is *you*, the goddamn American press.'

Thompson's words receded into the distance.

Raylan deeply inhaled the cool air from the Hindu Kush Mountains, which blanketed Kabul at night. He emptied his umpteenth glass of whiskey and looked out over Hotel Serena's dimly lit swimming pool and courtyard garden.

He'd spent much of the evening looking at the document Helai Durani had given him in the National Museum's vaults. Granted, it was written in English, but that was about all. The instructions to assemble a Meccano kit were more exciting. In boring legalese, Helai had gathered stacks and stacks of evidence. Her arguments sounded unshakable, but if you used your common sense, you could tell that something was off.

It reminded him of the Five O'Clock Follies in Saigon. Every day at exactly five o'clock spokesmen for the American army leadership gave a military press briefing to the hordes of journalists there on the ground with them. And how they did it and where they found the godforsaken nerve, nobody knew, but time and again they managed to turn their losses on the battlefield into what seemed like heroic situations or even glorious victories.

Transforming lies into news.

That's what they wanted.

After experiencing a number of these Five O'Clock Follies, it was clear to Raylan: as a journalist he would always choose the path the authorities definitely didn't want him to follow.

Commander Thompson had called him his worst enemy in Hué. And strangely enough, he had done this with a certain grudging respect. The same respect Raylan had shown for the Marines he'd tramped around with for three years.

Here in Kabul, the attorney general of the Department for the Organization and Defence of the Interests of Afghanistan, Aadel Gailani, apparently had no idea what kind of reporter he'd approached. To him, Raylan Chapelle was an internationally renowned journalist who'd written for *The New York Times*, *Life*, *Look* and *Paris Match*. The perfect figure to treat the world to an epic piece in which Afghanistan's budding democracy triumphs over a communist terrorist-group.

But Gailani could go to hell, Raylan thought. Just like in Vietnam, he would just go his own godforsaken way. Raylan lit a joint and stared at the hazy Hindu Kush in the distance. In his mind he was back beside Commander Thompson again, looking out over the River Perfume at the contours of the Imperial Citadel.

'I'd prefer to spare that old city,' Thompson had muttered. 'But in this war I have little if any say. The brightest minds have dragged us into this mess, but they're apparently not bright enough to get us out. This whole goddamn army is fucked up: from the White House all the way down to my own command, but you didn't hear that from me, understand? They're expecting us to sack the city. But at what cost? In just a few days I've lost more men than during the whole damn war. And more will die. Tomorrow, the day after tomorrow. As long as the Stars and Stripes waves atop that damn citadel tower.' He took a long pull on his cigar. 'Chapelle, you're a fucking pain in the ass and you know it. But you're the only one who can make sure that the home front knows what the hell is going on here, how history is playing out.'

Last night Raylan had fought off sleep. He'd rather hear Thompson's voice booming in his head than see the burning monk over and over again in his mind. Whiskey, nicotine and weed had helped him stay awake. While the sun slowly crept out from behind the mountain ridges, a muezzin with a shuddering cry called believers to morning prayers.

Raylan didn't have a lot of time to do in-depth research for his article. It had to be ready before the judge ruled in two days. The article would appear in *The New York Times* on the last page of the foreign section with the headline 'ALLEGED ATTEMPTED COUP PUNISHABLE BY DEATH'. Death penalty or not: no American back home even knew where Afghanistan was, let alone gave a damn about it.

It was seven o'clock in the morning and already unpleasantly warm when Raylan took a seat opposite Askan Vaziri's lawyer in his dusty office. The lawyer was convinced it was a conspiracy. How did the security service find out about the plans? This could have only happened through an infiltrator. Most likely someone on the payroll. The government had made a pact with the security service. They were using Askan Vaziri as a pawn in an ideological war against the Soviet Union's threatening influence. With this trial they wanted to set an example for young people about what they would be up against if they questioned the government's current course. 'And then again,' the lawyer suggested. 'The sketches and accompanying notes for an attack on the royal convoy were only meant hypothetically. How do they say that again in your country, Mr Chapelle? Oh yes, to serve as an eye-opener. What's wrong with that? The constitution guarantees us freedom of speech.'

Okay, an attempted defence that shouldn't be brushed aside easily, Raylan thought, but one that was perhaps too obvious, given this lawyer was being paid for with funds from the People's Democratic Party.

Less than thirty minutes later, he was standing in front of the hermetically sealed-off building of the party newspaper *The People* with another document Helai had given him. It was intended to provide him with access to a maximum-security prison complex later that day. But Raylan hoped that the policeman guarding the premises would be so impressed by its official-looking character that he would give him access. A quick glance at the document and two simple words were enough to make it clear to Raylan that his attempt was pointless.

'Deh Mazang!'

Raylan tapped the sheet of paper and pointed to the building again.

'C'mon, man, this is a permit. I just want to pop in for a short visit.'

'This for Deh Mazang . . . Prison!' the policeman loudly snorted at him while pointing to the east of the city. With an uneasy grin Raylan removed a packet of cigarettes from his inside jacket pocket. When he flashed it in front of the guy, he glared at him as if he were about to punch him in the face.

'Motherfucker,' Raylan mumbled under his breath. He stuck a Lucky Strike in between his teeth and returned to the waiting taxi.

During Raylan's unexpected visit, the editor of the Bakhtar News Agency had been surprisingly unforthcoming. 'We're reporters, not judges,' he'd said. *The Kabul Times* reporter agreed. He looked more like a courthouse clerk than a journalist interested in getting to the bottom of a story: 'The facts speak for themselves, Mr Chapelle.'

They were all playing stupid, Raylan thought, when he walked into the auditorium of Kabul University early in the afternoon. Both the Bakhtar News Agency and *The Kabul Times* were funded by the government. Here at the university, also founded with government support and foreign money, it wouldn't be any different. He was therefore caught off-guard when he was not only courteously greeted by the Professor of Anglo-Saxon Languages, Noor Qadiry, but also heard that he'd take him to a place which, as he himself said, 'would reveal everything there was to know about Askan Vaziri'.

'They'll never stop,' Qadiry said, crossing the campus square with Raylan. Everywhere, groups of students were busy making banners and painting signs. Some had bandages on their heads, others were walking around with bruised faces. 'The government is trying to scare them off, but gets the opposite result. All this police violence motivates them even more to take to the streets and demonstrate. No one seems to be concentrating on their studies any more. I've been giving my lectures of late to an almost empty room.'

The newly planted trees on the yellowed lawns were a pitiful sight up against the campus buildings. Apart from this complex there weren't any other structures for miles around. The empty barren plain around the university was symbolic of how isolated the world of these students was.

'This used to be farmland,' the professor said. 'Now it's the intellectual heart of the country. But you won't find any farmers' sons here. They all go into the army. Poor people can't afford to send their children to university. We have the most modern facilities and the best teachers here, if I may be so immodest. This place offers young people perspectives that until recently were practically unknown to them.'

'Sounds like a paradise. So why are they becoming so radical?'

'They're developing a new culture and want to change everything, just like all the students on the campuses in America who are demonstrating against the Vietnam War. In Paris they occupy the Champs-Élysées because they want to get rid of a president old enough to be their grandfather. This form of protest is spreading across the world, including here, where an old king still rules. These young people want change. The vast majority of them think that communism can bring about these changes. And they want these changes today rather than tomorrow. The elderly among us call this impatience or radicalism. I call it youth, Mr Chapelle. Youth.'

Amused, Raylan watched as two young women hoisted their newly painted banner in the air and were met with loud cheers.

'Are these young people really a threat to the current regime?'

'A few weeks ago, I would have strongly denied this,' the professor replied.

'And now?'

'Now, I don't know, I really don't. The speed of the radicalization on such a large scale . . . I've never experienced this before.'

They walked through a long, deserted corridor, past the only classroom that was used. Raylan saw a group of smartly dressed students, the majority of whom were young women. They listened attentively to a professor with a white beard who was writing quotes on the blackboard in elegant handwriting.

'They're studying the poetry of Hafez,' Qadiry said.

In the university library, the professor pointed to a large oval space full of bookcases. 'This is the place I wanted you to see with your own eyes. The students call it the "Ark of Askan". Here you'll find all the books he has read and studied in recent years. They are for the most part a gift from the Russian Cultural Centre, which also financed the translations.'

Raylan walked along the full shelves, where books on Marxism, Leninism and Stalinism were sandwiched between the impressive works of the Arab philosophers Al-Kindi, Al-Farahi and Ibn Khaldun. *The Communist Manifesto* by Karl Marx and Friedrich Engels standing side by side with Leo Tolstoy's *War and Peace*. The professor pointed to a complete section dedicated to the ancient Greeks. 'That's how old the idea of a classless society is. In his book *The Republic* Plato describes a situation in which men share all their possessions, including women and children.'

A little further on, Qadiry pulled a book off a shelf. 'This is a work by Nikolay Tikhonov, one of the founders of Soviet literature. Ballads about immense heroism and courage. And look here . . .' He showed Raylan a strip of paper with writing in Dari that was folded inside the book cover. 'Askan isn't shy about giving his opinion. *Read this book, because it changed my life.*'

The professor carefully reinserted the book on the shelf.

'Askan also organized discussion evenings when he was here. Not only for students and professors, but also for people from outside the university. He wanted the knowledge that was gathered here to benefit the entire population. He was busy setting up a literacy programme. All Afghans who were unable to read and write – and that's the vast majority of the country – needed to be empowered as citizens, he thought. It is . . .'

With a deep sigh he put his hands on his hips.

'I'm not a lawyer, Mr Chapelle. I teach English. But what I can tell you is that Askan Vaziri is an idealist with two left hands. He's not a biochemist who assembles bombs.'

'In other words, you think he's innocent,' Raylan said.

'Innocent until proven guilty. That's how justice should work. But before he'd even set foot in the courtroom, Askan had already been found guilty. The trial against him is actually meant as one big symbolic warning for all young Afghans: "You may participate in this burgeoning democracy as long as you obey the rules. For any form of contradiction or radicalism will cost you dearly".'

They heard quick, light footsteps. A girl with long dark hair, dressed in jeans, ran into the library, hesitated a moment when she saw Raylan and the professor but then proceeded further in the direction of Askan's Ark. She greeted the professor, quickly exchanged a few words with him in Dari, after which she pulled a book off a shelf.

'*The Fight for Freedom,*' Qadiry told Raylan. 'Askan's most famous book of poetry.'

'He's my hero,' the girl said in broken English. Only then did Raylan recognize her: she was the one who'd tried to persuade the young policeman in front of the courthouse by engaging him in discussion. Before Rayland could say anything to her, she ran out of the library as quickly as she appeared.

'What did I tell you?' Qadiry sighed with a look of melancholy. 'Youth.'

Raylan stared at the rows of books. 'So practically everything I see here is from the Russian Cultural Centre?'

'For the most part.'

'With his hand on his chest Raylan bowed slightly to Qadiry. 'Thank you for enlightening me, professor.'

Once he was outside he saw the girl join the last group of demonstrators who were heading into town. Chanting slogans with the others, she entered the desolate no man's land that separated the campus from the city.

The Russian Cultural Centre in the Kart-e-Char district reminded him of a bunker built by Egyptian pyramid designers. A fearless concrete city palace asserting its right to exist. The monumental stairwell, characteristic of communist architecture, looked like it was primarily intended to make you feel more and more insignificant the higher you went. In the megalomaniac entrance lobby, the floor covered in grey tiles, a life-size portrait of Lenin greeted Raylan and a cranky Russian receptionist suspiciously studied him from behind her desk. She looked as if she could sing the bass part in a Cossack choir.

Time for bluff poker.

'Raylan Chapelle, *New York Times*,' he said with the superiority of someone who is used to people the world over being able to understand him in English. 'I'm writing an article about Askan Vaziri, who will probably be sentenced to death soon. According to my sources, he has connections to this centre.'

'Do you have an appointment?'

'No.'

'I'm sorry. Without an appointment . . .'

'Brush me off, my dear, and I'll drag this centre's reputation abroad through the mud so badly that your boss will send you to back to Moscow tomorrow with a one-way ticket. The choice is yours.'

She looked at him as if he'd just spat her in the face, picked up the phone and spoke in a muffled clipped tone. It sounded like she was requesting permission from military headquarters at the Kremlin to personally decorate the leather jacket of the unshaven, wild-haired man standing in front of her with live grenades.

'You wait,' she barked threateningly after she'd hung up.

Raylan surveyed the hall. He saw a man appear on the other side. Striding quickly and confidently, he cut a razor-sharp diagonal across the lobby'. His light-grey suit hugged his honed body. Undoubtedly a Spetsnaz guy, skilled in special combat techniques, capable of using his little finger to hurl unwanted visitors down a flight of stairs. To Raylan's surprise, the man reached out his hand to him. His English had that familiar syrupy Russian undertone.

'Grigori Michailov, coordinating director. What can I do for you, Mr . . . ?'

'Chapelle. Raylan Chapelle.'

An arrogant look crossed his angular face.

'American, I understand?'

'I write for *The New York Times*.'

'I prefer *The Washington Post*.'

'What can I say? It's a free world.'

The response came in the shape of a thin smile.

'It's not customary for people to just show up here without an appointment . . .'

Raylan interrupted him, 'I'm writing a background article about the case against Askan Vaziri.'

Michailov raised an eyebrow.

'The young editor of *The People*, who allegedly was planning an attack on the king,' Raylan explained.

'Right, yes.'

'He appears to have ties to this centre.'

There was a slight hesitation, immediately followed by a chilly response. 'Comparisons can easily be drawn between the party ideology of Soviet communism and the ideas of the People's Youth Organization of Afghanistan. However, as a Russian centre of science and art, we stay out of the country's political affairs.'

'C'mon, really? Everything you Russians do is political.'

'From the somewhat paranoid point of view of an American journalist, I can imagine it looks like that to you. Yet, let me assure you that nothing could be further from the truth.'

Raylan looked at him and smiled. With all due respect, Mr Michailov, your place here is filled with communist literature and revolutionary art, you screen *Battleship Potemkin* every night, and you're trying to tell me you don't have any influence on the so-called People's Democratic Party of Afghanistan?'

He glanced at his state-of-the-art quartz watch.

'Mr Chapelle, I don't think this is the right time or place to have this discussion with you. I'm sorry, but I have more important things on my mind.'

'What are your books doing in Askan Vaziri's library?'

'I'm afraid I don't follow you.'

'Almost every book belonging to that young man is embossed with a red star and a hammer and sickle. The largest part of his communist collection appears to have been financed by this centre.'

A scrutinizing glance was followed by a casual smirk.

'The Russian government has supported Kabul University in various ways. Part of the library, including translations into Dari, was a gift to the country.'

'So there's a connection after all.'

'A coincidence, not a connection.'

'It means that this centre has directly or indirectly contributed to indoctrinating a young idealist, filled his head with ideas and beliefs that drove him to take an action that is considered to be a danger to the state here.'

'If I understand you correctly, you're trying to seize upon a domestic situation to portray this centre in a bad light.'

'I'm simply saying that one plus one equals two.'

'It's what we would call slander, Mr Chapelle. You know we can sue you for that?'

From the corner of his eye, Raylan saw a guard appear. A broad-shouldered young Russian with the head of a condor. Michailov subtly gestured to him.

'If you want to sue me for being a journalist, I'd say, go right ahead, Mr Michailov.'

Michailov signalled to the condor that he should get on with it. Raylan felt a hand on his shoulder, an iron grip.

'One more question,' Raylan said.

'And that is?'

'You acted like you didn't know Askan Vaziri. Yet you knew he's a member of the People's Youth Organization of Afghanistan.'

Michailov glared at Raylan as if he wasn't the director of a cultural institution, but the boss of a Siberian penal colony. Bull's-eye, thought

Raylan right before the condor forcefully escorted him outside and shoved him down the steps.

'If you have any more "questions" like this, best you make an appointment with him,' said Michailov, who was now standing at the top of the stairs next to the condor. 'I wish you good luck with your article.'

Raylan barely felt any pain once he scrambled to his feet again. Grigori Michailov, he realized with some sense of excitement, had just done something you should never do in the presence of a journalist: he'd lied though his teeth.

He hobbled past the last houses in the Deh Mazang district, which were built against the foothills of the Asmai Mountain. He had to squint to be able to see anything in the glare of the low-hanging sun. When he reached the gate of the prison complex he stuck a Lucky Strike between his lips. The interpreter with the horn-rimmed glasses, who was waiting for him, nervously shook his head.

'No time. They're expecting us.'

Raylan flicked open his Zippo, lit his cigarette and enjoyed the smoke filling his lungs. The interpreter loudly knocked on the gate. A porthole slid open. After a short conversation the entire gate followed. With two fingers Raylan snuffed out his burning cigarette and returned it to the packet. After having his identity checked and being frisked, he was instructed to take a seat in a musty waiting room until the prison director and his assistant showed up. The warden was a chubby man in his fifties wearing an expensive pinstripe suit. His assistant – who had hunched shoulders and wore a threadbare brown suit – looked considerably poorer and masked a terrier-like hostility with a wafer-thin smile.

They showed him a number of outbuildings, in which men in prison garb wove carpets, tooled leather or welded pewter pots and pans together. The Deh Mazang prison was apparently a large group of workplaces, which, thanks to an army of cheap labour – mainly petty criminals, beggars and vagrants – turned a huge profit. Clearly, this money hadn't been spent on the restoration of the buildings, which dated from the beginning of the century. Signs of neglect were visible everywhere, from loose electrical cables and leaking ceilings to walls with peeling paint. Halfway through, Raylan lost his patience and tugged on the interpreter's jacket.

'I'm not here as a tourist. I've come to interview a suspect.'

'Very rude,' whispered the interpreter, who, nervously twitching, conveyed Raylan's message, after which the director immediately ended the tour and, with an expression as if someone had just grabbed his balls, led them through the bare corridors into his office. With disgust, Raylan looked at a tray that was holding a large teapot and saucers full of sweets.

'Thanks for the tea, guys, but now I want to speak to the prisoner.'

'Very rude,' mumbled the interpreter, but he also conveyed this request. The director ditched his twisted grin for good and in snappy sentences instructed his assistant to bring 'the ungrateful American and his sidekick' to the prisoner. After passing three metal gates they ended up in the maximum security area of the complex, where Askan Vaziri was waiting for them, chained to a chair behind a table.

'You've got ten minutes,' lisped the assistant.

Raylan sat down opposite Vaziri.

'My name is Raylan Chapelle, I'm a journalist and I want to hear your story.'

After the translation, the youngster stared at Raylan with hollow eyes.

'For weeks I'm kept in isolation,' he replied in perfect English. 'Yesterday you were given a VIP seat in the courtroom. Today you're sitting here in front of me. You must be very important to them.'

'Who do you mean by "them"?'

'Daoud Khan's elitist puppets. What did they promise you in return?'

'Let's get this straight, my friend: I'm not on anyone's payroll.'

'Only speak Dari,' the assistant commanded.

Raylan looked at him and continued in English. 'I really don't have time for this bullshit, Askan. I want to know if you condone violence as a means to an end.'

'Of course,' answered Askan. 'Through the armed struggle, we want to return the country to its citizens.'

'That's why you recited that poem in court?'

Askan nodded.

'That was tantamount to an admission of guilt, do you realize that?'

'I'm not like Hafez,' Askan said in a tired voice that seemed to get less audible with every word. I don't preach peace and harmony. I despise the open materialism of the feudal elite and the corrupt practices they keep in place. The only effective answer to that is the class struggle.'

'I might as well be reading the recruitment folder of the Communist Party.'

'Continue in Dari, otherwise this conversation is over,' the assistant grunted.

Raylan ignored the order and offered Askan a cigarette. 'Imperialistic Lucky Strikes, kid. I'm afraid I don't have much more for you.'

'*Bas*,' said the assistant, 'enough', and he stormed out of the cell.

'Not good,' the interpreter muttered. 'Not good, no.'

Raylan put the cigarette between Askan's lips and gave him a light. 'I've been given access to some documents related to your case. You know what I see? Apart from the fact that you're a bit of an elitist smart-ass, you couldn't hurt a fly. Besides, I bet you're so clumsy you can barely replace a light bulb, let alone build a bomb. That's not the story the public prosecutor wants me to believe. You know what I mean?'

'By wanting to destroy its opponents, the system ultimately destroys itself from within. I've put my life entirely at the service of the revolution. If that means I have to die, I'm willing to die.'

'Every revolution has its own martyrs. Is that what you're after: writing poems surrounded by a bunch of virgins in heavenly paradise? Do you want to become a *shahid*, a martyr?'

'Cowards die a thousand deaths because of fear. The brave only die once for a good cause.'

'Oh, man . . .'

Raylan sprung to his feet. The nagging pain behind his eyes now spread throughout his head. Damn it, Askan the Martyr had wet dreams about the New Man and if necessary was willing to sacrifice his blood for some naive utopia. For the first time Raylan saw the bizarre resemblance between the hippies who flooded Afghanistan and young people like Askan, who took to the streets with their red banners. They shared the same boundless confidence that an earthly paradise was still possible. Whether it was the hippie heaven in Goa or Kathmandu, or the classless society in Russia or China. These were paradises where everyone was considered equal, where supposedly there were no more class or race conflicts and all privileges had been abolished. They'd forgotten for the sake of convenience that Adam and Eve had let themselves be driven out of that paradise and that there was no going back, for anyone.

For the first time Raylan felt there was a deeper reason why he was sitting opposite Vaziri. He felt that if he managed to shed light on one story, he'd be able to discover the meaning of the other.

The story of Isobel and himself.

Actually he only wanted one thing: to turn back time and not duck for cover in the courtyard in Muhrad Khane as he had, but to grab her hand and flee together before all those frightened demonstrators clashed with the riot police, obstructing their access.

Approaching footsteps could be heard in the corridor. Raylan sat down again opposite Askan.

'You're both a nightmare and a gift from heaven, Askan. A nightmare for the authorities here, who are more than happy to hang you from the highest gallows as a symbol of evil. But with all your ideals, you're also a gift from heaven for your communist buddies in the Kremlin, who could use a martyr to instigate a revolution in their neighbouring country. No matter how you first got involved in this, you're being used. And I want to know who's behind it. Is it Michailov?'

Askan Vaziri's face went white for a moment. The door handle was forcefully pulled down. Raylan leaned as close as possible to the youngster. 'Askan, listen, you're not someone who organizes a coup, you write poems. Talk to me. Who are you trying to protect?'

The door flew open. A whole delegation marched in: director, assistant and two guards. The prison guards grabbed Askan and dragged him out of the cell. The director gestured that Raylan's time was definitely up.

As the gate of the prison complex was slammed shut behind him, he removed the last cigarette from the packet, lit it up and sauntered down the sloping road in the direction of the old city.

There was no question about it, here in Kabul he'd now established his reputation as a pain in the ass!

6
Farah

Not far from the gate of the heavily guarded ministerial building she'd found both the taxi and Nehal again. She'd asked her to head south-east, to Pul-e-Charkhi, where thirty years ago her father had been dumped like garbage into an anonymous mass grave.

They'd driven through the outskirts of the city, where eight-storey grey concrete buildings had been thrown up practically overnight. With their bare windows and doorways, they looked like empty bunkers.

'After seven years and billions of dollars in aid, we don't even have sewers yet. You see these streets? It's as barren as the moon around here!' Nehal cried.

But Farah was deaf to her complaints. She sat silently in the back of the taxi, consumed by conflicting emotions and doubts about the choices she'd made.

During the confrontation with Goldwater this morning, she'd shown immense restraint, and the same with Shakoor at the Ministry just now. But how far was she supposed to go to achieve what she wanted? How many of her ideals was she supposed to renounce just so she could guarantee an unknown boy's safe return home?

'Are you sure you want to do this?' Nehal sounded glum. 'We could turn around. I'll take you back to your hotel and I won't charge you for it. This is a terrible idea. Nobody wants to be here.'

'I do,' Farah muttered, staring silently into the middle distance.

They drove across an endless plain where the wind had free rein, a desolate lunar landscape of rubble, bordered in the distance by jagged mountain ridges and the high walls of Pul-e-Charkhi prison, where the Americans had moved their most dangerous terrorists from Guantanamo Bay. On the other side, the watchtowers of the military base, where the 201st Corps of the Afghan National Guard was stationed.

They stopped at a pale-green flag that marked the site of a large rectangular pit.

Farah stood right by the edge and looked into the pit. It had been excavated with the precision she knew from archaeological digs. There was no trace of bones or the remains of footwear and clothing. The only reminder that something had been hidden there for many years came from the fluttering scraps of dark canvas under which the bodies had lain.

She heard a horn. Nehal was motioning her over. Dusk was falling.

Stubborn as she was, Farah stayed put and allowed her mind to wander back to that night, more than thirty years ago, when the young lieutenant had stopped here with his truck full of corpses.

The lieutenant got out of the truck with its camouflage tarpaulin covering a cargo bed. He ordered the four soldiers who'd followed him in a jeep to remove the bodies from the army truck. Having turned off the headlights, they worked by the light of the moon and the stars.

In pairs, the soldiers would pull a body out of the shapeless heap in the cargo bed. One soldier held the body by its feet, the other by the armpits. They'd carry the corpse to the pit, practically dragging it across the ground. Beside the edge, they rocked it back and forth. Each time the soldiers let go of a body it seemed to hover motionless in the air for a split second before landing with a dry thud on the bottom of the pit three metres down.

She knew that what she saw before her were snippets of what she'd read in the lieutenant's witness account. But that didn't stop her from wanting to shout at the soldiers that they were mistaken, that the man in the beige linen suit they were throwing over the edge of the pit right now wasn't dead at all, that she'd seen him only recently under a waringin tree in Jakarta, that he'd always been around, for thirty years, always in the same suit, which had remained bright and intact. But those soldiers couldn't hear her, and she saw his battered body fall on top of the others.

Again there was the sound of a horn, more insistent now.

A soldier walked to the edge with a baby wrapped in bloody rags and slid backwards into the pit. He placed the child next to the adults with its face in the direction of Mecca.

The horn sounded three times.

A large tarpaulin was spread over the bodies. The earth was quickly scattered across it with spades. The lieutenant took measured steps from the grave to the edge of the road. He'd counted each one. Ninety in total. He turned around and looked at the loose earth.

'Farah. The curfew.'

She stared into Nehal's worried face, felt a hand grabbing hers. In the distance, she saw a jeep heading towards them.

'Come, *hamshera*.'

Nehal had left the engine running and now accelerated, shifted gears and shot away. Before long, they were doing over 100 kilometres per hour when a text message from an unknown number appeared on her display: *Is your phone secure?*

She typed back: *Prepaid.*

Seconds later her ringtone went off. The same number. She answered and heard the voice of the man who'd been so reticent last night while they were eating Philly cheese steaks and drinking Budweiser. The same man who'd cut open his knuckles punching a tree and confused her this morning with an unexpected tenderness in his eyes.

At first glance, it looked as if the sky over eastern Kabul was being sliced by wildly fluttering birds. But you could tell from the abrupt zigzagging that this was a trick of the eye. The whimsical shapes were fighter kites made of brightly coloured paper. They were attached to cords of over a hundred yards long, which boys on the ground were setting on a collision course with other kites using short, snappy hand gestures.

The autumn wind blew sand from the hill across the square on Tepe Maranjan plateau not far from King Nadir Shah's tomb. It was at this marble mausoleum with its monumental columns and black metal dome that she'd see Mason again.

Farah had followed his instructions. From Pul-e-Charkhi prison they'd made their way back to the city. As Mason had predicted, the jeep had followed them for a while. They appeared to shake it off as they approached the hustle and bustle of the old town. But it only meant that they were now being followed by another car. Mason reckoned that from the moment she'd exited through the gate at Eggers, she'd been under constant surveillance.

On Qalai Fatullah Street, she'd calmly stepped out of Nehal's taxi and had visibly settled the bill. Then she'd taken her time to cross the street to a clothing store with the sign SARAH AFGHAN. The smile that greeted her on entry told her that the owner must have recognized her from Mason's description. The woman took her into the back, through the large sewing workshop, where about seventy women were making burqas and other traditional clothing. It was a vicious cycle. During the Taliban regime, women and girls weren't allowed out without a burqa. When they could do so again after the American invasion, many Afghan men would harass them in the street with lewd comments and indecent proposals. Most women didn't want to wear a burqa at all, but as soon as they went out uncovered, they were fair game. Years after the 'liberation' the burqa industry was still running at full tilt.

Garments had been laid out for her in a small room. An anthracite-coloured *khimar*, a long cape-like cloth that would cover her neck, shoulders and breasts. A *perahan tunban*, the long, loose-fitting shirt that many men wore, and equally wide shapeless cotton trousers. She pulled it on over her own clothing, and after she'd removed what little make-up she was wearing the shop owner shepherded her out the back and through a maze of little alleyways to the street parallel to the main thoroughfare, where Nehal was now waiting for her.

They'd taken the long way, constantly checking the mirror to make sure they weren't being followed. Police officers were stationed in strategic places around the square, where, armed with fully automatic weapons, they calmly surveyed the scene. This festival of wind and air combat was an open invitation to suicide bombers. If in the middle of the crowd you blew yourself straight to heaven instead of your kite, you achieved the maximum terror effect.

She stood on the edge of the square and looked up at the sky. The multicoloured kites circled one another, waiting for the right moment to cut their rivals' cords. That was what *gudiparan bazi*, as this form of kite fighting was called, was all about. Each kite flier had rubbed his cord with a paste of finely ground glass, rice and glue. Once hardened, this mixture made the cotton razor sharp. And that was vital, because the cord was the only weapon in this pilots' air duel. She saw that the boys had tied pieces of leather around their hands and fingers to keep their skin from being cut to the bone. As she walked on to the square, searching the crowd for the man she was due to meet, she thought of the last time she'd been surrounded by kites

It had been just a few weeks ago. In the Netherlands. On the square in The Hague.

She'd walked around with her old friend Uncle Parwaiz, who'd once tightly held her hand and shown her the collection in the National Museum of Kabul. He was going to be naturalized as a Dutch citizen that day. He'd looked up at the kites, as happy as a child. But a few minutes later the silver Bentley had driven past, leaving Parwaiz clutching his chest with both hands, as though wanting to tear his shirt to pieces.

He'd taken the man in the back seat for a ghost from the past. Parwaiz had fallen to his knees on the paving stones and died instantly. The shock of recognition had paralysed his heart.

If only she could have told him that the man in the back seat wasn't the one who'd once interrogated and tortured him in the dungeons of the national security police in Kabul. She wanted so badly to tell him that it hadn't been General Michailov. That man was dead.

But his bastard son was still alive.

The man who'd recently been after her life.

Valentin Lavrov.

She was startled by the cheers. A white kite flew past its purple rival and with a single fierce tug cut its cord. A group of ecstatic boys, armed with a branch tied to a stick, rushed towards the stricken kite.

Two firm hands grabbed her shoulders and pulled her back so she wouldn't be trampled by the boys.

She looked him in the eye. Heard his clear voice. The insistent yet gentle command.

'Walk slowly and keep your eyes down.'

She thought of the way he'd ordered her to leave the boy in the barracks last night. His pent-up rage. She'd sat next to him in the jeep. Had felt his hand on her back. Now he was walking next to her, in a *shalwar kameez* and with a *pakol* on his head, a traditional round woollen cap. She thought of him standing at the intersection after the car accident the day before, amidst the chaos, in his camouflage gear. The calm and decisive way he'd acted as commander was now the way he quickly and inconspicuously steered her through the crowd here, keeping track of everything and everyone around them while he simultaneously spoke to her.

'This place is crawling with plain-clothes police. Afghan security service. Best if they don't notice us.'

She nodded.

'You're one of the few women around here. That's why I asked you to put on what you're wearing now. Women still don't go out in public very much, and when they do, they're usually covered from head to toe. Having contact with a woman all but equals proposing to her.'

'You're not going down on one knee again, are you, Mason? I'm not dressed for it.'

She could tell by his voice that he was grinning.

'Look at all these boys around us.'

They were halfway across the square, and she could see them everywhere, whichever direction she turned: boys known as *charka gir*, who held the wooden spool around which the kite's line was wound. She saw the fliers who controlled the kite in the air. And surrounding the kite fliers were the boys with sticks and branches ready to sprint to a crashing kite.

'Boys are readily available and approachable. A pretty boy is a status symbol. If you want to increase your social standing as a man you must own a boy.'

She had trouble avoiding his gaze. A cut kite fell from the sky like a dying bird.

'But I thought homosexuality was a mortal sin in Islam?'

'A homosexual loves men. And boys aren't men, certainly not when they're dressed as girls. You play with them. They give you pleasure. And as a man you're entitled to pleasure. Allah says so. Problem solved.'

'Under the law it's illegal to own a dancing boy.'

'In the thirty years you've been away, they've played fast and loose with the law. The authorities especially. They refuse to make any structural changes.'

She turned to face him. He immediately looked the other way.

'Last night, Mason. Was it that you wouldn't or couldn't do anything about it?'

He walked on slowly.

'You're forgetting the other option.'

She kept walking beside him.

'And that is?'

'I'm not supposed to do anything about it. Orders from above.'

'Goldwater?'

'And higher up.'

'Christ.'

'Not that high.'

His eyes. His smile. A split second. Then he turned away again.

She clapped her hand to her mouth to hide her smile from curious onlookers.

'Keep looking straight ahead.'

'I called my editor-in-chief last night. He said that when Afghan militias are stationed at a base such as Eggers, there's a good chance that those at the top have reached some kind of understanding not to intervene when parties with dancing boys are held. So I assume he's right.'

'The Taliban are our priority. We've established and trained Afghan militias to fight the Taliban. Once we're out of here, they must be in a position to take charge. As long as we're here, we have to maintain the best possible relations with the Afghan authorities. That means putting our norms and values second to those of the Afghan government. It's too bizarre for words. We came to Afghanistan to fight the Taliban, and yet we're supporting Afghan commanders whose behaviour is just as reprehensible.'

Loud cheers were heard. A group of exuberant boys ran past them. A kite had fallen to the ground. The boys were fighting for it.

She thought of what Edward had told her.

I'd bet that to this day it's still happening systemically within the ranks led by commanders such as Hafami. And the Americans have to live with that reality, whether they like it or not. Which brings us back to the behaviour of that gunnery sergeant of yours.

It was as if Mason could hear her thoughts. He stood still and kept his eyes averted. There was something in his voice she hadn't heard before. 'You know what it is? The sound of mortar attacks or the screams of the wounded – those I can handle. I signed up for that. But the sound of a boy moaning as he's being raped in a barracks at night, yet I'm not allowed to step in . . . That's something I can't bear.'

They were standing at the edge of the plateau, looking out over the city. The sky above was now full of fighter kites. She saw the pain in his eyes. The powerlessness too. And she understood the anger he'd been unable to contain the night before.

'A week ago a woman turned up at the gate. She'd lost her mind. Her husband had been a member of Hafami's National Guard. He'd been killed in a Taliban attack, and Hafami had attended his funeral. He'd shown a warm interest in her son, a little kid barely seven years old . . .' Mason shook his head with a grimace. She saw the anger welling up again. 'The things they did to that kid . . .'

They stood still beside each other. Sand blew up against them. Cheers rose behind their backs.

'My oldest just celebrated his seventh birthday . . . You know what I mean?'

She felt her heart beating faster. They remained silent until he calmed down.

'I recorded the woman's story and personally handed the report to Goldwater.'

'What did he have to say about it?'

'He said he'd pass it on to the appropriate authorities.'

'In other words, nothing's being done about it.'

'Everything is swept under the carpet.'

They watched two large fighter kites circling each other. They were the biggest in the sky. Hunter and prey, prey and hunter – they kept swapping roles in a life-and-death struggle.

'I have information for you. Rumours were doing the rounds before Hafami even got here. You can't believe everything you hear, but from the day he rolled into Camp Eggers with his militia and his entourage of tea boys, about six months ago, it all kicked off straight-away. Nightly parties. An MP of ours went to check but wasn't allowed inside because it's officially Afghan territory, that kind of bullshit. Another MP got into a fist fight with Hafami's men. Goldwater had him transferred out but did fuck all else. That's when I realized there were other interests at stake. In my capacity, I have access to the files of the Military Intelligence Service. I decided to create my own secret file on Hafami.'

She shook her head. 'You're running a big risk, Mason. By giving me that intelligence you're flouting the policy of your superiors. If the military leadership finds out, you'll be dishonourably discharged. Or sent to prison. Why are you doing this?'

'The moaning in my ears, to rid myself of it.'

'Then why didn't you do anything for that boy last night?'

'I could have taken him away from there. But I know for sure that my role would have ended right there and then. A general like Hafami is much more powerful than a gunnery sergeant like me. I would have been transferred, and the incident covered up by both our army command and the Afghan authorities. And I don't know what would have happened to you, but we certainly wouldn't be standing here together.

The cogs in her head were spinning. Acting on Mason's information would fly in the face of her agreements with Edward. As word spread that she was investigating Hafami, the chances of working with Shakoor and the Ministry of the Interior would be lost for ever. It would make it impossible to one day reunite Sekandar with his family.

'I promised my editor I'd give it a rest. And I don't want to risk you getting thrown out of the army, or worse, ending up in prison,' she finally said.

High above their heads, the hunter had devoured his prey. The big kite that had furiously circled its opponent only moments before now fluttered down utterly powerless. The boys with their sticks and branches ran like mad down the flanks of the hill and disappeared in clouds of whirling sand.

'Don't worry about me,' Mason said.

'Are you sure?'

He flashed her a cynical grin.

'How do I get hold of those documents?'

'Go to the old bazaar this afternoon.'

'And then what?'

'You'll find out. Burn the documents as soon as you've read them.'

'How do I get in touch with you afterwards?'

'I'll call you.'

With an unexpectedly abrupt movement, he turned around. Before she knew it, he'd disappeared into the crowd.

Confused, she walked past a young kite flier. Suddenly she felt deeply moved by how intensely he'd concentrated while competing with an invisible opponent somewhere hundreds of yards away. She stopped and looked at him, and she saw it in his eyes.

The only reason for flying his kite.

For the fight.

However young most of these boys were, high up in the sky their sharp lines and vivid kites made them all warlords. Fighters who kept challenging each other.

Even the kite fliers who'd had their cords cut dozens of times would over and over again get ready for a new fight. They'd make an even sharper cord, a different kite, and fly it. It was symptomatic of the way most people here lived their lives.

Just like the boys and men around her, she'd been born in a land of struggle, of tenacious struggle, constantly entering a new fight to win it. A country that over the centuries had driven out powerful occupiers.

Now she had to decide for herself whether she was up for another fight.

She looked at the young kite flier and thought of Parwaiz and the advice he'd given her on that last day in The Hague: *In your heart of hearts you know what choice you're going to make,* bachem. *Follow your heart.*

While the kites continued to come to blows above her, she walked back to the side of the road where Nehal was faithfully waiting in her dusty Toyota.

7
Raylan

1968

In the entry hall of the National Museum, Parwaiz Ahmad was waiting next to the statue of King Kanisha and courteously bowed.

'*As-Salaam-Alaikum, aghaye* Chapelle.'

'*Wa-Alaikum-Salaam, aghaye* Ahmad.'

This time they didn't walk through the halls and down the spiral staircase to the museum vaults. Instead, Parwaiz escorted his American guest to the top floor. There he led him into the oval boardroom, which was sober but tastefully decorated. On either side of the large table, which also served as a desk, were stacks of books. An oriental upholstered sofa on a large red wool carpet was the centrepiece of the room. Windows, the entire width of the space, offered a magnificent view of the old city. Beams of sunlight fell across the wall opposite the windows, bringing a metres-wide mural to life. Barren mountain landscapes, luscious valleys and cityscapes, wartime scenes, trading caravans and colourful historical events covered more than half of the surface.

'Work-in-progress,' Parwaiz said with a modest smile. Actually, it's only a sketch of our long history. He pointed to the abstract-looking collection of strange shapes and colours at the beginning of the painting. 'This represents what remained after Allah created the world, which didn't seem to fit anywhere. But it was also a shame to throw these away. In all His wisdom He then swept those pieces together, and so Afghanistan was born.'

Parwaiz moved his hand slowly, as if he wanted to use that one gesture to illuminate the entire panorama.

'According to the Afghan calendar, we're currently living in the year 1347. More than twenty-five dynasties have tried to influence our history: Genghis Khan, Tamerlane and Babur, to name only a few.'

'Let me guess,' Raylan said, pointing to a long line of marching soldiers with classic Greek features. 'Here Alexander the Great and his army are crossing the Hindu Kush.'

'Alexander was a tragic idealist,' Parwaiz said. 'He hoped to establish a kingdom in which he could unite the East and the West. But that proved impossible.' He nodded at the procession of figures in psychedelic colours towards the end of the painting. 'Even the hippies, the first foreign force to take possession of our country without violence, won't manage in the end.'

Parwaiz was about to elaborate on this, but stopped speaking the moment the door swung open unexpectedly. With a formal nod he said goodbye to Raylan, went over to the woman in the doorway, exchanged a few words with her and then silently pulled the door closed behind him.

Helai's glistening dark-blue dress cascaded over her body. The other times he'd seen her she'd been wearing long sleeves. Now her arms were bare. Her golden skin seemed to be glowing from deep within. Raylan could once again smell that hint of caramel.

'Thank you for coming.'

'I understood it was important.'

'I spoke to the young man,' he said.

'Not just him, I heard.' Her voice was stern.

'We agreed I would write this story my way,' he sighed.

'That's right, but that still doesn't justify unacceptable behaviour.'

He looked away and stared outside. 'If I have to censor my every move as a journalist, because I antagonize others by doing my job, I might as well throw in the towel. Is that what you want?'

The sky above Kabul was so blindingly blue that he had to squint. She silently lowered the blinds. The light was now more subdued, and made everything softer – her voice, her eyes, everything. A light shadow fell across her face. 'Why did you want to see me again, Raylan?'

He wiped beads of sweat from his forehead. Not now, he thought.

He mustn't succumb to the temptation to wrap his arms around her hips and firmly press her against him.

'I'm sorry if my investigation has caused you any problems, but this case is more complicated than just the facts. Askan Vaziri might be a communist crusader, an idealist revolutionary . . .'

'He's a wolf in sheep's clothing,' she interrupted him. 'And we have laws here to protect us against anybody who thinks he can take the law into his own hands without suffering the consequences.'

'By only serving the law, you end up failing the democracy. Askan Vaziri is not an assassin. He's a pawn who's allowing himself to be used in a power struggle.'

'A power struggle. Between whom, then?'

'The Americans and the Soviets.'

'And where do we fit in, the Afghans?'

'Your king has chosen a pro-Western course. The Shah of Iran is a close ally of the American White House. The Soviets are gradually being surrounded by neighbouring countries that increasingly fall under America's sphere of influence. To prevent that, they have to do more than just build a new airport, a residential area or roads. They use subtle but effective methods that mainly impact young people, with the aim of radicalizing them. The social unrest that has now arisen as a result of the state's handling of the Vaziri case mainly works to their advantage, not yours. Vaziri has assumed the role of martyr. He is prepared to sacrifice his life to advance a massive popular uprising. And such an insurgence is much more threatening to the country or to the rule of law than one anti-government article in a communist youth newspaper. Do you understand?'

She stared at him in despair.

Raylan gazed at the battles on the mural. 'The day I got to Vietnam I saw the self-immolation of an old monk on a square in Saigon. He set himself ablaze as a protest against his government, which oppressed the Buddhist majority of the country. In the weeks that followed, other young monks followed his example. By setting themselves on fire, they eventually mobilized an entire people.'

Helai shook her head. 'Askan Vaziri is not a monk. He's student, a poet, a romantic with a blind belief in communist ideology.'

'He's become the leader of an expanding anti-government movement. Thanks to him, thousands of young people are already taking to the streets. When Askan is sentenced to death, there will be tens of thousands, maybe hundreds of thousands. Forces you'll hardly be able to control any more, and that could put an end to your fragile democracy.'

'Why are you saying all of this?'

'Because . . . you can change this.'

'And how do you propose I do that? Should I go to court and say, 'Forget what I said in my plea, that youngster is not a danger to the state, he's just a romantic madman with a communist screw loose in his head. He's been used as a pawn by our own security service or by the Russians. Let him go, is that what you want?'

Raylan realized that his body was starting to tremble. The image of that monk was seared into his retina. He could again hear the roaring flames, the stench of human flesh being consumed by fire penetrated his nostrils, the chanting of young monks in a circle around their burning leader echoed in his head. 'I'm sorry . . .' he murmured. 'I . . .'

He dropped on to the sofa, cradled his head in his hands, leaned forward, took a deep breath and sucked the air into his lungs.

Helai came and kneeled on the floor opposite him and handed him a glass of water, which he gulped back with two Anafranil. He looked at her hands, which she'd gently rested on his thighs. He could feel their warmth through his jeans.

The chanting of the monks drifted into the air, the sea of flames was extinguished. He leaned towards her, close to her mouth. She didn't pull away. When he pressed his lips against hers, she took his hand and placed it against her chest. Her heart was beating fast. He heard the slight quiver in her voice.

'The first time I saw you . . .'

'You were angry.'

'I was caught off-guard. You were everything I . . .'

'Despised?'

'Admired.'

'I don't understand. You seemed . . .'

'Upset. I was. You suddenly appeared in court in the middle of my arguments.'

'I'm sorry, I . . .'

'No, I'm glad you came.'

'Why?

She caressed his cheek and spoke in a tone as if she were about to make a long-awaited confession. 'At Columbia University, we had our own community. The young women from Afghanistan, we looked after each other. We all came from the same circles; we knew each other's parents. We thought we were very modern. But . . .'

'There's always a but.'

'Everything in America is so different from Afghanistan. Here I'm not an individual, which was expected of me in America. I'm primarily a member of a family. Here, family means everything. The fact that I could study abroad as woman might seem very progressive to you. Yet, even if I wear Western clothes and make-up, I am and remain an Afghan woman, raised very protected with strict moral values and high expectations. On my first day in New York I immediately noticed how conservative I was, how traditional and withdrawn. I was jealous of the straightforward way the American male and female students interacted as if they were each other's equals. It was so relaxed, so effortless . . . I wanted to be like those young women, but I couldn't pretend to be something I wasn't.'

She looked at him with a slightly mocking smile.

'My mentor said he found my intelligence "remarkable" and my naivety "refreshing". It sounded like an insult at first. But I came to understand what he meant. I perceived that new world the way an amazed child stares through a pane of glass. I may have been studying in New York, but I didn't really live there, I wasn't an integral part of it. I could dream about the freedom of the West, but it didn't change the fact that I was an Afghan: with my own language, my faith, my culture, my family. There was figuratively a barrier between me and the world.'

'What held you back the most?'

'A fear of freedom. I was afraid I would lose myself if I gave into my desires to break free, afraid to disgrace my family as well. My father had high expectations of me. He paid for my trip, my stay, my tuition. Everything. Disappointing him would have been the worst thing I could do to him and to myself. So I concentrated on my studies, knowing once I finished that here I would have to measure up to other expectations awaiting me.'

'A career as a public prosecutor. That's something to be proud of, isn't it?'

She shook her head. 'My degree wasn't meant to foster a career, it was a requirement for a good marriage. My parents wanted their daughter to be the perfect candidate for a desirable husband from their social class in society.' Her smile had disappeared. She looked at him with an unexpected sadness in her eyes. 'I'm getting married in three weeks.'

'To whom?'

'A man you recently met. At the department.'

'Gailani?'

'Yes.'

'Why him?'

She let out a long sigh.

'I'm perfect marriage material for him, the ideal woman to show off at galas, parades and official occasions, smart enough, well-educated but Afghan enough that our traditions aren't compromised. The ideal mother for his children. It's a match that both families are very happy about. Hardly anyone here marries for love. A wedding ring justifies your existence in the family and bestows a respectable position in a world so very far away from yours . . .'

She stroked his face and looked deep into his eyes.

'You have the bluest eyes I've ever seen. And with those eyes you burst into the courtroom and turned my world upside down. You represent all those young men I barely dared to look at in New York, who were reading a book in the sunshine on the campus lawn, openly flirting with their fellow students, playing basketball with friends, and whose sweat you could smell when you walked past them. The same guys who sat staring into space, bored to tears by their classes and who boarded the downtown bus to go see concerts by The Doors, The Byrds and Country Joe and the Fish.'

She brushed a strand of hair out of her face and smiled shyly. 'In your eyes, I see the freedom that for years I didn't dare to choose for ... The freedom I will never know here.' Her smile faded, and her gaze became serious. 'I must enter marriage an honourable woman. That's what our tradition demands. But my heart says something completely different.'

'What does your heart say?'

She looked at him with piercing eyes. 'That you should be my first. Not the man I'm going to marry.'

The vulnerability with which she said this touched him. He leaned towards her and tenderly kissed her on the lips.

She'd laid down on the sofa and allowed his hands to stroke her neck, slide along her shoulders, over her arms, over the smooth fabric of her dress, to rest for a moment on her breasts, to explore even further: along her back, over her hips, her thighs. The sensation he was experiencing was remarkable. Every touch was new to him, but at the same time felt familiar, as if he'd caressed her body many times before. This surprising familiarity encouraged him to discover more. He carefully took her head between his hands and let the tip of his tongue playfully slip in and out between her lips. It made her smile. He gently bit her lower lip, looked for her tongue again, and when he found it, he rolled it around with his tongue as if in a slow-motion mating dance.

She ran her hands down his back, to his buttocks and back up to his chest. Feeling her way, she unbuttoned his shirt and unfastened his belt, and as she did, she felt bold enough to caress the bulge between his legs. After he'd removed his shirt, she stroked his bronzed upper body, and smiled at its firmness. She assisted him as he undressed her, and he in turn was surprised by the voluptuousness of her warm, light-brown body. He kissed her pert breasts.

As their mouths searched for each other again, their teeth collided because they both smiled with pleasure at the tenderness of the primal desire they aroused in each other. For a moment, it seemed as if she was startled by his erection. Her body was tense. With her eyes closed she pulled his body on top of hers, his face up against her face.

'I want you ...'

'Are you sure?'

189

She bit her lip. 'Very sure.'

He carefully started to enter her; he could feel it would be difficult, she was very tense. He stroked her face. 'It's okay, Helai. You make the rules here.'

She looked at him with a smile and relaxed. He went a little further: gently, slowly. She groaned and looked at him with her eyes wide. He withdrew again. He was consumed by desire but held back. He didn't want to hurt her. Then he felt her hands clutch his buttocks and push him deeper inside.

She let out a cry of pain.

He reacted immediately.

'No, no,' she sighed. 'Don't stop.'

He felt her pelvic muscles tightening, as if she were pulling him deeper inside her. He gently rocked his pelvis back and forth and bit her fingers, which she stuck in his mouth, as if this might help him cope with the excess of pleasure he was experiencing. He was so aroused by now he felt like they'd been fused together. He'd crossed a line and there was no way back. He started moving faster and faster. She lay beneath him, with her mouth open and her eyes shut, and she touched his body much like someone who was blind, so she could take everything in.

'Look at me,' he sighed.

She opened her eyes, and even before he could indicate to her that he couldn't stop himself from coming, she just nodded and smiled. And as he came inside her, she pressed him against her so hard that it seemed like she would never let go of him again.

The moon was already hanging above Kabul when they left Parwaiz Ahmad's office and headed downstairs through the museum's ancient statues, now steeped in shadow. At the bottom of the stairs, Parwaiz Ahmad was waiting for them. Helai briefly touched Raylan's hand and then disappeared into the vaults.

He silently followed Parwaiz through the ground-floor rooms, wondering why this man of all people had assumed the role of intermediary. But perhaps this question was completely irrelevant in a country and culture where men and women had grown up and lived strictly separated from each other for centuries. Despite the new modernity there was little if any possibility for a woman to be seen in public with any man other than her husband or a family member. He'd taken advantage of the hospitality of this honourable man, who without a doubt, sensitive as he was, must have noticed that much more had happened between his two guests than they'd originally agreed to. Raylan was left with a bitter feeling of shame.

'My apologies, Mr Ahmad,' he said when Parwaiz held the door open for him.

'Apologies are unwarranted,' he formally replied. 'God be with you, Mr Chapelle.'

'And with you, Mr Ahmad.'

From the balcony of his hotel he stared at the place where heaven and earth touched each other. There, just above the mountain tops, where the day took over from the night, there was a glow, golden like a promise. It was simply an illusion. Today, seven young people were told by a judge that their lives were about to end.

He took a cold shower, got dressed, and with the *Kabul Times* tucked under his arm walked around the corner to a food stand, where he routinely waved to the owner Mahfuz, who enthusiastically greeted him. 'Hello, Steve!'

Apparently Mahfuz didn't care what his only American customer was actually called. With his roguish grin, he-man appearance and deep blue eyes, he apparently saw Raylan as a dead ringer for the Hollywood star Steve McQueen, whom he undoubtedly knew from the billboards adorning the façade of the Behzad cinema, where *Bullitt* was showing.

The canvas above his head fluttered in the wind. He sat down at a low table, smoothed out the front page of *The Kabul Times* and stared at the photo of the seven young suspects. The accompanying article was unequivocal: by plotting an attack against the king, these seven staff members of the Communist Party youth newspaper had committed high treason.

He realized how differently his article would portray this story. What was described in this government mouthpiece as high treason was, for him, an uncensored expression of freedom of speech. The plan to kill the king, as Askan Vaziri and his accomplices had described, was nothing more and nothing less than a symbolic appeal to oppose the social inequality in the country. If, as a government, you really want to defend democratic principles, you must allow these kinds of statements to be made, however extreme they might seem. If the court goes ahead and condemns Askan Vaziri and his fellow accused to death today, Afghanistan's young democracy will have done itself more harm than good.

He resolutely folded his newspaper closed. Mahfuz presented him with a bowl of *kala wa pacha* – soup made from the legs, heads and entrails of cows and goats. It was the most nutritious breakfast he could imagine and it gave him energy for a whole day.

Mahfuz watched with nervous anticipation as he took a first bite. 'Good like last time, Steve?'

Raylan nodded enthusiastically. Because his mouth was full, as an extra compliment he wanted to give Mahfuz a thumb's up, but in the nick of time he realized that in Afghanistan this means fuck off.

Alongside the busy road a row of men shuffled by. They were hauling huge bundles of cotton on their backs, which had come from the cargo bay of a brightly painted lorry. Across the street a few boys were stacking a cartload of oranges so high against the front of a fruit shop it looked like a shiny orange fortress. A rather dignified elderly man passed by. On his head he carried an enormous round bowl piled high with naan breads. This was seemingly a day like any other. At first sight, everything seemed to be exactly as it has been for hundreds of years. But if you looked more closely, you could see that most people were walking faster than normal, that the street vendors in their turbans covered in dust from the mountains were in more of a hurry to have shoppers pay up, and people were a bit more fervent than other days about throwing stones at the mangy stray dogs with their sad eyes.

The Vaziri case was happening out of sight, but it had an effect on everyone. Only nobody here on the street had the luxury to think about it. They had to survive, make it to the next day, feed their families – those were the main priorities. All this in a feudal system in which more than three-quarters of the country was in the hands of a small elite: big landowners who had a say in just about everything.

Also in the courts.

Raylan looked at his watch, realized he was already late, slurped his bowl of soup empty and pushed his stool back.

'You go, Steve?'

'Be back tomorrow, Fuzz.'

He opened his folded Persol 714 sunglasses and walked into the blistering heat in search of a taxi that could take him to the courthouse as quickly as possible.

Near the Royal Palace, he got a glimpse of where King Nadir Shah had been murdered in 1933. Soldiers in dark-green uniforms who routinely kept watch each day in front of the fences of the hundred-year-old royal palace now grimly stood there with their rifles readied. People had started streaming into the city. The People's Democratic Party of Afghanistan had announced that a huge protest was planned for today. Buses from Herat, Kandahar and Mazar-e-Sharif delivered the party members. Together with workers from the oil refineries in Shebarghan and the textile factories in Pul-e-Khumri – who'd travelled hundreds of kilometres on foot to march through the streets of Kabul for the first time in their lives – they walked to the courthouse to demonstrate against the anticipated death sentence of their communist comrades.

It seemed like all the side streets leading to the main road were quickly becoming overcrowded with protesters singing at the top of their lungs. With a frustrated gesture, the taxi driver stopped his car. Raylan hastily gave the man behind the wheel a handful of afghani, got out and mixed with the demonstrators. After little more than a hundred metres he could barely go any further. Police three rows deep were positioned across the entire width of the street. An impenetrable helmeted barrier of shields and raised batons.

He could hear loud singing coming from behind him. A legion of tens of thousands of chanting demonstrators, waving red banners and Afghan flags, formed a huge front together with the students. They threateningly advanced towards the first police cordon, which, under the loud cheering of the demonstrators, started to retreat metre by metre. Raylan sought cover in a doorway so that he didn't get crushed by the crowd.

By the time the protesters had reached the second cordon around the courthouse, the atmosphere had become grim. The cries fell silent. The uncertainty in the masses was almost palpable. Should they take advantage of the momentum and storm the courthouse?

At that moment, the large doors at the top of the courthouse steps swung open. Raylan recognized the man who came outside: the defendant Askan Vaziri. He spread his arms, almost in a state of disbelief, and addressed the crowd in Dari. Soon there was deafening cheering. Demonstrators fell into each other's arms. Some of them spontaneously burst into tears.

A young demonstrator shouted to Raylan: 'Free! Free! They've all been freed!'

Raylan pushed his way to the front of the police cordon by the stairs, waved his press card high in the air and was eventually let through by a police officer. As fast as he could, he mounted the stairs up to the large entrance door, where a guard hurried him inside.

The chaos, the shoving and noise in the courthouse lobby were at least as great as what was happening outside. Searching in vain for the interpreter with the horn-rimmed glasses, Raylan pushed his way through the crowd and with a confident stride went via the courtroom into the long corridor, where he knocked on the door of Helai's office.

She was dressed in the same suit as the first time he'd met her and gave him a shocked, almost frightened look. A very clear signal. He was in the wrong place at the wrong time.

'*Azizam, i ki ast?*'

He recognized the voice of Aadel Gailani.

Helai forced a smile. Her English-language attempt at being cheerful sounded almost painful. 'It's that American journalist.'

She opened the door wider. Raylan entered the room. Backlit by the setting sun stood the robust silhouette of Aadel Gailani.

'Admit it, Mr Chapelle: you doubted our judgement,' Gailani said, as he walked towards Raylan and shook his hand. 'You thought we'd sentence them to death, didn't you?' With a loud laugh he gave Raylan a friendly slap on the shoulder. 'C'mon, man up, admit it!'

'Indeed, everything pointed to a death sentence,' Raylan said. 'What changed?'

'Condemning Askan Vaziri to death, making him a martyr, would have been too much of an honour,' Gailani said, flipping open his silver cigarette case decorated with the exotic nude. 'And if I've learned anything from Machiavelli, it is that mercy always works best when it's preceded by an immense amount of fear.'

He offered him a kretek. Raylan shook his head, after which Gailani lit one himself and then grinned at the crackling sound. 'We gave them a good scare,' he continued. 'We showed them what the consequences of their actions could mean. Now we'll ease up on them. Let's see what they do: will they stay caged up or break loose like a pack of wild dogs?'

Raylan now understood where the suspicion he'd felt when he'd first met this man originated from. Gailani saw freedom as a temporary relaxation of an authoritarian grip, a cloaked dictatorship, and not as a form of actual participation.

'Does the acquittal apply to everyone?' Raylan asked.

'With this caveat,' Gailani replied. 'Askan Vaziri packs his bags and relocates to the Soviet Union.'

'Voluntarily? Or is it an expulsion?'

'Let me put it this way: the seeds planted among us by the Russians are better suited to the soil over there, not here.'

'You're not answering my question.'

'That's all I'm at liberty to say.' His response sounded ominous. 'State secret.'

'And the ban on their newspaper *The People*?'

'Lifted. But you must understand that we plan to keep a close eye on everything.'

'Freedom of expression,' said Raylan with a cynical grin. 'But within limits.'

He could hear Gailani's breathing in the charged silence that ensued. Raylan wondered if he'd actually convinced Helai with his appeal yesterday, or whether the outcome of the trial had been a predetermined plan, as Gailani suggested. Or was it perhaps possible in this country with such a precarious legal tradition that the judge had made an independent decision after all? Anyway, it seemed wiser to him to leave the entire matter as is, to wrap up the Vaziri case and to see his romantic diversion with Helai as a cherished, secret memory.

'Of course we look forward to your article, Mr Chapelle.'

Helai broke the silence the same way she'd spoken to him the first time: in the business-like and measured tone of the determined public prosecutor she was supposed to be. It somehow felt reassuring. In this forced role play they'd all now adopted their familiar poses without revealing anything deeper underneath. The perfect moment to leave the room.

She went to the door first. Before she pushed down the handle, she briefly glanced at him. In her eyes he thought he recognized a hint of tenderness.

Once outside the courthouse, he was soon immersed in the crowd, where the confusion, and undoubtedly also the relief, had to be at least as great as his own.

The centuries-old tradition was no longer practised. But the cannon, which used to fire a shot from the side of a mountain in the southwest of the city at twelve noon, was still there. A shot from the so-called afternoon cannon in those days was the signal that everyone could retreat to their home, inn or tea house to escape the worst of the afternoon heat.

In his revised article, Raylan had simply made it clear that the young democracy of Afghanistan had passed its first litmus test by not prosecuting the communist newspaper's seven staff members. He'd sent it off to *The New York Times* by telex. No cannon would now be able to stop him from wandering through the city at this particularly scorching hour. He needed to soothe his restless spirit.

Tomorrow he was going to find an apartment or boarding house, just like he'd done in Saigon. He knew it would have to be in Murad Khane, the neighbourhood he'd always associate with that wondrous encounter with a young Dutch woman. In the meantime she must have left the country via the Khyber pass, along the Himalayas in the direction of the Kathmandu Valley or she was now doing sun salutations on the beach in Goa.

A group of giggling girls in school uniforms crossed the street. A donkey stood as still as a statue on the side of the road; on his back an enormous open jute sack filled with oranges. An old lorry, colourfully painted with birds, flowers and crescent moons, drove by, honking its horn. He waved back to the men in the cargo bay. To his surprise he realized he could recapture his carefree mood of a week ago, when he was just going about his business with his typewriter case and his rucksack.

He'd only been in this city for a very short time, and yet it seemed as if he'd already spent years leaving his mark here. It had to do with the chaos hiding under the apparent friendliness. A threat that was less visible than in Saigon, but which felt equally familiar to him. He'd come to Kabul to write his story about the mechanisms his own government had employed to cause a war in Vietnam, which they were determined to continue even against the express wishes of the American people. After barely a week in Kabul, he was already convinced that sooner or later all hell could also break loose in Afghanistan – a war that might be as far-reaching as the one in Vietnam.

He put that thought out of his mind and wandered for a while along the banks of the River Kabul, eventually ending up on the square in front of the Pul-e Khishti Mosque with its blue dome glistening in the bright sunlight. A group of people in the middle of the square attracted his attention. Dozens of pigeons fluttered into the air as he approached.

In a large circle men, women and children were standing around a young woman. Seated on a stool, she was sketching the portrait of a man who was proudly posing. Half-hidden behind other's backs, Raylan carefully followed her every move, her gaze and the critical way she examined the portrait before handing it over to the man, who in turn showed it off to the crowd, after which he thanked her with a pile of afghanis and made room for the next person.

Raylan saw his chance.

While she bent over to get a blank sheet of paper from her sketchbook, he quickly sat down on the stool opposite her. While still not looking up, she slowed her movements. For a moment she simply sat still and then she turned towards him.

Instead of the immense surprise he'd expected, she reacted with a smile that was as disarming as the first time they'd met.

'Hello, Ray.'

'Hi, Ise.'

For a while they just sat there in silence, smiling at each other.

He finally asked, 'How about drawing my portrait?'

She shook her head, leaned forward and pulled a sheet of paper from her cardboard portfolio case, which she turned in his direction.

He found himself staring into the observant eyes of his drawn likeness.

'Your face was engraved in my mind's eye,' she said.

The clear water in Hotel Serena's courtyard pool played with the shapes and lights as if it were a liquified funhouse mirror. With his feet in the water, Raylan sat on the edge looking down at his surrealistic reflected image. He made a filter from a narrow strip of cardboard he'd cut from a bookmark. He distributed some crushed weed along the rolling paper so the joint was thicker at the end than by the filter.

'Clearly, not your first time,' said Isobel, who'd been quietly observing him.

Raylan lit up, inhaled deeply, and as he passed the joint to her with a solemn gesture, he slowly exhaled. 'Did you know I'd turn up?' he asked.

'I didn't know. But I hoped you would.'

'Do you always get what you wish for?'

She filled her lungs with smoke. 'Generally not,' she said with a slightly pinched voice. 'But if I sink my teeth into something, I sometimes have a reasonable shot.'

She looked at him, and he could read the teasing in her eyes. 'You still haven't told me what you thought of your portrait,' she said.

'Dashing.'

'And anything else?'

'Confronting.'

'People always have a façade. What they conceal, that's their true face. The eyes are a reflection of the soul. If you look closely, you can see someone's essence in their eyes.'

'And what do you see in my eyes?'

'Sadness.'

He gestured that she should give him back the joint, took a long drag and said, 'The world makes it hard to be anything else but sad.'

'So why are we even here? To be unhappy?'

'To carry our load?'

'Oh dear, an Atlas Complex.'

'Yeah . . . Why not?' After a second drag he handed the joint back to her. 'What made you go travelling, Ise?'

'I suppose to meet you.'

'Seriously.'

'I am serious.'

'What was the motivation?'

'Piet Mondrian.'

'Who?'

She let out her infectious laugh. 'Mondrian was a Dutch painter. Everyone at the art academy where I studied thought we should make art the way he did: abstract. The only problem is that I love the world the way I see it. I love real people, from flesh and blood. And besides, I come from the land of the Dutch Masters as well. Rembrandt is my hero. I believe in tradition and craftsmanship.'

'Let me guess: that wasn't appreciated.'

'I was excluded, made fun of and rejected in a myriad of ways. And instead of succumbing to self-pity, I thought: I'm outta here. Painting and drawing were my way of discovering the real world. I dropped out of art school and boarded the Magic Bus.'

'So, is the reality you seek here in the East?'

'God created the Garden of Eden in the East. Here the Vedas were written and Zarathustra proclaimed that people have the ability to choose the path of goodness through good deeds, good thoughts and good behaviour, long before Muhammad and Jesus were born.'

She handed the joint back to him. He took a long puff and for a while stared in silence at the erratic reflections of light on the water. 'Have you ever heard of the River Perfume?'

'No.'

'It flows through Huế, which was once the imperial capital of Vietnam. Literally a crown jewel. Of no military importance whatsoever.

Yet the North Vietnamese took the city. Actually as a PR stunt. If the Americans didn't recapture Hué they would suffer an enormous loss of face. So they went for it. By the time they drove out all of Ho Chi Minh's ruthless commie guerrillas, more than half of this ancient city lay in ruins. Everything was covered with a thick layer of sludge. In the canals, the streets, even on the lawns around the Imperial Palace – nothing but dead people. The imperial library had literally been blown up. Pieces of books and loose pages were scattered everywhere you looked. It was as if the dead had all written farewell letters. We found a shallow mass grave. The Viet Cong had shot thousands of civilians because they suspected they'd worked with the Americans. And in the middle of that field, a small boy was digging in the ground like a dog looking for a buried bone. Each time he uncovered a face, he stopped for a moment, stared at it and continued digging right beside it. Not one of the GIs in the vicinity knew what to do. I approached the boy and squatted right in front of him, but he simply kept digging. He didn't even slow down. When he uncovered another dead face, I gently took his hand. He didn't move, he just stared down at lifeless eyes. Then I took his other hand. Only then did he look at me, but he didn't see me. He looked right through me. I picked him up and carried him away. The ground I traversed felt unstable. I didn't even have to hold on to him; he clung to me like a monkey. When I wanted to hand him over to a medic, he wouldn't let go of me. I . . . He . . .'

Raylan sighed, took a long drag of the joint and felt Isobel's hand glide along his arm. Her voice was as soft as the grasp of her hand on his hand.

'What you did for that little boy . . .'

'What about it?

'A child, totally desperate . . . and you lifted him up, took him in your arms and cared for him . . .'

'That's what you're supposed to do . . . in such a situation.'

'Let me tell you something, Ray . . . ?'

'Yeah?'

'At that moment, for that little boy, you were a kind of god.'

'I don't want to be anyone's god.'

'You were there for him, whether you like it or not. It's something he will never forget. And when he's older and having a difficult time, he'll think of that moment; then he'll think of you. And that will give him strength.'

She took the joint from him, inhaled, and whispered while staring at the smoke she was exhaling. 'Lift me up, Ray . . .'

'You don't even know me . . .'

'I've known you my whole life. And the life before that, and perhaps all my lives before that. You're mine and I won't let you go any more.'

'That doesn't sound like a hippie philosophy.'

'What do you mean?'

'I thought hippies didn't believe in ownership.'

'I'm not a hippie. I'm Ise. And I don't care if you think I'm a fool, a hippie or whatever. Tonight I'm yours, and you're mine.'

'And tomorrow?'

'We'll worry about tomorrow, then.'

She snuffed out the joint by dipping the roach in the water and started to undress.

'What are you doing?'

'I need to tell you something else about myself. I can walk on water.'

He looked up at her, now standing over him in only her undies she first let one foot glide above the water and then the other. With a dull splash she disappeared, only to come to the surface again, laughing and laughing. She brushed her wet blonde hair away from her face, gesturing that he should come in after her, and with a skilled breast-stroke cut through the water to the other end of the pool.

Never in his life had he undressed so quickly. At a sharp angle, he dived for the mosaic tiles at the bottom, thinking of how Sirens with their enchanting voices lured sailors to shipwreck on the rocks around their island. He touched the bottom with his fingertips, pushed himself off again and let himself drift upwards in her direction.

When he came closer to her, she wrapped her arms and legs around him, and he heard her voracious laugh, which would no doubt wake everyone in the hotel, but he didn't give a damn. He loved her laugh and let himself be smothered in her embrace.

PART THREE
An Army of Eagles

I
Raylan

1975

The ringing of the Bakelite telephone on the bedside table put an end
to the already short night of sleep Raylan had managed to induce
with a bottle of Armagnac and a handful of Anafranil. The voice of
his Vietnamese informer, Hoang Dang, sounded excited.

'Have you heard?'

'For Christ's sake, Hoang. No idea what you're talking about.'

'It was on Armed Forces Radio. They said it was 105° F in Saigon
and then they played "White Christmas".'

It hit him like a sledgehammer. Adrenaline rushed through his
body. 'Okay, Hoang. I'll meet you at the agreed location. Travel light.'

Raylan slammed down the phone and jumped out of bed. He got
dressed, buckled his boots, dropped his press card and notebook into his
shoulder bag, raced down the hotel stairs and hurried northwest towards
the Old Market, Ton That Dam. In the distance he heard the dull echo
of explosions. With their 130 mm long-range towed field guns, courtesy
of the Soviet Union, North Vietnamese troops were obliterating the
South Vietnamese army's last line of defence on the outskirts of the city.

It had been clear for weeks that the war was coming to an end, but
nobody could have imagined it would happen so quickly. 'White
Christmas' was the signal for Operation Frequent Wind, a large-scale
evacuation of remaining Americans and all the Vietnamese men,
women and children who were connected to them through work,
marriage or close family ties. If Saigon fell into the hands of the North
Vietnamese Liberation Army, they'd all be in immediate danger.

Above him the rotor blades of large Chinook helicopters hammered the sky. Accompanied by Cobra gunships, they flew back and forth between Saigon and the South China Sea, where the aircraft carrier USS *Midway* was positioned off the coast. The thousands on the evacuation list would be transported from agreed pickup points to the ship. The number of people who needed to be evacuated was estimated at around 1.6 million. Such a massive undertaking was out of the question since the North Vietnamese had bombed Than Son Nhut airport a few days earlier.

Employees of the US embassy had issued assurances that an orderly and well-controlled evacuation would be initiated. If he managed to get Hoang, his wife and their two-year-old daughter into the embassy, they would be picked up there by one of the helicopters. The closer he got to the building, the busier it became. Hundreds of panicked people rushed through the streets in the direction of Thong Nhat boulevard, where the mass hysteria was overwhelming. Thousands were congregated around the American embassy compound. Marines from the Seventh Fleet futilely tried to stop people from climbing over the shut gates and the walls topped with rolls of razor wire.

Raylan looked around, observing the chaos and the fear, raised his right arm as far as he could, put his other hand against his mouth and shouted Hoang's name. He was taller than most in the crowd and stood out with his blond hair. In no time, his call was answered. He lifted Hoang's crying daughter on to his shoulders and instructed Hoang and his wife to hold on to him as tightly as possible. He then forced his way through the panic-stricken crowd in the direction of the gate, over which he saw some of his colleagues scrambling. Once there, he held the child in the air as high as he could. The outstretched arm of an American colleague took her from him and lifted her over the wall. Then it was Hoang's wife's turn. Several arms helped her over, and she too disappeared alongside the gate's edge behind the wall. Then it was Hoang's turn. Like a parcel being delivered, he was helped over. At the top of the wall, Hoang turned around and held out his arm to assist Raylan. But he placed two fingers against his right eyebrow and saluted.

'Stay safe, Hoang!' Then he turned around and made his way back through the madness, into a Saigon in a state of total disarray.

The entire night American helicopters flew over the city. If he stayed he'd be putting his life at risk, but after ten years Raylan didn't want to miss seeing what would happen to the city once it was taken by the communists. He saw the desperate people of Saigon, who knew there was no longer a way out, looting pharmacies. With large quantities of stolen sleeping pills and tranquilizers, they chose death over falling victim to the retaliations the North Vietnamese would undoubtedly unleash as soon as they took the city. Others sold all their jewellery on the street or by the boats in the harbour, hoping to buy their way to freedom. People burned papers that indicated they'd had close ties with the Americans. South Vietnamese soldiers left their boots, discarded uniforms and weapons in the middle of the street and hightailed it, barefoot, back to their families. A crying mother tried to force her baby into his arms.

By morning, the last US Marines had themselves found refuge on the roof of the American embassy. When they flew over the heads of the forsaken Vietnamese in the last helicopter, looters were already ransacking the first floors of the embassy building. Less than an hour later, Raylan saw the first vehicles of the North Vietnamese Liberation Army driving via Thu Do street into the heart of the city, right past Lam Son Square, where ten years earlier that old monk had set himself ablaze.

'Canadian press!' Raylan respectfully called to the boys in their North Vietnamese camouflage uniforms, who looked at him suspiciously. Their impenetrable faces gave them the innocent appearance of choirboys, but he knew better. They sent their tanks over the wide boulevards through the city in the direction of the Independence Palace. There President Duong Van Minh told the North Vietnamese army commander that he was prepared to surrender. 'You don't have any government to hand over to us,' he answered, and was immediately carted off to prison.

By 11.30 that morning the red flag with the yellow star of the North Vietnamese Liberation Army waved above the city. A war that had raged for two decades ended overnight without a bloody battle.

The next morning Raylan was awakened by the tinny sound of triumphant patriotic songs blasting from countless loudspeakers hung in the deserted streets by the Liberation Army. There was no way to send his reporting of the events. All telex and telephone lines had been cut off. He was politely, but persuasively, asked to take his place in an Antonov passenger plane together with other journalists who'd stayed behind, and they were all flown to Wattay International airport in Vientiane, Laos. The new communist regime had little use for the prying eyes of foreigners during their political purges.

Raylan was startled awake by a dull sound resembling an exploding hand grenade, followed by a short shockwave. They'd hit an air pocket. He was sweating profusely, and his heart was working overtime. He'd lifted off from Vientiane with a single question in his head, to which he knew he had no answer: how would he ever leave behind a war that had abruptly stopped after ten years? It had become an inextricable part of his life.

He'd come to this war of his own accord. But the burning monk on Lam Son Square had immediately robbed him of any free will. He'd originally stayed for three years. But for the past seven years he'd flown back and forth between Kabul – which he now considered home – and his work assignments in Saigon, knowing that one day he might come back minus an arm or leg, completely burned out, or – worst-case scenario – in a body bag. But it wasn't like he had a choice: he felt a compulsion . . . that damn war kept tugging at him. Free will had given way to obsessive behaviour.

He wanted to focus the world's attention on the war in Vietnam, hoping people would eventually take some responsibility. His reports were desperate cries from a doomed world. A world of body-counts, dead Vietnamese suspected of collaborating with the Viet Cong tortured to death, desperate families fleeing their bombed-out villages, innocent civilians caught in the crossfire. He'd spoken to them all. They'd entrusted their stories to him. Thanks to those stories he was able to inform the world about what was really happening in Vietnam.

And if he happened to be in the area again, even months or years later, he'd visit those he'd met to see how they were doing, would hear that the father had died, the children had joined the North Vietnamese Liberation Army or fallen victim to their reprisals. On those occasions he arrived with vegetables, meat or rice and regularly hid some money under a sleeping mat or in a drawer. Not because he wanted to pay them for their information, because that went against all his journalistic principles, but because he wanted to help them in any way he could.

He thought about the times he'd helped carry young marines from the battlefield to the helicopters. They kept believing they were fighting in Vietnam for God and Fatherland. *Semper fidelis*, always faithful. Obedience was their motto. Raylan, as a journalist, had exactly the opposite attitude: *diffidere in perpetuum*. Forever mistrustful. Disobedience to all forms of authority had become his professional motto.

The war played such a dominant role in his consciousness that it sometimes seemed like the key to everything wrong with the world and everything that could be made right again was to be found in Vietnam. Now that the war was over, he was left in a vacuum in which there only seemed to be room for guilt, regret and powerlessness.

By getting on that plane it felt like he'd betrayed all those people he'd met in Vietnam over those ten years. He'd made sure that Hoang, his wife and their child had been lifted over the wall of the American embassy, but he'd left them there, without considering what would happen to them next. He'd left so many people behind in his pursuit of even more news that just told the same story over and over again, without having made a fundamental difference.

Through the thin patchy fog Raylan saw the snowy mountain ranges quickly approaching. He automatically braced himself. Every landing at Kabul airport remained a perilous undertaking. He sighed a breath of relief once he reached the bottom of the flight stairs. A taxi took him to the northwestern district of Kart-e-Parwan to the Hotel Intercontinental, which was built on top of a hill. Like some modern-day fortress, it towered above the ever-expanding capital. The Intercontinental's policy was one of extreme discretion. That was the main reason he always booked a room for one night here under an alias and paid in advance.

His hotel bed's snow-white sheets sharply contrasted with the blood-red cushions and the velvet curtains. On the moss-green wall above the bed hung a painting of flowering poppy fields. The net curtains hung in such thick folds in front of the windows that the city seemed enveloped in a thick fog. He stood in the middle of the room on the Persian carpet with only the noise of the air-con around him and noticed how extremely tense he was. A glance at his watch indicated there was more than an hour left. After stacking the cushions on the wide bed, he began a series of rituals that he knew would sufficiently calm his nerves while he was waiting.

He enjoyed a joint and after each drag took a sip of whiskey from his hip flask, topped off with an Anafranil tablet. He then opened the balcony windows so the smell of weed would be dissipated by the mountain wind and took a long hot shower. He carefully dried himself off, put on only his jeans and started lathering his face. With a new blade and lukewarm water he shaved off a week's worth of beard. He was almost finished when he heard a knock at the door. In a startled reflex he cut himself. He then rinsed away a narrow streak of blood on his right cheek that had mixed with the foam.

When he opened the door she was right there in front of him. A thin, elegant dress in muted colours with three-quarter-length sleeves hung loosely around her body. She had a transparent black scarf with a red-floral motif draped over her dark hair. And as he stared at her, he thought about how he'd clung to this moment for the past few months – months that had tested his patience and desire. Now that she was within arm's reach he couldn't imagine that whatever might follow could be any more intense.

'You're early,' he said, feeling his aftershave sting the fresh cut.

She smiled uneasily and assessed him with her eyes, as if she should apologize. She then leaned forward and gave him a passionate kiss on the lips. He retreated a bit to allow her the space to come in and closed the door behind him.

'I couldn't wait.'

He kissed her just behind her ear and caught that familiar scent of caramel. She wrapped her arms around him and dug her nails into his back. He wanted to cling on to her, rest his head on her belly like a little boy and weightlessly float away on her warm body until everything was quiet in his head. He pressed her close to him, her firm breasts against his chest.

'I heard it's over,' she said. 'The war.'

He shook his head. 'Don't talk now . . . First us.'

Their rendezvous, whenever he returned from covering the war, always began with undressing each other in complete silence. Whispers, sighs, panting. Touching, caressing, clinging to each other.

He could feel her body through the silky fabric of her dress. He lifted the skirt and stroked her smooth thighs while her hands skilfully unbuttoned his fly. She pulled down the coarse denim and playfully folded her fingers around his balls, as if weighing how heavy they were. Her tongue penetrated his lips, looking for his. In the seven years of their clandestine encounters, she'd essentially let go of all shame. Here with him, Helai was absolutely free. Hotel rooms served as walled sanctuaries where she could be whoever she wanted to be: an outspoken woman demanding pleasure, who asserted herself without being punished, who was rewarded for what was considered morally improper behaviour elsewhere.

Her fingers tousled his hair. With both hands, she pulled his face towards her and looked deep into his eyes. 'Where are you?'

'I'm here,' he replied.

'Here? With me?'

'Where else?'

He wanted to kiss her, but she stopped him. 'I missed you.'

'Same here.'

She shook her head. 'The jury isn't convinced.'

He smiled and felt his temples pounding. 'I want you, here and now.' He said it with as much longing as possible in his voice. She opened her mouth and let his tongue glide inside as he unbuttoned her dress, unhooked her bra and buried his face between her breasts.

Every time they stripped naked in front of each other, they were months older and something had changed – more weight, more gravity – but the fiery desire they shared in familiar rituals remained unchanged, the surprising predictability of what would come next but always the slightest bit different.

Helai forced him down on his back and straddled him. He felt her lips all over his chest, a bite in his nipple, her tongue in his navel and her lips closing around the tip of his penis. He stared at the ceiling, while trying to ignore the approaching whir of Chinooks and the chanting of hundreds of monks, until he saw her face appear right above him. A worried look in her eyes.

'It's over, Raylan. It's over. No more war.'

He really wanted to shout that she couldn't be more wrong; she was so naive. But he stayed silent, brushed a lock of hair from her face, reached for her mouth and kissed her. She lay down under him, guided him inside; her panting exciting him even more. He tasted the sweat on her skin, but what normally tasted salty was now like muddy water. There was barely a trace of her caramel sweetness. Instead, the stench of burning gasoline penetrated his nostrils. The sound of flickering flames filled his ears. Time for all of it to stop. Now that he was inside her. She'd take over. She would make everything disappear; once again transport him back to the here and now.

But the flames flared higher. Fighter planes flew low, dropped their napalm. He moved inside her even harder. He wanted to breathe freely again, without the stench of napalm, without shrieking mothers fleeing their burning straw huts with their screaming children. Now they were all standing around the bed and staring at him with blank faces. He had to exorcize them, and the only one who could help him do that was her. He moved faster and faster. His breathing quickened. It looked like she was ablaze. She looked at him with big, frightened eyes, clawed the air to reach him. But through all the smoke he could barely see her. In the barrage of flamethrowers and machine-gun fire he could barely hear her.

He couldn't stop now. Only she could provide what he needed.

Then he heard it: her begging him to stop. He felt her hitting his chest with her fists. The room spun around him. His despair was released as a primal scream. He fell on his side next to her. As she slowly crawled out from under, he gently moved his head back and forth and cried to himself.

She went into the bathroom. He heard the water running. He slowly got to his feet and dizzily staggered towards her. She was standing under the shower with her arms crossed over her breasts, her back slightly bent. He saw that she was crying. He wanted to go and comfort her. She held out her arm to deter him. On her face, disillusionment, anger and fear fought for priority. He raised his arms, as if to make clear that she had nothing to fear, and retreated backwards into the room.

The ringing in his ears, the pounding of his heart. With small thuds he banged his head against the glass window. He held his breath to keep a frightened scream from escaping his lips. He just stood there, until he heard the shower stop and she approached him from behind.

Her voice sounded broken. 'I don't know what's going on . . . the last few times . . . but it's . . .'

Now, just breathing hurt terribly. Best to keep quiet. He was afraid he'd say the wrong thing.

'It's like you've become someone else . . .'

Slowly he turned around and watched as she got dressed. 'I'm sorry,' he murmured.

She put on her shoes and stood in front of him. Her eyes were red from crying. He wanted to touch her, but she raised her hand, even more decisively than in the bathroom.

'That time I saw you come into the courtroom . . . I knew right away. I wanted you. But I got more than I bargained for. You brought the dead with you as well. Every time we met, there were more of them. And now I know they'll never let you be.'

She put on her scarf.

'Please stay,' he said.

She shook her head.

'We never promised each other anything. We did this as long as we both enjoyed it. I can't help you any longer.'

She took her sunglasses out of her bag, put them on and walked to the door.

'Don't walk away,' he said. 'Not now.'

She turned around.

'Everything happens for a reason. Come to the palace tomorrow with your wife.'

With a soft click of the door she was gone.

*

213

They looked impressive in their dark-green Presidential Guard uniforms. Wide epaulettes on their shoulders, striking headgear, with a golden eagle on the red band spreading its mighty wings. But most remarkable about these men were their snow-white gloves and the almost deferential concentration with which they held the two narrow crates between them. They accompanied them as if it were a procession, lit by uniformed torchbearers, who guided them through the dark alleys of the old Murad Khane district, past the armed soldiers standing guard every ten metres to ensure that all the residents stayed inside.

Raylan was at the end of an alley behind a police barricade amidst a crowd of curious onlookers and saw the procession approaching. He flashed his precious unlimited visa at a policeman. '*Ma inja zindagi mikonam*. I live here.' But the man wasn't the least bit impressed with his *taskort* and waved him off with an arrogant gesture. Raylan was about to jump over the barrier, when he caught sight of the slight figure of Parwaiz Ahmad. Leading a group of foot guards, he exited the alley first. Ahmad was the one who'd coordinated the transport of some of the portraits Isobel had painted to the presidential palace. When he saw Raylan, he fell out of character for a moment. His voice shot up a bit.

'*As-Salaam-Alaikum, aghaye* Chapelle. I thought you were still in Vietnam.'

'*Wa-Alaikum-Salaam, aghaye* Ahmad. I'm here, as you can see, and I'd love to go home,' Raylan said, nodding in the direction of the bewildered cop. 'But it doesn't look like it's going to happen, if it's up to this diligent civil servant.'

'That would be a sour note on what promises to be a lovely evening,' Parwaiz replied. After instructing the guards on how to securely fasten the two crates in the back of the waiting lorry, he addressed the agent on duty with the appropriate reserve and made it implicitly clear that only one person was in charge here, and that was the man with whom Raylan was now walking into the alleyways of Murad Khane. Parwaiz seemed to feel very comfortable in his role as civil commander. Actually, the lack of a uniform was the only thing that distinguished him from the guards.

'Are you sure you didn't miss your calling?' Raylan asked with a grin.

'In a case like this, which unites the national interest and the arts, extreme discipline and absolute obedience are desired, Mr Chapelle. The painting of the president needs to be hung in the palace without any problems arising, and the artist's husband should not be treated like a troublemaker.'

'Much appreciated, Mr Ahmad.'

'*Qabel nadara*,' he replied with a smile. 'You're welcome.'

Because of the soldiers who'd positioned themselves every ten metres in the network of alleys, it felt like they were parading past a guard of honour, magically lit by the torchbearers walking ahead of them.

'You are no doubt very proud of your wife,' Parwaiz cheerfully mentioned. 'A commission to paint state portraits of the entire presidential family is an incredible honour. Have you seen the final results?'

'I'm sorry. I've been away for almost two months.'

'Compared to the recent official photo, Daoud's new portrait is much more humane. Exactly what our president wanted: that he be seen as a man of the people.'

'Despite his blue blood?'

'What do you mean?'

'He may have deposed the king, but he is and remains his cousin.'

'I have faith in the future. Are you still an arch-pessimist?'

'I've just seen Saigon fall to the communists. Sorry, I'm not in such a festive mood.'

'But the war is over, and you were against the war.'

'That's right. But I'm also against communism.'

They'd arrived at the entrance of the house. '*Khosh amaden ba khanetan.*' With a courteous gesture Parwaiz stepped aside for Raylan. 'Welcome home.'

As he walked down the long narrow corridor to the studio, Raylan heard a scurry of footsteps coming up the stairs, accompanied by an excited boy's voice: 'Daddy, Daddy!' And before he knew it he felt the warm liveliness of a little boy, clinging to his father like a monkey in pyjamas. Raylan hugged him tightly, lifted him up in the air, then put him down and planted a big kiss on his forehead.

With endearing looks, hardly matching their stern uniforms, the guardsmen watched as he walked hand-in-hand with his son to the studio, where Isobel was waiting for them surrounded by her large paintings. She hugged Raylan, wiped away a tear, swept a lock of hair from her face and signalled the men to approach and crate up the last painting to take with them.

Together with the small blond boy Raylan went up some stairs that led to a room on the top floor where on the coarsely plastered walls, a painted Afghan mountain setting slowly transformed into a Dutch polder landscape graced by an old farmhouse. He grabbed his rucksack and pulled out a present: dog tags, two small metal plates with a stamped name and date of birth.

The boy read out loud: 'Paul Chapelle, February 15, 1969.'

Raylan smiled at his son.

'May I keep them on in bed tonight?' Paul asked excitedly after hanging the chain with the tags around his neck.

'No doubt handy if you get lost in dreamland,' Raylan replied with a wink.

'But I never get lost. I always come home. Just like Nils,' exclaimed Paul and from under his pillow he removed a thick book with an illustration of a little boy on the back of a goose: *The Wonderful Adventures of Nils*. A tale about a Swedish peasant couple's son who is magically turned into an elf-like creature and, riding on the back of a tame young goose, Morten, travels with a flock of wild geese flying north for the summer.

Paul's dreams could very well be about any chapter in the book. It was as if he himself had experienced all of Nils' exciting adventures, encounters, dangers and wise lessons about life. Still, he couldn't get enough of hearing the same story over and over again. Especially when Raylan read it to him.

'Once there was a boy ... long and loose-jointed and tow-headed ...' Raylan began. 'He liked best to make mischief.'

He paused for a moment to look at his son, who rubbed his fingers over the stamped name on the metal plate as if it were braille, and he was struck by how much Paul had grown since the last time he'd seen him. And especially by how much he'd missed him. The boy had a myriad of questions about what was going on in that country at war, which again and again pulled his father back there. Raylan wanted to spare his son the horrifying truth, but Paul always asked if his dad had ever fired a gun, who Agent Orange was and why every North Vietnamese was called Charlie.

Raylan couldn't help but wonder how his son saw him. As an often-absent father, an idealized hero or a complete stranger who he called Daddy? He saw Paul's eyes almost closing and flipped ahead to the moment when Nils, after a journey full of adventures, returns home reborn: *'"Welcome!" added his father, and not another word could he utter. But the boy still lingered at the threshold. He could not comprehend why they were so glad to see him – such as he was. Then his mother came and put her arms around him and drew him into the room, and he knew that he was all right. "Mother and father!" he cried. "I'm a big boy. I am a human being again."'*

He planted another kiss on Paul's forehead, gently closed the book and quietly slipped out of the room.

Raylan lingered downstairs in the hallway. Parwaiz and the guardsmen had carried the last painting outside and gone on their way. Slowly he returned to the studio, where Isobel was waiting for him among the large canvases depicting the buildings and the people of Kabul, painted in earthy colours, in shades of ochre and sienna. Each painting was a serene aspect of everyday life at the crossroads of past and present.

'Home is where your heart is, but if you don't follow your heart, home is nowhere to be found,' she'd once said.

He knew every nook and cranny of the house, yet he walked around it like a stranger. The entire time he'd lived there, seven years, he'd chosen to flee again after only being home for a few weeks. Flee to Saigon, feverishly flee to war. Not once had Isobel stopped him.

She smiled at him. The smile of a woman who probably knew him better than he knew himself. She came and stood before him. Her fingers caressed his face, and she kissed him very gently on his lips.

'You're home,' she said, and he felt himself go weak in the knees, as if all his resistance broke down the moment she uttered those words.

She handed him a glass of whiskey and lit a joint.

'How was it to leave there?' she asked.

'It was complete chaos . . . Every man for himself.'

'I meant for you, personally?'

'I don't know . . . Everyone was in such a hurry. So was I. How we left Vietnam is tantamount to betrayal. Anyone who cooperated with the Americans in any way now has a target on their back. Roundups, purges, re-education camps. It's going to continue until there's not a single anti-communist left. I can't help but wonder if I could have done more.'

'Stop tormenting yourself with questions like that. It's a waste of energy. You were there as a reporter. You did what you could.'

He shook his head despairingly. 'Every time I returned to Saigon, all these years, I thought: maybe now I can do something, something to change the system. Something, if only a little something . . . however small . . . And now that it's over . . .' He pressed his palms firmly against his face and massaged his temples with his fingers. 'I wish I could stop the memories. If I could just stop remembering the dead, maybe they would cease to exist. But I'm always surrounded by them.'

'Now, too?

'I can't even remember a time when they weren't there.'

He took some Anafranil pills from his chest pocket and swallowed them with a gulp of whiskey. 'They're dead. And yet they're still here. They keep coming back. What is it going to take to get rid of them?'

He saw no pity in her eyes. She looked serious and confident.

'They're waiting, Ray . . .'

'Waiting? For what?'

'Until you do something.'

He felt an unexpected anger rise to the surface. 'What the fuck am I supposed to do?'

'Stop trying to shut them out,' she said calmly. 'Open the door, invite them in, give them a voice and listen to them. Listen to their stories, write down what they have to say. That's why they haunt you, why they keep returning, why they don't want to leave. They don't want their deaths to be in vain. All these years you've let the living talk; now let the dead have their say, and the world will listen.'

She took a long drag, held the smoke in and handed the joint back to him. He walked the length of the panoramic mural: past the men bending their heads towards Mecca on the banks of the River Kabul; then men with bloody aprons in a sun-drenched courtyard slaughtering a sheep; the veiled women in the square in front of the Pul-e Khishti Mosque behind a swarm of flying pigeons. He thought of his incessant longing for the unknown, his constant need to flee. Just like his relationship with Helai had been about fleeing, from the moment it started until the very end.

'Why didn't you ever try to stop me when I wanted to go back to Nam?' he asked.

'Your whole being breathes war,' she said in a resigned tone. 'But you want something more, something most people don't care about or can't do. Your conscience compels you to serve the truth.'

'The war was a false promise,' he said. 'It's all been one big lie.' He turned to her. 'I lied to you too.'

'About her?'

He was stunned. 'How . . . ?'

'It doesn't matter. I've always known. And in some bizarre way, I'm also grateful to her.'

'Why?'

'She made sure that most of the war stayed outside this house. When you got back from Vietnam, she first purged you of all the misery . . . so afterwards you could come home . . . to us.'

'I'm sorry,' he said, and he silently stared at his feet for a while. 'More than I can say.'

She stood right in front of him, her arms hanging by her side, vulnerable while at the same time filled with strength.

'It's about time you came home, Ray.' She passed him the joint. 'Let's talk more tomorrow.'

She caressed his cheek, and what he saw in her eyes was much more than sadness. It was pain. He wanted to touch her, keep her there with him, but he was frozen in place with the joint in his hand and only watched as she walked out of her studio.

2
Farah

2009

In the narrow, dusty streets of Shahr-e Naw district, the tarps covering the stalls flapped about in the strengthening wind. Being here without a male companion was the most reckless thing a woman could do.

Farah was walking into the heart of a black-market trading network, which had been in business since Russian troops invaded the country in 1989. In those years, complete tanks, lorries and jeeps were traded as separate parts and offered up for sale here. Since 2001, vendors profited daily from the vilified American presence in their country. At knock-down prices you could get all sorts of military goods that had fallen into the hands of criminals and swindlers before they reached the American army camps. These intermediaries sold the items to local distributors, who then passed them on to merchants at a mark-up. There they stood, with their weathered faces, surrounded by war trophies. Steel-capped combat boots, camouflage gear, bullet-proof vests, khaki-coloured helmets, all-weather sleeping bags and quick-drying underwear.

This is also where the Taliban's errand boys came to do their shopping. As well as brand-new GPS sets, night-vision goggles and long-range laser rifles, they bought the police uniforms worn by suicide bombers who marched into hotel lobbies, shopping centres and restaurants to blow themselves up.

Farah was acutely aware of how vulnerable she was. For the umpteenth time Paul's warning flashed through her mind: *Two female journalists were killed last week.*

She could still turn around, return to the relative safety of Nehal's taxi and drive off without so much as a thought about the dossier that was waiting for her somewhere around here. She could forget that last night she'd seen a little boy who reminded her of Sekandar. That she'd done nothing to protect him from the horrors awaiting him.

She'd refused to sign the document that would have prevented her from publishing anything about what she'd seen and experienced in the Afghan division of Camp Eggers. And that refusal had made her a liability to the American Army Command, a journalistic time bomb.

'Goldwater will have you followed,' Mason had told her. 'Every step you take, every contact you make, they'll be on you.'

She looked at the stall owners who'd boxed themselves in with big plastic bags of 'Meals-Ready-to-Eat'. Many of them contained pork, but they were still in great demand. The same was true for the shrink-wrapped donuts, bottles of maple syrup, packets of breakfast cereal and the big bags of protein supplements for bodybuilders. Soap, shaving foam, American Crew shampoo, deodorant sticks and *Baywatch* DVDs with a scantily clad Pamela Anderson displayed prominently on the cover completed this dumping party for Afghan men.

After yesterday's accident, the riots had spread throughout the city. The offices of foreign NGOs were attacked; traders just outside the gates of military camps were beaten up and denounced as traitors. But here, at this huge bazaar where the American presence was so pervasive, here of all places people were left in peace.

But that didn't apply to her.

Although she'd draped the dark-grey khimar as loosely as possible around her head and upper body, had all but concealed her curves with the loose-fitting cotton trousers and shirt and had removed all her make-up, she could feel innumerable male eyes darting all over her body. Eyes that tried to undress her layer by layer, like Hafami had done last night.

It would only take one of these staring men to engineer a confrontation, place a wandering hand somewhere on her body and she'd react with instinctive and unexpected force. And in this public domain ruled by men that would be tantamount to a death warrant. Only recently, a woman who'd put up a fight when a stranger had touched her up had been molested by a large group in reprisal. It had happened in broad daylight.

The bazaar snaked deeper and deeper into increasingly dark and dingy alleyways. She tried to manoeuvre through the throng of people, cautiously steering clear of physical contact and avoiding stares. She knew that in this very place, at this very moment, she was doing the one thing she shouldn't be doing: flouting every single agreement she'd made with Edward last night.

Why hadn't Mason simply given her a USB stick when they met? And why had he asked her to come here alone? It was a test: she could think of no other reason. He probably wanted to know how far she was willing to go, how determined she was to penetrate into this labyrinth reeking of open sewers to obtain his information. She was determined to prove that she was up to the task.

Keep going, look straight ahead. Her eyes darted around, surreptitiously scanning her surroundings for her contact, who ought to be waiting for her around here. Doubt began to creep in. As she crossed a narrow junction, the overcrowding and chaos made it hard to breathe. Her chest felt tight with the noise, stench and growing uncertainty. How would she be able to spot someone on the lookout for her if she couldn't look people in the face? She almost tripped over a legless man sitting on a piece of plastic. He pointed to a creased photo attached to the sodden piece of cardboard in front of him: a proud soldier surrounded by his wife and five children.

Someone bumped into her from behind.

She felt a hand grabbing her arm.

Just as she was about to yank herself free she stared into the eyes of her assailant – a young woman – and heard her panicky voice.

'*Yak chize beret daram*. I have something for you. Quick!'

She allowed the woman to take her hand and pull her into an alleyway. After a hurried dash through a maze of streets, they arrived at a peeling door, behind which two photocopiers produced a terrible racket. The greasy smell of burned printing powder drifted into her nostrils, but it was a welcome change from the rotten stench outside. Before she knew it, a package tied with string had been pressed into her hands.

When she walked out through the shop's front door with the parcel under her clothes, she had no idea what its contents were or what upheaval they might bring. But she knew one thing for certain: there was no going back now.

During the drive back to the hotel, she'd left the parcel intact; she hadn't untied the knotted rope to flick through the photocopied sheets. She'd calmly walked into the hotel, the bundle concealed underneath the elastic waistband of her loose-fitting trousers.

Believing it possible that someone might have trailed her and was now sitting in the lobby, she'd heeded Mason's advice. *Play the game. Act like you don't know you're being followed.* She struck up a conversation with the bashful receptionist behind his mahogany counter and asked if she had any mail. Stupid question, she realized. Nonetheless, he began to rifle through a stack of envelopes, reading each of the addressees' names out loud, until he came to the last one and gave her an apologetic look. He then asked whether she liked Kabul and if she cared to eat in the hotel restaurant tonight.

In her room, she'd first carefully checked to see whether anything had been moved and whether the contents of her safe looked exactly the way she'd left them. Reassured, she'd then hung the DO NOT DISTURB sign on her door.

By now the sun had disappeared behind the mountain ridges. Of all the lamps in her hotel room, she'd left only the one in the bathroom on, with the door ajar. She was sitting in the middle of the bed, bathed in the light from the other room.

In the past she'd often sat in her room like this, in a slender shaft of dawn sunlight, hoping that she'd be able to forget her loneliness again that day, the feeling that she didn't really belong, that she didn't fit in with the people and the world around her. That she was an imperfect child. Being showered in morning light made her feel strong.

Now, more than thirty years later, she summoned the light again. Its artificial counterpart this time. But it came close to the desired effect. She wanted to make sure she had the inner peace and strength to assess what she was about to read as a journalist without getting emotionally carried away. She'd carefully opened the parcel, and the loose sheets now lay on a pile in front of her.

Mason had been meticulous. Copies of the military code of practice pertaining to sexual offences. The transcript of the statement by the woman who'd come to Mason to report General Hafami. The key parts of the secret file that US Military Intelligence had compiled on this high-ranking Afghan.

She was surprised to find that, in preparation for their tour of Afghanistan, American Marines were given detailed instructions on what to do in the event of a sexual assault within the ranks but received no guidance whatsoever on the correct course of action when witnessing rape or sexual abuse by the local population.

The factual tone in which the account of the widow Roshan and her seven-year-old son Idris had been recorded made it all the more heartbreaking. The story of a child regularly waved off by his trusting mother as he was driven away by an Afghan soldier in a jeep infuriated her. It was the same fury and the same powerlessness she'd felt that night at Camp Eggers. An inevitable response. But that fury could get in the way of an impartial assessment of the material.

She took a few deep breaths and began reading the profile of the man who saw it as his right to use children as objects of pleasure.

General Hafami belongs to the largest ethnic group in Afghanistan, the Pashtuns, who are known for their fighting spirit. After the Russian occupation of Afghanistan in 1979, Hafami became the undisputed leader of the clan of warlords, who for ten years fought the Soviet army with secret American support. When the Russian troops withdrew, the warlords became caught up in an internal power struggle over who should rule the new Afghanistan. In the bloody civil war that followed, much of Kabul was razed to the ground. The Taliban put an end to that conflict and became the warlords' new common enemy. It was only after the attack on the Twin Towers in New York in 2001 that America started its offensive against the Taliban while the warlords – with plenty of US dollars and material support – united in the Northern Alliance. Together with the US Marines they eventually managed to drive the Taliban into the mountains. As a reward for his efforts and in exchange for a ceasefire, Hafami was given a significant role in national politics.

Here she abruptly stopped reading.

The document mentioned the name of the man who'd greeted her with such gallantry and reserve that morning in the lobby of the Ministry of the Interior.

Ashraf Shakoor.

It turned out that he and Hafami had established a provisional local government after the fall of the Taliban. In close cooperation with Hafami, Shakoor had put Hamid Karzai forward as a presidential candidate. Once president, Karzai had rewarded both men's loyalty with prestigious positions.

She thought of the photo she'd held in her hands after Shakoor had briefly left her alone in his office. The one that showed him as minister of the interior, standing next to Hafami.

She heard a tapping sound. Small red drops fell on to the last page of the secret military report. She recognized the metallic taste of blood on her lips. Blood splashed from her nose on to the paper.

In the bathroom, she washed it off her face, stuffed cotton wool into her nostrils, sat down again and read on.

We can conclude with a probability bordering on certainty that General Hafami has a significant stake in the Afghan narcotics trade. Additionally, many in Hafami's military unit are guilty of, among other things, establishing illegal checkpoints, extortion and systemic sexual abuse and exploitation of young boys.

She was having difficulties breathing, removed the cotton wool from her nostrils and took a few large swigs of water. What she read next came as a surprise: *Hafami temporarily removed from office.*

Based on the intelligence gathered, the US military authorities had managed to put enough pressure on President Karzai to secure, pending a judicial investigation, Hafami's temporary suspension. But barely two months later the investigation was dropped by presidential decree for lack of evidence. Hafami was rehabilitated and returned to the highest echelons as general of the Afghan National Guard. The fact that he was allowed into Camp Eggers meant that the Americans too had caved in to the Afghan president's demands.

She lay back on the soft bed and tried to take it all in. There was only one possible conclusion. From that moment on, Hafami must have thought he was above the law. Enjoying the protection of the country's senior politician, he considered himself untouchable.

She sat up and looked for her phone. When Paul finally answered, she breathed a sigh of relief.

Judging by the hoarse sound of his voice, she could tell he'd been smoking too much and had probably drunk gallons of coffee.

'Sorry I didn't call you back earlier,' he said after a stifled yawn that betrayed she'd woken him up.

'How are you?'

'Aside from the fact that every single muscle in my body aches, that I almost drowned in the Moskva and was forced to wear a tie in some crumbling Russian castle, I'm actually doing exceptionally well.'

'What happened?'

'I spoke to that informant.'

'The man investigating the motorcycle gang?'

'Yup ... But those guys must have known something was afoot. They almost ran me down, really. But by then I'd already been given the info on a USB stick.'

'How did you escape?'

'At breakneck speed, literally ... on a motorcycle.'

'And what was that you said about the Moskva?'

'They chased me. Shot my rear tyre to bits somewhere along the riverbank. A police patrol boat picked me up.' He sighed. 'Locked me up in five-star police accommodation, with room service, jacuzzi and sensual massage ...' She heard the cold cynicism in his voice. 'Yup, they really messed me up. But I managed to hold on to the USB stick. Solid proof that Lavrov was behind the attack on Anya.'

'What did you do?'

'I struck a deal. The head of the secret service, who questioned me a while back about your role in the hostage situation at the Seven Sisters, this Alexander Arlazarov ... I passed the information on to him. That probably saved my life.'

'Jesus, Paul, now what?'

'Believe it or not, but this Arlazarov is playing a double game, at the very least. He had your old passport. And the letters.'

'Raylan's . . . ?'

'Yes . . . They've been keeping tabs on me for a long time, but the remarkable thing is . . . somehow or other we have a common interest when it comes to Lavrov. I don't know what it is, but I'll find out. I have a new lead. We're closing in on him. We're gonna nail the bastard!'

In the silence that followed, she heard the sighing of the ventilator.

'How's Anya?'

'Not much change.'

'Not much?'

'None, really. She's . . . There's . . .' The sob in his voice was unexpected.

'Paul?'

'If she recovers . . . and I say "if" . . . she probably won't be able to breathe unassisted.'

Her heart tightened, and for a split second the pain in her chest was unbearable. Over the past few days, she'd been counting on the fact that Anya would come around again, gradually recover and eventually even go back to work. Then she'd be able to visit her and clarify the whole situation. Explain exactly what had happened in the catacombs of Jakarta, the pressure she'd been under that led to her divulging Anya's name. It looked as if she'd never be able to do that now. She'd have to carry the guilt for what had happened to Anya for the rest of her life.

'Is there no chance at all? No hope?' she asked.

'As good as none . . .'

'As good as?'

'The doctors are hedging their bets. But . . .'

She wanted to wrap her arms around Paul, hold him. But they were separated by thousands of miles. 'I wish I could be there with you,' she finally said.

'I know, but you've got your own business over there . . .'

'Has Edward spoken to you?'

'No . . . Why?'

'He said he'd call you.'

'About what?'

'About . . . what I've discovered.'

'What have you discovered?'

'A *bacha bazi* network, run by an Afghan general.'

'Jesus, you never stop, do you?' There was that aggression in his voice again, the same as in their previous phone call.

'I have classified intelligence that the US military knows about the network, but isn't doing anything about it.'

'Who's your source?'

'A gunnery sergeant.'

'And he just happened to pass you information?'

'He's been working on it for months. It's a secret military file on the general. His name is Hafami and he's the biggest crook here, but condoned by both the government and the Americans.'

He sighed again, more deeply than before. 'We had agreements. You, me and Edward.'

'I know.'

'Then why do you ignore them?'

'I know what I'm doing, Paul.'

'Is that so? Do you really?'

'What do you mean?'

'Don't you realize, after what happened to Anya, that . . . Oh damn it, Farah, do I have to spell it out for you?'

'Are you saying that what happened to Anya is my fault? I know full well it is.'

'No, that's not what I'm saying, God damn it.'

'Then what, Paul? What are you saying?'

'You're turning yourself into a walking target. And I don't want to see you . . .'

She understood what he was getting at and wanted to reassure him and say that it would all work out, but she also knew it wouldn't be that easy. For the time being, nothing would work out, and she knew it. 'You and me, Paul . . . We're journalists.'

'There's one on a ventilator here.'

'You don't understand. I *have* to do this.'

She heard him stomping out of the room, the echoey sound in the hospital corridor. 'You have an obligation towards Edward and me.'

'But what about Sekandar? What about him? We agreed that we'd do everything possible to help him return safely. I don't want to send him back to a country where one of the top army commanders allows boys to be raped.'

'Aha! So now we suddenly have a higher purpose. We're going to purge the Afghan army of paedophiles.'

'I don't want us to fight, Paul.'

'Then what is it you want?'

'I want you to understand me . . .'

'Hold on. You've been away for barely two days, you simply ignore all of our agreements and now you ask me to understand you?'

'Then what do you want me to do?'

'Do what you have to do. I've had it with you.'

'Listen, Paul, I don't want us to . . .'

There was no point in saying anything else. He'd already hung up.

3
Paul

His mobile phone still in hand, he lingered in the corridor of Piro-gorov hospital and cursed himself for how he pushed everyone he loved away. With that same powerless feeling he returned to Anya's side, looked at her just lying there. He could touch her, but she remained unbearably far away. He couldn't take it. After a kiss on her forehead he walked out of the room.

A taxi took him to Ulitsa Arbat, the former aristocratic and liter-ary district of Moscow, dotted with antique shops, boutiques and small cafés, all once full of self-proclaimed philosophers, bohemians and intellectuals. Here in this intricate network of alleyways and side streets he'd walked with Anya and at one point she suddenly stopped and pointed upwards like an excited child.

'Look!'

He'd followed her finger in the direction of an old building with a narrow Juliet balcony. There her favourite writer Rybakov had writ-ten *The Children of the Arbat*, the story of an idealistic young communist, Sasha, who was sentenced to three years of hard labour in a Siberian work camp because he'd published a newspaper.

'Here we are!' she'd roared in the direction of the balcony. 'The Yank and me . . . ready to take on the world.'

On the street corner they'd listened to the poignant lament of a folk singer and an accordionist.

Oh Arbat, my Arbat, you are my destiny, you are my happiness and my sorrow.

She'd wrapped her arms around him as if she'd never let go again.

FRIENDSHIP it said in large Cyrillic letters above the weathered door of the antiquarian bookshop. When he went inside, an old-fashioned bell let out a dull ring above his head. He inhaled the smell of musty paper. Every horizontal surface was covered with books. Art and literature, encyclopedias, Marxist-Leninist classics, reference works on history and politics. On the wooden counter, sagging under the weight of a heavy copper cash register, stood an ivory bust of Pushkin in addition to classic editions of Chekhov and Turgenev. Shostakovich's *The Dawn of Humanity* playing on an old suitcase gramophone filled the gloomy, dimly lit space, which seemed bereft of other customers.

A small, stocky man appeared from one of the aisles. His bald head was covered with strands of grey hair comically combed to one side. With a cigarette butt between his lips he stared at Paul as if he were seeing a ghost. 'What can I do for you?'

Paul found himself enveloped in a haze of tobacco and alcohol. 'I'm interested in *For Merit to the Fatherland* by Sergey Kombromovich.

The man grimaced and smacked his lips 'Our first national hero, Grigori Michailov. Forgotten Knight in the Order of Glory.'

'Forgotten?'

The wilful look in the shopkeeper's eyes turned to melancholy. 'You know, hardly any young people come to my shop any more. They're no longer interested in their past. What they don't realize is that you can only let go of your history once you've given it a good hard look.'

He gestured that Paul should follow him and marched ahead through narrow aisles between the metres-high bookcases, which were all packed to capacity. At the very last case, which was leaning slightly, his crooked index finger irritably pointed upwards.

Paul grabbed a wooden ladder and carefully climbed past the lower shelves to the highest, removed one of three editions from the row of books and blew the dust off it. Was there a sadder fate? National heroes, showered with knights' orders and medals because of their merits on the battlefield, who still end up somewhere on a neglected shelf at an antiquarian bookshop.

He paid for the book. The owner clumsily stuffed the rouble bills into the cash drawer, frowned, raised his hand and disappeared down the aisle between the bookcases again.

Paul was already halfway to the door when he heard something behind him. He turned around. With a triumphant gaze the man held up the back of *The Great Lie* and with his yellowed index finger demonstratively tapped the photo of the writer.

The little bell rang dully above Paul's head when, without reacting further, he stepped outside.

Club Mayak owed its name to the Mayakovsky Theatre on the ground floor. With its old wallpaper, worn-out furniture and the ornate, but slightly off-key Bösendorfer piano in the corner, it seemed more like a down-and-out jazz musician's living room than the favourite hangout of journalists, artists and actors.

You'd find them here almost every Wednesday and Friday evening, Anya and him, usually in the company of other journalists. What started out as heated discussions about all the possible and impossible abuses in the world invariably turned into midnight booze fests, in which beer, vodka and cheap house wine were soaked up by stuffed cabbage rolls and pierogi, and in which passion took on varying unpredictable forms. He thought of one time when, drunk out of his mind, he'd crept behind the piano to play a special version of 'Strangers in the Night' for Anya, forgetting that he couldn't actually play the piano. Then there were times when Anya would stand on the table and sing 'Katyusha': *... to my dear one ... the one who Katyusha loves so ...*, swearing she'd never leave him except in a coffin. But then there were the countless other times when, out of jealousy, anger, sorrow or desire – all legitimate as far as she was concerned – she'd smack him in the face, faster than he could duck, and then she'd walk away as if it were the last act of a Greek tragedy. Summer or winter, she always did this without a coat, knowing he'd come after her, hang his own jacket over her shoulders and then escort her to her apartment, where they'd spend hours making up in ways even unknown to the *Kama Sutra*.

At a table in the farthest corner he took large sips of his beer, wolfed down a hefty serving of shashlik and skimmed through the boringly written biography. Surprisingly, he already knew many of the facts thanks to the research Farah had done weeks ago in Amsterdam after the sudden death of her old family friend Parwaiz.

Grigori Michailov: born 23 October 1943 in Saratov. Educated at one of the Suvorov military academies, the Moscow Higher Combined Arms Command School and the Frunze Military Academy. The kind of career that left you with the distinct impression little Michailov knew exactly what he wanted to be when he grew up.

A military hero.

Strangely enough, after the Frunze Academy he'd disappeared from the radar. And no matter how cleverly the author tried to get around it, if you put the years next to each other you could clearly see gaps between the period Michailov appeared in Turkmenistan as an intelligence officer and the point at which he was appointed vice-chairman of the Central Military Commission in the North Caucasus. From 1968 he surfaced as general coordinating director of the Russian Cultural Centre in Kabul, a role that seemed as far removed from the military as one could imagine. This changed on 27 December 1979, when the Saur Revolution developed into a civil war. Michailov was promoted to commander of the Russian armed forces. That same day, 1,800 tanks, 2,000 armoured vehicles and 80,000 Soviet troops crossed the Afghan border.

It was the beginning of a nine-year display of Russian might in which more than 15,000 Soviet soldiers and one and a half million Afghans were killed, and that would eventually end in a humiliating military retreat. Before the eyes of the world press, Michailov, who meanwhile had reached the rank of colonel general, was with the last of the Russian forces to return to Russia from Afghanistan in February 1989 via the Friendship Bridge over the River Amu-Darya.

After serving as commander of the military district of Kiev for two years, Michailov was appointed minister of defence in November 1993. Barely a year later, in that capacity, he proclaimed he would conquer Grozny within two hours. That boast led to a war lasting more than two years, in which thousands of young Russian soldiers died and tens of thousands of Chechen civilians became victims of mass atrocities and carpet bombings, which were directly ordered by Michailov.

The third and most dramatic fact was the bombing in February 1996. With limousine and all Michailov was blown up right in front of his Moscow apartment. The dream of that little boy who wanted to be a military hero ultimately became the obituary of a man who, with the blood of thousands on his hands, needed to be gathered up in bits and pieces. The deadly attack was attributed to Chechen rebels but never officially claimed by them.

Paul closed the book, finished his beer and strolled into the late Moscow evening.

Upon his arrival at the hospital, the evening staff had just changed to the night shift. Paul asked the ICU nurse who checked Anya's monitor if he could spend the night in the room with her. After she'd finally consented, he slid a chair close to Anya's bed, listened to the even sound of the ventilator and rested his hand on her upper arm.

She felt warmer than usual.

You can do this, he thought. You're my fighter. You've always fought for everything. For your causes, your life. Even for love. 'I'm fighting with you,' he whispered in her ear.

He'd managed to convince himself. It could take weeks, maybe months. But eventually she'd open her eyes again. And as soon as she realized what had happened, she'd immediately demand that the needles and tubes be removed from her body. Then he would help her out of bed, carry her up the stairs to her apartment, then dive into the kitchen and make her chicken Kiev and scallops, which they would eat in bed together. He'd have to feed her, because she'd lost a few fingers, but he'd teach her how to pick things up again, even how to type once more.

He would be there for her in every way he could. Like he'd once been there for his mother, in the months after his father's death, when she'd wandered half-naked across the fields at night, distraught with grief and groaning like a wounded animal. He'd gone looking for her, and when he'd found her, confused and barely approachable, he took her back to the farmhouse, placed her under a hot shower, dried her, put her to bed, and stayed with her until she fell asleep. This is how he'd once cared for Isobel, returned her to life. He'd be there for Anya in the same way.

He was certain of it. There would be no goodbyes.

He was now holding the bundle of letters Arlazarov had given him. He hesitated about opening them. They weren't his property. But they were from his father, in his own words. The content of the letters might give him the opportunity to get to know an unknown side of the man he'd last seen thirty years ago, as he walked away from him in Schiphol airport's departure hall.

He untied the two silk ribbons from the parcel, removed the red velvet bits of cardboard and folded open the first letter. Paul immediately recognized the handwriting. Firmly written words on lined paper quoted the fourteenth-century Persian mystic Hafez.

O minstrel, say good fortune is now mine. The face of my Beloved is reflected in my cup.

Raylan was a man of words, but those words always served his work. And his work was war. Not love.

Only a great poet can speak his heart in this way.

Then why don't you keep your mouth shut, Paul thought, but he couldn't stop reading.

A war reporter abroad sometimes needed someone to make it through the night, but at home, in Kabul, where Raylan had a wife and a child waiting at home?

There of all places?

Another woman.

The best I can do is quote Hafez, in the hope of giving you a glimpse of my happiness.

Helai Durani.

The joy of having met you and the joy of being allowed to love you.
Farah's mother.

Paul folded the letter, put it back in the bundle and stared at Anya for a long time – lying there, defenceless, on life support. He stroked her arms and her hands. It seemed as if they were now even warmer.

He read the second letter. Then the third and also the fourth. Strangely enough, he couldn't tell if Raylan and Helai had actually had a love affair. The exchange suggested that their relationship had been purely platonic.

In the fifth letter he came across a striking fact.

In 1978 Raylan spent three days in Moscow.

He'd given some lectures there, but the letter suggested that there must have been more going on at the time.

I've got wind of the fact that in Kabul a coup is being readied to overthrow the state, a revolution with direct links to the Kremlin. The young man who you once sought the death penalty for plays an important, but yet unclear role in this. It hasn't been possible to find any further evidence of this. I can't say anything more, for if I were to publish anything about it, I'd be placing your future and Farah's in immediate danger.

Paul reread that last sentence several times. What did Raylan mean by that?

A high, shrill beep brought him back to reality. The nurse rushed in, checked the equipment and ordered Paul to leave the room while the doctor on duty and two assistants hurried to her bedside. From behind the window in the hallway, he saw the doctor giving Anya an injection and instructing his team to prepare new infusions.

A quarter of an hour later the doctor returned to talk to him. His explanation sounded calm. Anya had contracted a fever, probably due to acute pneumonia.

'The most common complications with a coma are respiratory infections and septic shock, in which bacteria enter the bloodstream.'

'How serious is that?'

'Serious.'

'Life-threatening?'

'That risk is present.'

'There's nothing you can do about it?'

The doctor looked at him as reassuringly as possible. 'We have to wait and see how she reacts to the antibiotics, keep a close eye on even the slightest changes. Unfortunately, we can't do more than that at this moment.' The man briefly squeezed his upper arm as a sign of encouragement. 'Except for medical staff, nobody is allowed in her room for now. Perhaps you'd better go home and get some rest. We'll call you if there are any developments.'

Paul nodded and watched the doctor join his assistants again. He kept an eye on all of them until they disappeared at the end of the corridor. He wasn't really sure why he did that. Maybe out of sheer fatigue, or perhaps because he thought that as long as he had them in his sight there was hope.

He gazed through the window of Anya's room again. The other night, he'd been granted a new lease of life. But what did it matter when he had to helplessly watch from behind glass while her life ebbed away into nothingness?

He heard the echo of her passionate voice in his head. She stood on top of the table at Café Mayak and, with her wine glass spilling over in her hand, she smiled at him.

I'll never leave you, my fuckin' Yank!

4
Farah

2009

The walled gardens of Bagh-e Babur nestled against the Kuh-e Sher Darwaza mountain, to the southwest of the old city centre. Having climbed most of the terraces, Farah was now standing in the shade of a pomegranate tree. Her view of the snowy mountains was obscured by columns of black smoke rising up from several neighbourhoods. The wind carried the constant noise of sirens. She was just rearranging the orange silk scarf around her head when she heard his deep, somewhat raspy voice right behind her.

'Are you sure you weren't followed?'

She'd got into the habit of taking a detour from her hotel before getting into the car with Nehal, who'd exchanged her taxi for a jeep covered in dents and scratches. Farah turned around with a slight look of reproach.

Mason was smartly dressed, strikingly so, wearing black leather shoes, a white shirt hanging over loose-fitting grey trousers and a long, darker-grey jacket on top of it all. In this mix of traditional and modern he could easily pass for a local businessman and walk into a bank with a sleek briefcase. But with his dark eyes, square jaw and olive skin he still looked to her like some Polynesian warrior in civilian clothes. Mason took off his sunglasses and pointed to the inscription on the façade of the mosque behind her.

'Can you tell me what that says?'

Without taking her eyes off him, she translated the text.

'Only this mosque of beauty, this temple of nobility, constructed

238

for the prayer of saints and the epiphany of cherubs, was fit to stand in so venerable a sanctuary as this highway of archangels.'

His baffled frown made her smile.

'I used to come here as a girl. I know the text by heart. According to the Koran, the paradise of heaven consists of a series of terraces. The higher you go, the more beautiful the terraces.'

With the same outward calm he'd brought to the chaos following the collision at the T-junction two days ago, he now looked around him. He was probably less interested in the garden's geometry or aesthetics than he was in the chance she might have been tailed and in potential threats. While he scanned the area, she noticed his long eyelashes. It was only when she saw his lips move without hearing a word of what he was saying that she realized she'd been overtly staring at him for some time.

'Sorry?'

'. . . so we're actually standing at the highest point of an artificial heaven.' He motioned with a nod of the head. 'C'mon, we shouldn't stand around here too long.'

She followed him up the steps, through the huge wooden door with its iron fittings, past the marble wall with its many little holes beautifully filtering the light. An oasis of peace and quiet inside the earthly paradise. Together they stood in front of the final resting place of the Great Mughal Bagh-e Babur, the garden's founder. Mason's curious inspection of the tomb reminded her of the way he'd leaned over the cradle of new-born baby Farah yesterday morning. The same unexpected tenderness in his eyes.

She turned to him with a look of mild reproach. 'It was a test, wasn't it, sending me so deep into that bazaar? You wanted to see how far I was prepared to go.'

'No, that wasn't why. I didn't have much choice. Within the military's admin system, paper printouts and digital copies of files can always be traced. Everything has a digital watermark. I've been smuggling excerpts from files from the Ark into the city for some time now, making copies at various small businesses so they can't be traced back to me. But I had to get you a copy as well. I took my own dossier into that shop in the alleyway. The guy running the place seemed trustworthy. A fistful of dollars doesn't hurt either. He photocopied the whole file, which I then left behind for you. His sister kept a look-out for you. She knew what you'd be wearing. And I told her you had blue eyes.'

Mason unscrewed the cap from a plastic bottle of water and handed it to her. It was only after the first sip that she realized how thirsty she was.

'You haven't read everything yet. What I gave you is just the tip of the iceberg. One of the reports mentions a boy who was found, or whatever was left of him. Too horrific for words. The kid, it turns out, had been picked up by the police and locked in a cell a couple of days before his death. Shoplifting, a minor offence. But after a visit from "a senior official" he disappeared without a trace.'

'What's Hafami's role in this?'

She saw the tension steal over Mason's face. His jaws tightened, his nostrils widened, his pupils narrowed. It was the same look he'd had on his face when he jumped out of the jeep the other night. 'He was that senior official. There's talk of a video circulating; it's changing hands for a lot of money.'

'What kind of video?'

'It shows the boy being killed after . . .' He looked away. 'Sorry . . . I've seen a lot in my life, but some things are just too much to bear.'

The call to prayer could be heard from the towers of an adjacent mosque. For a while, they looked out across the garden in silence. When Mason spoke again, he did so in a dark tone of voice she hadn't heard from him before.

'The Pentagon is pursuing a military strategy centred around cooperation with the Mujahideen warlords. In practice that means they give those warlords, like Hafami, the freedom to maintain public order as they see fit. The most recent report published by Human Rights Watch suggests that crimes like abduction, rape, intimidation, theft, extortion and murder aren't committed despite, but mainly because of, those warlords. Men like Hafami are receiving bags and bags of US dollars because he's supposedly fighting the Taliban. But in reality, he's instructed his men to arrest mostly innocent people and pretend they're Taliban supporters. He has them tortured to force their families to pay a ransom. It means that he lets many of the real Taliban go free while netting cash from the innocent . . .'

He paused and took a few gulps from the bottle. They both looked on in surprise as a group of women, oblivious to the riots in the city, noisily installed themselves and their children on the grass for a big picnic.

'You know,' Mason resumed. 'I took an oath. I've sworn allegiance to my country and I'm willing to die for it because I believe in the values we represent. But when I see how we squander those values by entering into alliances with low-lifes like Hafami, then it's my duty to do something about it.'

'And jeopardize your career in the process.'

'So be it.'

She saw the rage in his eyes. For a moment she was lost for words. She wanted to put an arm around him, console him, tell him she admired his courage. But she held back. For a while they sat side by side in silence. A dull explosion could be heard in the distance. Mason leaned forward slightly, rested his hands with spread fingers on his forehead and temples, took a deep breath and started to tremble.

'What's wrong?'

No answer came. He was miles away. When she gently put her hand on his shoulder, he groaned softly.

'We hit an IED once,' he said as he sat up again.

'I know. Gaby told me.'

'If this pain were to hit me during an operation, it would endanger my men. I can't have that on my conscience. I have to report it. But I keep putting it off.'

'Why?'

'My mission isn't done yet. Or that's to say . . .' He turned to her with a self-conscious smile. 'Ours, I hope.'

'I'm shocked by what I read here,' she responded at once. 'It flies in the face of everything I stand for. I can't just forget this and walk away. But I don't have the backing of my own newspaper.'

'Why not?'

'They think it's too dangerous. For me.'

She hadn't been able to sway Edward with journalistic arguments. And he'd made no effort to understand her. The man who'd hired and trained her, who'd always supported her, refused to even consider it. He'd instructed her to drop whatever investigating she was doing and get on the first plane home after the reburial.

'They're probably right,' Mason said. 'Publishing these documents will make you an enemy of the US army and an adversary of the Afghan government. You won't even be able to attend your father's reburial. So I understand if you decide not to pursue this.'

She put her hand on his shoulder. 'Come with me. I want to show you something.'

Together they descended the stairs and walked towards the eastern wall. The women on the grass fell silent as they passed, but a little later their almost hushed whispers could be heard, followed soon after by high-pitched giggling. Three excited little boys chased one another in the shade of the trees.

'Look,' she said once they'd reached the highest point and had a clear view of the terraces. 'The Great Mughal loved gardens. Everywhere he conquered land, he had gardens created. From the west coast of India to the Gulf of Bengal and from Lahore in the Punjab to central India. Gardens to exclude the chaos. I grew up in a garden like that, a hundred times smaller than this one, but surrounded by the same kind of old, overgrown wall. As a child I thought I'd always be able to keep the world at bay; I didn't know any better.'

She turned to face him. 'Then an American turned up. A journalist. He never knew it, but he was the one who, many years later, gave me the courage to tear down that wall and to also become a journalist. And look at me now, here of all places, standing next to another Yank. A Marine no less. Someone I shouldn't trust in my profession. And vice versa. Yet here we are. And do you know why?'

He threw her a questioning look.

'Because from here on in we're a team, Mason. You and I. That's why.'

The old house was hidden deep inside a residential area that had spread its tentacles across Kabul's eastern mountainside like a giant octopus. The windows were boarded up. The former front door had been bricked up. A heavy wooden gate now hermetically sealed the entrance to the courtyard.

She'd banged the black metal knocker on the wood three times. A shutter slid open. Two dark eyes stared at her suspiciously.

'My name is Farah Hafez. I have an appointment with Roshan.'

The shutter closed again. A heavy lorry thundered past. The ground shook. The gate remained closed. She was about to knock again when she heard footsteps and a woman's voice on the other side. A beam slid away, the lock was undone, the hinges groaned. The gate opened just wide enough for her to quickly slip through. The guard immediately pushed it shut again and slid the beam back into place, across the middle of the gate.

Standing before her was a woman in an ankle-length black linen dress. Her face was smooth and ageless and she wore her ash-grey hair in a bun. She carried a bulky leather shoulder bag. Her black-framed glasses made her look a bit severe, an effect she immediately neutralized with an amiable smile.

'*Khosh amaden*. Welcome. My name is Mariam. I work here as a child protection officer. I'm sorry to have to receive you in this way, but we're still getting threats from men who consider these refuges to be places of depravity. According to protocol, I have to search you now. Do you mind?'

Without waiting for an answer, Mariam quickly patted her down over her clothes from top to bottom, and then gave the all-clear to the man at the gate. He was a *chaukidor*. Day and night he watched over the women and children living here.

'Shall we?'

Mariam smiled and gestured towards the driveway leading to the courtyard. Her manner inspired confidence and made Farah feel as if they were old acquaintances.

'What's a child protection officer doing in a refuge for widows?' Farah asked.

Mariam smiled. 'You know that when an Afghan woman loses her husband, she effectively loses everything. Her place in society, her future and for all intents and purposes her life. But people often forget that her children are just as much the victims in all this. Just when they're at their most vulnerable, their whole world collapses.'

Farah listened to her with mixed feelings. It might have been thirty years ago, but Mariam's words penetrated a deep sorrow.

'I understand,' she said.

'My organization, Save the Children, works with the Centre for Widow Protection,' Mariam continued. 'This refuge is the first project to support both the widows and their children. The women receive vocational training, so they can find a job, earn money and live an independent life. We also help the children. Every day a van picks them up here to take them to a special school. I check in to see how they're doing as often as I can. Idris, the son of Roshan, who you will soon meet, has been traumatized. He's going to school for a few hours a day, but we still have a long way to go.'

Her last sentence was followed by a deep sigh.

They entered a spacious inner courtyard, where three young women were slapping wet clothes against a large stone, before wringing them out and letting them dry in the sun. In a corner, a few girls were immersed in a game that she used to play a lot. It was called *mancala*. It involved capturing as many of your opponent's pebbles as possible by moving them between hollows in a rectangular board. She'd played the game with her classmates during breaks at school, with her girlfriends in the afternoon and occasionally with her mother at home in the evening. In the months following her husband's death, Helai had become increasingly absent-minded. Playing mancala with her wasn't much fun any more. Farah remembered the evening they played their last game. Tears had come to her mother's eyes and she'd grabbed her hand.

'We must flee, sweetie. Otherwise we'll all be killed.'

A cheer from one of the girls triumphantly putting down the winning pebble wrenched her from her thoughts. She followed Mariam into the building, which was made up of a number of interlinked houses. A maze of small rooms and corridors, filled with a hodgepodge of old sofas and carpets, with a few new things such as a coffee maker and a fire extinguisher mixed in. In the most beautiful room, which appeared to be reserved for receiving guests, was a Persian

244

carpet with a bird motif. Five cushions had been arranged in a circle and a small hand-crafted wooden bow was displayed on the wall alongside a leather quiver.

The slightly nervous woman who was waiting for them there couldn't have been more than thirty. She had a slim, pale face and intense, carefully made-up eyes. Her light-brown hair fell well below her shoulders. She wore a long, light-blue skirt and a roomy blouse with gold-coloured embroidery, three rings on her fingers and a copper bracelet. Roshan's appearance was highly unusual for an Afghan widow.

'Even here at the house, the other women can't get used to it,' she said after greeting Farah. 'They think that because I'm dressed like this and wear my hair down I'm happy about my husband's death. But I don't feel like mourning for the rest of my life, as I'm expected to do.'

She brushed a stubborn lock of hair from her face and pointed to the bowl of *shor nakhod* on a low side table. Farah looked at the salad of potatoes and chickpeas topped with chutney, mashed coriander and spring onion. Mariam picked up a dented thermos and poured green tea into three large glasses.

'I read Sergeant Mason Williams' report,' Farah said, as she sat down on the cushion opposite Roshan.

Roshan looked at her inquisitively. 'Are you with the government?'

'No, I'm a journalist.'

'But I already told the American sergeant everything.'

'I know, but Sergeant Williams is bound by the camp's regulations. He had to pass the report on to his superiors, and they in turn had to pass it on to the Afghan authorities.'

Roshan looked disappointed. 'I think I know what that means.'

'We can't allow for nothing to come of this. Your story must be heard. Not just in Kabul or on a national scale, but internationally.' She saw the surprise on Roshan's face. 'I write for a foreign newspaper. If your story gets published abroad it would really increase pressure on the authorities to take action against Hafami. *Khodem kar mikani?* Are you prepared to work with me?'

For some time, Roshan regarded her without a word. When a baby started crying in another room, she abruptly got up and left the room.

'Her daughter is three months old,' Mariam sighed. 'Becoming a widow is a punishment in itself, but being widowed while pregnant is several degrees worse. And if that wasn't enough, she was rejected by her in-laws when they heard that she'd filed a complaint against Hafami. In all fairness, you can understand why. There's a chance that one of the relatives might kill her son Idris . . .'

'What?'

'Whether or not it happened against his will, Idris committed *zina*: sex outside of marriage. It's a violation of family honour and punishable by death. Sergeant Williams is aware of sharia law and immediately put Roshan in touch with our organization.'

'So Roshan is here thanks to him?'

Mariam nodded and began to divide the salad across three bowls. Roshan timidly entered the room again, this time with a baby on her arm. She sat down, pulled up her blouse, and put the child to her breast. Farah waited for her to look up again. When she did, her eyes were sad. 'How can an article in a newspaper, even when it appears abroad, have any impact on a man as powerful as Hafami?'

Farah briefly glanced at Mariam, who responded with an approving nod. 'I've read a number of secret reports on Hafami. If we publish them alongside your story it could lead to charges. And this time the authorities won't be able to turn a blind eye to them. Your account could make the difference.'

Roshan looked away and gazed lovingly at her child while she breastfed. Farah wanted to do what she thought a good journalist had to do: not force anything but be of service. Roshan needed to feel safe with her. She waited quietly for Roshan's eyes to meet hers again. The woman took a deep breath.

'*Bya shoro konem*. Let's start.'

Farah felt her body relax, asked if it was okay to jot down a few things and pulled out her notebook and pen. 'To begin with, I'd love to know what kind of man Kareem was.'

Roshan displayed a bashful smile. 'I liked him straightaway when he was first introduced to me. He was really . . .' Her eyes wandered as she pondered this, and then she blushed. '. . . clumsy. But in an

246

endearing, fuzzy-feeling-in-my-stomach kind of way. Kareem was different from other men. He had sensitive eyes. And I thought that was remarkable, because he was training to be a cadet at the ANPA, the Afghan National Police Academy. He'd wanted to be an engineer, but his family was too poor to pay for tuition. Still, he was proud to be a police cadet.'

Roshan let her gaze wander again. Her tone became more subdued. 'Every morning before he went to work, I saw a different expression appear in his eyes. Harder. As though he was trying to protect himself from what he would be seeing that day. When he came home in the evening, he sometimes wasn't able to let the tenderness back in. Then I knew he'd seen things he didn't want to talk about.'

For a moment Roshan seemed to be somewhere else entirely. When she looked at Farah again, her eyes were dull. 'I don't know what the last thing he saw was. The day he died, I mean. I hope he was looking up at the sun when it happened, the mountains in the distance or perhaps a child that reminded him of Idris.'

The baby had stopped drinking.

'They say he must have been killed instantly.'

Roshan lifted her child, rested it against her shoulder and started patting the girl gently on the back. 'It was the deadliest attack since the Taliban were ousted from Kabul,' she said with a sigh. 'The explosion completely ripped off the roof of the police building. Forty policemen died and at least thirty civilians.'

The infant burped a few times. Roshan gave her the other breast. Her voice was unsteady, and its near-monotonous tone suggested that however many times she'd told her story she needed to search for the words all over again.

'They brought Kareem home on the back of a pickup. Idris ran inside and shouted that Daddy was staring up at the sky and wasn't moving. He'd been killed by flying debris and broken glass and they hadn't even bothered to close his eyes. They carried him inside and then they left again. He was lying on the table, covered in blood. I took Idris over to a neighbour. Then I tried to remove the shards from Kareem's body . . . I washed him and wrapped him in a sheet.'

She lifted the baby again and rested her against her shoulder.

'The president said the victims of the attack were *shahidan*, martyrs. The Afghan state would pay for the funeral of all the slain police cadets. There'd also be a special fund to assist the victims' families.' She shook her head in despair. 'Kareem has been dead for five months now, and I haven't heard anything since.'

She rocked the baby in her arms.

'I'm grateful to Allah for granting me this short time with the love of my life, but I can't accept what happened to Idris afterwards.'

'Can you tell me about that?'

Roshan shook her head. 'Not with her in the room. She's still far too small to understand a word, but I don't want her to ever find out what happened to her brother.'

She rose to her feet and walked out of the room with the sleeping baby in her arms. In the ensuing silence, Farah heard a dull thumping, as if someone was rhythmically hitting a wall with the palm of their hand. It was her own heartbeat. She took a few bites of her salad but noticed she was having great difficulty bringing the spoon to her mouth. Her right hand had trembled ever so slightly while taking notes.

It took a while for Roshan to return, but when she walked back into the room it was with the determined look of someone who'd decided to choke back her reluctance and to share what she'd rather forget. She sat down opposite Farah and launched into her story.

'The day my husband was buried, Hafami came to us. I felt honoured to have such a distinguished general attend the funeral of an ordinary officer. I noticed that he lavished a lot of attention on Idris, but I didn't think anything of it. He asked Idris to take good care of his mummy now that his daddy was gone. Idris said that he missed his daddy very much and that he couldn't go to cricket matches with him again. That's when Hafami offered to take Idris one time. I never thought he would, but a week later a soldier turned up at the house in a jeep. I remember . . . I'd dressed Idris in his favourite cricket shirt. He was so excited when he left . . . It was eleven in the evening when they brought him home. He was in a total daze. I didn't know what to do. I thought . . .'

She rubbed her nose and eyes. Mariam wanted to put a comforting arm around her, but Roshan discreetly pushed it away.

'I don't know what I was thinking ... I had no thoughts. I was pregnant, I'd lost my husband, I didn't want to go back to my family. When Hafami called a second time to collect Idris, I thought it would be all right ... as long as they didn't bring him back too late. And although it was earlier this time, I saw that he'd been crying. I asked him about the game, but he didn't say anything. Nothing at all.'

A long silence fell.

'How often did they take Idris?'

Roshan stared at her, but it wasn't clear whether she actually saw Farah. 'I didn't count the number of times ...'

Something in her intense gaze shifted, and her eyes seemed to fill with despair.

'Am I a bad mother?'

'No. How were you to know what was really going on. You trusted the word of a senior military figure. Anyone in your situation would have done the same.' Farah leaned forwards and reached for Roshan's hand. When their fingers touched, they clung on to each other. 'How did you find out?'

'Only after the last time. Idris was quieter than ever. I felt it was much more than just grief for his father. That he wasn't having a nice time when he went away in the soldier's jeep. I heard him cry on the toilet. He was crying with pain. He was bleeding. I took him to a doctor. He said: "I don't know how to tell you this ..."'

Roshan blankly stared past Farah, tears streaming down her cheeks. Her voice was dull and monotonous.

'He said he thought ... that ... all kinds of things had been inserted into him ...'

And so they sat for a while, in silence, their hands intertwined.

Mariam took a cardboard folder from her bag and handed it to Farah.

'I spoke to the doctor who examined Idris. This is his medical file.'

She handed the folder to Farah, who opened it against her better judgement and started reading. The business-like wording about the cause and nature of Idris's internal injuries hit her like a sledgehammer.

When she looked up after reading, the figure of Roshan in front of her was swaying as if the house were floating on waves. She tried to stand up. Mariam leaped to her feet and helped Farah to a musty out-house, where she emptied her stomach into a hole in the concrete floor.

Back in the room Roshan took her hand and asked if Farah would please forgive her for upsetting her.

'I am upset, but it's not your fault,' Farah replied. 'Quite the opposite. I'm grateful that you confided in me.'

They sat a bit closer together.

'There are a few more things I'd like to know. Is that all right?'

Roshan nodded.

'After you discovered what had happened to Idris, what did you do?'

'I was at my wits' end. I didn't know who to turn to. I couldn't go to the police. The perpetrator *was* the police. That's when I decided to go to the camp. I speak a few words of English. At the gate I said that my husband was stationed there and that I had important information about his general, and that I didn't want to tell it to an Afghan policeman or soldier, but only to an American. Mason was standing at the gate and asked what was going on. At first I thought he was an Afghan, because he has the same brown skin as us. But he was wearing an American uniform.' Roshan gave her a timid smile.

'I think,' Mariam said, 'you were wise not go to the police. If, as a woman, you have no evidence of rape but still press charges, you can be accused of *zina*, or adultery. If you'd gone to the police to report it, there's a good chance that Idris would have been found guilty.'

'I have a very important question,' Farah said, 'and I want you to think about your answer carefully. I can publish this story under a different name. But the people in Hafami's circles will know it was you. And there may be other media that want to interview you. They'll need to know your identity. Are you prepared to let me to use your real name?'

'I've already given it some thought. Like I did when I went to the camp. I don't care what happens to me, but Idris has his whole life ahead of him. It's all or nothing. I'd be a coward if I didn't reveal my identity.'

'Is Idris here?' Farah asked. 'I'd like to see him.'

Roshan nodded. They got up. Farah pointed to the small bow and arrow quiver on the wall. 'Can I borrow these?'

Idris was sitting on a stack of pallets piled up against a mulberry tree in the small garden at the back of the courtyard. He was staring at something in the sky, but whatever it was it was invisible to anyone but the boy.

'This is Farah,' Roshan told him. 'She's going to help us.'

He looked at her and she saw that his eyes had the same vacant expression as Sekandar's when she'd last seen him in the Netherlands. And with the same inward-looking gaze he asked, 'Can you help my daddy come back, ma'am?'

Farah leaned towards him. 'I can't make your daddy return, Idris. Nobody can do that. But I can make sure that the men who took you are punished.'

He looked at her in disbelief for a while. 'How?'

She sat beside him and put down the bow and quiver. 'Do you know the fairy tale of the eagle and Prince Badan?'

When he shook his head, Farah started telling him the story.

'A long, long time ago there was a powerful emperor who lived in a large castle with an enormous garden. He had one son and his name was Badan. He was a very brave little fellow, just like you. One day the emperor was walking around the garden with Badan when suddenly an eagle fell from the sky and dropped at their feet. Writhing around its neck was a poisonous snake. It was hissing and about to lunge at them, but Badan took his bow and shot an arrow straight into the viper's head, which then fell dead to the ground. The eagle spread its wings and said to Badan, "You saved my life and in return I will one day save yours." And with a grateful screech he disappeared into the clouds.'

She gently stroked his shoulder. He moved a bit closer to her.

'Years passed, and Prince Badan became emperor. One day enemy forces invaded the country. Thousands of soldiers stormed the palace. Badan's army was much smaller, but he refused to surrender. Armed with his bow and arrow, he rode out at the head of hundreds of horsemen towards their opponents when he heard a terrible screeching above. The sky filled with an army of eagles. And at the head of it flew the eagle he'd once saved from the snake. Now he came to Badan's rescue and together they defeated the enemy.'

She looked at him and saw that he was impressed by the story. 'Do you want to be just as brave as Prince Badan?'

Idris nodded.

She rose to her feet and picked up the longbow. 'Come, I'll teach you how to shoot like he did.'

She positioned him in front of her, with his feet apart, and showed him how to hold the bow in a resting position. Then she placed an arrow on the string. She got him to hook the fingers of his right hand around the bow's string in such a way that it nestled exactly in the first groove of his middle digit. Then she turned his torso and the bow towards the tree in front of them.

'We aim for the snake. The snake has disguised itself as a man. He's standing right in front of us. It's the man who did bad things to you.'

Idris grew pale and started trembling.

'You don't have to be scared now. I'm here with you. I'm helping you. I'm your eagle.' Standing behind him, she raised his left arm, with which he held the bow, to shoulder height and got him to draw the string in a straight horizontal line. She kept both his shoulders as low as possible. The bowstring touched the middle of his nose and chin. Bow hand, draw hand and elbow formed one straight line.

'Keep breathing, easy now, yes that's it. Pull back the bowstring and aim for the man.' She felt the fear in the slender boy's body slowly turn to quiet anger. 'Aim for his head. Between his eyes. You're going to make him disappear from your life for ever.'

The little boy's rage and her own merged in the fluid motion with which they released the arrow together. It flew in the direction of the imaginary man standing before them.

Farah's lips were dry. Whenever she swallowed it felt as if her throat was filled with sand. Her face was flushed. Since they'd driven away from the refuge, she hadn't said a single word to Nehal. She had a sense that if she were to open her mouth one long scream would roll out. A scream without end.

Nehal slammed on the brakes. The junction in front of them was overrun with men. Hundreds of clenched fists were raised in the air. An American flag waved above burning car tyres. Fifty-two stars became smouldering holes, after which the textile burst into a myriad of flaming particles. The poisonous stench of burning rubber crept into the jeep. Sirens swelled from afar. An army helicopter whirred right above their heads.

With a firm tug at the wheel, Nehal extracted the car from the pandemonium and veered into a dusty maze of narrow streets. With every corner they turned, they appeared to be penetrating deeper into an oppressive labyrinth. Farah thought of the decisions she'd made in the past few days, which now drew her deeper and deeper into a web from which she could barely free herself. She was wrenched from that thought when Nehal swerved and just managed to avoid a completely veiled woman who crossed the street with her child by the hand. Immediately afterwards, she turned into one of thousands of bumpy side streets and ended up on the ring road, where they careened past crowded buses, clapped-out taxis and gleaming white SUVs, until she reached a junction and took a road up one of the foothills of the Hindu Kush.

Farah uttered a sigh of relief. As the city receded below them, they looked out over an endless plain of rust-brown roofs with the late afternoon sun reflected in the windows of some glass office towers.

On a plateau some two hundred metres above the city, Nehal switched off the engine. Behind a fence of cut-up mesh Farah saw the desolate contours of an immense, empty swimming pool. Bibi Mahro Hill Pool.

The Russians had built it thirty years ago, thinking it would lend Kabul Olympic allure, but it had since crumbled into an empty pit of cracking concrete slabs. A tall, peeling diving platform rose up into the ash-grey sky like a wagging finger. The pool's once-blue walls had faded and were riddled with bullet holes.

A handful of boys were kicking a football against the pool's sloping interior. All of them sported the worn-out shoes, frayed trousers and cheeky manner typical of street urchins. Three skateboarders whizzed dangerously close to the edges of the empty pool.

Nehal walked over to the diving platform and nimbly climbed the narrow metal stairs, all the way up to the highest level, until the foot-balling boys some fifteen metres below were reduced to tiny, scampering figures. Disorientated and slightly dizzy, Farah stepped on to the narrow concrete platform. The silence pounded her eardrums. She held her breath. For a moment it looked as if Nehal might walk off. But right at the edge, she turned around and sat down cross-legged with her back to the pool. With an almost ritualistic calm, she pulled a thermos flask out of her bag, unscrewed the cap, poured tea, held it up and offered it to Farah, who sat down on her knees in front of her and took the cup.

Below them the boys had stopped playing football. At the outer edge, where the hill plateau sloped steeply into the abyss, the three skateboarders were standing as still as statues. With one hand just above their brows, shielding their eyes from the sun, they peered at the two women high above them.

'I come here regularly,' Nehal said. 'Time stands still for me up here.'

The city was shrouded in a grimy smog of dust and exhaust fumes. In places it was mixed with black smoke from burning car tyres. Army helicopters in the distance cut through the haze.

Nehal started humming. Farah recognized the melody. It was an old battle song.

This is our home, the house of lions and tigers. This is the land of high mountains and green views and rivers.

'Who taught you that song?'

'My mother. She's the reason behind my visits here. She was four-teen when her parents told her she was engaged. She didn't get to see her husband until the wedding party. He was more than twenty years older. She had a son before she had me. My father told her to give me up. Having a girl was a disgrace.'

'Then what?'

'She fled to Kabul. Taking me and my brother with her. How she survived with two young children in those first few years, I don't know. When Abdullah was ten, he started taking care of us. Neither he nor my mother ever locked me up in the house, like most men do to their wives, daughters and sisters. I was allowed out, to run around and play with Abdullah and his friends. Just like a boy, really. I looked like a boy too. My mother thought that was fine. At least it gives you freedom, she said. My mother was a very beautiful woman. I'd see her unveiled at home, see her body when she washed. I didn't look like her. I was the spitting image of my father, the man she hated. But she never let on. She was always kind to me. Some evenings she'd lock herself in the bedroom with me, and then she'd take out an illicit hand-mirror and do my make-up while singing the song of the lions and the tigers for me. And then I'd sing along.'

'Why do you come here to reminisce about your mother?'

Nehal looked away. One by one, the boys down below slinked off, leaving the pool looking even more deserted.

'When the Taliban came to power, women were confined to their homes. Girls were no longer allowed to go to school. My mother and I had to stay indoors. Abdullah went out every day to do odd jobs. One day he came down with such a high fever that we were afraid he might die. In her desperation, my mother went out into the street to find him a doctor. The Taliban were roaming the city in small Toyota pickups to whip men who didn't have the right beard length, to slap the faces of people who dared to smile and to arrest women who didn't completely cover up in a burqa and then stone them afterwards.'

She paused to take a breath and looked at Farah; her eyes were hollow and vacant.

'When they stopped my mother, she supposedly cried hysterically for a doctor. They shut her up and brought her here, to this very spot where you and I are sitting now. Lorries used to come here, loaded with political opponents, as well as homosexuals and intellectuals. All those who were branded apostates. They were blindfolded and forced to stand here. The executioner would recite verses from the Koran before pushing them off the edge. My mother had shown a lack of respect by shouting for a doctor. Women weren't entitled to medical assistance. She refused the blindfold and, if the stories are to be believed, stepped off the platform while the Koran was still being read. She didn't make a sound as she fell.'

Nehal sighed and stared straight ahead without a word. 'As a child

I had a notebook and a few colouring pencils. I hid them behind a brick in my room. At night I'd remove the pencils and draw by the light of a candle, sketching what life would be like once the men with the beards were gone. I made drawings of what my mother would look like when she came back. I was reminded of those old drawings when I glanced at you through my rear-view mirror. The same head-strong expression, the same determination.'

They could hear rumbling in the distance. The sky above the mountain ridges had turned pitch black. A cold wind swept down along the mountain sides.

'You know, *hamshera*, whatever happened to you and whatever will happen to you in the future: always refuse to spend your life in fear. No matter how savage our times may be, lions and tigers won't be dominated. We can only live fully if we fight, each and every day. You're a fighter, just like my mother. I bet she thinks it's an honour for me to be here with you.'

The dark clouds drifted closer. The rumbling in the distance sounded more ominous now. They looked in the direction from which black smoke continued to rise.

'The best remedy for all this misery,' Nehal said. 'A tidal wave.'

She firmly rescrewed the cap on to the thermos flask, put it back in her bag, held out her hand and looked questioningly at Farah, who rose and pulled Nehal to her feet.

5
Raylan

1975

For almost a hundred years Kabul had been the capital of emirs and kings. They literally built their power and wealth into a majestic realm: the Arg-e-Shahi, Citadel of the King. The walled stronghold in the northeast of Kabul had in less than a century become a city within a city. It included an array of palaces, rooms for the Royal Court, barracks, an armoury and even a prison. Since Prince Daoud Khan had banished his uncle, King Zahir Shah, two years earlier after a nonviolent coup and declared the country a constitutional republic, for the first time in Afghanistan's history a president resided in the citadel.

From the back seat of a shiny government vehicle, Raylan watched the officer in the guard booth at the main gate thoroughly checking whether the identity cards of the passengers matched the names on the list of registered guests. In Isobel's case it was no more than a formality. As the artist behind the presidential portraits, which were to be unveiled this afternoon, she had already visited the Arg countless times before. Raylan and the young Paul were visiting for the first time, hence the delay.

Because of a large anti-government demonstration they had already been forced to take a detour through the city. Raylan had no patience for this kind of red tape. He wanted to get out of the car to give the officer a piece of his mind, when the man unexpectedly came out of the guard booth and returned their documents with an apologetic smile.

As the car pulled away the officer leaned towards the back seat and gave a military greeting to little Paul, who enthusiastically returned the salute. It was utterly thrilling for the boy to be a guest today in what he himself called 'the castle'. He looked with wide eyes at the stately round palace that appeared before them as soon as they drove under the entrance gate into the citadel grounds.

'The Kuti Baghcha,' Isobel said. 'The very first palace ever built here. With windows facing in all directions. And there' – she pointed to a slender minaret – 'is the mosque. With a roof made of wood from the ancient forests of Paktia.'

'And that?' Paul asked excitedly, as they drove past an impressive building with arched windows.

'The royal library,' Isobel replied. 'It's filled with books and manuscripts hundreds of years old.'

In a flash Raylan saw the charred remnants of books, lying on the scorched grass next to the library building riddled with bullets in the Imperial Citadel of Hué. He remembered that little boy on his knees brushing the earth away from the dead faces in the shallow mass grave. The countless associations with a war that still raged in his head.

They drove into the northwest section of the Arg-e-Shahi, where he could already see the contours of the presidential palace when Isobel asked the driver to stop. 'We'll walk the last stretch,' she said resolutely, and then they all got out.

In this walled part of the city, at an altitude of almost two thousand metres surrounded by barren mountains, Raylan was surprised by what he saw: a park filled with flowerbeds of daisies, fragrant roses from yellow to vermilion red and *sinjid* trees laden with the most delicious jujube berries. Under the shade of plane and pomegranate trees, he and Isobel followed Paul, who ran along the path in front of them towards a murmuring fountain.

Halfway, Isobel hesitated and turned towards him. 'I wanted you to see this place, Ray. It meant a lot to me when I discovered it. What does it remind you of?'

Raylan looked around, perplexed by her question.

'I'll tell you,' she continued. 'The courtyard of Hotel Serena, the night you took me to the swimming pool there.'

He felt his stomach knot up because he knew he'd disappointed her by not knowing the answer. He could hear it in the sound of her voice.

'I didn't bring you here to see some bigshot pull a sheet away from my painting and then say all kinds of interesting-sounding nonsense about it, because I don't really give a damn about any of that. I wanted to show you this place because it's where I've spent a lot of time thinking about what has changed between us in the last seven years . . .'

'Sweetheart, I . . .'

'No, I want you to listen to what I've got to say, Ray. I've always believed in you, and wanted to help you in any way I could. I've even tolerated another woman in our marriage, because I kept hoping it might help you deal with your demons and that would protect our marriage. Even someone blind can see you're being eaten up from inside by that bloody war. But all this time I believed that when it was all finally over in Vietnam, everything would change, that you would change. Stupid, naive me. The war there may be over, but the war inside you rages on.'

'But . . . what we talked about yesterday, about . . .'

'That it's good to give the dead a voice, to tell the world their story?'

'Have you suddenly changed your mind?'

'No, I still believe in that. It's good to fight for the truth . . .'

He saw tears in her eyes.

'But . . . ?'

'I now want you to fight for us too.'

She turned her face away for a moment, wiped her hand over her eyelids and then looked at him with the same determination as before.

'I want you to fight for Paul. He needs his father. And to fight for me. Because I need the man I fell for at first sight . . . Look at me, Ray. You're the love of my life. But I no longer want a man to flit in and out of our lives while he's turning into a shadow of the person I once knew. I'll always care for you, but if you think I will be a momentary safe haven for you, you're wrong. I deserve more than that, and so does Paul. Go off to war again if you can't resist, but then don't you dare come back to us. Choose the other woman if you so desire, but then don't come home. Choose us, stay with us, share our lives. But for good.'

'Mummy, Daddy!'

Speechless, Raylan looked at little Paul, who was standing at the edge of the fountain, overjoyed and half soaked. The boy held out his arms to them as Raylan caught a glimpse of soldiers in Presidential Guard uniforms approaching from behind. Raylan ran towards Paul, grabbed him and firmly pressed his wriggling body against his chest. Only then did he see a breathless Parwaiz Ahmad among the guards, who wiped the sweat from his forehead with a handkerchief.

'Finally, finally,' Parwaiz sighed. 'We heard you'd left the car. Is everything all right?'

'But of course, *aghaye mehraban*, dear sir,' Isobel replied before Raylan could utter a word. With a relaxed smile she gave him two kisses.

'I'm sorry,' Parwaiz said. 'But I'm the one responsible for organizing all of this.'

'Do you live here too?' Paul asked innocently.

'No, I ...' The tension on Parwaiz's face seemed to fade as he looked at Paul. 'The president lives here with his whole family.'

'Is he coming to the party?' Paul asked. 'The president?'

'Certainly,' Parwaiz said with a tender smile. 'He's the most important guest. Do you know what you're going to say to him?'

'*Ma'ham yak wakhte eto khane mekhayam*,' Paul said grinning. 'I also want a house like this later.'

Smiling, Parwaiz took Paul by the hand, and while giving the boy some advice in etiquette, he led them up the wide palace steps into the marble hallway, through an endless corridor where portraits of all the kings and emirs hung, until they arrived in the large reception hall. It was filled with men in dress suits, tuxedos and uniforms. Most of them were accompanied by their wives, all dressed in elegant evening gowns.

The Presidential Guard cleared the way to a podium on which a lectern stood, as well as three paintings draped in red velvet. Isobel received incredulous looks because of her bohemian appearance, her shimmering eyeshadow and crimson lipstick. With every movement, her ankle-length beige dress, made of semi-transparent layers of crepe, fluttered around her body like a fairy's gossamer gown.

Tender glances, especially from the women, were bestowed on the little boy next to her, with his long blonde hair and shirt with its fluttering swan design. The looks of disapproval were reserved for Raylan, who had shaved for the occasion, but with his messy hair, haggard look and boots under his jeans, had largely ignored the strict dress code. The only concession he'd made was to wear a white shirt that Isobel had purchased for him, especially for this occasion.

But it wasn't the suspicious eyes glaring at him that made him freeze in his tracks. It was the screaming in his head, coming from the crowd in front of the gate at the American embassy in Saigon. He felt the weight of Hoang's little daughter on his shoulders again. For a moment he couldn't breathe. He turned around and found himself standing face to face with that Vietnamese woman in tears, trying to force her child into his arms. He wanted to push her away, when he realized in the nick of time that it was a waiter offering him a drink from a full tray. Raylan hoped it was alcohol and grabbed a glass, when he recognized with a start the man walking straight towards him with an amused look on his face.

Aadel Gailani had put on weight but still moved with elegant grace. His hairline had receded, and there was a hint of grey around his temples. His handshake, however, was firm. Just like at their last meeting, seven years ago, he gave Raylan an amicable pat on the shoulder. 'Who would have thought that a Dutch woman, whom you once considered missing, would ever paint the state portrait of the first Afghan president?'

'*Encounters are like road markers to a future that has long been mapped out.* Those were your words then,' Raylan replied.

'The will of Allah. Kismet. I remember it like yesterday. Already seven years ago, almost to the day.'

'In the meantime the Supreme Being has taken good care of your career. From the country's attorney general to interior affairs minister. Congratulations. I hear you have your office here at the palace?'

'Correct. A way to demonstrate my loyalty to the president.'

A murmur went through the crowd, and they both looked in the direction of the lectern, where there was some commotion. While Isobel was busy shaking hands with a number of high-ranking guests, Paul had climbed on to the stage with the idea of already removing the cloth covering the portraits.

'My son,' Raylan said. 'Just as impulsive and impatient as his father.'

'What's his name?'

'Paul. I'd have called him John, but my wife won that battle, so Paul it was, her favourite Beatle.'

'I take it you're very proud of her.'

'I am.'

'It must have been hard being separated from her for such long periods when you were in Vietnam.'

Raylan wondered where Gailani was going with this and answered, 'More than you can imagine.'

'But you're still going strong. What's your secret?'

'I don't have a secret.'

Gailani gave him an enigmatic smile. 'Come, come, Chapelle. Every man has his secrets.'

Impossible, Raylan thought. This fellow couldn't possibly know what's going on. 'May I ask you a question?' he said to change the subject. 'Today of all days, the People's Democratic Party has organized a protest march against your president. All the left-wing politicians he'd included in his government as a thank you for their support during the coup two years ago he has now fired and replaced with conservative ministers. What possessed him to do such a thing?'

'It was a deliberate decision,' Gailani calmly said. 'The communists let their delusions get the best of them. They were using the president as a springboard to eventually seizing power themselves. By firing them, the president has demonstrated who's really in charge of the country. But your question implies that you doubt his decision.'

'I think Daoud has made a crucial mistake. By pushing aside the communists like this, it's suddenly abundantly clear he only used them to gain power himself. The harmful side effect of this is that he alienates himself from an important demographic: the young. And they represent the future of Afghanistan.'

'I remember when we first met, I tried to impress on you that in a society such as ours that has little experience with democratic values, radicalization quickly occurs, both on the left and the right. We must nip that radicalization in the bud even if it's the young people. Take, for example, the recent uprising in Panjshir Province. A handful of rebels robbed a local bank in the name of Allah and proclaimed an Islamic Republic in the market square. Our rapid intervention sent them scurrying into the mountains like dogs with their tails between their legs.'

'Don't underestimate the strength of extremists,' Raylan said. 'You can banish naive revolutionaries like Askan Vaziri, set legally elected communist ministers aside or drive young Muslim fanatics into the mountains, but you haven't won the battle yet. On the contrary. Because with every powerful punch you deliver, you can expect a much stronger counter-reaction. In Vietnam I saw how far people were willing to go to fight oppression. They were willing to die if necessary. That's a strength no army can match, no matter how powerful. In Vietnam we had all the military resources, capabilities and manpower. It was hubris, the belief that we were invincible, that eventually cost us the war. Your president is now in jeopardy of making a similar mistake.'

At that moment three dull thumps sounded in quick succession. Even before Raylan could acknowledge his reflex to take cover, he saw what was going on. A man in a dark-grey suit tapped the microphone at the lectern to check if it was on. 'Ladies and gentlemen. Your attention, please. For the president and his wife!'

Two uniformed sentries opened the double doors, and he entered the great hall, with his wife on his arm. Daoud Khan was a serious-looking man, sophisticated and politely distant. He graciously greeted Isobel, and he shook Paul's hand, who whispered something to him that made him smile. Shortly afterwards Raylan saw Parwaiz coming towards him together with Paul.

'Your Excellency,' Parwaiz said, greeting Gailani, and then he turned to Raylan. 'I believe your son wishes to go to a certain private location. Would you care to accompany us for a moment?'

'Do you have to pee, boy?' Raylan asked as they exited the hall.

'No,' Paul said confused, 'but this nice man said he'd show me something special if I came along and didn't say anything.'

'I'm sorry,' Parwaiz said. 'I needed a reason to talk to you in private for a few minutes. The speeches are exceptionally long, and I promise that you will be back in time for the unveiling.'

They turned a corner. Raylan saw a courtyard garden surrounded by an arched walkway. In the middle of the garden stood a girl with long black hair. Swirling around her were butterflies in all sorts of colours but she seemed to be completely absorbed in a series of slow movements, which reminded him of Asian martial arts.

'What's that girl doing?' he heard Paul ask.

Raylan wanted to answer, but stopped when he saw the woman waiting for them in the shadows.

The sky above the courtyard of the presidential palace was windless and bright blue. The blinding sunlight glided over the brick arches of the arcade that surrounded it. Raylan had to squint so he could see the dark-haired girl moving gracefully and slowly amidst the stifling heat in the garden.

There was light everywhere. And that light brought the butterflies in the garden to life. With their wings spread wide, they sat on the lavender plants, the orpine and holy rope soaking up as much sun as possible. As soon as they were warm enough they flew into the air, off to suck nectar – with their long rolling tongues – from the deep purple flowers of the summer lilacs or to flutter their colourful wings around the girl, who was focused on her slow choreography.

Parwaiz bowed to Paul. 'This is what I wanted to show you,' he said.

'The butterflies?'

'The girl. Do you want to know what she's doing?'

'She's fighting ghosts.'

The answer seemed to make Parwaiz more nervous than he already was. He glanced in the direction of Helai, who was standing nearby, calmly waiting, and then quickly returned to Paul again. 'Do you want to be invincible?'

The boy nodded.

'Then go to her. She'll teach you.'

Paul looked at Raylan. 'Go ahead . . . I'll wait for you here.'

The boy walked along the gravel path into the middle of the garden. Parwaiz breathed a sigh of relief, quickly nodded in Helai's direction to indicate that his task was done and hurried away.

Meanwhile Paul stopped directly in front of the girl, which compelled her to stop moving. 'Your eyes are blue too,' Raylan overheard his son saying. He couldn't help but smile at the upfront way Paul said this. An Afghan girl with sea-blue eyes doing a kind of traditional fighting dance in the butterfly garden of the presidential palace in Kabul, imagining she's some mini-avenging angel – that's pretty impressive when you're a six-year-old boy. Your only choice is to act as tough as you can.

'This was all my idea.'

Raylan turned around. Helai had walked up to him. There was an undefined look on her face, a hint of melancholy. 'I wanted them to meet once, Paul and Farah.'

Raylan wanted to ask why, but was interrupted by a cry from the girl in the garden.

'Nako! Don't do that!'

They watched Farah try to stop Paul from plucking a blue butterfly from the sky.

'She's beautiful, just like her mother.'

'Thank you.'

'Her eyes are striking . . . for an Afghan girl . . .'

'Do you find that surprising with a mother who has two different coloured irises?' The smile with which Helai said this couldn't completely camouflage the tension on her face. 'My family is originally from Bactria, way up north. Blue-eyed children are still born every now and then. A throwback to the time when soldiers from Alexander the Great's legion mixed with the local population.'

A silk scarf with a floral motif was wrapped around her head, and she wore a floor-length golden-brown dress with gracefully flared long sleeves. Although the dress completely covered her body, the form-fitting cut and elegantly draped fabric accentuated her curves.

He wanted to touch her, not out of desire, but out of embarrassment for what he'd done to her in the hotel room, and he searched for words to explain himself, but none came. His hand hung helplessly in the air in front of her.

'I'm glad you came,' she said softly.

'I thought you were . . . I mean . . . I just . . .'

'I know what you're trying to say and I also know you can't say it.'

'I don't have the words . . .'

'There's no need . . .'

With a resigned smile she looked away from him in the direction of the girl, who was posing the way models do in fashion magazines, while the butterflies swirled around her. 'They're not attracted to you, the butterflies,' he heard her say to Paul. 'Because you frighten them with your dark soul.'

He felt Helai's cool hand on his upper arm.

'The sun is too warm. Come.'

She led him to a shaded alcove from where they could see the two children in the butterfly garden. Raylan wanted to light a cigarette to help his nerves, but as soon as he saw her disapproving look, he put his packet of Lucky Strikes back in his pocket.

'I once told you how I felt the first time I saw you . . .', she said.

Her eyes were sad, and for a moment it was as if time stood still and the past came to life in sharp, fleeting images. Again he entered the courtroom, where he saw her standing in front of him. An unapproachable woman in lawyer's robes, with eyes that drove him crazy and a beauty that made his heart skip a beat. Now, looking back, he realized what he should have known then: she would always be a stranger to him, and that was precisely the reason he would continue to long for her.

'It's bizarre and somehow it's not,' she continued. As soon as I saw you, with your fierce gaze and your tough-guy reputation, I got the feeling you were going to play an important role in my life. Something in me knew, as if it were predestined . . .'

He remembered when their eyes first met in the courtroom, how she was at a loss for words. The trembling of her hand as she brought a glass of water to her mouth.

'Coincidence,' he said, 'doesn't exist in your faith.'

He wished he could literally return to the moment of that first meeting, so he could find what seemed to have vanished now that they were facing each other here. Going back in time as a last-ditch attempt to fix his mistakes. With the knowledge he now had, he could keep her at a distance from the start, so that he'd protect her from what he'd finally afflicted on her. All these thoughts were spinning through his head as he watched the girl, who in a cloud of butterflies very slowly and deliberately showed a sequence of moves to Paul, who self-consciously looked on.

'We can't defy our destiny,' he heard Helai say. 'Our lives go the way they do. We can't blame ourselves for the way things went. You and I . . . We did our best.'

It was as if his throat was slowly being squeezed closed. He frantically searched for the right words, which he struggled to arrange into a question.

'You said it wasn't all for nothing. What did you mean?'

In the garden Farah suddenly got a bit more aggressive and smacked Paul on his cheek.

'Attack me,' she cried. 'Now!'

Raylan saw the boy ball his fists and start punching her. She fought off his first blow with her left arm. She blocked his second blow and then immediately got him in an armlock to stop him from moving. Paul tried in vain to wriggle loose. Raylan wanted go over to the two of them to intervene, but Helai stopped him. The girl loosened her grip, which allowed Paul to free himself. Oddly enough the boy didn't get angry with her. He basically seemed startled by her extraordinary strength.

'She learned all that from Aadel,' Helai said. 'Every morning they practise for half an hour under the apple tree in our garden. They have formed a curious alliance, although they seem to have nothing in common. The distance is painfully obvious . . . not just between father and daughter.'

'I hope there's some happiness in your marriage.'

She smiled wistfully. 'Not in the marriage. But don't underestimate a mother's love for her child.'

She looked into the garden, where Farah was busy explaining to Paul how she'd blocked his attack.

'Do you know what she can do like no other? Ask difficult questions: "Where are we from? Why did Allah make us? And if He created me, did He also create the apple tree? The world, the universe? And how?"'

Helai smiled endearingly, unconsciously crossing her arms, as if her heart were an invisible treasure she was trying to protect. 'One day I saw her sitting there, staring with that deep, dark look she sometimes gets, and I asked her what was going on. She looked at me and said, "I'm trying to imagine what everything would look like if it lasted for ever."' Helai shook her head and looked at Raylan melancholically. 'You have a six-year-old daughter and she's trying to fathom eternity . . .'

Meanwhile, Farah challenged Paul for a second time to attack her.

'Aadel wanted a son,' Helai continued. 'But we weren't blessed with a second child. He says it's my fault . . .'

Her smile revealed an exceptional talent for irony. 'It's remarkable how much she resembles her father,' she then said staring at Raylan. 'A passionate temperament, always wanting to climb as high up in trees as possible, constantly running away from home, too curious for her own good, distrustful, averse to authority, combative, critical and allergic to lies.'

She lovingly looked at Farah, who had Paul in an armlock again.

'You know, other girls her age keep a diary. She doesn't. She's got a scrapbook, full of articles she clips out of newspapers. She jots down all kinds of information. I wouldn't be surprised if she becomes a journalist later, just like her father.'

Her voice sounded both soft and intense, and that's the way she looked at him.

'She's yours, Ray. Farah is our child.'

Despite the heat, a cold shiver shot down his back. And instead of words that might express disbelief, surprise or even the inability to grasp what she had just told him, only a sigh came out of his mouth.

'I can't prove it,' she calmly continued, 'but I just know. A woman knows something like this. Look at her, Ray. She's got your eyes. She's the reason I've always come back to you, no matter how hard you've made it for me.'

Confused, he stared at the girl in the garden, who patiently instructed Paul how to respond once she attacked him again.

'I can feel free when I'm with you,' Helai said. 'But I also know that I'll never know true freedom. I was only a port-of-call you passed through every time you returned from the hell of war, making it easier to go home to your wife and your son.'

Farah approached Paul menacingly.

'Neither of us wants our marriages to end in divorce,' Helai said. 'We know only too well why and whom we married. I don't want to raise my daughter in poverty and shame, but to give her all the opportunities life has to offer. Maybe someday she'll truly be free.'

With a comforting gesture, Helai rustled Raylan's hair. She looked into the garden, where Paul, to his own amazement, had managed to get Farah in an armlock. The two were standing so close together it looked like they were embracing.

'You'll keep going out into the world, always chasing the truth . . . That little girl there in the garden, that's my world, my truth.'

Paul slowly let go of Farah, faced her and bowed to her in the traditional way.

'You're passionate about being a journalist, have a great sense of justice,' Helai continued. 'Yet, you cling to the dead so tightly . . . you can barely see the living. Our last time in the hotel room . . . The worst thing wasn't that you lost control of yourself, but that I saw death in your eyes. You overwhelmed me with death.'

Farah silently returned Paul's greeting while the butterflies with their shimmering wings hovered around her.

'You're the love of my life, and the father of my child,' Helai said. 'But I can't see you any more. It hurts too much.'

The distant sound of applause echoed through the corridors from the great hall.

'You must go now,' she said. 'Isobel is about to make her speech.'

Her eyes were clouded in tears, and he leaned forwards, but when Helai retreated he took her hand and kissed it as softly and tenderly as he could.

As he walked back towards the ceremony with Paul, he thought about how much he'd like to explain to his son that he'd just had a mock fight with a girl who was his half-sister, but he knew that he would never do that.

'Go on ahead,' he said to Paul, and as the boy ran to the hall, Raylan turned to take one last look at the girl with the blue eyes and jet-black hair who silently watched him walk away.

6
Farah

2009

She surveyed her surroundings. She shouldn't stand around here too long, because women and news media were a deadly combination. The guard in front of *The Afghan Press* building, which was surrounded by large coils of razor wire, had slung his automatic weapon over his shoulder and was checking her passport while he talked to someone inside via his radio.

She tried getting his attention. 'Can't I just go through?'

'Stay where you are.'

Before she'd set off for Afghanistan, she and Edward had talked about what he should do in the event she was abducted or killed. It was the first time they'd taken such measures. What questions he might ask to confirm she was still alive if he had to negotiate a ransom. She'd never seen him look more miserable than when she'd placed the proof-of-life list of questions only she knew the answers to on his desk.

Never thought it would come to this, Hafez.

She pricked up her ears. Among the traffic chaos behind her, she picked out the deep, dull roar of a diesel engine. She turned around. A black Cherokee Trailhawk with tinted windows slowed as it approached.

'Ms Hafez?'

She looked into the pretty face of a young woman with curly black hair and almond-shaped eyes.

'My name is Halima. I've been instructed to search you.' She pointed to the guard. 'He's not allowed to do that.'

'No problem, go ahead.'

The young woman stood there looking flustered.

'Have you done this before, Halima?'

'To be honest, no.'

Farah stood with her legs slightly apart, lifted her arms out to the side and said: 'Just pat me down with your palms.'

Halima's hands moved uneasily over her body. She was so nervous she even giggled as she stroked Farah's thighs. With a flushed face she then straightened up again and looked at the guard, who irritably motioned for both of them to go ahead.

In the doorway, Farah turned one more time. The black Cherokee was now right in front of the building. She waited for someone to get out, but the doors remained closed. She memorized the registration number. Then came the misgivings, the vague premonitions, the doubts as to whether it had been wise to come here. But after their call Edward had left her with no other choice; she had to get her article about Hafami published somewhere else. She had no professional network other than the *AND* she could call on. The copy of *The Afghan Press* she'd bought yesterday had sparked this idea.

Unlike most other newspapers in Kabul that relied on financial backing, *The Afghan Press* was a large independent newspaper that not only published in English but also dared to be critical of the current government. It struck her as an ideal platform. After hearing her name, the managing editor she'd spoken to on the phone immediately agreed to meet.

She walked over to Halima, who was nervously waiting for her. 'Aside from you and Ferozi, who else knows about my visit?'

'Nobody. I'm the only one Mr Ferozi confided in. Your articles about that Russian oligarch inspired us all. It's not often that an Afghan journalist makes the front pages of international newspapers. It's an honour to welcome you here, and to frisk you.'

'That wasn't frisking, Halima. That was caressing.'

The young Afghan woman's timid smile was disarming.

At the end of the corridor she knocked on a door. Without waiting for an answer, she swung it open.

The organized chaos of Ferozi's workspace reminded her of

Edward's office in the old *AND* headquarters. Shelves laden with stacks of files, a desk buried under paperwork and an outdated computer under a modular ceiling close to collapse.

Managing editor Zahoruddin Ferozi got up from behind his desk. He was tall and wiry. Although he tried to be jovial, she also sensed a certain apprehension in him.

He nodded to Halima, who then closed the door.

'She's one of my most talented photojournalists. Can you imagine, thirteen and she received a public flogging by the Taliban for not wearing a burqa. If anyone proves that cruelty is a motivator, it's her. She knows no fear and has been producing quality work for many years. Halima could be your younger sister.'

His grin was almost as broad as the arm gesture towards the two fake leather chairs in front of his desk. 'We're fellow journalists. *Ma famil astem*. We're like family. Have a seat.'

She sat down.

'As Halima probably told you, we've read all your articles about Valentin Lavrov with great interest. Your call came as a complete surprise. You mentioned a serious issue that you wanted to discuss in private. What can I do for you?'

'I have a big story and I'd like to work on it with you.'

'Why not publish in the *AND*? You work for them, right?'

'It's a domestic matter.'

'Can you be more specific?'

As ever, her right hand automatically flitted over her head. Running her fingers through her curls had always been the most soothing thing she could think of, especially at moments when she didn't feel entirely at ease. But instead of curls, she now encountered the fabric of her headscarf covering her cropped hair.

'Practices within the Afghan National Guard.'

'What kind of practices?'

'Sexual abuse. *Bacha bazi*.'

Ferozi was silent while his gaze darted around the room. 'Rumours about *bacha bazi* practices within the ranks of the Mujahideen have been circulating for years. You can say what you like about the Taliban, but they certainly made quick work of this form of paedophilia.

However, now that the Taliban have been ousted, *bacha bazi* is back with a vengeance. In fact, it's considered to be one of the most popular pastimes among the political and military elites. So before we continue, Ms Hafez, let me ask you this: how reliable are your sources?'

'They're solid. Why do you ask?'

'Here in Kabul, unlike the rest of the country, the media are still relatively free to report on various issues. Some topics however, such as religion, homosexuality and paedophilia, are rather risky, and that's putting it mildly. Add warlords and politicians to the mix, and the subject becomes lethal. Writing an article about child abuse by a high-ranking military officer is equivalent to signing your own death warrant, if you know what I mean.' He shifted uncomfortably in his seat. 'With all due respect, Ms Hafez, I hope you understand my reservations.'

'Yes,' she said. 'I certainly do. But hopefully I can also satisfy you that we're not looking at a one-off incident. I'd rather not name names at this stage, but it's happening high up, right at the top of the command structure.'

Ferozi looked shocked and seemed unaware of his trembling fingers drumming on the desktop. 'If it's the person I think you're referring to, then we'd better not ever mention that name. Is he personally involved?'

'One of the abused boys identified him.'

She thought of the photo of Hafami she'd shown Idris after letting him shoot the arrow into the tree. 'Is this the man who hurt you?' she'd asked. 'Think of Prince Badan and point to him if it's a yes.' And Idris had tapped the photo with his finger, right in the middle of Hafami's forehead.

'Practising journalism in Afghanistan amounts to taking your life in your hands,' Ferozi said grim-faced. 'It's like balancing on the edge of an abyss. If for whatever reason the authorities see the reporting as a threat, they'll do everything in their power to stop publication. Threaten you, intimidate you with anonymous phone calls, make it impossible for you to attend press conferences, things like that. As a managing editor, I'm having to navigate this on a daily basis. I remain hopeful that I can continue to address issues such as human rights, corruption and abuses of power. Otherwise my work would be mean-ingless. But a very large group of leaders and authorities see freedom of expression as a threat to their interests. And those interests, Ms Hafez, are so substantial that they're prepared to kill if necessary.' He leaned over his desk towards her. 'The power of the man you're investigating . . . you don't know the half of it.'

'How far does that power reach?'

'Potentially very far. You have a Russian colleague who was laid into with a lead pipe and who's now in a coma. That's a warning, a taste of what might happen to you, and to me too, if we were to join forces for your investigation.'

'Isn't that our journalistic duty, *aghaye* Ferozi?'

'It certainly is, *khanum* Hafez. But first I'll have to be swayed by the evidence that you've gathered. And I'll need access to all of your sources.'

The premonition she'd felt earlier on entering the building now came back to her like a boomerang. 'You want me to disclose my sources to you?'

'I need to be one hundred per cent sure that they're completely reliable.'

'They are, you have my word.'

'I'm afraid your word alone isn't enough, I'll have to judge for myself.'

'Unfortunately, I can't agree to that. I protect my sources – with my life if necessary.'

Ferozi leaned back, looking demoralized.

'That's no more than your journalistic duty, I understand that. Just as you'll understand that as the managing editor I have a duty to pro-tect the reputation of my newspaper.'

For a while they sat facing each other in silence. When she finally peeled herself out of the sticky leatherette armchair, she thought she detected a hint of relief on his face.

'I respect your position, *aghaye* Ferozi.'

With his hand on his heart, he answered her slight bow.

'*Khanum* Hafez. I'm glad we met. It was an honour. And should anyone ask about our conversation: it was merely a journalistic tête-a-tête. Between fellow wordsmiths. We never spoke about your investigation.'

Disappointed, Farah walked past the other editorial offices to the exit, remembering something Edward had once said to her: *Truth is subjective and gets us nowhere. It's facts we're after.*

She remembered exactly when he'd said it: sitting opposite him in the old *AND* building as a third-year journalism student. It was the first time he'd flashed her that grin, the one that was both heart-warming and ironic. The grin of a man used to speaking to trainees who were all so keen on making it as journalists they were practically bursting with idealism and ambition.

'I want to go for the truth, Mr Vallent,' she'd said to him. 'Just like Raylan Chapelle. He's the reason I want to become a journalist. I want to join the newspaper Chapelle wrote for. And I want to work for the man who supervised him.'

His grin had vanished instantly. She saw his nostrils flare, the fist closing in front of his mouth. They sat facing each other; neither said a word.

'Chapelle wanted to cover a war,' Edward had said after a long pause. 'But he became a part of the story. The war was what drove him and what ultimately killed him. If you join us here ... and I'm saying *if* ... I don't want you to also be lugging around some war with you one day. If only because that would mean all the time and energy I'd spent on you had gone to waste.'

She was supposed to have been his star pupil, a figurehead of objective journalism. Edward had taught her how to arm herself with facts, how to carry out detailed and thorough research and how to protect herself by always maintaining a semblance of impartiality.

And that's what she'd done. Until now, that is.

A car accident, a military camp, a dancing boy in the middle of the night. None of this was causally related. It had been a purely random sequence of events. But she'd been carried away by it all. She could no longer exclude herself from the situation she was investigating. She was knee-deep in it. Any form of objectivity had become impossible for her. Impartiality had become an illusion a long time ago.

She realized that now.

Edward hadn't abandoned her. She herself had crossed a boundary.

The chaos of the city was overwhelming. Farah looked around. To her relief, the black Cherokee had disappeared. She spotted Nehal's car about a hundred metres away. She made her way over.

At first, the dull roar of the engine behind her just sounded like one of the many SUVs driving around the city. But the sudden braking noise, the opening doors and the rapid footsteps were different, alarming. Before she had a chance to turn around, hands grabbed her, yanked her bag from her arm and pulled a smelly cotton hood over her head. She wanted to scream, but along with the air she inhaled she also sucked the cotton into her mouth, so she could barely breathe.

She was dragged into the car and thrown on to the back seat. Doors slammed shut. The car pulled away with screeching tyres. Hands roughly pressed her face against the seat, pulled her arms back and tied her wrists together. The hands clawed at the shiny fabric of her skirt. She could feel the fingertips clutching her briefs and tugging at them.

The hood over her head stifled her resistance. The claustrophobia left her breathless and sent her heartrate soaring. She could no longer hear her own screams. She was convinced she was about to suffocate. Using every last ounce of strength, she flexed her abdominal muscles, pushed off and thrust her hips up as hard as possible.

She hit a head.

The hands let go.

She turned around and started wildly kicking her legs. Hit the head again. Repeatedly.

But then a noise made her stop. It was a familiar sound. She'd first heard it during the hostage situation in Moscow: the metallic click of a gun being cocked.

She froze.

Then came the punch.

Square in the face. The monotonous rumble of the car engine, the male voices and even the sound of her own breathing faded. Until all that was left was a deep, dark silence.

*

A few slaps in the face brought her back around. A masked figure hovered above her. Hands grabbed her by the head, pulled the hood down again, yanked her out of the car and hauled her along echoing corridors. The smell of mould crept through the fabric of the hood.

'*Estad bash!*'

They came to a halt. A bunch of keys rattling. The rusty sound of a door being unlocked. A whoosh of air when the door swung open. The stench that met her: a blast of sour sweat, urine, excrement. She retched. When the heavy door fell shut behind her, the noise reverberated like the inside of a cathedral. A violent shove between her shoulder blades forced her to carry on walking.

The men barking around her sounded like a pack of hungry wolves. Metal clattered against metal. She was shouted at and called a whore and she stumbled. Two arms on either side kept her from falling. Another door hinged open and fell shut again, so now the yelling was muffled. It made her aware of her own ragged breathing. Her skin hurt, a chafing sensation around her buttocks and between her thighs. The sudden thought: how long had she been unconscious? What had they done to her?

Yet another door opened. Cold air wafted towards her. A room that felt like a tomb. Another pair of hands grabbed her and removed the rope from her wrists, only to cuff them behind her back again, attached to a chain this time.

The hood was pulled off her head. Stale air filled her lungs. The masked man disappeared behind a slamming door.

Clatter. An overweight man with bushy eyebrows, a heavy beard and a cleft lip emptied her shoulder bag on to a metal tabletop. Judging by the look on his face, the catch was a bitter disappointment: a satellite phone, press pass, credit card, Afghan banknotes, two pens and a pencil. That was all. Mason's report, her pad with the notes from her conversation with Roshan and her prepaid mobile were missing. On Nehal's advice, she'd left them all in the car with her.

The man standing in front of her was tall and lean. He had a stern expression, protruding ears, drooping shoulders. Wisps of thinning hair stuck to his shiny forehead. The most striking thing about him was his nose: his long, thin face appeared to be constructed solely to lend it support. He was the one who stank of urine.

He turned his head a little. His cold eyes fixed on hers. His thin, chapped lips pursed ever so slightly when he firmly tightened the steel cable behind her. The chain she was attached to turned out to be connected to a pulley. The hoist could pull her hands up above her head and dislocate her shoulders. If they wanted to, they could hang her by her wrists.

She was trembling like someone with a fever. '*Wakil* ...' It was barely more than a whisper. 'Lawyer.' The man in front of her brought his sweaty bonce closer. His dry lips parted and the sound that came out of his mouth escaped through his nostrils as well. It vaguely resembled laughter but was more like a deflating tyre. Then he slapped her in the face with the palm of his hand, right between her chin and her ear. 'What were you doing at *The Afghan Press*?'

Distraught, she gasped for breath.

'Why am I here?'

'I'm the one asking the questions.'

He tightened the cable. She winced. The pain shot through her vertebrae like a jolt of electricity. The cable pulled her hands behind her back further up. In a reflex, she leaned forwards and stood on tiptoe.

'Who did you meet at *The Afghan Press*?' The stench from the screaming man's mouth drifted towards her, a spray of saliva hit her in the face.

'Several people.'

'Names.'

'I'm not ... I don't know them.'

With the back of his hand, fingers close together, he punched her in the stomach.

'Names!'

The pain permeated every fibre of her body. It was the combination of the cramp in her arms, the unnatural contraction of her shoulder blades, the convulsion of her upper body. She struggled to remain standing.

'What were you doing at *The Afghan Press*?'

'I told you . . .'

'Who did you speak to?'

'I . . .'

'Names!'

He grasped her by the chin and forced her face upwards. 'We'll strip you naked, douse you in cold water, again and again until your nipples are frozen stiff, like icicles, and fall off when I as much as point at them. And when we're done with you, you'll wish you'd never been born.'

She was breathless. All her barriers were down. Every movement, every sound hurt. She'd better watch out. Control the anger that now aimlessly raged through her body and made her feel desperate. In her mind she heard the voice of the old Indonesian woman, Satria.

Anger is an energy, but feed it too much and it will destroy you.

Time stood still.

She was back in the dressing room of that old theatre in Amsterdam. Her loose-fitting, black satin trousers fastened with a belt around her hips. Her hands inside the wide sleeves of the jacket. The sash securely tied around it. Her martial arts outfit. An invisible, but impenetrable coat of armour.

That's how it had been. That's how it had felt.

No anger. Only the power of conviction. A silent force.

The man was still standing right in front of her. She saw his mouth move. More slowly, it seemed. He was shouting. Yet his voice sounded distant. She registered his movements. He grabbed her by the shirt, pulled her up and slapped her in the face.

She didn't feel his hand. He didn't seem to touch her. The pain was far away now.

No fear. No anger.

Not even surprise when a third man entered her field of vision. She recognized him by his stocky build and closely cropped hair. She smelled his Old Spice aftershave, saw the shock in his eyes.

Agent Sam Harcourt's voice shattered her imaginary armour.

'Stop!'

The hoist came down. The soles of her feet touched the floor.

Harcourt shouted: 'Don't you ever act without our authorization again!' Mendosa was standing beside the man who'd emptied her shoulder bag. With a single gesture he made it clear that everything had to be put back in.

She lowered her head and tried to fight back the tears but couldn't stop them.

Harcourt untied her and placed his hands protectively on her shoulders. 'Are you able to walk?'

She nodded. With great care, he escorted her out of the concrete room. The corridor they walked down was narrow and high. Closed cell doors on either side and a net suspended above its entire length. Through the mesh she could see the three storeys above.

'We'll take you to the area reserved for women.'

'Why?'

'This is the men's section.'

'I mean, why have I been detained?'

'I'll explain it to you in a minute. But first you need to be examined.'

'Why? I want to get out of here.'

'Security reasons. If anything happened to you during the process . . .'

'I want to get out of here!'

'First we have to get some clarity about what happened.'

She felt a rage building. 'I'll tell you what happened. I was kidnapped in broad daylight, had a hood pulled over my head and I was being tortured.'

She abruptly turned away from him, held on to the wall with both hands, closed her eyes in an effort to stay on top of her emotions, took a few deep breaths, turned around again and stared at Harcourt with a feral look in her eyes.

They sat opposite one another in a hollow-sounding room inside Pul-e-Charkhi prison. Mendosa slid a plastic cup with tea towards her. She picked it up. Her hand was still shaking, and she spilled some as she took her first sip. She blew her nose on one of the paper tissues Harcourt had piled before her. Then she looked at each one of them in turn.

'Our current information,' Harcourt began, 'suggests that the Afghan Intelligence Service has evidence that you're engaged in activities that are seen to pose a threat to state security. During your interview with Secretary-General Shakoor from the Ministry of the Interior, you apparently implied that you suspect the head of the National Guard, General Hafami, of improper conduct.'

'You know how I ended up in that camp. So you also know that it wasn't my idea.'

'You made a choice. And choices have consequences. You should know that. You're a journalist.'

'Should I have left the woman in the crashed car to her fate?'

'There you have it: you made a decision. Just like you refused to sign the journalists' Code of Ethics.'

'I'm not obliged to sign anything. And certainly not a gagging order. I wasn't asked to come to Afghanistan by the US army. The Afghan government invited me.'

Mendosa leaned forward. 'You told us you refused the government's invitation.'

'I didn't turn down the invitation itself, but I declined to come here and do their bidding. I won't let any politician or general silence me.'

'Signing would have made a world of difference. Now it looks as if you're trying to discredit the US military.'

'How?'

'By assuming that certain Afghan customs, which became obsolete a long time ago, are practised and tolerated on US-run bases.'

'*Bacha bazi.* I saw it with my own eyes. Obsolete? My arse, Agent Mendosa.'

'You saw boys dancing?'

'I saw an Afghan soldier take a boy into a barracks. The boy was dressed and made up as a girl. It takes little imagination to figure out what he was meant to do. A group of horny men was waiting for him inside.'

'Why Hafami?'

'He was the one who threatened me.'

Harcourt pulled out a leather folder sporting the emblem of the CIA and opened it. 'According to our report, the Afghan camp security handed you over to Gunnery Sergeant Mason Williams in a confused state. Is that correct?'

'I wasn't confused. I was being threatened. Sergeant Williams had come looking for me.'

Harcourt regarded her impassively. 'Did you have any further contact with Williams the next day, or the days after?'

'Why do you ask?' She looked at Mendosa, then at Harcourt. Both were poker-faced.

'Answer the question, Ms Hafez.'

'No, I didn't have any more contact with Sergeant Williams.'

The way Harcourt looked at her spoke volumes. He clearly didn't believe her. 'Why don't you just tell us where you've been in the last few days and who you've spoken to.'

He spoke to her the way you speak to a naughty child. She turned her face away from them and looked at the screen in front of the window, which was so dusty you could barely see through. The sun coloured it rust-brown. A spider weaving a web caught her eye.

She tried to get a handle on her thoughts. There were two possible reasons why she'd been detained. The first was that they were up to speed on all of her activities and contacts. That could mean that Mason was also being interrogated somewhere else at this very moment. But if that were true, why didn't they just confront her with their evidence? Why were they only insinuating things? That pointed to the second possible reason: they'd been unable to map her comings and goings in the past couple of days. In that case, Mason's strategy had worked a treat. Goldwater and his security services were exasperated. So now they were trying this approach. First they had her undergo a traumatic experience that would bring her close to breaking point. The abduction, the stab at torture. Then the unexpected charge of the light cavalry coming to save her. Harcourt and Mendosa couldn't have been in the area by chance. The paternal arm around her shoulder, the protection, the calming tone, the tissues and the tea.

Good cop, bad cop.

She turned to face the two men opposite her again.

'If I tell you what you want to know, will I be free to go?'

The truth, she thought. Nothing but the truth. Anything to get out of this hell hole as quickly as possible.

She'd decided to come clean with them.

She told them about the identification of her father's belongings at the Ministry of the Interior. Secretary-General Ahmad Shakoor's refusal to help her locate Sekandar's family. She talked about how she'd stood by the edge of the mass grave where her father had been found, and the fascination with which she'd watched the fighter kites on Tepe Maranjan plateau. The childhood memories that surfaced as she walked through the Babur Gardens the next day.

The truth, she thought. Nothing but the truth.

Or at least a big chunk of it.

Harcourt ran a finger down the transcript of her first interrogation until he found the line he was looking for and quoted aloud, 'I want to be able to write freely about my country.'

His scrutinising gaze. 'Is that why you stopped by *The Afghan Press* this afternoon? To write "freely" about "your country"?'

She'd kept Mason and Nehal out of her story, but she couldn't gloss over Ferozi's existence. He was her weak link. She had no idea how the nervous-looking managing editor would behave if figures such as Harcourt and Mendosa were to apply pressure. But she was determined to set out her version of the truth.

'I have a Dutch passport. My roots are Afghan. I'm a journalist. Now that I'm in my home country, I want to know what it's like to work as a journalist in Afghanistan. I spoke to Mr Ferozi about that.'

That was no lie.

Mendosa produced a cynical grin. 'Am I right in thinking you applied for a job?'

'A job application isn't the right word. I wanted to explore my options.'

'Ms Hafez . . .' It came out sounding tired. 'We asked you to stay out of trouble. Do you realize how much trouble you'll be in if Mr Ferozi contradicts your story?'

She continued to look them straight in their stoic faces. 'And do you realize how much trouble you guys will be in when it's revealed that journalists like me are abducted in broad daylight by masked agents of the state security service, without being charged and without the bastards taking any notice of the Geneva Conventions? Despite my appalling treatment, I've told you what you wanted to know. I have nothing to hide. I know my rights. If you don't charge me with anything, you'll have to release me as quickly as possible.'

'Friends for life,' Harcourt said. He got up and left the room. Mendosa drummed his fingers impatiently on the tabletop. Okay, not another word now, she thought to herself.

The door swung open. Using two fingers, Harcourt signalled that she should stand up. What next? She was prepared for anything. Had they interrogated Ferozi? Had Mason been detained? Had they picked up Nehal?

Harcourt and Mendosa's footsteps ricocheted off the long corridor's concrete walls. A plump guard in a faded green uniform walked ahead of them, a heavy bunch of keys tied to her hip belt. The wind blew sand from the courtyard through the barred windows into the corridor. The bright sun cast streaks of light on the floor. The small cells on either side were crammed full of women. Back to back, sitting motionless on mattresses. Plastic bags containing their personal belongings hung on nails on the wall. The cell doors were open.

Curious glances, blazing eyes, some of them red-rimmed. Faces filled with anger and despair. Almost none of these women were here for murder, drug trafficking or any other serious crime. She knew that. Most of them were victims of a corrupt and medieval legal system. If you had money or political power you could get away with murder and buy yourself free. Most judges and prosecutors had never seen a law school from the inside. They'd been appointed by family or friends. Women who reported crimes or who'd been charged with something were found guilty in advance.

Because they were women.

Nobody did anything to protect them. Violence against women was legitimate, just like the violence unleashed on her now seemed to be considered normal. She was only a few steps away from being released. She knew what she had to do as soon as the heavy prison gate was closed behind her. The real criminals were out there. And she'd go after the biggest one of them all.

She kept walking.

A few more metres.

The guard unlocked the final door. Under the hot afternoon sun, they walked through a mesh corridor towards the gate. She still couldn't believe it. Was it a test, another tactic aimed at breaking her? They might well drag her back inside again. She'd withheld facts, misled her interrogators.

They came to a halt right in front of the gate. Mendosa thrust her shoulder bag into her hands. At Harcourt's signal, a guard opened a separate door in the large gate.

She didn't move.

7
Paul

The immense hall of Moscow State University gave him the glum feeling of insignificance. From behind her desk, the plump receptionist looked at him with a sardonic grin.

'Hello, Bruce.'

'Good morning, Demi.'

'You're looking even worse than the last time. Maybe I should call an ambulance?'

'No, need. Just the sight of you heals all my wounds.'

'I'll tell our press director you're here, *moy negodyai*, my poor devil.'

Paul leaned on the counter as she pressed the keys on the intercom and with a discreet tone indicated that 'the cowboy' had arrived. She blushed when she noticed that Paul kept staring at her and casually waved him away. For some reason it did him good to be able to charm a somewhat older woman even under these circumstances.

'Daydreaming, Bruce?' Now she was staring at him.

'I was imagining us together.'

'Don't get your hopes up.'

She resolutely pointed behind him. When he turned around he saw the somewhat shabbily dressed, balding man with the artistic goatee and brown horn-rimmed glasses coming towards him. As if Sergey Kombromovich had been waiting just down the corridor.

'So you went into the woods, Mr Chapelle . . . Unafraid of the wolves.'

'You called it,' Paul replied. 'But not without fear.'

'Yet you did it.'

'Because I adhere to my motto.'

'And that is . . . ?'

'Feel the fear, but do it anyway.'

It could have been the beginning of an interesting conversation lasting all the way from the lobby, down the long corridor on the fourth floor, until they reached the panelled room with leather armchairs and a magnificent view of a park. But unlike the last time, they stopped chatting. Neither of them was interested in making small talk when there were much more serious matters to discuss.

After Sergey Kombromovich had locked the door of his study he looked at Paul seriously.

'I know why you're here, my dear fellow.'

'I suspected as much,' answered Paul, taking one of Raylan's letters out of his jacket and showing it to Sergey. 'At our last meeting you told me that my father was here to give lectures. My colleague Farah was in possession of a number of letters that Raylan had written to her mother at the time. This one is from April 1978. In it, he writes that he'd accidentally stumbled across something important.' He saw the surprise on Sergey's face as he stared at the letter. 'Can you tell me what my father was looking into?'

Sergey pointed to one of the armchairs by the window. Once Paul had taken a seat, he sat down opposite him and returned the letter.

'After his lecture at the university your father met an Afghan man, who was officially registered here as a student, but who was used by the KGB to recruit fellow citizens for a communist coup in Afghanistan.'

'You mean the Saur Revolution?'

Sergey gave him an almost solemn nod.

'It turns out that Michailov was the secret architect of this coup. His plan to turn the country into a Russian buffer state was brilliant. He recruited young Afghan officers, had them brought to Moscow, supposedly for military training, but in reality they were involved in the preparations for the coup. The armed forces were to provide military support for Afghanistan's new communist elite.'

Sergey Kombromovich stared out of the window and uncomfortably shifted his weight in the chair.

'What was eventually to become the Saur Revolution was a gigantic machine whose wheels had been secretly turning for years. Nobody, certainly not an American journalist, was allowed to interfere with this grand scheme. Using blackmail, they tried to make it impossible for your father to continue his investigation.'

'Was Michailov involved in the blackmail?'

Sergey looked at him thoughtfully.

'To ask the question is to answer it.'

Paul leaned forward and looked at Sergey attentively. 'What about Michailov? There's a gap between the time he completed his military training and when he served as director of the Russian Cultural Centre in Kabul. What happened?'

Sergey sat down again.

'Michailov graduated *cum laude* from the strictest military training institutions. He was immediately recruited by the GRU, the Glavnoye Razvedyvatel'noye Upravlenyje, an extremely secret military intelligence organization founded by Lenin. Even the highest-ranking politicians couldn't gain access to their intel without extensive security clearances. The organization built an international network of elite military agents, all of whom were tasked with infiltrating foreign political circles in order to spread communist ideas. Michailov's appointment as director of the Russian Cultural Centre in Kabul fitted that strategy perfectly.'

Sergey slowly got up.

'But that's not the only aspect of his life the censors demanded I disregard in my book. And that brings us to the main reason for your visit.'

Sergey went over to the bookcase, grabbed a few books from the middle shelf, behind which a small safe appeared to be hidden, and took out a large dark-brown envelope that he gave to Paul.

'The secret police report on Michailov's death. On the last page is the conclusion of the then investigating detective.'

Paul thumbed to the end. The first thing he saw was the name of the detective in question. He looked surprised.

Sergey Kombromovich stared back, unmoved. 'Alexander Arlazarov and I are ... old friends ...'

'Old friends ...' Paul felt no need to inquire further and concentrated on the conclusion. 'Michailov was stabbed to death, it says here. But I thought that ... I mean, it was an assassination.'

'That so-called terrorist attack took place when Michailov had been dead for two hours,' Sergey said in a flat tone. 'In reality it was murder, my friend. More specifically: patricide, a murder to make even Oedipus green with envy. Alexander had to let his prime suspect, a prominent young man who enjoyed diplomatic protection from the Kremlin, walk away. His superiors took him off the case as soon as they realized what was going on. The KGB took over. In the middle of the night, Michailov's body was put in his limousine. Explosives were placed under the car. They detonated them remotely. Thereby transforming a murder into a terrorist attack.'

Sergey pointed to the document Paul was holding.

'All the findings are there. Including the name of the prime suspect.'

'I assume I already know who that is.'

This time it was Sergey's turn to look surprised.

'You were talking about a kind of patricide that Oedipus himself would be jealous of. Valentin Lavrov was a bit too talkative when my colleague Farah visited him in Moscow weeks ago. Turns out he's Michailov's bastard son.'

'A tragic history,' Kombromovich murmured, 'which began in Makhinjauri, a Georgian village on the Black Sea. In the 1960s and 1970s it was a popular spa for rich communist party bosses and high-ranking military. Young spa workers tried to create a better future for themselves by becoming romantically involved with them. And hey, a man like Michailov, who eventually rises from being a general to a government minister, surely he doesn't want to be reminded of the bastard child he fathered in such a backward village? Vakurov, Michailov's right-hand man, came from that region. He'd introduced Michailov there and apparently felt responsible for the welfare of the fatherless boy. Vakurov had Valentin's mother marry his cousin. He was also the one who paid for Valentin's first years of study in

Moscow. Anyway, it formed the basis of a career that, thanks to his perseverance and loyalty to the Kremlin, made Valentin the leader of a global energy consortium. Lavrov used his untouchable position to put an end to the life of the man who must've always known of his existence, but who never so much as glanced at him.'

Paul tapped the police report.

'You've kept this report all this time, my friend. Why?'

Immense fatigue sounded in the sigh Sergey let out.

'At the time we both had a wife and young children. But Alexander and I both knew that a moment would come when the truth had to be told. Not so much to ease our own consciences, but to show that we are increasingly governed by lies. Incidentally, it isn't necessary for me to say that you're never to share which sources you've consulted in order to obtain this information.'

'I'm a journalist. I protect my sources . . .'

'With your life if necessary?' A slight smile appeared on Sergey's face, which now relaxed for the first time.

'If necessary.'

'You seem like a man who isn't afraid to go down a dark path teeming with wolves. That, I suspect, is why Alexander chose you for this.'

'Chose me . . .' Paul repeated thoughtfully. 'You mean I'm the messenger?'

'Whatever you want to call it . . . Somebody has to do this.'

'But still, my dear friend Sergey, what purpose does this information serve after all these years?'

Sergey got up and walked to the window. With his arms outstretched he spread his hands on the windowsill and leaned slightly forward as he looked out over the park.

'For a Russian nationalist, and there are still many in prominent positions in the army and political circles, this murderous act will always be unforgivable. Publication of an article about this would certainly sound the death knell for Valentin Lavrov. It's much worse than corruption, intimidation or the siphoning off of billions of roubles. It's an issue of national honour.'

Sergey turned to Paul and crossed his arms.

'Moreover, the fact that our own president has protected him all this time isn't exactly going to strengthen his position. We have elections coming up in three months.'

With a serious face, Sergey Kombromovich extended his hand to Paul.

'*Moy dorogoy*, my friend, you're now holding enough evidence to make Valentin Lavrov disappear from the stage once and for all. I wish you much success and happiness with this endeavour.'

In the centre of Moscow, four lanes of traffic had come to a standstill, nobody was going anywhere. Paul, in the back seat of a taxi, felt his mobile phone vibrate in the inside pocket of his jacket. On the screen he saw the number of Pirogorov hospital. He answered and tried to concentrate on what the nurse was saying to him, but the first few words hit him hard.

'*Serieuzniye oslozjneniya*. Serious complications.'

The taxi driver refused to ride over the pavement. Paul threw open the door and started running.

He could no longer hear his own footsteps when he stormed into the hospital's ICU twenty minutes later, gasping for breath. The only sound that registered was a loud thumping. His heart was pounding in his ears.

The doctor stood right in front of him in the corridor and spread his hands in front of his chest as a sign that Paul was not allowed to go any further. Or was it a gesture of consolation? Paul couldn't see him clearly. His eyes were glazed over.

He saw the doctor's mouth moving but didn't hear what he was saying.

It wasn't necessary.

Paul already knew.

PART FOUR

The Father and the Blond Fighter

I

Paul

2009

He slid open the heavy curtains. Light poured into the room in a beam of suspended dust particles. Anya was staring at him. Behind her the cork wall was covered in newspaper clippings, photos and notes. She hated most photos of herself, but not this one. Paul still knew exactly where he'd taken it. At the editorial offices of *Moskva Gazeta* he'd sat diagonally across from her and with a degree of caution he pointed the lens at her while she sat at her laptop trying to make a deadline. She'd looked up and treated him to that bittersweet 'I see what you're up to' smile. But she didn't stop him. And when he clicked, her eyes revealed more than just the fanaticism he was so used to seeing.

They also showed trust, which was the only reason that photo was still hanging there, even after he'd left for Johannesburg.

When I look at myself, I see you in my eyes.

He removed the drawing pins, smoothed the photo and put it on a big wooden table beside a stack of newspapers. Her muesli bowl and coffee mug were still standing there, reminders of how much of a hurry she was in that last morning. He bowed his head, held her image so close to his face it began to blur and then he put the photo in his inside jacket pocket.

As he walked past the record player, he saw how carefully she'd stored his vinyl collection. Hip-hop and rap albums by the Russians Noize Mc and Oxxxymiron were sharing shelf space with jazz classics by John Coltrane and Miles Davis.

He took the Maroussia shower gel and eau de toilette that were in the wicker basket beside the sink in the cramped bathroom. When he looked in the mirror, he was startled by the hollow eyes in his ravaged face.

The worn wooden louvre doors of the wardrobe in her bedroom creaked when he opened them. He ran his hand along the leather jackets she'd bought at the flea market. When you entered her apartment, there was that dank smell of second-hand clothing. Anya adored old and worn-out.

'Does that apply to me, too?' he'd once asked jokingly.

'You're an old soul,' she'd answered. 'In a damn good body.'

He removed the leather motorcycle jacket with the diagonal zipper from the hanger. She'd once seduced him wearing a halter top, braless, on which the Russian flag had been hand-painted. He grabbed her tattered skinny jeans with the horizontal tears, convinced that this is what she'd want to be wearing to meet her maker.

Then he pulled open the dresser drawer in which she kept her only decent lingerie set. Anya wasn't into fine underclothing. She mostly wore bras and big pants that seemed to belong to an earlier era. This black lace set fitted her body like a glove.

'It was supposedly inspired by classical Russian ballets,' she asserted as if she were a connoisseur. In any case, she'd had to convince herself and cough up quite a few roubles to buy the set. She'd planted herself on the sofa right before he arrived home, scantily dressed in her newest purchase.

'I'm celebrating me, myself and I,' she said.

Her breasts were partly visible under the embroidered crimson flowers on the transparent black tulle.

'Want to see more?'

'No,' he whispered, and he knelt down in front of her, closed his eyes and ran his fingertips along the embroidery. Then he felt her nipples go hard against the supple fabric.

'Liar.'

Her voice was husky. Slowly he unfastened the back clasp. He kept his eyes closed. In a circular pattern, he gently licked her breasts. She pulled him towards her, searching for his mouth. He gently bit her lips.

Then, agonizingly slowly, she pushed him away and stood in front of him. Like a blind man reading Braille, he tugged at her string. She pulled it down to the floor and tossed it aside with her foot. Then she opened her legs and pressed his face between her thighs where his tongue lingered until she climaxed.

He looked at her, lying there. On that steel table in a green tiled room, under the bright white light of a round fluorescent tube. Her head raised; the bandage had been removed. Part of her scalp was shaved as a result of the autopsy carried out on her body. They'd opened up her skull. Purple-blue bruising was visible on the right side of her face, a Y-shaped incision went from her pubic area straight to below her sternum, and from there diagonally upwards to her shoulders on either side.

'Are you sure?'

The nurse's voice. She'd introduced herself as Khristina. A big woman, with grey-blue eyes and lots of dark brown curls.

Paul nodded and pointed to the diaper Anya was wearing.

'But this has got to go.'

'The dead no longer have control over their bladder or intestines,' Khristina said.

He went over to the table where he'd left Anya's clothes, grabbed the lingerie set and held it up.

'I want her buried in this.'

Khristina looked at him for a while – neither disapproving nor approving, but with that neutral professional expression of people for whom dealing with the dead was simply a daily routine. The look in her eyes seemed to soften somewhat. Finally she gave him a quick nod, opened one of the cabinets and pulled out a box of cotton wool.

'Turn around.'

'Why?'

'Out of respect for her. Believe me, she wouldn't want you to see this.'

He stood with his back to the table until she said he could turn around again. The diaper had disappeared into a pedal bin, the box of cotton wool was now half-empty.

Khristina passed him latex gloves.

Paul shook his head. 'It's the last time I'll touch her. I don't need gloves.'

She gave him a brief probing look, then casually dropped the gloves in the bin, filled a stainless-steel bowl with lukewarm water and handed him a washcloth. 'You brought something special with you to wash her with, right?'

He nodded.

'Be gentle. The skin is fragile; the blood doesn't clot anymore.'

He mixed the Maroussia shower gel with the water and inhaled the scent of sandalwood.

'Start at her feet and from there wash along her legs up to her face.'

Even through the washcloth Paul felt how icy cold Anya's feet were. He gently rubbed along her legs, her thighs, went over her belly, her breasts, swept a strand of hair from her forehead and washed her face. He went to stroke her short hair. *Most men like long hair because it's feminine, doll-like, but I've always found it boring.*

Khristina stopped him. 'If the head wound starts bleeding, we're in trouble. Time to dress her.'

They were at the foot of the table. Khristina had Anya's expensive undies in her hand. 'Lift her legs carefully.'

Hesitantly, he did what she asked.

'Higher. Otherwise I'll never be able to dress her in this little nothing.'

He held Anya's legs so high, they went up in the air.

Skilfully Khristina pulled the undies up to Anya's buttocks.

'A present from you?'

'No, she gave it to herself.'

'She beat you to it.'

She looked at him slightly amused. He was still holding up Anya's legs.

'You can lower her legs now and then slowly turn her towards you.'

He did what she asked as carefully as possible. Their actions had something of a cautious choreography, performed in unspoken trust between two people who a few minutes earlier had been total strangers.

He carefully laid Anya on her right side. Khristina pulled the undies over one hip and turned Anya towards her, so that Paul could pull them over her other hip.

They put on her skinny jeans using the same technique. He got a vision of Anya as a kangaroo hopping through the bedroom in an attempt to wriggle into her favourite jeans.

Khristina gave him the bra, grabbed Anya under the armpits, extended one hand further to keep her head straight and placed her in a sitting position. It looked like an uncomfortable hug with Anya passively letting her arms hang down.

'The straps,' Khristina said.

He slowly slid the bra strap around Anya's right arm, then leaned towards Khristina, who patiently helped manoeuvre and slide it up around the other arm. As he covered Anya's breasts with the embroidered cups, her head nodded slightly, as if she were keeping an eye on things. He was struck by how pale she looked, but also by her calm expression, as if a small part of her was still aware of what was happening to her at this moment.

He decided Anya should wear her black hoodie so he could conceal the swelling on her head by pulling up the hood. Khristina carefully camouflaged the bruises on Anya's face with a skin-coloured mist from an airbrush gun. Following her instructions Paul then applied a very thin layer of lipstick and eye shadow.

He took a step backwards and gazed at Anya peacefully lying there, just as she sometimes did on the sofa at her place, asleep with the blue light of her laptop illuminating her face.

It hit him hard. The realization that a part of him was now forever locked away in her lifeless body.

2

Farah

2009

The sun cast long shadows. The wind whipped grains of sand into her face. Pul-e-Charkhi plain stretched out in front of her, vast and inhospitable. Without a word, Harcourt and Mendosa had waited for her to walk through the prison gate of her own accord, knowing that her release would be coupled with another humiliation.

She'd have to make her way back to the city on foot.

In the distance, she saw the fluttering green flag that marked the emptied mass grave. She mechanically put one foot in front of the other. Keep moving forward. Keep walking. Don't stand still.

A cloud of dust was approaching fast. An old Ford Ranger. The driver slowed down. The reflective windscreen obscured his face, but she knew he was scrutinizing her from head to toe. As a woman on her own she was an incredibly easy target on this deserted plain. She kept going, determinedly, without looking up.

He drove past.

She breathed a sigh of relief. But then she heard him take a sharp turn behind her. He pulled up alongside her at a crawl. The window on the driver's side rolled down. A deep voice. Calm and authoritative.

'*Dakhel sho*. Get in.'

She didn't so much as glance at him and kept walking. 'She said you were proud, but this beats everything.' She could tell by his tone of voice that he was grinning.

She jerked her head towards him. Jet-black eyes. Stubble on his

300

square jaws. Short, cropped hair. Broad shoulders underneath an army green T-shirt. She put him in his mid-thirties. But you could never really tell with Afghans; they often looked older than their actual years.

'Who do you mean by "she"?'

'Get in and you'll find out.'

'Do you work for Nehal?'

He nodded his head at the rear-view mirror and slapped the outside of the door with the flat of his hand. Looking over her shoulder, she saw the black Cherokee pulling away from the prison gate and heading towards them.

'Either you get in, or I'm driving off. It's up to you.'

After she quickly got in on the passenger side, he stepped on the gas. Once at speed, he patted the heap of faded brown textile lying between them on the front seat. 'For you. Put them on.'

She checked out the *salwar kameez* trousers, the matching shirt and the flat felt cap. Men's clothing.

'There aren't any women where we're going.'

'Where are you taking me?'

He glanced at his rear-view mirror again. 'You'll find out soon enough.'

'At the very least tell me what you're planning on doing.'

He shook his head with a mocking smile. 'You can get out if you prefer. You'll get another lift in no time.'

In the mirror, she saw the Cherokee emerge out of a rust-coloured sand cloud. She began to pull on the trousers. It was actually easier than she'd expected. They were big enough to slip on over her own clothes. The belt needed considerable tightening. The shirt was equally shapeless, but then that was the whole point. She pushed the *pakol* as far down on her head as possible.

He looked her over and nodded his approval. 'I've never had such a beautiful man in my car.' He handed her a plastic water bottle, from which she drank thirstily.

'Leave some for me, will you?'

'If you tell me your name.'

He chuckled again. For the first time, she studied him carefully. He was muscular and had a huge tattoo on his right bicep: a dragon with fierce wings and a fire-breathing human head. A *simurgh*, a mythical bird.

He gestured for the bottle.

'According to Islamic law, tattoos are mutilations, and therefore forbidden.'

'I know.'

'Then why do you have a *simurgh* on your arm?'

'It helps me in battle.'

'Are you at war?'

'Who isn't around here?' He put the bottle to his mouth.

'Who are you fighting?'

'*Amrikaya*. But also the Taliban. And all the corrupt politicians and businessmen who are selling our country down the river and making off with all the money. The hate preachers, it's them I'm fighting. We're a proud nation. We can no longer allow fear and hatred to rule our lives. We have to get a grip on ourselves. We have to work on our potential.'

'You sound like a politician.'

He turned to look at her and saw her grin.

'One I might actually vote for too.'

He laughed out loud, tossed the emptied bottle under his seat and held out his hand.

'My name's Malid.'

The steep slopes of Mount Badam Bagh appeared before them. They were west of the city and fast approaching a large crowd. Thousands of men had gathered at the foot of the mountainside in vans, pickups and four-wheel drives. Their animated screaming and shouting were drowned out by the barking of huge bull mastiffs and Afghan shepherds. Once kept to protect herds and bite wolves to death, these creatures with their docked ears and tails were now bred, pumped full of steroids and trained to bring in big money. They were restrained with chains and wide leather leads. Bundles of gambling money quickly changed hands among small groups of men.

'Why are we here, Malid?'

'You'll find out in a minute.'

He parked the Ranger beside a cluster of pickups and peered around, visibly tense. The Cherokee, which had been trailing them at the same distance the whole time, was now slowly moving towards some cars parked nearby.

He opened the door. 'Stay close to me. Don't look over your shoulder.'

They walked side by side through a throng of men, who'd formed a large oval around a sandpit. The excitement mounted. Two dogs the size of calves, with sharply filed teeth, were led into the arena. A large green cloth was held between them, so they couldn't see each other yet. An old man with a white beard stood in the middle of the ring. Gesturing dramatically, he swung a long stick through the air.

The cloth dropped.

The dogs charged at each other.

She was unable to look away, fascinated by the blind rage with which one dog immediately sank its teeth into the other's neck. The weaker canine soon tried to surrender. But its opponent failed to notice, yanked it to the ground and kept biting. Men rushed over to try and prise the dogs apart. When they finally managed it, the distraught owner bent over his bleeding hound, which lay whimpering in the sand.

Malid tugged at her sleeve to indicate that they had to move on. They approached a group of men standing beside some pickups. They booed as the crying man left the arena with his dog in his arms. Malid leaned back against the side of a white van and knocked on it as inconspicuously as possible. The side door slid open. With an equally casual but urgent nod, he told her to get in.

'*Zud!*'

She hesitated. In the dim interior, she saw a boy wearing the same brown *salwar kameez* as her.

'Quick!' From inside, a hand grabbed her tightly and pulled her into the van. At the same time the boy jumped out. The sliding door slammed shut.

She found herself face to face with Nehal.

It had only been a few hours since she'd pulled her close on the tallest diving platform of Bibi Mahro Hill Pool. Inside the van's stuffy load space, littered with toolboxes and metal pipes, she did it again. And once more, it felt awkward. But that didn't stop her from putting her arms around the young woman. It was the only language she could speak right now.

Nehal was patient with her outward show of emotion and passively accepted her embrace. She clearly didn't know how to respond to this kind of emotional display. Farah released her.

'I saw it happen,' Nehal sounded dejected. 'They pulled over. Two men. One grabbed hold of you. The other put the hood over your head. I followed them all the way to the prison. That's when I contacted Malid. I . . .'

She averted her head.

'What is it?'

'I keep thinking . . . I should have prevented it.'

'But how?'

'That's the thing: no idea. Anyway, what's done is done.'

Farah turned towards her. It was a strange feeling to be saved by a woman who didn't want to be thanked for it. Or worse, whose every word and gesture implied that she'd failed. Perhaps that's what explained the bond between them, she thought to herself. Both had an uncontrollable urge to save others. And kept thinking they were falling short.

'What did they do to you?' Nehal asked.

'They threatened me with torture. I don't know if they'd have gone through with it, but they tried to intimidate me with the prospect. They have their suspicions, but no proof. Not yet anyway.'

Nehal leaned over to the window beside the sliding door and lifted the roller blind ever so slightly. In the distance, they saw Malid and the boy in the brown *salwar kameez* walk past the rows of men in the direction of the parked Ranger. They got in and slowly drove away. Shortly afterwards, the black Cherokee set off in pursuit of the Ford.

'I'd love to see their faces when they realize they've been hoodwinked,' Nehal said and firmly rapped her knuckles twice on the wooden partition of the driver's cab. The engine started. The van carefully reversed and then drove off. Whenever they turned a corner, they could hear the shrill sound of the metal pipes banging together. They were sitting on one of the toolboxes, but tumbled off every time the driver unexpectedly braked or accelerated with a jolt.

Nehal did her best to be heard over the noise. 'You're not going back to your hotel. We're taking you to a safe house.'

'Where?'

'If I told you, it wouldn't be a safe house any more.' Her laughter was as bubbly as ever.

They sat huddled together: two quiet, exhausted women in the stuffy load space of a van that felt like an oven on wheels. They were driving through a city they couldn't see but could hear all the better, and that bore as many scars as their own souls.

A huge workbench occupied the garage where they got out. Parked inside it were a jeep and two more vans as well as Nehal's taxi. Nehal greeted the man who'd driven the van and introduced him to Farah as her brother. He was just as short and stocky as his sister and he had the same thunderous laugh. He ran an air-con installation company. The plan was for him to go to her hotel and smuggle Farah's personal possessions out under the cover of quickly servicing the AC system. She gave him her room number, key card and a list of the essential items he had to bring back. Then she stepped out through a side door with Nehal.

Her surprise elicited a booming laugh from Nehal.

They were in Murad Khane.

The old heart of Kabul. She'd walked here as a child, holding her mother's hand, through these pedestrianized streets that connected the bazaar, the places of worship, the caravanserai and the residential homes. It had all been built in the eighteenth century for the king's courtiers, servants, secretaries and administrators. After the Russian invasion in 1979 and subsequent wars, this part of the city had become one big ruin. For years, the buildings that weren't hit by rockets and mortars had been buried under towering piles of garbage and debris. Three years ago, it had been decided to rebuild the houses from the ground up and to partially reconstruct them in the original, centuries-old style.

The house with the courtyard where Nehal lived with her brother and his family was surprisingly large and cool. Thick mattresses and red velvet cushions lined the walls of the main room. Oil lamps burned in the clay recesses, illuminating little figurines. They walked up through a number of smaller, low-ceilinged rooms until they reached the flat roof where laundry was drying and large pots with an olive tree and white oleander flanked a big dovecote.

The old quarter stretched all the way to the river. The noise of the city was muted here, like the sound of a distant ocean, an illusion that was regularly shattered by shrill honking. The sun slunk behind the mountains.

Nehal came and stood next to her. 'My mother's father was born here. He died here, and when I die, it will be here too. This is our home. Wherever we go, we always come back here. This is your safe house.'

'Why?'

Nehal smiled. 'The way of the Pashtuns.'

'*Pashtunwali?*'

Nehal nodded.

'But that tradition goes way, way back . . .'

'It's as old as these hills.' Nehal's booming laugh again. Then she became serious. 'I cherish my heritage the way I cherish this house.'

Nehal opened the little door to the dovecote, stuck her hand in and made a slow sweeping motion. Fluttering wildly, the pigeons took to the air and flew up into the violet evening sky in a wide arc. The two women watched them in silence.

Farah enjoyed their silent covenant. Some people talked because they were afraid of silence. Some gossiped about others so they didn't have to reveal anything about themselves. Yet others were always on the go, working night and day, just so they wouldn't be confronted with how empty their lives really were. One half of the world seemed to be fleeing from itself, while the other half was circling aimlessly around itself. Yet somehow this woman had the ability to make her feel at home without too many words.

Her mobile phone buzzed.

Paul.

She hesitated a long time before she answered. She felt it in every fibre of her being: this was about Anya. Yet his cold cynicism took her by complete surprise.

'We both have a funeral to attend soon, how about *that*?'

She gasped for breath, unable to respond.

'The doctors say she didn't feel any pain. Clinically, she was already dead . . . the whole time I was sitting beside her, holding her hand, the machines were keeping her alive.'

She listened to his voice, ravaged by alcohol, cigarettes and grief, and stared into space.

'I loved her. Not like I used to. It was different, or more . . . I don't know . . . What I'm trying to say . . . I don't know what I'm trying to say. I'm going to miss her so much . . . Maybe that's what I'm trying to say.'

She was finally able to utter a few words. 'I'm so sorry.'

It was quiet for a moment. And then, 'Sorry? What for?'

'That I can't be with you. For making things so difficult for you.'

'Do you ever make things easy for anyone?'

'No . . .'

She heard his breathing and the sound of the Zippo as he lit a cigarette. Then he inhaled deeply, exhaled and carried on talking. 'Maybe we're more alike than we think.'

'What do you mean?'

'When we want something, we go for it, blind to any risks.'

'What's wrong with that?'

'Nothing. But we drag others down with us. And when they die, because of us . . . Then what's the point of it all? God damn it.'

In the long silence that followed, she desperately searched for words. 'Paul . . . ?'

'Yes . . . ?'

'Maybe we ought to stop asking what the point is. We can't help it. We are who we are. We can't undo the past. We're going to wake up tomorrow, get dressed and do the things we have to do.'

He took a drag of his cigarette. He held his breath for a moment before exhaling again. 'Is that our life?'

'If you have a better idea, I'd like to hear it.'

'No . . .'

'I'll come to you.'

'No, I'll be all right.'

'I'm not asking, I'm telling you.'

'No, I'm telling you . . .' He started coughing. Then she heard a muffled curse, followed by sounds that suggested he'd slipped the phone into his trouser pocket and had walked off with it, but she knew that wasn't the case. He was pressing his phone against his jacket so she wouldn't hear him cry.

She shook her head to tell Nehal, who was staring at her worriedly, that something was wrong.

When Paul spoke again, she heard the despair in his voice. 'You're the only one who . . .' Then again those sounds that were supposed to camouflage his grief.

'Paul?'

Another pause before he resumed. 'Sorry, Fah. I'll call you later.'

She listened to the soft crackling on the line and stared out over the city, which now seemed to be silent too.

'What was that?' Nehal asked.

'A colleague of ours, a good friend in Moscow . . . Dead. I have to go.'

That's when she heard the ping of a new message. Assuming it was Paul, she looked at the text on her screen.

RCC. Darulaman Road. 8 p.m. Alone.

She didn't recognize the sender's number, pressed call to find out who it was and got through to voicemail. Zahoruddin Ferozi, the managing editor of *The Afghan Press*. She spoke after the beep, 'Mr Ferozi, I just received a message claiming to be from you. Can you call me back, please?'

She looked at Nehal. 'RCC. Darulaman Road. How fast can we get there?'

It took Nehal exactly fifteen minutes to get to Darulaman Road, to the concrete complex with its sharp angles and walls peppered with mortar holes. The former Russian Cultural Centre, where in the 1980s Soviets and Afghans met for lectures, films and the dissemination of the communist ideal, was now a decrepit ruin. Through the holes in the walls she saw the silhouettes of down-and-out drug addicts. In the smoky glow of wood fires, they were shooting up or breathing in the blue fumes of liquid evaporating on bits of foil.

She checked her watch. Two minutes past eight. Ferozi hadn't returned her call. She hesitated.

'This isn't the kind of place where a man would arrange to meet a woman,' Nehal observed.

'Perhaps that makes it the ideal location,' Farah said. 'Nobody would suspect it.'

Nehal looked at her in horror. 'Are you really planning to go in there?'

Farah nodded.

'At least use this to cover your nose and mouth,' Nehal said, handing her a scarf.

But even ten scarves wouldn't have masked the horrible stench that filled the gloomy dump. The floor was littered with rubble, glass, cigarette butts and used needles. With her mobile's torch she illuminated the silent ghosts that sat huddled, crouched down or with their backs against the wall, staring glassy-eyed into space. She felt Nehal's hand on her arm, urging her to turn around, and shook her head. She had to keep going.

Eventually they found Ferozi in the basement.

Although his eyes were wide open, she knew he could no longer see them. He was lying motionless on a piece of cardboard, on his side in an unnatural, contorted position. His swollen hands were covered in blood. When she looked closer, she saw that all his fingernails were missing. Nehal wanted to take her away, away from this place, but she couldn't stop staring at him. She kept telling herself that what she was seeing wasn't real. That it wasn't her fault that this man was lying here.

Her phone buzzed. Ferozi's number appeared on her display again. She was trembling as she answered. She instantly recognized Ashraf Hafami's voice.

'Sooner or later, everyone relents. Ferozi did, and you could be next. We have the boy. You can save his life by taking tomorrow's first flight out of the country.'

Before she could utter a word, he'd broken the connection.

We have the boy.

She dialled the refuge's number and got Mariam, the child protection officer, on the line. In the background she heard Roshan's hysterical screaming.

That's when she knew Hafami's threat was true.

She also knew she couldn't leave the kidnapped boy to his fate. Hafami wasn't the kind of man who'd keep his promise. In fact, it would suit him better if Idris, as an important witness against him, were to be found dead somewhere by the side of the road the following morning. She had to do everything in her power to prevent that. She wouldn't be booking the first flight out to Moscow, as she'd said to Paul.

We're a team, she'd promised Mason. If there was ever a moment to act on this, it was now, tonight.

Less than an hour after she'd called Mason Williams and told him her confusing story, he was standing beside her. He firmly shoved aside carbon filters, spray cans, tools and a small rusty toolbox, unfolded a large transparent sheet of tracing paper and spread it out on the workbench in Nehal's garage. Dust particles whirled up in the light of the lamp she was holding over the hand-drawn floor plan. At a scale of 1:100, they were looking at the top view of a walled villa on the banks of the River Kabul.

'Hafami's working palace,' Mason said. 'Our buddy has a total of three palaces. His family home is in Wazir Akbar Khan Park and he has a colossal villa in Mazar-e-Sharif. But this is his private fiefdom. This is where he has all of his staff meetings, where he receives his criminal pals and political cronies, and, if the rumours are true, this is also where he hosts his private *bacha bazi* parties. The odds are that the boy was taken here.'

His finger slid to where the thick dark lines at the front of the compound were interrupted by a narrower line. 'There are two ways of getting into this place.' He tapped the black line. 'The main entrance, or' – at this he moved his finger in the opposite direction and indicated a point right outside the compound's wall – 'the stage door, aka the sewer tunnel.'

He pulled a dark wetsuit out of the large commando rucksack made of waterproof PVC and held it out to her. 'Your outfit.'

'What about you? I'm not going on my own.'

He grinned and lifted the corner of his shirt under his military fatigues. She spotted the matt black of his long johns underneath it.

'Like we said, we're a team.' Then he bent over the drawing again. 'It's looking promising. Due to the extreme drought the river level has never been lower. The tunnel will take us straight to this spot here.' His finger pointed to a dark square right beside the swimming pool. 'The engine room.'

'How about security?'

'This location isn't known as a top priority. The other two compounds are much more heavily guarded, because they house his entire family. This complex just has two or three permanent guards. It's only when they're expecting important guests that extra security is deployed. Always members of the local police force.'

'What do we do when we find the boy?'

'We take him with us. Via the same route.'

He took a small parcel from the rucksack: a junior wetsuit, a foil blanket, a first aid kit and a stretcher made of rope. 'I'll carry him out on my back, if necessary.' He folded the drawing and put it back in the bag. 'Any questions?'

'A couple hundred. I'll save them for later.' With a grin on her face she walked to the side of the jeep, opened the door, draped her black scarf over the window as a curtain, and squirmed into her wetsuit. She couldn't tell whether her body was shaking because of adrenaline or sheer terror. Probably a combination of the two.

'One more thing,' Mason said, after she'd put on her shirt and loose-fitting trousers over her wetsuit and had tied the scarf around her head. 'Breaking into such a secure complex is normally a matter for well-trained Special Ops. I'm taking you because I have faith in you. Because of your *pencak silat* training and how you rose to the occasion after the car accident.' He looked at her intently. 'But you have to promise me one thing. You do exactly as I say. No more and no less. Deal?'

She nodded.

He repeated his question, this time directing it at Nehal, who'd climbed behind the wheel, having already decided she was going to drive. She gave him an annoyed look.

'No make deal with *Amrikaya*,' she replied in broken English and smiled with a giggle. 'But with you I do.'

It was strange not to see Nehal behind the wheel for a change. A chilly night wind blew in through the open windows of the old Jeep Wrangler as Mason drove them into the city. He pointed to a small shimmery spot in the clear sky.

'We've got zeppelins hovering above the city. Aerostats. They can pick up and analyse pretty much all mobile communication. But by the time we sent those things up in the air, the Taliban had long since dumped their mobile phones and closed their email accounts. Now they communicate like the Mujahideen did in the 1970s, during the Soviet occupation of Afghanistan. They pass on their instructions, threats and warnings orally. Or by letter. Commonly referred to as night letters. They're passed from hand to hand and burned after reading. Our very expensive toys are just hanging there like washed-up junk.'

'Afghans always smarter than Americans,' Nehal commented from the back seat.

'Let's see if you're right,' Mason said while slowing down for a roadblock staffed by an Afghan army unit. The curfew was already in effect. Anyone on a public road without a valid reason was stopped and arrested.

The soldiers gestured urgently for him to drive right up the concrete blocks, but instead Mason stopped the jeep some fifteen metres in front of the barrier. He'd stepped out of the car before they'd even had a chance to aim their fully automatic rifles. Farah watched intently from the dim interior of the jeep as he calmly approached the clearly nervous men. The giant American in military fatigues who looked like an Afghan firmly asked for the *qomandon*, the commander. His posture reminded her of when she'd first seen him at the Butcher Street T-junction. One of the soldiers rushed to the nearest house and returned with a stocky man in uniform – the *qomandon* – who stomped straight over to Mason.

The men saluted. In the short conversation that followed, Mason visibly alluded to the jeep once. Then he leaned over to the other man, as though confiding something in him. She saw that as he did so he greased the other's palm. Both men then saluted again and parted.

As Mason calmly returned to the jeep, the road was cleared.

'Keep your eyes straight ahead,' he said as he got in and navigated the jeep between the concrete blocks.

The silence after they'd driven away from the roadblock lasted several minutes. Until Farah finally asked, 'What did you tell them?'

'That I was taking two senior politicians to a secret meeting. That your identities had to remain secret due to kidnapping threats. And just to be on the safe side, I slipped him some money.'

'In that case you should give me money too,' Nehal said. 'If I'm supposed to be a politician, I want to be paid as a politician.'

Her loud laughter reverberated through the jeep.

They'd reached the northwestern bank of the river. The walls around the villas here were higher than they were elsewhere, and the barbs of the razor wire on top probably even sharper. The individual compounds were separated by plots of wasteland strewn with rotting garbage while weeds covered half-dead trees. What little could be seen of the villas behind the walls was bathed in the pale-blue glow of the swimming pools that were always illuminated. No cars were parked out on the street.

'Private security patrols this area,' Nehal said. 'Any parked car is a potential bomb. It's towed away at once. If you get out, I'll keep driving around.'

About a hundred metres from the compound, Mason stopped the jeep, jumped out and together with Farah headed towards the riverbank, while Nehal began her first tour of the neighbourhood.

Underneath one of the trees, among the rampant weeds, Mason began to take off his fatigues and boots. Farah looked around and in one smooth motion pulled her shirt over her head before taking off her trousers and trainers and putting them in the rucksack. When they stood facing each other, both in their matt black wetsuits, she felt self-conscious. Their thin neoprene suits were little more than a second skin.

Mason leaned over. Almost tenderly he inserted the bud of the wireless headset into her ear. His touch sent a quiver through her body. From afar came the sound of a deep and rapidly approaching rumble. Mason placed his hands on her shoulders and pushed her down. They made themselves as small as possible. A patrolling combat helicopter swooped over low. The greasy layer of oil on the river water glistened in the glow cast by the searchlight beam.

They waited for the chopper to ascend again on the other bank and disappear from view behind the taller buildings before they stood up. Mason swung the rucksack over his shoulder and took her hand. He carefully guided her across the wet and mossy rocks, and by the time they reached the entrance of the tunnel the water was up to their waists.

The sewer was closed off by a galvanised iron fence, secured in a rough brick wall. From behind the fence the smell of putrefaction wafted towards them. Mason tried several lock picks until they finally heard the cylinder lock click and the metal chain come off.

He looked at her to see if she was ready. She nodded. She waded after him into the low tunnel. The light from their head lamps attracted insects; they circled around her head with a vicious crackling sound. The whiff of methane gas produced by decaying sewage waste entered her nostrils. And all around she heard the shrill squeaking and rustling of rats scuttling away along the dripping walls. Her fear of small spaces made her heart race.

She thought of Roshan's story, the anger it had aroused in her. She thought of Idris, who was probably being held somewhere in this complex. This was about them, she told herself. Not about her. She walked on in silence, stooping under the vaulted ceiling until Mason came to a halt.

They stood before a wall with a jumble of drainpipes sticking out. Mason illuminated the cast-iron manhole cover above their heads and started pushing it with all his might. She tried to help him, but however hard he pushed and cursed the entire world, the lid wouldn't budge from its concrete casing.

Then came his scream.

Out of nowhere and deafening.

3
Raylan

1976

Only the bluish flames made a sound. Spreading in all directions over the monk's orange habit, penetrating the skin's lower layers and reaching the deep tissues – the muscles and bones. Riveted to the ground in lotus position, the monk rocked his upper body, as if to control the unbearable pain without letting out a single cry. He turned his head a quarter and looked Raylan straight in the eyes. His voice barely rising above the hissing and crackling.

'We want . . . to bring . . . peace . . .'

Raylan was astonished by the calm with which the man being consumed by the fire spoke to him.

'They say we're communists. They're ripping up our flags . . . ransacking our temples, attacking us . . . destroying our statues . . .'

Here, the monk's words faltered. His head had turned black and he could barely move his twisted mouth.

'I sacrifice my body to the fire . . . to keep alive . . .'

His final words trailed off into nothingness. The last flames pushed his charred body backwards against the asphalt.

The lamentation of the other monks in the square and the sound of approaching sirens were drowned out by the staccato tapping of iron hammers striking hard against the ink ribbon of his Remington Travel-Riter. At the speed of a hundred characters per minute, Raylan's fingers raced over the keys to pass on the burning monk's dying words to his newspaper.

. . . to keep alive the hope of freedom and peace . . .

Once more he found himself on Lam Son Square in Saigon. This time not tortured by a memory that had haunted him in nightmares and anguishing flashbacks for more than ten years, but as the earnest seeker of half-forgotten answers. From behind his typewriter, he undertook a journey back in time to do what he'd promised Isobel he would: give the dead a voice.

Under cover of long-range missiles, in a landing craft he again crossed the River Perfume in Huế with the marines of Alpha Company. They were packed together, sitting on crates of ammunition, heavy weapons and explosives. On their green camouflage helmets and bullet-proof vests he read their battle nicknames: Leatherneck, Jarhead, Born to Kill, Deadeye, Ghost, Magnet Ass, Short Round. Boys who hadn't started this war, but they were tasked with finishing it. In their teens and twenties with a deep-rooted faith in America's greatness and goodness.

'We're here to bring you democracy,' one of them called.

'And to wipe out the commies,' another added.

'We're here to kill all the gooks!' shouted a third.

They all had that dull look in their eyes of boys who would continue denying, to their last breath, what they knew deep inside: that any one of them might die today.

And as Raylan ascended the riverbank crouching with them through a mayhem of falling bombs, shots and bullets bursting bodies apart, he hit the keys of his typewriter harder and harder. With each new stroke, the senseless deaths of boys dropping around him took on a different dimension.

That of a fiery indictment by a seasoned war correspondent.

Raylan wrote as if his sanity depended on it. While he plugged away on his Remington, in his thoughts he roamed a smouldering crater landscape where there'd once been rice paddies. The nearby village had been reduced to ashes by a napalm bombing. The scorched earth was littered with the charred bodies of villagers on their way to their fields. A lone GI with a bandana around his head and a machine gun perched on his shoulder emerged from the fiery smoke. Smirking, he told how he'd been deployed to Vietnam as a rookie, 'to win people's hearts and minds'. With a casual gesture the kid swung the machine gun off his shoulder and aimed it at a bomb crater where a handful of sobbing women and children had taken refuge. 'But in this godforsaken place you can't tell your friends from your enemies, damn it!'

And he started shooting. Until the weeping in the crater was completely silenced and only the hammers hitting the ribbon could be heard.

Among the burned-out ruins of the Imperial City of Huế, Raylan was again reminded of that little boy brushing dirt with his bare hands from the faces of the dead in the shallow mass grave. He picked up the boy and took him to the military field hospital, where a doctor examined him. All that time Raylan had grasped his hand and anxiously listened to his frightened whisper. 'The men came when we were sleeping. They dragged Mummy and Daddy outside ...'. And Raylan imagined the Viet Cong with their kill lists breaking down the doors of people living in Huế to cart them away in open trucks to collection points in the city where large pits had already been dug. He demanded an explanation from the young commander in charge of the operation. 'Why are you separating parents from their children?'

'Under the new social-communist order, collaborators pose a great threat,' replied the man with his inscrutable enemy face. And with a calculated gesture he ordered the soldiers to take up position in front of the group of men and women at the edge of the pit.

The soldiers raised their rifles.

'You're killing your own people!' Raylan shouted.

A second order sounded. Then shots rang out. In the ensuing silence, the clicking of typewriter keys, capturing everything for posterity, was all that was left.

Sometimes Raylan took a break from his journey. By then evening had arrived unnoticed. Or he'd worked the entire night and saw the dawn light fall through the windows. Then he drank his coffee and flipped through the pile of notebooks and diaries lying beside him on his desk and he came to the conclusion that he no longer needed them. All his memories, no matter how gruesome and confronting, had been recorded by his subconscious. Ten years of reporting on the Vietnam war turned out to be a universe through which he could travel freely with his

Remington as a time capsule. An experience that was more intense than the surge of adrenaline he got every time he jumped into a helicopter, jeep or army lorry on his way to the front lines again. Now he could get much closer to everything without endangering his own life, spread his wings and soar, allowing him a bird's eye view of the landscape.

There were times when he abruptly got up from behind his typewriter and left the house feeling desperate. Then it was unbearable to realize how naive and obstinate he'd been. All that time in Vietnam he'd continued to hope that through everything he and his colleagues wrote the world would eventually see the total pointlessness of the war. He was so obsessed with that idea that he didn't realize his own life was gradually being destroyed by the war.

Effortlessly, he jumped in and out of helicopters. He knew how to take notes, how to deal with death, but no one had ever told him anything about being a father. That woman on his last night in Saigon, who'd begged him to take her child to safety, appeared in his dreams. The next morning he wrote about all the fatherless children produced by the war and he thought of his own son.

All these years he'd been a father to Paul in name only.

Having come to this realization, he roamed for hours through Kocha-e-Kharabat – the street of musicians and dancers in Kabul – where the strumming of an old fifteen-string lute accompanied the lamenting songs of well-known local singers. This calmed his nerves and gave him unexpected insights.

He rushed home and ambushed Isobel with his wild idea. He'd give Paul the time of his life, an experience he'd never forget.

'Go ahead,' she said. 'And do your best to be the father he needs.'

Through clouds of dust he drove the BMW into the mountains, with Paul tucked under a blanket in the sidecar beside him. The journey took them over the roughest roads, past hills strewn with boulders, along steep cliffs, through dry riverbeds and across desert sand, until they arrived on the flanks of the Pamir Mountains in the northeast. A desolate area, which Marco Polo and Alexander the Great had once passed through, and where Kyrgyz nomads now herded their sheep, goats and yaks in caravans to take them to traders in Pakistan to exchange for food and clothing. Here, at an altitude of more than three thousand metres, in front of a stone hut used by the Kyrgyz and Wakhan nomads travelling their trade route, Raylan had real contact with his son for the first time ever.

He tried to hide how uncomfortable he felt, made a campfire, boiled water for tea, coffee and rice, and had Paul try roasted yak. An icy wind rose up as the daylight faded to deep crimson. The mountain peaks crested through slowly drifting clouds, and the sparks from the fire jumped so high it almost seemed like some childlike attempt to touch the stars.

He looked at his son, who after his last bite stared into the distance. A child now part of something much bigger than himself. His face was bathed in an orange-red glow from the fire; his head full of thoughts a father could barely fathom.

'You okay, boy?'

Paul nodded.

'A penny for your thoughts.'

Paul turned his head towards Raylan. 'Did you always want to be a journalist, Daddy?'

All those times he'd run away from home as a child, further and further and longer and longer, until a day came when he didn't return. At a later age that restlessness took complete control of his life. Being a journalist seemed, above all else, to legitimize never settling down in one place.

'I didn't know I was going to be one, a journalist. It just turned out that way.' Raylan could see in Paul's eyes that he wasn't satisfied with the answer.

'That's not what I asked you.'

Grinning, Raylan shook his head. He wanted to stroke Paul over his hair, but the boy avoided him. Uncomfortable, he took a sip of his coffee, which by now was lukewarm and tasted bitter. 'I'm not proud of what I've done, if that's what you're getting at.'

'No, I didn't mean that. I was just asking . . .'

'. . . if it was my heart's desire. Well, I don't know . . . Honestly, it really wasn't about wanting. I had to do it. If you know what I mean?'

Paul stared ahead and shrugged his shoulders.

'Sorry I might not always give you the answer you want to hear, son, but that's the way it is. I can't make much more out of it. Why the curiosity about this?'

Paul obstinately stared into the fire. 'Because I want to be one too,' he finally muttered, 'a journalist, just like you.'

Raylan didn't know what to say. His greatest desire was for his son to live a life beyond the reach of everything he'd been confronted with in his profession. A life in which the stability of a family and the certainty of a safe future were the measure of things. Not the chaos and pain he'd experienced. He thought long and hard about how to react. He didn't want to discourage Paul but certainly didn't want to encourage him either. 'Maybe one day you'll discover what you're really good at,' Raylan finally said.

Paul reacted crossly. 'I know exactly what I want.'

It was the forcefulness with which he said this, the certainty in his eyes, that made Raylan realize just how determined his son was. He stood up, put more wood on the fire and then sat down next to him.

'If that's what you want, really want, I'm sure you'll make an amazing journalist. At least you're not afraid. You're prepared to take risks . . . I think you got that from your mother.'

'So what did I get from you?'

'Being as stubborn as a donkey.' Raylan grinned. 'And believe me, that can be tricky. The world around you demands you adapt, that you do what everybody else does. And that's exactly what you shouldn't do.'

He felt Paul shiver and put an arm around him.

'Wherever you go, whatever you do, choose your own path. Keep believing in what you think is right.'

Raylan looked up at the sky, now a cloudless expanse with countless stars. He heard Paul cautiously choosing his words.

'Sometimes, when you're writing, I hear you crying. Why?'

'Because . . .' Raylan said trying to find the right words. 'When you're writing, it's as if everything happens all over again. I can show you the world, child, I can tell you about so many things, and I will, but I'll never be able to explain to you what a war does to people. All I hope is that you never have to experience one.'

Silently they stared into the fire, which flickered in the wind.

'Will you promise me something?' Raylan asked. He looked directly at Paul. 'That you'll never go to war of your own free will?'

Without reacting, Paul slowly turned his head away.

'Promise me?'

Raylan looked at his son, who just silently stared into the fire, and shuddered.

4
Farah

2009

There he stood in the sewer tunnel, his eyes filled with disbelief about what was happening in his head. Mason Williams pressed both hands against his temples as hard as he could, as if that might stop the pain. Slowly he slid down along the wall. Farah caught him to the best of her ability. His voice was hoarse. 'First aid kit. Syringe.'

She remembered what Gaby had confided to her at Camp Eggers – *roadside bomb, severe concussion, cluster headaches* – and grabbed the rucksack, unzipped it, rummaged around and by the light of her headlamp saw a glint of transparent plastic, the case with the pre-filled syringes. He unzipped his wetsuit. Gasping for breath, he gave her instructions.

'Pull off the blue shield. Orange tip on my belly. At a right angle. Push.'

She heard the click. The needle shot out of the pen. As soon as the Sumatriptan flowed from the syringe under his skin, an electric current seemed to course through his body. His blood vessels narrowed. He gasped for breath.

She pulled out the needle and disinfected the spot where she'd injected him.

'Breathe in for four seconds. And out for six.'

Slowly his body began to relax. His breathing became more regular.

'We'd better abort this mission,' she said.

He looked at her, stubbornly biting back the pain. 'Not without the boy.'

It took three long minutes for Mason to more or less return to his senses. Then he started to cast light on to the pipes. The quiet resolve with which he did this infuriated her. But he finally found one that seemed large enough to crawl through. He started unscrewing its grille. In the glow of her headlamp she saw that the tubing gradually went upwards. They'd have no choice but to climb in on their backs.

He gave her a final look. With a crooked smile he squeezed into the narrow pipe. His head was the first to disappear, followed by his upper body and then his legs. On his command she shoved in the bag, which he pulled along with his feet. Through her headset she could hear his heavy breathing. Then his voice. Muffled but forceful. 'Get in.'

The pipe was smooth, making the climb harder than she'd anticipated. She couldn't get much purchase on it. Every centimetre was a triumph. She thought of those ventilation shafts she'd crawled through in Jakarta. This tubing was even narrower, but Mason's voice and the faint glow of his flashlight kept her claustrophobia at bay. Her fingers were just strong enough to push herself off from the surface.

She'd advanced a few metres. It couldn't be far now.

An engine kicked in. The heavy throbbing of a pump. Seconds later, a powerful water jet with the unmistakable smell of chlorine gushed over her. She held her breath, felt the first signs of panic and heard his voice just in time. 'Raise your left arm.'

She did as she was told, slid her left arm up with difficulty and felt his hand grab hers. If he lost his grip the current would drag her into the sewer tunnel. His other hand grabbed her shoulder. Then he pulled her up through the raised maintenance hatch and helped her out of the pipe. He didn't let go until she signalled that she could stand on her own.

Their wetsuits and boots were covered in oil and reeked. They'd be leaving a trail. The stench alone would betray their presence. Better to remove them.

They moved as far apart as possible, with their backs to each other, and quickly got changed.

A second.

Perhaps even shorter. Holding what they'd peeled from their

323

bodies, they were acutely aware of each other's presence. A brief, breathless moment, when everything seemed to fall away.

Time, guilt, powerlessness.

Immediately followed by their ragged breathing, while Farah quickly put on her bra and knickers, pulled the shirt over her head, fastened her trousers, and tied the black scarf tightly around her head.

Mason quickly stuffed their diving gear into the rucksack, zipped it up and swung it over his shoulders.

'C'mon.'

The engine room was close to the swimming pool. Seven brick steps curved gently upwards. Mason stopped abruptly, pulled a small aerosol out of the rucksack and sprayed a light mist on to the first four steps. Green laser beams appeared in the vapours. After a muffled curse, he pulled out a rope, flung it over a heavy metal pipe above the steps, secured it and was about to climb up when he froze. He had to grab the rope so as not to fall.

She reached out to him. 'What's wrong?'

'Dizzy . . . Side effect of the Sumatriptan.'

They stood like that for a while, until she felt him relax again. He grimaced at her. 'On with the show.'

He took hold of the rope again. After a few short, fast breaths, he hoisted himself up and crawled along the raised stone edge. When he gave the all-clear, she followed behind him.

The nymphs around the pool were the first thing she saw. Their wings half unfolded as if to welcome her. She heard a soft hissing. Hot air, intended to dry the swimmers, was released through small holes in the stone wings.

Beyond an illuminated fountain stood a two-storey building, constructed of pink granite and fringed by Corinthian columns of marbled limestone. Each floor had a wide, covered landing with a balustrade. A spiral staircase on either side of the building connected all levels. Stone eagles marked the corners of the flat roof.

Mason pulled out a gadget the size of a mobile phone. With the utmost concentration, he aimed its antenna at various parts of the building. Even the stone eagles at the corners didn't escape the beady eye of the EDF, an electronic device finder capable of detecting the presence of hidden cameras. Even switched off, the minicams reflected the laser beam and betrayed where they were located. The LEDs lit up to reveal they were installed everywhere, even inside the eyes of the stone eagles. But none were operational.

On Mason's sign they crept up the outside staircase.

With the help of his lock picks, he managed to open the first room. A click and a turn of the knob, and the door hinged open, which Mason then closed behind them as softly as possible. No torches: with only net curtains in front of the windows any light would be visible from outside. While standing on the deep-pile carpet of a room all but dominated by a huge bed, with a ceiling mirror to match, they waited for their eyes to adjust to the dark.

Mason detected the first spycam on the mirror above the bed. The EDF also lit up when he checked the painting on the wall opposite the bed. It was an ancient-looking image of a man wearing a long robe in a blatantly erotic pose with a youngster meekly bending over. The eyes of the man penetrating him were filled with lust, those of his prey with submission.

Mason whispered. 'It's in the eyes.'

'What is?'

'The camera. It's hidden in one of the pupils.'

They discovered a third spycam in the marble bathroom, concealed in the immense wall mirror.

As well as the ingeniously hidden cameras, the explicit paintings and the garish decor, the rooms on this floor shared another disturbing feature: not a trace of the boy.

They were about to head to the second floor via the outside staircase when they picked up a deep, dark growling noise. This was followed by the creaking and squeaking of a hydraulic gate sliding open. A jet-black Cherokee with tinted windows slowly crunched across the gravel path to the front of the villa. There it waited until Hafami came out and got in beside the driver. Two guards armed with Kalashnikovs flanked the opening wrought-iron gate. The driver accelerated and left them in a cloud of dust.

On Mason's instruction, Farah used her mobile to contact Nehal and whispered the make of the car and registration number to her. 'It's Hafami. Follow him.'

'What about you?'

Mason gestured for her to break off the connection at once. The guards walked from the gate to the outside staircase. On the first floor, they each went in different directions. The younger of the two continued up to the next floor. Doors opening and closing. The sounds of a routine security check.

Farah and Mason crept across the landing to the outside staircase on the other side. They checked to see if anyone was on the ground-floor level, slipped in through a sliding glass door and froze in their tracks.

They found themselves staring down a tiger, its mouth wide open in a silent roar.

5
Raylan

1976

When they returned from the trip to the mountains, their faces were tanned and healthy, while the look in their eyes was softer. Paul described to his mother in vivid detail what he and his father had experienced in the wild. But neither talked about what they'd discussed as 'men'. Paul was still too young to know the words for these things. Raylan had never learned to use them.

Silently they cared for their third travel companion, the BMW R27.

'Always treat your motorbike like a friend,' Raylan had advised as he hoisted Paul on to the gas tank in front of him in the Pamir Valley. The boy imagined himself a knight who could give his iron horse the spurs by reaching for the steering levers. Raylan had felt his son's excitement through his leather jacket and realized how much Paul resembled him.

He was certain of it: the urge to discover the world had been passed on to Paul through his genes. Though Isobel also contributed by shortly after his birth wrapping the baby in a large shawl, binding it to her body and dragging him everywhere in Kabul with her sketchbook and pencils. Undoubtedly, she'd also passed her empathic curiosity about people on to him, as well as her openness to the many beautiful things in the world.

'Be the father he needs,' she'd said.

If Paul was serious about following in his father's footsteps later in life, it was never too soon to start. He picked Paul up from school, and together they drove along a wide boulevard in the direction of a narrow white column. It stood in the middle of a marble plaza surrounded by a small park.

'Have you ever taken a good look at this?' he asked, as Paul climbed out of the sidecar.

'I think so.'

'Then I'm sure you know its significance?'

Paul shyly shrugged his shoulders. Together they walked up to the pillar, which seemed to loom higher and higher.

This is the Independence Pillar. For centuries, foreign armies have caused havoc in this country. Alexander the Great was one of the first, Dzhengis Khan followed, the British were the last. They were defeated more than fifty years ago. And then the Afghans said, enough is enough. From this day forth our country will be independent. And this monument is a testament to that freedom.'

Then they drove to the National Museum, where a short while later they stood together with Ahmad Parwaiz in front of a painting depicting the legendary Battle of Maiwand in 1880. Parwaiz told Paul the compelling story of the girl who waved the Afghan flag on top of the hill, while below her the Afghan army battled the British.

'Malalai is sometimes called the Afghan Joan of Arc,' said Parwaiz, who almost had a heart attack when he saw Paul pressing his nose against the canvas.

'What are you doing, *bachem*?'

'Seeing if she's got blue eyes like that girl in the butterfly garden.'

A few days later, Raylan was with Paul on Jadayi Maiwand Boulevard, where a military parade was held every August on Independence Day. But it wasn't August yet, and no troops deftly paraded in close ranks. Instead, hundreds of young people chanting slogans, with their fists raised in the air, marched through the streets and demanded the resignation of President Daoud.

'Groups congregate to protest almost daily these days,' Raylan said. One time they're from the Communist Party, another time the Islamic Youth Organization and then a branch of the trade union gets its turn again. Everyone seems to be used to it, but these gatherings are getting more and more numerous and the shouting louder and louder. And do you know why? Afghanistan may be independent, but the country still doesn't belong to the people. These youngsters are the future of the country. The government allows them to study at university but won't listen to them, and their chance of getting a job is slim. Actually, their participation in society isn't welcome. They want to change that. Not just for themselves, but for everyone. So they take to the streets more and more often, with their fists raised in the air. Because they're angry. And what happens when you get angry?'

'You prepare for a fight?'

Raylan was watching the protesters. 'Exactly. And that fight's gonna happen, kiddo. Not today, nor tomorrow, but soon. And then it won't be just a fight. By then it'll be a revolution.'

They went to Shahr-e Naw Park, where Raylan did a workout with Paul he'd picked up from the Marines in Vietnam. To make Paul mentally stronger and increase his stamina, they ran an obstacle course of their own making that included a climbing frame, a sand hill and a wide, dry ditch. At each hurdle, Raylan thought up something extra, such as push-ups, rugby tackles and some playful wrestling exercises. All of it an introduction to what he really wanted to teach his son: free fighting techniques, which he'd witnessed in raucous bars, in alleyways and on military bases and had made his own.

'You've learned from your mother that we have to be kind to each other,' Raylan said, resting his hands on Paul's shoulders and pulling him towards him. 'But in reality people aren't all that kind. They'll grab you when you least expect it. Has happened to me a bit too often. So that's not going to happen to you. I'm gonna make sure you're prepared for whatever hits you.'

With a sudden move he gave Paul a hard shove. The boy was so stunned he almost lost his balance. Raylan assumed the posture of a fighter, with his fists protecting his upper body and face.

'You're my enemy. C'mon, punch me.'

Paul looked at him in bewilderment.

'Well, don't just stand there like you're afraid of the world! You're my son. And *my* son isn't a weakling. Hit me!'

All at once Paul reacted aggressively. He was so quick that Raylan only just managed to block the right angle to his chin. He did this decisively, using his left arm, and then extended the flat of his hand at Paul's face.

'Right hand over the nose, fingers towards the eyes.'

As he demonstrated this, he forced Paul's head backwards and brought his knee towards his crotch.

'Next, you hit him hard in the balls. Got it?'

Raylan let go of Paul and took up his fighting posture again.

'One more time.'

Paul looked at him horrified.

'C'mon. Hit me again.'

His son's frustrated reaction came spilling out.

'No!'

Raylan lowered his fists.

'What do you mean, "no"?'

'This isn't for me . . .'

'Then what is?'

'What the girl in the butterfly garden was practising.'

It was as if Paul had punched him in the stomach with that remark. Raylan imagined her in front of him again. Her long black curly hair. Those sea-blue eyes. His eyes. Helai's words echoed through his head. *That little girl there in the garden, that's my world, my truth.* It was also his truth. But not one he was prepared to share with his son.

The boy stood with his hands on his hips to give his words more power.

'I want her to teach me to fight. Not you.'

'That's not possible, kiddo.'

'And why not?'

'I don't know where she is.'

'In the palace. She's in the palace!'

'We can't go in there.'

'You can't go in there, but Mummy can!'

Raylan was flabbergasted by the intensity with which Paul reacted.

'Just stop now.'

'No, you! You've got to stop!'

All the boy's frustration of the past few years was now released.

Tears welled in his eyes, snot dripped from his nose. He clenched his fists. 'You were never there, and now you suddenly think you can boss me around. Mummy takes care of me. And she's much better at it than you are!'

Raylan reacted without thinking. His words came out much louder and colder than he wanted.

'You think you're a tough guy? But when things get a bit rough, you're happy to be a mummy's boy again.'

Paul's voice wavered as he randomly started pounding Raylan with his fists.

'You're a bastard. Go back to your war!'

Paul abruptly turned and ran away.

Raylan wanted to follow and give him a piece of his mind, but he was shocked by the aggression he felt towards his son. Together with that realization came the dismay, and with the dismay the unavoidable panic. He noticed his entire body was trembling. He frantically searched in his trouser pocket for the strip of Anafranil tablets. He'd been cutting back on the pills, but now – right now – he didn't have a choice. He needed them. Not two, like usual, but five. He pressed the tablets out of the strip and finely chewed them because he didn't have any water with him. Gasping for breath, he sought support at the nearest tree.

He concentrated on his breathing.

Breathe in for four seconds, out for six.

He lost track of the time. Once he calmed down, he looked around again. Paul was nowhere to be seen.

The first thing he did was to return to the spot where he'd parked the motorbike. But Paul wasn't sulking in the sidecar; the bucket seat was empty. He ran back into the park. His heart almost bursting out of his chest. He shouted Paul's name so loudly that passers-by reacted terrified. At the other end of the park he kept looking around like a wild man. Sweating profusely, he ran back to the BMW, rode around the park twice, then stopped at every alleyway and criss-crossed every street in the neighbourhood.

No trace of his son. The sun slid behind the mountains. Panic and a rage beyond his control had him by the throat.

6
Farah

2009

There were several tigers, mounted in various menacing poses. They lined the hallway of Hafami's villa, which led to an oblong room with a lofty, Gothic ceiling. High-backed leather chairs were arranged around an oval table. The walls boasted painted scenes of heroic battles. It instantly took Farah back to the mural in Uncle Parwaiz's living room in the Netherlands: the historic panorama of Afghan wars going all the way back to Alexander the Great's invasion.

The guards could be heard at the front of the villa. They'd finished their rounds and entered the hallway. Mason gestured that Farah should follow him. They walked through a marble corridor past a lounge-like sitting room, a huge kitchen and an adjacent dining room until they reached a steel spiral staircase at the back of the building that led them to the basement.

The corridor opened on to a luxurious space decorated to look like an exclusive nightclub. The padded bar was inlaid with gemstones and generously stocked with bottles of liquor. The beams of their two torches swept across seven oriental daybeds and converged on a stage measuring roughly four by four metres. To the right of the stage was a separate platform full of musical instruments on stands. She recognized the fifteen-string lute, the harmonium and the Indian drums. The images of half-naked dancers on the walls strengthened her conclusion.

'This is a *qush-khana*.'

Mason looked at her, not understanding.

'A special room where the *kataah*, the owner of dancing boys, invites his friends and colleagues to come and watch the show.'

All this time the LED lights on Mason's EDF were going into overdrive. The small room was littered with spycams.

Behind the stage they discovered a passageway inside a wall. Having been painted the same black as the concrete wall around it, the bay with the metal door was barely noticeable. The lock, which had a control panel with a keypad and was made of inch-thick steel, gave the impression that it was a safe.

Footsteps could be heard on the spiral staircase.

Mason quickly rummaged in his rucksack. He pulled out what looked like a calculator. He inserted the cable attached to it into the door lock. Figures appeared on the display. It only took seconds. A soft click signalled the unlocking. The heavy door opened with difficulty.

The room they now entered was square with dim blue lighting. The only sound was the soft whirring of small fans inside three NAS modules next to one another. In the middle, on a metal desk, sat a laptop. Farah immediately woke it from sleep mode. The names of the different NAS modules appeared on the screen. They spoke for themselves.

Sugar Boy. Candy Dancer. Everlasting Desire.

She thought of those boys forced to dance for the men in the *qush-khana*, the paedo pictures in the rooms. Her trembling fingers worked the laptop's touch pad, trying to gain access to the NAS, but it required decryption.

The voice of one of the guards could be heard from the room with the stage. He was communicating with his colleague upstairs via his hand-held radio. Mason tried to close the door with his back, but the lock had other ideas. There was the sharp scraping of metal-on-metal when the door hit its steel frame.

The sudden silence in the *qush-khana*.

A sure sign that they had been discovered.

She looked at Mason, who gestured for her to take cover beside him against the wall. *You have to promise me one thing.* Running over to him now would make too much noise. *You do exactly as I say*. She looked around. It was impossible to hide. The door handle moved.

She obeyed a bizarre impulse.

The barrel of his Kalashnikov. She was looking straight down it. Farah could tell from the eyes of the guard aiming at her that he'd been prepared for anything.

Except for the woman opposite him, who'd hastily removed her shirt. Her black lace bra showed much of her breasts.

His hesitation may have lasted no more than a hundredth of a second.

But it was enough.

With his left hand, Mason grabbed the guard by the hair and yanked his head back as far as he could, while elbowing him hard in the neck with his right arm. The man collapsed. His Kalashnikov clattered to the floor.

After this quick-thinking action, Mason remained bent over him, breathing heavily. She saw that he was sweating, put her top back on and walked over to him. 'Well, I hope that's not because of me.'

He produced a feeble grin. 'I wish it were.'

Using tie wraps he deftly bound the man's hands behind his back, then secured his ankles. He covered the man's mouth with breathable tape. The younger guard's voice came over the radio. Mason looked at her for answers.

'He wants to know what's going on.'

'What should I say?'

'*Alarme kazeb. Hech gap nest.*'

He grabbed the radio, pressed the speaker button, and repeated the words as faithfully as he could. '*Alar ... me ka ... zeb. Hech gap ...*' He looked at her, unsure of himself, and copied her lip movement. '*... nest.*' Then he immediately switched off the device. 'Christ. What did I just say?'

'Fa-alse alaaarm. Over and ... ou-out.'

'Oh fuck ...' As quickly as he could he started pulling the hard drives out of the NAS modules. 'We have to take them with us. All of them.'

There were twelve in total. They went into the rucksack along with the laptop.

Footsteps approached from the corridor above. Mason looked at her. 'I screwed up big time, didn't I?'

With their backs pressed to the wall, they stood on either side of the wide door opening on to the *qush-khana*. Farah could tell from the way the young guard had descended the steps that he was on the alert. He hesitated before he went any further. He whispered into the radio.

When he didn't receive a response, he must have sensed that something was up. When he reached the doorway, he sounded irritated: 'Samir?'

They both held their breath. There was undoubtedly a reason for his hesitancy. Perhaps he'd never set foot in here before. Maybe he thought his older colleague was giving him a hard time. Whatever it was, it threw him off his guard.

That lack of alertness should have done the trick when Mason landed the side of his hand on the young man's neck. But it didn't.

She watched it unfold before her eyes. The youngster in the black guard's uniform spun around, raising his leg as he did so. His booted foot slammed full into Mason's fist, which he'd lifted in the nick of time to cover his face.

Mason ended up against the wall.

She must have screamed without realizing it, because the young guard immediately turned to her. Just then her right foot landed smack in his crotch, and he doubled over. She reached for his gun and yanked it off his shoulder. She hit his skull hard with the butt, hard enough to stop his moaning. She took some tie wraps from the rucksack, bound his wrists and ankles like she'd seen Mason do, then taped his mouth shut.

Mason had scrambled to his feet. He swore under his breath and had trouble breathing. She wanted to sling the rucksack over her shoulders, but he stopped her. 'Thanks. But please allow me.'

They glanced at each other. Without any discussion, they both knew. The boy they'd come to find wasn't here.

Mason put his hand on her shoulder. 'Let's go.'

They walked up the stairs, through the corridor and out via the entrance hall. As Mason began to fumble with the gate's opening mechanism, Farah involuntarily looked up and wondered if the silver-coloured zeppelin hovering somewhere unseen high above their heads had picked up any of their activities. Then she felt Mason's arm, turned and saw the gate swing open.

They stuck as close as possible to the walls of the other compounds. A car approached in the distance. It was driving too slowly for an ordinary civilian vehicle. They ducked behind a wall. The engine of the slowly passing car sounded familiar. Her mobile phone buzzed. It was Nehal. 'I followed Hafami all the way to the east,' she said hastily. 'He's in District 12, Proja-i-Gawdari. I got in touch with Malid. He should be driving somewhere near you right now.'

Now it dawned on Farah why the vehicle was moving so slowly and the engine sounded familiar to her. She didn't hesitate. Before Mason had a chance to react, she was out on the street. From the centre line she waved to the Ranger in the distance until she saw the bright-red glow of the brake lights.

7
Raylan

1976

Raylan had been driving around like a maniac for over an hour when he realized that Paul could blindly find his way through every alley-way in the old centre. Because of the network of small streets, their house wasn't even that far from the park via the shortest route. His last hope: Paul had gone home to Isobel, the only one who really understood him.

After he'd parked the motorbike, he ran into the alleys of Murad Khane. Standing out of breath in front of their house, he saw the glow of light in the window of the upstairs room. He stormed up the stairs. In front of Paul's room door, Isobel was already waiting for Raylan. From the compelling way in which she looked at him he concluded that it would be wise not to proceed any further.

'Not now,' she whispered on edge. 'Later. I'll see you downstairs.'

Without waiting for his answer, she disappeared back into the room.

Although Raylan's anger and fear had given way to the reassuring certainty that Paul was safe, what prevailed was the realization that he'd once again done something that would no doubt be irreparable.

Downstairs he found a half-full bottle of whiskey, which he greed-ily put to his lips. Quietly he walked into Isobel's studio and looked at the canvas drying in the middle of the room on a wooden easel. It was a scene in the Pul-e Khishti Bazaar. Two merchants rolled out a red carpet. Other vendors in the narrow, shady street stopped passers-by and praised their wares. Like a magnet, his gaze was drawn to the spot to the right of the middle. There, a sun-tanned man in jeans, a blonde woman in a blue kaftan and a blond boy stepped into a ray of sunlight. They seemed to come from another world.

He looked at his likeness on the canvas as if he were seeing a ghost. Then he looked at the woman with the sensual eyes. Her gaze was confident and her posture determined. He thought about what he'd put her through all these years.

She'd lived with a man who because of his addiction to war had slowly alienated himself from her, but who'd also had a mistress for years. A man who wasn't there for her and his child most of the time, and whenever he was home had one foot out the door again, ready to go back to his war.

Most women would have filed for divorce for less.

Isobel hadn't.

She'd stayed with him.

With his back against the wall, he slowly sank through his knees, until his buttocks hit the floor. He stared at the little boy in the painting, who seemed happy, vulnerable too, open to the world. The world against which he'd vehemently tried to protect him.

He thought of his own youth. He must have been Paul's age. He sat against the old oak tree in the woods, just as he now sat against the wall of the studio. It was the middle of the night, and he'd run away from home again. That time, too, he'd sworn to himself that he'd never go back. He rubbed the bruises on his upper body and arms and listened to the wind, which told him to go home. To protect his mother, if need be, to fend off his father's drunken fists. He knew a day would come when he could do more. A day when he'd strike back. So hard that his mum would never have to be scared again. Every day he practised in the barn for that moment. But it didn't come to that. With the money his mother had saved, she put him on the train to New York City. A one-way ticket. On the night his father's fatal blows rained down on her, he was already thousands of miles away from his mother.

Isobel's soft voice nearby, 'I know you're only trying to protect him.' She sat down beside him on the floor. 'And you want to do that by making him tougher.' It wasn't a reprimand he saw in her eyes. 'But he's got a gentle side too, Ray. And I don't want him losing that.'

He nodded with some difficulty.

She reached for the bottle and also took a sip. 'Protect him as much as you want, cherish him, help him develop his self-esteem, but do it softly and with care.'

'I just want him to be happy.'

'He already is. I saw it on his face when he returned from the mountains.'

He took another sip. 'Is he asleep?'

She shook her head. 'He's waiting up for you.'

With a long sigh he stood up. The ascent up the creaking steps took for ever. The door didn't seem to be made of wood, but of lead. Each footstep he took in the room felt heavier than the one before.

Paul had left the bedside lamp on and was lying on his back staring at the ceiling, his eyes swollen from crying.

'Hey, kiddo . . . I went looking for you everywhere.'

Raylan waited for a reaction, and when it didn't come carefully sat down on the edge of the bed. He wanted to put his arms around his son and say he was sorry, but he didn't know how.

'I know why you sometimes cry when you're writing,' Paul said. He turned his head on the pillow and looked Raylan straight in the eye. 'You've seen people die.'

'And there was nothing I could do to prevent it,' Raylan whispered, and bit his lip.

'Sometimes I cry too,' Paul said. 'Not like today, but when I think you're never coming home from the war.'

'But I'm here now.'

'Yeah, but you always leave again.'

'Not this time. If you want, I'll always be here, just like I am now.'

'Okay . . . but I have to go to sleep soon . . . and . . .'

'Don't you like having me around?'

'Yeah, but you don't have to teach me how to fight.'

'Okay, we have a deal.'

Paul reached for the big book on the table next to his bed.

'Will you read to me?'

Raylan opened *The Wonderful Adventures of Nils*.

'From the beginning,' Paul said. And he turned on his side so he could see his father.

8
Farah

2009

During the twenty minutes it took them to get to District 12, they drove past an array of eerie concrete carcasses of flats, walled villas cheek by jowl with mud-brick houses and a large open field full of tents and huts made of cardboard and corrugated iron.

'They keep arriving,' Malid muttered. 'The refugees from the provinces. Everybody wants to come to the city. As if there's no war going on here.'

Just before they reached the location where Nehal said she'd be waiting for them in her jeep, they saw a large SUV turn out of a gate. It shot past them at high speed.

Farah was the first to recognize the Cherokee.

'They must have sounded the alarm in the compound,' Mason said. 'There's no point in chasing it now. Let's see what Hafami's been up to here.'

Nehal pointed to the drab walled complex. 'I looked it up. Apparently it's an orphanage. He's been in there all this time.'

Mason walked to the wall and paused a few feet away from it, hands on his hips and his legs slightly apart. As he looked straight ahead a shadow slid across his face. 'He's here.'

'Who?'

'The boy.'

'How do you know?'

He turned towards her.

'I just know.'

On Mason's instructions, Malid positioned his back against the wall with his legs at a ninety-degree angle. Mason ran up to him but came to an unexpected halt halfway. He stooped and pressed his hands to his temples. Farah knew what was happening and wanted to run over, but just then he ran up again, placed his right foot on Malid's thigh and climbed over him. Mason pulled himself up on the wall, clambered over the edge with his right leg gripping the other side and extended his left hand in invitation for Farah to follow suit.

She'd never done this before, just like everything she'd experienced in the past few days had been new to her. Her father's voice. *Never take a step back. There is only one way to victory, and that is forward.* She ran up and placed her right foot on Malid's thigh. She'd gathered so much speed that her left foot hit his shoulder. For a split second, she was suspended in the air. Then she felt Mason's grip. The rucksack followed with a dull thud.

The courtyard was deserted. In places, the weeds were knee-high. A heap of car tyres. A flash of recognition. Sekandar's drawing of the improvised 'rock' of gathered timber, stacked tyres and boulders on which he'd perched as the eagle.

She followed Mason to some cracked windows, which were partially boarded up with planks. They peered inside. In the dusk she saw beds with coiled springs. There were bodies on them. Bodies riveted to the upright headboard with chains.

The building was a dusty, dilapidated maze. When they tiptoed into the dormitory, they heard sobbing in the dark. Farah knelt beside one of the beds, gently pulled down the blanket and saw the boy's body underneath recoil in fear.

'Don't be afraid, I've come to get you out of here.'

The boy rolled over. The chained silhouettes in the other beds moved with him. She switched on the torch on her mobile phone. Emaciated faces with inflamed eyelids stared at her, frightened and confused. The excited whispering in the beds grew louder and more restless.

Farah put her finger to her lips. 'Shh.'

She went from bed to bed, illuminating the big-eyed, anxious faces. Not a single one looked like Idris's. She tried to shush them, but it was too late. The murmuring had penetrated deep into the building. She could tell from the reverberation of a closing door, the sound of foot-steps approaching. And from the light of a torch cutting an elongated path through the corridor. The boys ducked under their covers.

Mason pulled her close. He was shivering as if he had a fever. 'You need to do it.'

'Do what?'

'Eliminate him. Take off your scarf.'

She did as he asked. He took the scarf in his hands and quickly showed her what to do. He wasn't up to it himself. She just nodded and pressed herself against the wall beside the door frame.

The guard's silhouette appeared in the doorway. He stood there for a moment. The beam of his torch skimmed over the motionless bodies under the covers. Then he walked into the room.

In one fluid motion she came up behind him, flung the scarf over his head, like Mason had shown her, and then yanked it with both hands. As hard as she could. The man reached for his throat. The torch clattered to the floor. She knew what to do.

Turn around. Pull the scarf over her shoulder. Do a hip throw.

He sailed over her. His head hit the wall. He crashed to the floor, where he remained. Mason picked up the torch, handcuffed the guy with tie wraps and taped his mouth shut. They dragged him into the corridor by his feet.

In a tiled room they placed the man on a chair and taped his hands to the armrests, flat and with his fingers splayed. Mason took an EOD Leatherman out of his pocket and unfolded the bit with the sharp point, the C4 Punch intended for prepping explosives. He inserted the tip of the multi-tool under the nail of the man's index finger. He came round as if shocked by an electric current. His eyes bulged with pain. The tape on his mouth smothered his scream.

Farah leaned towards him. '*Ma ura wadar mesazam ke stop kona.* I can make him stop.'

The man stared at her. She saw the contempt in his eyes. If he could have, he'd have spat in her face, no doubt about it. She nodded at Mason. The tip of the awl went under another nail now. Again, the man in the chair jerked as if he'd received another electric shock.

'It's up to you,' she said. 'Either you cooperate, or we carry on doing this.'

He nodded.

Farah held Idris's photo in front of his face. 'Where is he?'

The answer was incomprehensible. Farah leaned in closer. Too close.

The headbutt came as a complete surprise. It knocked her backwards. The room was spinning. Everything went black for a moment.

When she came to Mason was feeling her jaw, her forehead and finally her nose. Her eyes were watering. Her brain seemed to be shrinking before expanding again with full force, making her head feel as if it was about to burst. She was nauseous, saw his mouth move and heard him whisper.

'Hate me now . . .'

Mason placed his broad hands on either side of her face, turned it straight towards him and put his thumbs on her nostrils. The pain he caused with one judicious tug was accompanied by a horrible cracking sound, which made her think her whole face was breaking in two.

She screamed.

He held her face firmly with both hands until the worst of the pain was over. Then he gently rubbed his thumb from the bridge of her nose down to its tip.

'Thank me later.'

She realized what he'd just done. Her nose was straight again. No permanent damage. The tears kept pouring down her face. He sat down behind her, letting her lean back against him, and whispered in her ear.

'We'll soon know how many more guards there are. You just shouted the house down.'

She was sitting in front of him while he massaged her temples. It was an unexpectedly tender and intimate moment. She almost forgot where they were, what a dangerous situation it was. She felt this every time she was near him: this sense of being protected no matter the danger. The dizziness subsided. She relaxed and slowly let her head fall against his chest. She opened her mouth, breathed in and out and dropped her arms down by her side. She was now completely collapsed against him . . . her pillar of strength. In the middle of a danger zone, she felt as if they were completely alone.

The reality sounded more ominous. She heard the rusty hinges of what must be a heavy door groan as it opened and closed, followed by the crunching of sand between shoes and a dirty floor. Someone was about to enter the circle, the circle in which she'd briefly imagined herself to be safe.

Mason leaned forward, his mouth at her ear again.

'Wait here.'

She felt his hands slide off her shoulders as he stood up. She looked for something to hold on to. He helped her by guiding her hands to a water pipe that ran along the wall at hip height. She grabbed hold of it and exhaled gently. As soon as she was able to sit up unaided, he let go of her and crept out of the room.

She tested the sturdiness of the pipe and pulled herself up by engaging the strength of her legs. Then she heard the cry of pain from the corridor. The dull impact of fists and feet hitting a body that was no longer a match for the strength of another, fitter body, one not weakened by cluster headaches and the side effects of Sumatriptan.

The sound of someone falling to the ground. It was Mason; he was moaning.

The rush of adrenaline she felt eliminated any pain and fatigue and pushed any sense of danger to the back of her mind. She tiptoed into the hallway and saw the silhouette of the man who kept lashing out at Mason's collapsed body.

She made a snap decision.

Estimate the distance. Don't make a sound. Take a run-up. Push off with her left leg. Leap. Her right foot in his lower back. Her hands around his head. Her left leg over his shoulder.

Her reflexes outpaced her thoughts. It had been a long time since she'd done this. But the movements were anchored in her body.

She threw her right leg over his other shoulder and interlocked both her legs. The speed with which she'd come running allowed her to fall forward while hanging around his neck like a kind of millstone.

When they both hit the floor with a thud, she kept her thighs tightly clamped around his throat. She rolled on to her side, waited for the twitching to diminish and only let go when he was completely limp.

All this time, Mason had been watching hollow-eyed. He sat with his back to the wall, practically paralysed, his arms by his side, his legs outstretched as if they no longer belonged to his body. After wiping the blood from his open mouth, it was her turn to gently touch his face to see if anything was broken. Blood dripped from a deep cut just above his right brow. One of his eyes was starting to swell. She looked at him questioningly.

He nodded laboriously. Even that hurt by the looks of it. She rummaged for the first aid kit in the rucksack and dripped iodine on to a piece of cotton wool. She cleaned all the wounds and covered them with plasters. His right eye was now completely swollen shut. Then, stifling a cry of pain, she stuffed cotton wool into her nostrils to stem the blood trickling over her lips.

She rubbed his shoulder. His voice was little more than a whisper. 'Never seen . . . anything like those moves of yours.'

'Thank me later,' she said with a wink and tried to help him up, but he was in too much pain. She pressed the Leatherman into his hand. 'Wait for me here.'

Cautiously, she walked down the corridor, as if inching towards the edge of a ravine, lured by what must be hidden somewhere in the darkness, somewhere among the gritty debris of the abandoned rooms and the dilapidated furniture.

Mason had sensed it too. *I just know.*

A steel door. She carefully opened it a crack. Cold air drifted up through the ashen half-light. Her mobile-phone torch swept a stone staircase. She descended step by step.

Down in the underground passageway, she held on to the wall. She illuminated the space around her and then gently pushed open the first door. A hole in the concrete floor, a water hose dangling from the wall, dripping. She closed the door and walked on.

Out of the corner of her eye she spotted a ray of light. Her throat was practically choked with fear now. An immobile figure a few metres away. Gradually it dawned on her: she was staring at her own reflection.

It was a dressing room. The table in front of the mirror was a still life of powder boxes and other make-up items. A clothes rack was laden with gold-embroidered robes, uniforms and shimmering scarves. Another table was strewn with bracelets and anklets with little bells. A shiny black wig.

At the end of the passage, light slivered through a sliding door. It was dead quiet except for the throbbing in her head, the pounding of her heart.

She opened the door. The light came from two lamps. They lit a back wall depicting an iconic mountain landscape. She thought of the paintings in the rooms with the four-poster beds. When she saw the digital camera on the tripod, she realized what went on in here. Horrified, she tried to gather her thoughts.

The camera: a witness that never lied.

She extracted the memory card with a gentle click and put it in her trouser pocket.

She held her breath and listened carefully. There was something she hadn't consciously heard before. She heard it again, more clearly this time. Barely louder than a sigh. She walked in the direction it was coming from. A narrow corridor with alcoves that resembled cells. They were empty, except for the last.

Idris was lying on a filthy mattress splattered with blood, his right wrist attached to an iron chain. His face was white with fear. She kneeled in front of him and gently ran her hand over his naked, shivering body. His heart was pounding even faster than her own. When she wrapped her arms around him, she felt the terror in his body. 'Khalos shod. It's over.'

Her breath caught in her throat. She heard stumbling on the stairs.

She wanted to let go of him, but he clutched her with his free arm. The sound he made resembled that of a small, whimpering dog. His cold fingers clawed at her. The footsteps quickened.

A blinding light brushed over her face and that of the boy.

'Fuck . . .'

The hand on her shoulder, his heavy breathing, the one closed eye. Mason had followed her.

The lock picks did their job. The padlock on the chain popped open. When Idris's other arm was free he threw that one around her too and pressed himself against her, his teeth chattering non-stop.

She wrapped a blanket around him and lifted him up. Mason lit the way, as they climbed the steep stairs with the boy's trembling body held tight. She carried him through the corridors and across the courtyard.

Mason opened the gate.

They saw the shock on Nehal and Malid's faces, but there was no time for emotions, no time for explanations. She wanted to put Idris on the back seat, but he wouldn't let go of her. She was amazed that a young child could call up so much physical strength from sheer terror. Mason took an injection kit from the bag. The boy didn't seem to notice the needle, and a moment later his grip relaxed. She wrapped him in a foil blanket and lay his head in her lap. Then she looked over at the building from where they could hear the faint sounds of clinking chains and muffled calls for help.

'I'll take care of it,' Mason said. 'The boy comes first.'

'We can't leave the others here all by themselves.'

Malid's response was incisive. 'I'll stay here. You need to go. Now.'

Nehal started the jeep. The first pale light of the morning sun rose up behind the mountains as they drove off and left Malid in front of the open gate. In his hands the lock picks Mason had given him.

The night slid further down the mountain slopes. Dirt and dust blew against the Wrangler's windscreen. Nehal had stepped on the gas and was staring intently at the road ahead. Ever since they'd driven off, Mason had been on the phone, organizing a rescue operation for the other boys. Farah stroked Idris's damp forehead. The boy's breathing was becoming more and more irregular. Despite the oppressive heat in the car, the aluminium blanket he was wrapped in and the calming injection Mason had given him, his teeth were chattering, and he was shivering all over.

She thought of how she'd helped him draw the bow yesterday, the arrow pointing at the photo on the tree. *Think of Prince Badan.*

She felt Mason's hand on her shoulder. He held up his phone and handed it to her from the passenger seat. 'For you. Gaby.'

She took the phone and heard the tension in Gaby's voice. 'I'm on my way. Are you all right?'

'I am, but the boy isn't.'

'Describe the symptoms.'

'He's trembling all over, his skin feels cold, his breathing's irregular . . .'

'Sounds like shock. He may have internal bleeding. How did you lay him down?'

'With his head in my lap.'

'Is there anything you can put under his legs?'

At Farah's signal, Mason lifted Idris's legs a little, and slid the rucksack underneath.

'And don't give him anything to drink. It will only make the shock worse. Make sure he's in a stable position. See you soon.'

When she returned the phone to Mason, their hands touched. He threw her a reassuring smile. 'It'll be fine.'

She nodded and looked down into the troubled eyes of the traumatized child in her lap.

They were on their way to Afshar hospital on the southwestern edge of Kabul. Every month, American Medical Overseas Relief provided treatment for hundreds of children living below the poverty line. Mason knew the director well. He and his unit dropped by practically every week to deliver gifts and food parcels.

With its sand-coloured walls, the building looked like a fortress. The armed soldier on the watchtower must have spotted the Wrangler through his binoculars, as a guard immediately opened the metal gate and motioned Nehal through.

Three ambulances were waiting in the courtyard. Armed personnel from the hospital's private security firm got into their jeeps. Nurses were loading mattresses into the back of a lorry. As soon as their car came to a halt, Mason jumped out and greeted the heavy-set director. She gave the medical convoy her final instructions in Dari tinged with a thick American accent. Despite the speed at which everything was happening, they received a warm welcome. She gave Mason a concerned look. 'Someone should take a look at your face.'

'Those boys should be their priority. Is everything ready?'

'We don't have enough ambulances. That's why we brought in the lorry. We're almost ready to set off. Is this the boy?'

She pointed to the jeep, where Farah was helping two nurses lay Idris on a stretcher. That same moment, a military vehicle careened into the courtyard. With screeching brakes, Duncan parked right next to the Wrangler. Gaby jumped out and ran over to the stretcher. She bent over Idris and consulted the director.

'First I want to get a scan done. Then we'll examine him further,' Gaby said.

Idris groaned and feebly raised his right hand, clutching at the air before finding Farah, who bent over him and took his hand.

Gaby froze when she saw Mason.

'I'm okay,' he muttered.

'No you're not! You need to get yourself to the ER at Camp Eggers right away.'

She looked at Farah. 'And you need to have your nose X-rayed.'

Farah shook her head. 'The boy first.' She walked alongside the stretcher, still holding Idris's hand. They moved down a long corridor, with consulting rooms, waiting areas and wards on either side, until they finally arrived at the X-ray department. Only a few weeks ago she'd been in a similar situation. Her head close to that of another badly injured boy.

She repeated the words she'd used back then, almost like a mantra. 'The doctor's going to look after you now. I'll be here, waiting for you. All right?'

Idris was wheeled into the X-ray room. The doors slammed shut. Rapid footsteps echoed in the corridor, and two women came rushing towards her: Roshan and Mariam. She saw the desperation in the young mother's eyes: first her husband, now perhaps her eldest child.

'Roshan, I'm so sorry. I never meant to put your lives in danger,' Farah said.

'You found him. You did everything you could to rescue him. How is he?'

'They're examining him now.' She took Roshan's hand in hers. 'He'll pull through,' she said, also trying to convince herself. 'He'll pull through.'

Back at the entrance to the Emergency Department, she saw the mattress-laden lorry leave the courtyard, the last of the medical convoy heading towards Proja-i-Gawdari.

Mason handed Duncan the bag containing the laptop and the hard drives. She walked over and stopped right in front of him. 'Were you planning to leave without saying goodbye?'

Something resembling a smile passed over his damaged face. 'You know why they give hurricanes female names? Because they're unpredictable, erratic, impulsive, change course, and their force is lethal. I could use you in my unit.'

She put her arm around him, turning her face slightly so her nose wouldn't hit his chest when she tightly hugged him.

She kept watching, long after he'd disappeared around the corner of the courtyard.

9

Raylan

'That's where I boarded the bus that I left on eight years ago,' Isobel said. Together with Raylan and Paul she was on Dam Square in the heart of Amsterdam. Attentively, Paul followed his mother's index finger in the direction of an ice-cream cart, besieged by tourists.

'Did you go all the way to Kabul by bus?' he asked in amazement.

She nodded and laughed. A few weeks earlier she'd also surprised her son with the news that they were taking him out of school. Once she'd gone to live in Kabul, Isobel deregistered as a resident of the Netherlands. In this way she'd held on to her passport, but Paul wouldn't fall under the country's strict compulsory schooling. It gave them the freedom to realize all their plans and, if necessary, to educate Paul by themselves at home. For the time being they wanted to live in Kabul, but they also wanted to visit the Netherlands more often.

By now Isobel had made a name for herself as an artist in Europe. For this reason she'd decided to open a second gallery, besides the small one in Kabul. On the corner of Staalstraat in Amsterdam, to be precise. Close to the bridge with a view of the Zuiderkerk, an iconic Renaissance-style church. And it was hardly a coincidence that this location was once immortalized by the French painter Manet, whom she greatly admired.

On a canvas, worlds could exist that were considerably more profound than everyday life, Isobel believed. If you were receptive to this, you were open to the truth. In the Rijksmuseum, she took her two guys by the hand to see what she liked to call the essence of that truth: *The Night Watch*.

'The men in the painting are civic guardsmen, the militia that protected the city at night, just like the police do nowadays,' she whispered to Paul, who watched in wonder as Captain Frans Banninck Cocq's company with their banners and muskets raised appeared to come straight at him in the intense contrast of light and darkness.

For Raylan, the essence of truth was something completely different. It was the harsh reality behind the empty promises and explicit lies of politicians. To illustrate his point, he then took Paul to Nieuwmarkt. There, an army of locals gathered on the square to protect the rundown housing they called home from being demolished. They were preparing to stand up to a unit of the anti-riot police, who, in anticipation of the confrontation, were provocatively hitting their batons against their shields.

'Look, child,' Raylan said. 'This is what the city militia looks like nowadays. In name they're still protecting the city and its citizens, but in reality they're protecting the interests of politicians and businessmen who want to build a motorway right through this old town.'

They stayed close to Amsterdam in an old farmhouse. It had once belonged to Isobel's great-grandfather and was now looked after by her brother Edward. The farmhouse was surrounded by stretches of fertile clay soil and small ponds, bordered only by winding dikes, willow trees, hedgerows and a few farmhouses in the distance. Nowhere in the world offered a greater contrast with the hustle and bustle of Kabul's old city centre. But it was here, in this secluded polder landscape, that Raylan found the inspiration he needed to work on his manuscript.

The enormous barn, which had once housed the cows, served as a temporary studio for Isobel, who, with Paul in tow, scoured lumber yards in search of the right material for her frames. She taught the boy to saw a mitre joint, assemble frames and stretch canvas linen. Paul was also initiated into the age-old practices of finely crushing raw materials in a mortar and pestle and mixing the powder with a binder to make paint. As Paul became increasingly fascinated by the art world, Raylan realized his son resembled Isobel more than he'd initially thought. Paul's lack of toughness worried him most. Could he hold his own in a world that, Raylan believed, didn't care much for things like aesthetics and beauty?

It didn't take long for those fears to come true. It was on a rainy Monday. From the large room with the bay window Raylan saw Paul stumbling across the fields. It was a scary sight. The boy was covered in mud and duckweed. Reaching the yard, he fell shivering into the arms of his father, who undressed him, gave him a bath and then placed him in bed wrapped in thick towels.

The only words Paul managed to mumble were incoherent.

'Relax, kiddo, I'm with you. You're gonna be all right.'

Raylan sat him up, put an arm around him and gave him the soothing tea that Isobel had made. Patiently they waited as he told them an incoherent story in short bursts.

A bunch of boys in the neighbourhood had invited Paul to help with building a treehouse. But when the oldest, tallest of the group arrived on the scene, Paul was told to 'bugger off' because he 'wasn't from here'. Then that bully repeatedly shoved Paul until he fell backwards into a ditch.

'They made fun of me . . . said I looked like a troll and that Mummy is a witch.' Then he saw red, Paul told them. And he let loose on that older boy.

Raylan looked at Paul's swollen knuckles and immediately thought of that time in Shahr-e Naw Park when Paul had surprised him by violently hitting his fists against his chest. That memory sparked an unexpected moment of elation in him. Now he knew for sure: his son had the same spirit in him. The same fire that Raylan had in his heart, an all-consuming rage that as a boy he should have learned to control by pounding hay bales every day. He saw Isobel gesture that she was going to call the police. Once she exited the room, he took his time reassuring Paul.

'You know, Paul, there are fighters and there are cowards. Today you were a fighter. You proved your worth.'

'But I ran away,' Paul stuttered slightly. 'Real fighters don't run away . . .' He extended his bruised hand and rested it on his father's arm. 'I don't want to run off. I want to fight back.'

Raylan lovingly stroked Paul's head and carefully chose his words. 'Well, I can't teach you to fight like the girl in the butterfly garden, but I can teach you how to focus your energy. Because if you can't control your anger, it will always be used against you. Just give it some thought.'

Raylan was about to kiss him on the forehead when Paul pulled his father towards him.

'Never mind that girl . . . You can be my teacher, Daddy. I want to learn from you.'

The next morning, Raylan took Paul to the edge of a nearby pond and stood in front of him.

'Control. That's the most important thing. Having insight. Knowing what you're doing, no matter how you're fighting. But your best defence is unshakable self-confidence. Believing in your own strength. Not letting it frighten you.'

He first taught Paul about defence strategies, how best to work up a sweat, but despite fatigue to concentrate on your every move. 'Keep looking at yourself. Control! Keep moving!' Every day he taught him something new. Right leg in front, jab with the right hand, indirect punch left, groin kick with the left leg. Basic kicking and punching techniques, which he combined with quickening his motor skills.

One morning, after a few weeks of training sessions by the pond, he gave Paul a pair of vintage boxing gloves, which he'd bought at the flea market on Waterlooplein. He looked straight into the eyes of his son, who immediately put them on and stood before him filled with self-confidence.

'Now I'm going to ask you to hit me as hard as you can. Doesn't matter where,' Raylan said.

There they were, a father and a son. Facing each other. Two bare upper bodies, heaving in a tense rhythm. A man and a child keeping a close watch on each other above the knuckles of their raised fists. The son looking for an opening in his father's defence.

Only their slightly laboured breathing and the shuffling of feet on the clay ground were audible. The sound of the wind snapping a dead branch disturbed Raylan's concentration. It was the perfect moment for Paul, who threw a forceful right jab and clocked his father full in the jaw.

Raylan's reflex was to strike back hard, when it suddenly dawned on him: he'd got what he'd asked for. Rubbing his painful jaw, he looked at Paul, who was apparently dismayed by what he'd just done and began to laugh to release the tension. Raylan bowed to his son, wrapped his arms around him and pressed him against his chest.

'Bull's eye, kiddo. Good punch!'

And while clutching him tightly, he walked into the pond with Paul, who jubilantly raised his arms into the air, after which they splashed around in the water together.

The evenings on the farm were invaluable to Raylan. Edward would fill the whiskey glasses in front of the fireplace, and they debated and debated until they genuinely believed they could change the world.

What united them above all else was the common struggle against powers that wanted to reduce freedom-loving people to sheep. Combined with a mutual respect for each other's characters and work, in a short period this shared passion made them not only brothers-in-law but also firm friends.

Their conversations about Raylan's war experiences were often the run-up to heated discussions about the most important task entrusted to journalists: restoring their readers' trust in the truth. Because if there was one thing Raylan and Edward agreed on, it was that no religious faith, no system really had an answer to all that was wrong with this world.

And that was precisely the reason why the facts were of vital importance to a journalist.

Edward believed that until his dying day a journalist should remain objective. According to him, Raylan's manuscript was in danger of becoming much too personal.

'Then do something about it!' Raylan animatedly exclaimed after a few too many. 'Edit the damn thing for me!'

Edward fell silent and looked at him surprised. 'Are you serious?'

'From the bottom of my heart, my grumpy old friend.'

Edward poured himself and Raylan another whiskey. 'I believe . . .'

355

he said in a shaky voice, 'that under no circumstances could I refuse you. It's a great project, Ray . . . one I believe in. As I believe in you.' He raised the glass. 'But allow me to make you a counter-offer you can't refuse. I'm hiring you as the *AND*'s Afghanistan correspondent.'

Raylan choked on his whiskey and looked at Edward in astonishment.

'If I see how the Cold War between East and West has been developing in Asia in recent years,' Edward continued, 'I get the idea that what you've written about Vietnam might one day be repeated in Afghanistan.'

'I've had my fill of war, Ed.'

'Well, war doesn't give a damn about that. I'd wager a bet that some war will find you again. And when that happens, you'll be our man in Kabul. So what do you say to my proposal?'

They'd agreed he'd give it some thought, but once Raylan had returned to Kabul he immediately started working on a series of articles for his new Dutch employer. He wrote about the Kremlin's covert attempts to restore the discord in the Afghan Communist Party, about how the national assembly, the Loya Jirga, approved a constitution in which sharia was declared the highest law of the land. He reported on how all of Afghanistan's political parties were declared illegal, leaving the National Revolutionary Party – founded by Daoud Khan – as the only party. He reported on President Daoud's many trips abroad, from Saudi Arabia (where he went on a pilgrimage and returned with five hundred million dollars in economic aid) to Persia (where he sealed his friendship with the Shah plus a two-billion-dollar deal). He wrote about the unlawful but growing popularity of back rooms in Kocha-e-Kharabat, where men gathered to ogle slender boys dressed as dancing girls.

Every now and then, Raylan stood in the middle of the Paghman Gardens, under the masterfully bricked arch that looked like the Arc de Triomphe, and he observed the somewhat self-conscious body language of couples in love strolling next to each other. After that day in the butterfly garden, Helai was never far from his thoughts. He was reminded of what the poet Hafez had once written.

It is easy to forever exile longing from your life. But difficult to break with friends as precious as your own soul.

He imagined the man walking towards him who, in passing, always paused for a moment.

Wa-Alaikum-Salaam, aghaye Ahmad.

As-Salaam-Alaikum, aghaye Chapelle.

Their usual greeting every time their paths crossed. And just like the occasions before, Raylan removed an envelope from the inside pocket of his jacket and handed it to Parwaiz. And following suit, Parwaiz gave the same answer before he placed the envelope in the inside pocket of his jacket and continued on. 'I'll make sure this letter gets to the appropriate person.'

It was an evening in the middle of autumn 1977. The horizon above the vast polder landscape around Amsterdam seemed like an enormous canvas painted by Isobel. A thick layer of deep blue gradually gave way to purplish-pink, which then soared to just above the tips of the dark treetops in solid stripes of dark yellow. Against this background, Raylan saw the trails made by aeroplanes approaching Schiphol airport. A little further in the landscape, dark-brown sheep silently trotted between the fruit trees in the direction of the oaks.

It had been more than two years since Raylan had discovered what it was like not to constantly hop on a plane to Saigon, but to take a seat behind the Remington and travel back and forth through time. During the intense writing process he'd once again come face-to-face with all of them: the dead he now gave a voice to by pounding his typewriter keys.

Over the course of time, the dark hole which he regularly found himself in had become less and less intense. When his heart started beating alarmingly fast, he no longer took Anafranil but concentrated on his breathing.

Breathe in for four seconds, out for six.

In the distance he heard the faint rumbling of an approaching thunderstorm. He carefully pulled the last page of the manuscript out of the Remington and placed it on top of the pile of stories: the boy brushing dirt from faces in a mass grave, that GI with his machine

357

gun, the cold eyes of the Viet Cong commander, the platoons of Marines who'd died on the banks of the River Perfume, the general who'd taken it upon himself via body counts to be the bookkeeper of the dead and all the others – the guilty and the innocent – whom he'd met and spoken to in his ten years of service in Vietnam.

Raylan had let them all tell their own stories. Each account a different part of the truth.

He thought of the last words of the burning monk: *to keep alive the hope of freedom and peace.*

And on the cover page he typed the title: *The Great Lie*.

He walked to the living room, where he heard Isobel and Edward quietly talking. He stood in the doorway with the thick stack of paper in his hands.

Isobel got up and slowly came towards him. She carefully took the manuscript, placed it on a table and wrapped her arms around him.

'Welcome home, Ray.'

In silence she pulled him closer to her.

Farah

2009

In Nehal's garage, which Duncan had temporarily transformed into a crisis centre full of advanced hardware and software for deciphering the encrypted data on the twelve hard drives from Hafami's compound, she listened to Gaby's calm voice on her mobile.

Idris was in intensive care with internal bruising. He didn't need surgery.

She ought to feel relieved. She and Mason had managed to rescue both him and the other boys from Hafami's clutches. But she also knew that while Idris would recover physically, as would hopefully the other boys, the emotional injuries he'd sustained would probably never heal.

'I think you should see this,' Duncan said after she finished talking to Gaby.

He pointed to a laptop screen. She recognized Idris. His eyes were lined with dark kohl, his eyebrows ink-black, his thin lips blood-red. The long black hair that fell past his shoulders was shiny like only a cheap wig could be. The dark-red silk dress he wore fell just below his knees. The slim-fitting trousers underneath were fastened tightly around the ankles with straps decorated with little bells. He wore similar tinkling bracelets around his arms. He raised them hesitantly and slowly twirled around in his bare feet, mechanically, like a doll on top of a music box.

He stood in front of a painted backdrop that was supposed to represent a scene from an ancient palace. She recognized it from the depictions on the walls of Hafami's compound. But that wasn't what Duncan wanted to show her, she realized. And it wasn't the dancing either. It was the man who emerged behind Idris. He wore a long robe, just like the men she'd seen on the Persian tapestries. He clapped his hands, reached for the boy, began to touch him and then roughly yanked him closer.

The cursor on the timeline stopped. The image froze. Duncan looked at her, tormented. 'I advise you not to watch the screen now, but to listen carefully.' She looked the other way. Duncan clicked *play*. The camera microphone registered Hafami's furious voice. He was in the same room as Idris. '*Chi megi? Emkan nadara!* That can't be true!'

She heard his rant and realized what was happening: this was the moment when Hafami was told his compound had been broken into.

His scream was hoarse. '*Kamrara estad ko!* Stop the camera!'

Then it dawned on her.

The news of their break-in had been Idris's salvation.

On the screens of several interlinked laptops images flashed by in fast forward. All decrypted material from the hard drives they'd retrieved from Hafami's compound.

'It's just the same filth over and over again,' Duncan muttered. 'Older men and young boys. It all begins in that little room at Hafami's compound. A kid in girl clothes will twirl around a few times to that whiny music, and then . . . Well, then one of those brutes takes the little guy to a room, where you get to see all the abominations he commits from as many different angles as possible.'

Now she understood why the network of secret cameras hadn't been on during their break-in. The cameras only became operational when a politician, businessman or senior military officer visited at Hafami's invitation. They'd register every single detail of the guest taking a seat in the *qush-khana* and getting turned on by the clumsy dancing of a boy who'd usually been drugged, after which they could have their way with him in the private rooms.

The cameras offered him the ultimate means of blackmail.

After that one evening, every guest would be indebted to Hafami for the rest of his life. The secret of power was to know the secrets of others. If you knew them, and in Hafami's case literally possessed them, your power was absolute.

She was about to turn away when someone on one of the screens caught her eye: an athletic figure in bespoke tailoring entered the dance room. 'Can you enlarge this image?' she asked.

Duncan zoomed in a bit. The face became grainier, but she recognized the aristocratic features. 'Play it back.'

The video had no sound. The man sat down. But as soon as he saw what was about to happen on stage, he got up, as if stung by a wasp, and made his way to the exit. After a brief, fierce altercation with one of the compound guards, who tried to stop him, he disappeared from view.

She looked at the date and time at the bottom of the screen: *08-14-2008 22.15 pm*.

These digits signalled an important breakthrough.

A breakthrough that could change another child's future.

Farah purposefully strode behind the security guard and into the lobby of the Ministry of the Interior. This time she hadn't come here by invitation. She was the one who'd made the appointment. Or rather, who'd forced it. 'It's an urgent matter that can't wait,' she'd said over the phone. She *had* to speak to him, the man who'd made an error of judgement by going somewhere he wasn't supposed to be, where he *shouldn't* be.

The unease with which Ahmad Shakoor looked at her when she entered his office was in stark contrast with the courtesy he'd shown her during their first meeting. He couldn't know what she knew, but there was no doubt that he'd immediately read her body language. She'd decided to ignore the unwritten code that as a woman you should never look an Afghan man straight in the eye. She was sure now: he must have been aware of her kidnapping.

'Ms Hafez, I'm afraid I don't have much time for you. I understand you have highly confidential information that you want to share only with me?'

He still sounded just as affable – a man who seemed unshakable, who was used to giving orders, who didn't have to listen to others. But she wouldn't give him a choice. This time he'd *have* to listen to her.

'During our previous meeting, you asked me to make it possible for you to help me,' she began.

'I assume your presence here means you'll let me do that?' He took a sheet of paper from the stack on his desk and a pen. 'I took the liberty of asking General Goldwater to send me the documents you need to sign. It will save you a trip to Camp Eggers.' He showed her where to put her signature. 'Right there, please.'

She showed no intention of signing the piece of paper. 'I'd like to make it possible for you to help me. But not in the way you have in mind. I will continue my investigation into General Hafami.'

Perhaps the silence only lasted a few seconds. But for a moment time seemed frozen. So was Shakoor's face. As they stood there quietly facing off, she noticed how furiously her heart was beating and how fast the blood pumped through her veins. His confusion, she saw, was masked by a nervous smile.

'My dear Ms Hafez, you've got yourself into so much trouble that you're not in a position to dictate the rules of the game to me. Like I said, I'm very busy. Do you have anything else to say to me?'

The blatant disdain in his voice fanned her anger. She had to control herself now. Do everything to serve her plan. She kept her eyes fixed on him and said in a calm voice: '14 August 2008, a quarter past ten in the evening.'

He looked surprised.

'General Hafami's compound. The *qush-khana*, to be precise.'

His gaze remained inscrutable. 'How . . .'

'The how is irrelevant. But I'll say this, you decided to leave as soon as you realized where you'd ended up. Still, there's irrefutable evidence that you attended a *bacha bazi* party.' She took out her phone and showed him the footage. 'Cameras don't lie, Mr Shakoor.' She saw that he'd turned ashen and stopped the video. 'As a Pashtun, you're morally obligated to protect the weakest in society, not to run away from them. A Pashtun must always strive for the good, both in thought, in word and in deed.'

'This is blackmail.'

'No, this is an appeal to your sense of justice. Sekandar's family must be found. I don't care how, as long as it happens soon. I want them to be reunited. And you're the one who's going to arrange that.'

11
Raylan

1978

On the limestone façade of the *AND* building a golden sun was painted with a crowing rooster on either side; a legacy from the years when the company published both a morning and evening edition. But those glory days were gone. The *AND*'s current situation was less auspicious than the headquarters' art nouveau architecture might suggest.

Because of the overall economic slump the newspaper had been forced to downsize significantly. Only the evening newspaper now rolled off the presses. A large portion of the printing areas and editorial offices had been cleared out. What remained in the monumental main building were deserted rooms where piles of yellowed newspaper, leftover cans of printing ink and miscellaneous spare parts of an outdated offset machine now served as reminders of the paper's past glory.

On the first floor, in what had once been the boardroom, illustrious newspaper tycoons looked down from gilt frames at the group of guests that had gathered in a semi-circle around Raylan. Edward cleared his throat and took the floor. Years of abusing whiskey and cigarettes had given his vocal cords the timbre of an American crooner with one foot in the grave.

'Journalists and angels have something in common: both are messengers. They observe what people do, report on this and warn us about the dangers that might loom ahead.' With an ironic look, he glanced at Raylan. 'And on occasion they write a book.'

363

Raylan did his best to ignore the chuckles of those present. He looked at Isobel, who smiled at him reassuringly. It was as if she was signalling to him: *hold on. Afterwards you can have a drink, you no longer have to endure being the centre of attention. I'll give you my undivided attention, just me . . . fulfil your every desire.*

'A book,' Edward continued, 'that tells the story of a war that once started with higher ideals in mind, but by the end was only about killing as many people as possible. A book that illustrates how countless innocent civilians fell victim to American GIs, who actually came to protect them, but because of a horrific combination of circumstances were turned into their occupiers and murderers. A book that reveals the truth about a war that turned out to be one big lie. A book that I'm proud to present to you today.'

Raylan barely heard their applause either. For two years he'd been on a battlefield in his head, where he'd forced himself to relive all his traumatic experiences. He'd looked death in the eye over and over again, and now that his memories had been neatly divided into chapters and put to rest, an emptiness had arisen that he wanted to escape from as quickly as possible. What could he do to protect himself from it? What would it take for him to not jump on the first plane out to some military hotspot in the world? Rebuilding the stable of the old farmhouse into a permanent workshop for Isobel? Ploughing up a piece of land and growing cannabis on it? Writing another book?

He searched for Isobel's eyes again. For two years they'd spent time with each other on a daily basis, alternating between Kabul and Amsterdam. And although their worldviews were as different as the light and shadows in Rembrandt's paintings, they had found common ground in the fact that they each documented the truth in their own way. He wistfully thought back on those evenings when Isobel came out on to the roof terrace of their house in Murad Khane, always accompanied by a sketchbook, pencils, a bottle of whiskey and two glasses. And he was equally happy to set up his Remington in her studio and work on his manuscript amidst the smell of turpentine and wet oil paint, as she immortalized a market scene in Kabul.

As long as she could hold a brush, Isobel would continue to paint.

All her life. But despite all the good the past two years had brought him, Raylan had decided to never write a book again.

'It's a great honour,' Edward related, 'to be able to hand over the very first copy of *The Great Lie* to a budding journalist.' With a grin Edward looked at the blond boy, half bored, leaning against his mother. 'Paul, would you please come forward for a minute?'

The boy looked at him with confusion. Isobel briefly whispered something to her son and gave him a nudge. Hesitantly, Paul approached Edward. With a shy expression he accepted the book. Yet as soon as he turned back towards the group, he triumphantly raised it in the air like he'd seen sports heroes do with their trophies on television.

Raylan saw the spark in his son's eyes and remembered the words Paul had uttered by the campfire during their mountain adventure. *Because I want to be a journalist, just like you.*

In his mind he saw the boy in the sidecar of the BMW raise his thumb in approval as they raced along the road overlooking the Pamir ravine. And he again felt the small but strong fists with which Paul had hit him when they practised fighting techniques by the pond. And while Raylan watched his jubilant son run towards him with the hardback in his hand, he suddenly knew what happiness felt like: as fleeting and intense as the moment he caught Paul in his arms – with book and all – and lifted him high above his head.

Three weeks later, he stood in the narrow building with the glass shop window on Shir Ali Khan Road in Kabul. There where collections of poetry, novels, scientific reference works and children's books were piled in a disorderly heap, reaching the ceiling in what Afghans describe as the *andaruni*, or 'inner sanctum'. In this cherished house of the printed word, with a select group of guests around him, including Parwaiz Ahmad, Raylan wanted to bring everything full circle.

'I had the choice to live anywhere in the world,' he said, 'but I didn't really feel at home anywhere. Until, on the day I arrived, I walked through Kabul, a city full of unfamiliar streets, faces and a language that was completely foreign to me, but somehow it didn't feel like it. Although I knew I was seeing and hearing everything for the first time, it all seemed very familiar to me, as if I'd lived here before, in another life perhaps, and I'd come home again.'

He held the English version of *The Great Lie* at chest level, close to his heart, and looked at Isobel.

This is for you, my darling. I can't give you more than this. But know that I love you.

'That was also the day I met the woman who would determine the rest of my life and who ultimately inspired me to write this book.'

He was not a man of grand gestures, nor someone who needed a lot of words to say what he had to say. It all came together in that single moment, in that one gesture with which he pressed the book against his heart and then gave it to Isobel.

Just like that night at the old farmhouse, he'd expected her embrace to feel like a loving welcome home. And even though he could see she was doing her very best to be happy for him and she pulled him close to her body, everything else seemed to indicate that this meant goodbye. The two years that culminated in this embrace, which had been the happiest days of his life, were now definitely behind him.

With the uneasiness of a journalist who'd never wanted to be a writer and a writer who was longing to be a journalist again, Raylan signed a copy of his book for Ahmad Parwaiz.

'You must realize, Mr Chapelle, that all great artists are free spirits,' Parwaiz said, as Raylan signed the first page of his book for him. 'Well, you're a free spirit, and I believe with this book a true artist.'

'That's very kind of you,' Raylan replied. 'But really too much honour.'

'The modesty becomes you. *Khoda havez, doste azizam.* Greetings, my worthy friend.' With a bow, Parwaiz left the shop, as if he were urgently expected elsewhere, and Raylan continued to sign books for the people in the queue in front of him.

Until the flow of people stopped.

Two deep blue eyes looked at him impassively.

'Is it hard?' he heard a child's voice asking. 'Writing a book?'

She stood in front of him. He stared at her. Astonished at how beautiful she was. Her mother's looks. He also saw the restlessness in her gaze.

His own restlessness.

'Yes,' he answered, staring at her, in the silent hope that this single look would explain why their eyes were like mirror images. 'Perhaps as difficult as all those fighting techniques I saw you do in the butterfly garden. Remember?'

'I remember,' she replied. 'You're the father of that blond fighter with the dark soul. Where is he?'

Raylan pointed in the direction of where he'd last seen Paul, only to realize who was standing right behind little Farah.

It had been two years since their last meeting. Helai didn't look a day older. Even though she appeared calm, he could sense her nervousness, which seemed just as strong as his.

She placed the book in front of him as if it were a precious gem. 'Sorry about taking you by surprise, but I'm terribly proud of you. You've conquered your demons. It would mean a lot to me if you'd sign your life's work for me.'

From the corner of his eye he could see Isobel watching. A look of shock and acceptance combined. No trace of reproach or self-pity. His hand trembled. The war that had cost him ten years of his life, in which Helai was an important chapter without ever being mentioned, not even in a single footnote, lay open on the table in front of him. Ten years compressed into three hundred and fifty pages.

Rarely had he felt as misplaced as he did now, sitting here, with a pen in his trembling hand and a row of curious people staring at him. But this is what he'd wanted. This moment, this meeting, when she'd come to him so he could ask her to forgive him.

He wrote the first thing that came into his mind. *A war can give peace a chance*. He closed the book and returned it to her.

When she took it, she held his hand for a moment. 'I'll treasure this,' she softly said before he could say anything himself. 'Just like I treasure all my memories of you.'

She gave him a parting smile, turned resolutely and walked to Farah, who was now with Paul and Isobel. He couldn't hear the exchange. There was a slight commotion. Raylan's sight was now blocked by a man dressed in the uniform of the Presidential Guard, who was standing right in front of him. 'Mr Chapelle, I'm sorry to disturb you here. But I have orders to bring you to the presidential palace as soon as possible.'

The car travelled through a city that looked much like the place Raylan had so enjoyed that very first day. Yet this Kabul wasn't the same city as ten years ago. Much of the colourful life that Isobel had managed to capture in her paintings was fading away. As if a grey veil had descended over its people, buildings and houses in recent years.

The government vehicle passed the Independence Pillar and stopped in front of the Kandahari Gate, one of the six gates of the Arg, the ancient royal city. A single glance from the guard at the wheel was enough to allow the car to drive straight on to Dilgosha Palace, which towered majestically above the pomegranate trees. Two soldiers of the Presidential Guard accompanied Raylan to the top of the wide palace steps, where, surprisingly, Aadel Gailani was waiting for him.

'I'm sorry we had to bring you here at such an inopportune time,' he said, giving Raylan a firm handshake. 'But it's at the request of the president himself.' He let his gaze fall on the cover of the book, which the guard handed to him. 'Bravo, you've finally done what you came to Kabul to do.'

Gailani gave Raylan a reassuring smile and gestured that he should follow him. With steady footsteps he hurried in front of him through the long, white-plastered corridor, past the boardroom where the cabinet met, the official reception hall and meeting rooms, until they stopped in front of the door to the presidential office, which was opened by a servant after Gailani's measured knock.

Raylan walked into an oval space where metres-high windows looked out on to a lush garden with a murmuring fountain. The impressive mahogany desk was positioned so that the president sat with his back to the window – an imposing sight for those who first entered the room.

Nobody was at the desk. To the right, where two elegant sofas were facing each other with a frosted-glass coffee table in between, two balding, middle-aged men who'd stood up awaited a greeting. With his hand on his heart, one of them, whom Raylan recognized as President Daoud, gave him a slight bow.

'Mr Chapelle, I hope you can forgive me for having you so abruptly removed from the realm of the printed word, but, as you will soon understand, there is a good reason for this.'

'I already suspected that this would be more than just a private book signing,' Raylan replied.

Daoud looked at him in amazement and then gestured to the man next to him. 'My minister of foreign affairs, Samad Ghaus.'

'*Wa-Alaikum-Salaam*, Excellency Ghaus.'

'*As-Salaam-Alaikum*, Mr Chapelle.'

'Take a seat, please,' Daoud said. 'What can we offer you?'

Raylan sat down next to Gailani and glanced at the bowl of sweets on the coffee table next to a large samovar. 'Only tea, Excellency.'

While the servant arranged sweet tea for Raylan, Daoud looked at the cover of the book Gailani had just handed him. 'Intriguing title,' he said with a thoughtful smile. 'The lie is perhaps the most important weapon in the political arena, don't you think?'

'The lie, Mr President, is a journalist's worst enemy.'

Daoud leaned forward a bit. 'That's exactly why I needed to meet with you at such short notice. We appear to have a common enemy.'

The president crossed one leg over the other and nodded at his foreign minister that it was his turn.

'You're a highly respected journalist, therefore I'll assume I can be candid,' Ghaus said. 'You and I both know that the Soviet Union is playing a dirty game with our country. One hand generously provides money, builds new roads and housing, while the other hand secretly installs communist infiltrators in all kinds of positions in our country. Even the Parliament and the army haven't been spared. The purpose of this deception is obvious: to establish as thoroughly as possible a large communist front against our current government.'

'The Russians are manipulating our parliamentary system and the army to slowly but surely transform our country from the inside into a communist buffer state,' Gailani added.

'Is that why all communist ministers and Russian military advisers have been dismissed?' Raylan asked.

'Bull's-eye, Mr Chapelle,' replied Daoud, who placed the book on the coffee table and straightened his back. 'I'm still largely dependent on financial aid from the Soviet Union. But I don't want to become a puppet of the Kremlin. My friend Mohammad Reza Pahlavi, the Shah of Iran, has already promised me economic development aid in exchange for stability in the region. There is now a military cooperation programme with India. Three other countries, Saudi Arabia, Iraq and Kuwait, have promised their financial assistance. But the country we had expected the most support from, the United States, has so far been considerably less forthcoming.'

'President Carter first wants a promise that we will turn our backs on Russia,' Ghaus said.

'But it's a historical fact,' Daoud continued, 'that for decades our country has been linked in many ways to the Soviet Union. You do not turn your back on such a powerful neighbour, with such a large army, from one day to the next. It would be suicide.'

Daoud pulled out a pack of cigarettes and a box of matches. 'Try to imagine . . . I've been given this match by Russia. This cigarette is what America can offer me . . .' He struck the match, lit the cigarette and looked at Raylan inquiringly. 'Do you understand the metaphor?'

'You want to use your Russian match to light your American cigarette.'

Daoud took his time inhaling. 'The day after tomorrow, I will go to Moscow,' he said after he'd exhaled a few perfect smoke rings. 'I want to test Party Leader Brezhnev's ability to grasp my metaphor and see how nervous he gets.'

'An audacious initiative,' Raylan said.

Daoud inhaled again while lifting his chin. 'Would you like to cover my visit?'

Raylan firmly rubbed one hand over his stubbly beard, while gazing at the faces of the three men one by one. This was obviously a foreign matter, but it must have been Interior Affairs Minister Gailani who'd come up with this idea. He thought of his earlier meeting with Gailani, a decade before, when he'd been offered the Vaziri case on similar terms. Thanks to all the publicity, Gailani had profited politically at the time. It wouldn't be any different now. If this manoeuvre worked as he'd planned, once again the president would be immensely indebted to him.

'I have a problem with this entire matter, Mr President,' Raylan said. 'When I was writing about the Vaziri case all those years ago, Afghanistan still had a free press. Now we're at a point where just about anything resembling dissent has been banned by you. You've dismissed Parliament. The only newspaper left is a government mouthpiece. And there's only one political party left: yours. So why would an autonomous American journalist like myself suddenly turn up in Russia?'

'I understand your reservations,' Daoud calmly replied. 'Let me put it this way: in order to ultimately bring democracy and progress to my country, I was forced to take the emergency measures you've just outlined. You have no idea how deeply the communists have already infiltrated all layers of our society. Even ministries and army units. If I hadn't imposed all these drastic and unpopular measures, you would be sitting opposite a president with a hammer-and-sickle emblazoned on his pocket. I'm forced to walk a tightrope between two extremes ... without a safety net. But only with the full support of the United States can I set Afghanistan on a prosperous economic course and achieve democracy. That's why I must attempt the impossible. In Moscow, I must make it clear to a friend, who has secretly become my enemy, that our friendship can no longer involve one country dominating the other.'

'And what's my role in this?' Raylan asked.

'Your articles regularly appear in *The New York Times*, you're the Afghanistan correspondent for the *AND* and you've just written a book that promises to be an international bestseller. No Afghan journalist is currently able to get their coverage printed in a foreign newspaper. But you, my friend, are. With your help, I want to show my American counterpart in the White House that I'm very serious about his prerequisites for US assistance.'

Aadel Gailani set his teacup on the table and resolutely turned towards Raylan. 'I'd greatly appreciate it if you'd consider my president's proposal. Incidentally, on the occasion of your book's publication,

my ministry in consultation with the Russian Cultural Centre has organized an exclusive guest lecture for you at Moscow State University.'

Raylan had to laugh. Gailani was still brilliant at brokering deals.

President Daoud pushed *The Great Lie* towards Raylan. 'In any
case, Mr Chapelle, allow me the pleasure of reading a signed copy of
your book.'

12
Paul

2009

He didn't know how long he'd been wandering around town, but it hadn't stopped raining the entire time – those small droplets you could hardly see or feel but that soaked and chilled you to the bone.

The lights going on behind the windows of countless Khrushchyovka buildings with single-family flats almost made him long to spend the rest of his days somewhere there, living a desperate life as hopeless as the silhouettes he now saw moving behind the curtains.

A dark-grey vehicle sped past. Muddy water from a rain puddle splashed against him. The car slowed and stopped a few metres away. By the time he noticed the blue licence plate had no number, it was already too late. Someone stepped out, opened the rear door and gestured for Paul to get in. It was the same giant of a man in a black leather jacket who'd taken him from the police station on an earlier occasion.

A familiar voice sounded from the car. 'My condolences, Mr Chapelle.'

Paul leaned towards the man in the back seat. 'Don't take this the wrong way, Mr Arlazarov, but I'll just wipe my ass with your condolences.'

Arlazarov's smile resembled that of the Mona Lisa.

'I can appreciate your anger.'

'Is that so? I wonder if you understand anything about human emotion.'

Arlazarov extended his arm and beckoned him closer with his

index and middle finger. 'Please just get in, my dear fellow. To facilitate our conversation.'

'Thanks for the invite, but we're done talking for now.'

Paul turned around. The man in black was like a wall blocking his way. Passers-by did their very best to scurry along, their eyes directed at the pavement. Behind him he heard that Arlazarov was getting impatient.

'Chapelle, it's not like I have all the time in the world.'

The leather of the back seat creaked. Arlazarov observed the view of the city in passing as if he were its mayor. 'I heard your conversation with Sergey Kombromovich was constructive.'

'If you can call patricide constructive.'

'You don't seem so happy with Sergey's new information.'

'At the moment I'm not really into being happy about anything. I have to bury my girlfriend.'

Arlazarov rubbed his chin. 'Death is not the dying of the light. Rather it is switching off the lamp because the dawn has come.' He gave Paul a sympathetic look. 'Comforting words, don't you think?'

'I'm not in the mood for comfort. I need a drink. And a cigarette.'

'Wallow in your self-pity later, my dear fellow. First I have something to show you.'

They were approaching Bolotny Square. Large groups of mostly young people suddenly swarmed into the street from every direction. They forced cars to stop, unrolled banners and raised their fists in the air. Paul heard them chanting. '*Day nam pravdu ob Anye Kozlovoy!* Give us the truth about Anya Kozlova!'

'Look at them,' Arlazarov said. 'They pay rent, study, work, do their grocery shopping, go to the movies, to the pub. But tonight they've all gathered here together. There's twenty thousand of them, I suppose. And probably more will join in. They weren't prepared for this, the authorities. Citizens taking to the streets to demand their right to know the truth. And believe me, this time they're ready to be beaten up by riot police, carted off in vans and treated the same way you were in some godforsaken station. I'm sure you can relate to that?'

'Anya didn't want to die so people would chant and carry banners in protest. She didn't choose to die at all. She just wanted to do her work as a journalist the best that she could.'

'You hit the nail on the head. She did her job so good, she got herself killed.'

With a relaxed movement Arlazarov pulled out the USB stick he'd received from Paul the day before. 'Returned with an invaluable extra. Think of it as a token of my appreciation for your dedication as a journalist.'

Paul hesitantly took the USB stick. A group of young demonstrators walked by. One of them was holding a photo of Anya above his head.

Alexander Arlazarov stared out of the window deep in thought. 'Woodward and Bernstein were your heroes, weren't they? Did you ever ask yourself why their informant always met them in that Washington DC underground car park?' He turned his head. 'That gentleman was part of the establishment, but he could no longer defend the actions of one of the country's important people, the US president.'

Arlazarov kept his eyes on Paul. There was not a trace of arrogance. There was only seriousness. Bitter seriousness. 'This ride is over. What you do next is up to you. You can drown yourself in a bottle and whine to a bored bartender, or desperately try to rid yourself of loneliness with one of our whores, or you can examine what I've added to the equation.'

Before Paul could react, Arlazarov snapped his fingers. The car stopped, the man in the passenger seat stepped out and opened the rear door. After Paul got out, Arlazarov stuck his head through the open window.

'Death, my dear Chapelle, is not only the end, it can also bring about redemption.'

The window slid up. Immobile, Paul watched the car force its way through the standing traffic with the help of a flashing blue light. A young woman with white ribbons in her hand came up to him. She smiled shyly and held up this symbol of opposition.

'For you.'

He shook his head. She stared at him in bewilderment, then disappeared in the stream of demonstrators heading towards the square.

PART FIVE
Through the Looking Glass

I
Raylan

1978

On top of Borovitsky Hill, about forty metres above the River Moskva – where a settlement once stood surrounded by a stockade – Raylan Chapelle entered the Kremlin under the Tower of the Redeemer. As the last of the Afghan delegation he passed the guards beside the entrance of the neo-classical building where the Presidium of the Supreme Soviet was housed.

Inside, his footsteps echoed as if he were walking through an immense cathedral wearing riding boots. He looked up at the huge chandeliers. Like fanciful galaxies they floated just below the vaulted ceiling. Everything in this magnificent centre of centuries-old Russian power had always been elevated above the everyday reality of the common people. Ever since Ivan the Great had appropriated the symbol of the Byzantine emperor's two-headed eagle and given himself the title of tsar – a term derived from the name 'Caesar'– Russia's rulers with their delusions of grandeur believed that their power was God-given.

It was immediately apparent from the hall's larger-than-life icon depicting the lineage of the Russian leaders. Its full branches displayed medallions of Metropolitans and Tsars. It was a tree that would continue to flourish until it reached the heavens. Lenin, Stalin and their successors were the new tsars, only in the guise of communist despots.

It was the second day of the Afghan-Russian state visit and according to protocol the current party leader and the Soviet Union's head of state, Leonid Brezhnev, would meet with President Daoud. The Afghan delegation entered an oblong room with an enormous conference table and without any explanation was told to wait.

After fifteen minutes, the Russian delegation waltzed in. Brezhnev, who hadn't been present the day before to greet Daoud and his entourage at the airport, looked old and frail. He struggled to walk, and that wasn't all. With his stocky appearance and surly gaze he looked more like a bespectacled bulldog – who could still bark but was probably incapable of doing much else – than the dignified leader of around one hundred and thirty-seven million Russians.

In front of the TV news crews and flashbulbs hands were shaken and pleasantries exchanged. This was followed by strapping sentries clearing the room of all journalists. Minister of Foreign Affairs Ghaus gestured to Raylan that he should sit diagonally behind him in the spot where the interpreter normally sat. The instant the doors of the conference room were closed, the atmosphere dropped to freezing point.

'Mr President,' Brezhnev growled without giving Raylan even a glance, 'I see you have an American in your group.'

Daoud reacted diplomatically. 'An international press attaché of American origin who has lived in my country for ten years.'

'I'm well aware of who Mr Chapelle is, no need to explain ... I also know about his new book attacking his own government. Is he a communist by any chance?'

'As much as I am, Mr Party Chairman,' Daoud replied impassively.

Brezhnev looked around the table with a scowl. 'I bet there's not a single communist in your group. And to think it was the communists in your country who helped you to seize power less than three years ago. But as soon as their services were no longer needed, you ruthlessly shoved them aside. You also expelled our best military advisers from your country, allowing Indian and Egyptian experts to take their places. But who supplied you with all those modern weapons your military is now using? Who?!' With an irritated gesture Brezhnev wiped the sweat from his forehead. 'The proud Republic of the Soviet people! It was us. Those are our weapons. Soviet weapons.'

In his rage Brezhnev was speaking far too fast for the Afghan interpreter to keep up, so there were gaps in the translation. Brezhnev gasped for breath. His pockmarked face had turned red. He sat back in his chair. Daoud, with his air of nobility, who'd been silent the entire time, seemed barely fazed.

'We want nothing more than to see Afghanistan flourish,' said the Russian minister of foreign affairs, Gromyko, who now took the floor as diplomatically as possible. 'Afghan non-alignment is important to the Soviet Union and essential for the promotion of long-term peace in the region. We are prepared to be generous with the economic and technical assistance you need.'

'On one condition,' Brezhnev growled again. He then leaned his heavy body across the table and looked Daoud right in the eye. 'That you have those American spies operating on our southern borders removed immediately if not sooner.'

Raylan knew for a fact that he was referring to a number of seismology specialists associated with the French oil firm Total. They were carrying out research into the possibility of oil exploitation in the area.

Brezhnev nervously took a sip from a glass of water – or was it vodka?

Daoud's face went dark. When he began talking, his calm tone betrayed his rising anger.

'Let me remind you that you're talking to the president of a sovereign country. Your statement is clearly brazen interference in the internal affairs of Afghanistan. We will never allow you to dictate the direction in which my country must head. Not now, not ever. How and where we let our foreign experts work remains the exclusive right of the Afghan state. If that means withdrawing your economic aid in retaliation, then so be it. Afghanistan would rather remain a poor country free in its dealings and decisions than a prosperous but voiceless satellite state of the Soviet Union.'

Daoud didn't wait for a reaction, pushed his chair back and stood up. His example was followed by the entire Afghan delegation, as if agreed to in advance. Brezhnev was clearly taken aback and remained seated with a vacant look in his eyes.

As Daoud headed for the door, Gromyko rushed towards him and took his arm. 'Let's think this through for a moment, please.'

Ghaus quickly whispered something to Daoud, and after some

hesitation Daoud turned around, returned to the table and shook the baffled Brezhnev's hand.

'I was told you wanted to meet with me privately,' said Brezhnev with a forced smile, now that he seemed to have awoken from his torpor. 'Well, I'm at your disposal.'

'Thank you for the invitation,' Daoud replied raising his voice, which was clearly meant to ensure that all those present could hear what he was about to say, 'but there is no longer any need for such a meeting. None at all.' Then he turned around and proceeded to exit the room, leaving the Russian delegation speechless.

Raylan thought of what Daoud had said to him a few days earlier: *You do not turn your back on such a powerful neighbour, with such a large army, from one day to the next. It would be suicide.* That's exactly what was happening. The man now striding with his delegation through the echoing corridors of the Kremlin, in the direction of the front door, had just signed his own death warrant.

2
Paul

2009

It all went down like Alexander Arlazarov had predicted. Over the course of the evening the demonstration in Anya's memory on Bolotny Square grew into a massive protest against the Russian government. The atmosphere turned dire when men in bomber jackets and balaclavas appeared among the demonstrators. They were hooligans for hire deployed by the authorities. Armed with batons and brass knuckles, they started beating the protestors in the crowd. They set cars afire and smashed shop windows. That was the signal for the security forces, called out en masse, to heavy-handedly intervene without delay.

Protesters fleeing the scene were set upon with water cannons. They fell like pins at a bowling alley, and were sent sprawling across the slippery cobblestones, after which rubber batons hammered down on their heads, backs and limbs. Barred police vans then carted them off at lightning speed.

Miles from this violence, Paul stepped out of the subway station at Ulitsa Pokrovka and minutes later rang the doorbell of the old apartment complex where Roman Jankovski lived. The wide staircase that curled around the elevator shaft took him to the fifth floor. Roman was waiting in the doorway with the forlorn expression of a man intent on drowning his impotent sorrow in vodka.

A thick haze of cigarette smoke filled the sitting room. There was the dull murmur of the newspaper's entire staff who were grieving by binge drinking. Roman's wife Helena came straight over to Paul. The tired wrinkles around her mouth and eyes suddenly made her look years older. 'I actually believe you look worse than all of us put together,' she said, wrapping an arm around Paul. 'C'mon, you've got to eat something, and drink.'

Paul didn't move. 'Maybe later, Helena.' He leaned towards Roman. 'You and I need to talk. Alone.'

In Roman's study, where the same chaos of papers reigned as in the *Moskva Gazeta*'s newsroom, Paul finally worked up enough courage. 'I haven't told you everything that happened after I saw Lyov,' he said in a hushed tone. 'I didn't lose the memory stick. I, uh ... passed it on ...'

Roman looked at him amazed. 'Passed it on ... to whom?'

Paul sighed. 'Alexander Arlazarov.'

'The director of the FSB's Counter-Terror Unit? Damn it, Paul!'

'When I was fished out of the water by the police, I found myself in a potentially perilous situation. Then it popped into my head to use the info about Anya's murder on Lyov's USB stick in exchange for my freedom. You, of all people, know what the Moscow police are capable of. Anyway, I bluffed my way to Arlazarov. Turns out he still had an old score to settle with Valentin Lavrov.'

A speechless Roman kept staring at him. 'How did you know that?' he finally asked.

'Honestly, I had no idea. But after my first meeting with him, once I'd tracked down that student who was involved in Farah's video confession ... it sounds crazy, but even then I could sense that Arlazarov and I had something ... in common. In any case, a profound dislike of Valentin Lavrov.'

'Strange ...'

'Believe it or not, it's true. We share the same enemy.' Paul held up the USB stick. 'Tonight Arlazarov handed me more incriminating information about Lavrov. Anya's death went a step too far for him.'

Roman had his arms crossed and looked at Paul suspiciously. 'Why would the director of an institute that fights terror and crime provide you, a foreign journalist, with top-secret information? You're talking about a man at the highest level of the FSB. Why would he even give a damn about the death of yet another Russian journalist?'

'Arlazarov is a man of principle,' Paul replied.

'It's precisely these men of principle who turn out to have few, if any, scruples. They can't be trusted,' Roman bluntly replied.

Paul could no longer suppress his irritation. 'Have you forgotten who provided Bernstein and Woodward with crucial information in the Watergate scandal? It was the director of the FBI at the time. So how about getting off your high horse for a change?'

Roman Jankovski silently stared out of the window. Paul came and stood beside him. 'Arlazarov was first obliged to abandon his principles twenty years ago. He had to free a murderer who was a protégé of the Kremlin. All this time, it has gnawed at him. Arlazarov is now the FSB's director. And that killer from long ago is now the CEO of an international energy conglomerate. Our investigation shows that Valentin Lavrov, just like all those other oligarchs, transferred millions in tax money to anonymous foreign accounts. But the Kremlin continued protecting him. Arlazarov wasn't allowed to prosecute Lavrov for that either. So he was forced to set his principles aside a second time.'

'Now, I understand,' Roman said, turning towards Paul. 'It was just a matter of waiting for the third time: the day a half-drowned journalist arrived on the scene with evidence that Valentin Lavrov was behind the order for Anya to be beaten to death.'

Paul pulled out the USB stick. 'Alexander Arlazarov only has a few more years before he retires. He wants to spend his old age in that crumbling castle of his with a clear conscience. I came straight to you because I thought you'd be interested in the secrets this holds.'

Roman Jankovski grabbed the USB stick, walked to the door of his study and locked it from inside.

The photos on the stick were made with a telephoto lens. In a grainy image, a helicopter landed on top of a huge industrial building, which was almost completely scaffolded. On every corner of the old complex stood a high white chimney.

'Battersea Power Station. A former coal-fired power plant near the Thames in London,' Roman said, rubbing his hands, clearly pleased with himself. 'I know that building from an old album cover. *Animals* by Pink Floyd. The place is now being converted into a complex of luxury flats.'

'And who do we have there?' Paul pointed to the man stepping out of the helicopter in the second image. 'Our dear friend Valentin.' His finger then slid in the direction of another man, who was waiting for Valentin Lavrov twenty metres away. He was wearing a long black coat. His distinctive close-cropped head with its wide jaw line and dark sunken eyes loomed well above Lavrov.

Roman hit the desk with his hand. He headed over to an old bookcase and started rifling through a pile of folders until he pulled one out and opened it. With an expression as if he'd just hit a hole-in-one, he placed a photo in front of Paul. 'Alexei Ardahev. Became a multi-millionaire in the 1980s thanks to interests in the oil industry and the media.'

'Wait a minute,' Paul said. 'The one who got into trouble a year and a half ago by announcing he was going to run in the next presidential election?'

Roman nodded. 'Shortly after that announcement, Ardahev was accused of large-scale tax fraud. A predictable counter-move by the Kremlin. To avoid being arrested, he fled the country with his wife, children and wealth. Britain gave him political asylum. In London, he bought two newspapers. For the most part he filled them with critical articles about Potanin's economic and political bungling. The Russian court sentenced Ardahev in absentia to life imprisonment.'

Paul crossed his arms and looked at the two men on the rooftop of the old industrial building as if he'd just caught them red-handed. 'So Valentin Lavrov had a meeting in London with a former media tycoon who's considered a traitor by the Kremlin. Let's see where this takes us.'

He double-clicked on the audio file below the images.

In the background Handel's *Messiah* could be heard as Big Ben chimed a melody in the distance. Despite the wind, Ardahev's dark voice was clearly audible as soon as the sound of the bells faded.

Dear friend, our alliance is only as strong as its weakest link. You know that, I know that. The project simply can't tolerate a weak link. There is unrest in the ranks.

Since when?

Since the hostage-taking in the Seven Sisters. We're wondering what part you played in that. And especially what that female journalist had to do with it. Right before, you were spotted with her in the Pushkin Museum.

Paul stopped the recording. 'As you can hear, this is about Farah.' He stared at Roman, waiting for a reaction.

It was only a few weeks ago. He pictured her again. In the immense hall of the Pushkin Museum, wearing that cocktail dress she'd borrowed off Anya, Farah squeezed through the artists and members of the Dutch trade delegation. She was out of breath, and her long jet-black hair was tousled. He knew how vulnerable she'd felt at that moment. He recalled the expression on her face when they made eye contact right before Lavrov whisked her away, as vibrating mobile phones were pulled out and the news of the hostage-taking in the Mass Media Centre of Moscow State University reached everyone in the room. The panic in her eyes.

'This meeting must've taken place right after the hostage incident and before Lavrov went to Indonesia,' Paul said. He clicked *play* and continued listening to Ardahev's booming voice.

What's your connection to this Hafez?

She approached me to be the guest editor of a special art supplement. But actually . . .

Actually, what? Damn it! I saw the press conference given by her colleague, that Paul Chapelle. You had her planted in that hostage situation by your right-hand man Vakurov. You forced her to give a statement to the camera as one of the black widows. Whatever possessed you, only God knows, but with your actions you put our entire project at risk. You're being investigated, my friend.

Silence. Static. Wind.

When Valentin Lavrov began speaking again, his voice sounded icy calm, as if he were trying to suppress his rage.

Is that why we're here? Because of a journalist?

Static.

You're well aware that I'm waiting for a final agreement from the Dutch government on the gas hub that will allow us to play a larger role in Europe. And we're close to signing a huge nuclear deal with Indonesia. Let's call these trophies, which I'm collecting on behalf of

President Potanin. *And once these deals are completed, that whole incident with Hafez in the Seven Sisters is as relevant as yesterday's news. Nobody will ever discover the truth about what happened there.*

Ardahev's voice sounded hoarse.

Best you listen to me, friend. I don't want to look out over this fucking town for a moment longer than necessary. I want to see Moscow again. And I want to see it from the Kremlin. Got it? I want everything to go the way I want it to go from now on, the way we planned it. Is that understood?

There was another long silence. After that Lavrov's voice sounded for the last time.

You worry too much, Alexei. It's going to be all right. I always make sure things turn out okay.

Static. Silence. End of sound clip.

Paul felt agitated and paced back and forth in the study.

Roman stood thoughtfully bent over his desk, rubbing his beard, staring at the images on the computer screen. 'Those images . . .'

'What about them?'

'Why are they so grainy?'

'Ever worked with a telephoto lens?'

'And the voices?'

'A long-distance microphone always picks up some wind and city noise. But what's wrong, Roman?'

'Is this really Lavrov and Ardahev? Perhaps the material has been manipulated?'

Paul came and stood right in front of him. 'This intel is solid.'

'Okay,' Roman said, pointing his finger at the men on the roof of Battersea Power Station. 'Assuming these two are indeed Lavrov and Ardahev. Then perhaps Anya was murdered for an entirely different reason.'

'What do you mean?'

'She was investigating something, Anya. I was the only one who knew about it.'

'Investigating what?'

'Icarus. Code name for a secret society of Russian tycoons who've fled abroad in recent years. Most of them are prominent opponents of Potanin. They want nothing more than to break the Kremlin's power and return to their homeland under a new regime. Alexei Ardahev, according to Anya, was the mastermind behind that plan.'

'Was?'

Roman clicked open an icon on his laptop. A black-and-white photo from an article in *The Sunday Times* appeared on the screen. The mangled and burned-out wreckage of a Jaguar in the verge on a deserted English country road. The caption read: *Russian newspaper tycoon dies in mysterious car accident.*

'And he's not the only one we can tick off the list.' Roman scrolled down to another newspaper photo of a London mansion in an upmarket suburb. A smaller inserted photo showed its owner, Pavel Vertinski, another media tycoon, also a member of the Icarus Society. 'He was killed five days ago during a "violent break-in". No signs of a burglary, of course.' Roman turned to Paul again. 'Someone is cleaning house.'

'Someone?'

'The FSB, would be my guess . . .'

'Arlazarov?'

Roman silently nodded.

'But why share this information with a journalist?'

'Think, Paul. What did Sergey Kombromovich say about the material he gave you?'

'That it would bring down Lavrov. So?'

'You were well on your way to nailing Lavrov to the cross. And you had a relationship with Anya. It looks like Arlazarov has personally chosen you to eliminate another member of Icarus. This time no accident or so-called forced entry. Also no poisoning, but in Lavrov's case a much more effective means: a disclosure. Or rather, several. Patricide, corruption, planning a coup d'état. Mixed together to form the ultimate fatal cocktail.'

'Damn it, Roman, we're talking about a man who beat me half to death in Johannesburg, tortured Farah and finally got Anya killed.'

'In recent years I've lost some of my best journalists, but I refuse to be involved in a retaliatory expedition organized by the FSB. I've always respected your choices Paul, even when you hightailed it to Johannesburg unexpectedly and left Anya. But now ... Look at you. You're a bundle of rage. Out for blood. You'll come to regret it. Put it out of your head. Go home. Forget it. Anything is better than being the plaything of an FSB director.'

They faced each other in silence.

'I'm sorry,' Paul said resting his hand on Roman's shoulder. 'But I have to do this.'

Roman removed the USB stick from the laptop. 'Then do what you have to, Paul. But this time you're really on your own.'

Paul dropped the stick into his jacket pocket, reached for Roman and embraced him.

'Give Helena a kiss from me.'

In the stairwell he lit a cigarette, deeply inhaled a few times and then slowly walked downstairs. It was still raining. From the direction of Bolotny Square, police vans with flashing blue lights whizzed by. As he saw them pass, he thought about what Alexander Arlazarov had predicted.

It was going to be a long, restless night in Moscow.

3
Raylan

1978

On Red Square, people stood in an endless queue waiting to shuffle past the embalmed founder of the great communist society inside the marble Lenin Tomb. Some had flowers or a wreath in their hands. Raylan even discovered a bride and groom among those in line. Bells rang and reverberated between the great Kremlin towers and the colourful domes of Saint Basil's Cathedral.

'Mr Chapelle?'

In front of him stood a shabbily dressed young man with stringy dark hair and an artistic goatee. He was so thin, his brown corduroy trousers and jacket were far too baggy on him. From behind horn-rimmed glasses with thick round lenses he looked at Raylan curiously, while holding up the Russian translation of *The Great Lie* and tapping his finger against the picture on the back flap.

'The one and only,' Raylan replied. 'And you are?'

'Your university liaison, Sergey Kombromovich.' The sympathetic-looking young man extended his hand to Raylan and bowed slightly to illustrate the importance of the encounter. 'Please follow me. It's not far.' He led Raylan in the direction of Alexandrovsky Park.

'It's already an honour to escort you, but it would mean even more to me if you would sign my copy of *Bol'shaya Lozh* after your lecture,' Sergey said almost childishly while rubbing the book in excitement, as if it were his favourite cuddly toy. Raylan knew first impressions never lied. Sergey Kombromovich was as likeable as he was emaciated.

Somehow he had an intuitive feeling about what had happened in the Kremlin conference room.

'May I ask how your meeting was?' he casually inquired.

'In one word,' Raylan said, 'alarming.'

'They're too old,' Sergey sighed, 'our leaders. With the age and attitude of our grandfathers. The very idea of change gives them stomach cramps. They're holding the country back, interfering with progress. We need to be rid of them and preferably as soon as possible.'

'And who or what will take their place?'

'We will,' Sergey replied. '*Ad meliora!*' As if by magic, he seemed to have overcome his diffidence. 'A new generation will rise up, Mr Chapelle. And what binds us together is our unbridled curiosity. If I remember correctly, Einstein once said something along the lines of "People like you and I never grow old no matter how long we live, because we are like curious children exploring a great mystery." When my generation takes charge, everything will be fine again.'

'And when do you think that might happen?' Raylan reacted calmly. 'Before Russia invades Afghanistan?'

Sergey abruptly stopped walking and looked at Raylan in astonishment. 'Is it that bad?'

'Less than thirty minutes ago, the Afghan president symbolically flipped your granddads at the Kremlin the middle finger and strutted out of the room with his entire delegation. Unless there's a small miracle, Russian will soon be the official language of Afghanistan.'

Sergey shook his head in dismay. 'Haven't they learned anything? I mean, look at history, read your book, and you see that if we invade Afghanistan, we're doomed to make exactly the same mistake the Americans made in Vietnam.'

'Do you really think your generation can prevent another war, Sergey?'

'I refuse to stop believing in a better future. But it will only happen if there is huge opposition against the old guard. I hope you'll at least lend a hand in that regard?'

'How?'

A proud smile appeared on Sergey's pale face. 'All those young men and women now waiting for you in the lecture hall dream of one day becoming the kind of journalist you are. Today you can show them what kind of an influence a journalist can have on the world. What it could mean for all those innocent fellow human beings if they could also look beyond the web of lies, like you've done. You discovered how your own government managed to manipulate people for years by hiding the truth. You've opened the eyes of so many people. Then open the eyes of those in that lecture hall today.'

'I'll do my best.'

'You're my hero,' Sergey shyly said. 'And I'm not alone.'

Raylan had never had anything like this happen with a stranger, but because of Sergey's unrestrained honesty Raylan experienced something that could best be described as a fatherly feeling. 'You know, Sergey, I think if you'd been there in that conference room at the Kremlin today, it would have gone much better.'

'It's not up to me, Mr Chapelle.'

'Well, see to it that one day it is, kid.' He encouragingly slapped Sergey on the shoulder as they proceeded along Mokhovaya Street, where a university building in late eighteenth-century classical style loomed before them.

'First it was the palace of Ivan the Terrible,' Sergey said. 'Catherine the Great then purchased it for the State University. The great fire of 1812 reduced it to ashes. A few years later, they rebuilt it from scratch in exactly the same style.'

'Impressive,' said Raylan, seeing a handsome young man coming straight towards them. He was tall and athletic and dressed in a smart blue suit with a red tie. His handshake was as forceful as his gaze.

Welcome, my dear Mr Chapelle. My name is Alexander Arlazarov. I was the one who organized your guest lecture.'

Arlazarov was the sort of young man who made you feel like you were talking to the head of the department, or even better, the director of the university. He had the sophistication of a con man smart enough to exude exactly the opposite. At least his English sounded much better than Sergey's. The two briefly exchanged some words in Russian. Judging from how they looked at each other and the subtle way in which Alexander briefly patted Sergey's jacket, Raylan picked up on a sultry kind of atmosphere between these two very different characters, a dead giveaway that they were more than just friends.

Alexander Arlazarov smiled at Raylan as if he could read his thoughts. 'A shame we don't have more time to get better acquainted, my dear Chapelle. Sergey has no doubt already told you that the lecture hall filled to capacity within minutes of the doors opening. Shall we not keep your audience waiting any longer?'

They quickly mounted the outside steps, walked through the lobby and finally navigated a maze of corridors with creaky stairs until they reached the old lecture hall, which was the size of a modest amphitheatre and indeed filled to the rafters. A euphoric murmur went through the crowd as soon as everybody realized the long-awaited American journalist had arrived.

'It's as if we have a rock star in our midst,' Arlazarov said. He looked at Raylan, who rubbed his chin. 'Is something wrong, my dear Chapelle?'

Raylan stared into the crowd and grinned. 'I forgot my goddamn guitar.'

On the elevated platform in the lecture hall, Raylan slowly gave the room a once-over. They were seated everywhere, close together on the old benches and worn-out wooden steps, all the way to the top of the highest row. Young Russian students, most of whom stood up to spontaneously applaud him. Raylan glanced at the blackboard diagonally behind him. In Cyrillic capitals, someone had written the title of his book with thick chalk. He took a sip of water from the glass on the lectern and encouragingly nodded to Sergey Kombromovich, who would serve as his interpreter.

'As a journalist I profess to speak the truth . . .' He waited for Sergey to translate his first sentence and then continued with his introduction. 'But when you are listening to a man standing in front of a blackboard with the words *The Great Lie* displayed in giant letters, you might not be inclined to take him seriously. So I apologize for my pre-emptive action.'

Raylan followed through by resolutely wiping the letters off the board, as a wave of laughter rolled through the room, then faded again, after which all eyes were expectantly focused on him.

'Someone asked me the other day if I was opposed to war. The answer is simple: if freedom of speech is at stake, I'm prepared to start a war to protect that right. I'm a journalist, not a pacifist. He waited a while for his words to fall, looked around and made eye contact again. An American general once said to me, just before he ordered his troops in Vietnam to recapture the Imperial City of Hué from the Viet Cong: "To liberate the city, we have to destroy it. They're counting on it. Just like they're counting on you to provide front-page headlines." After which he added, "The North Vietnamese aren't my worst enemy ... My worst enemy is *you*, the goddamn American press."'

Raylan paused again, while Sergey translated his last words, and surveyed the room. He relished the sparkling eyes of the curious students in attendance, precisely how Sergey had described his generation. That's why a piercing look he caught in the middle of the fifth row was all the more striking. The dark eyes staring at him radiated not only curiosity but suspicion and disapproval. Moreover, it was a look that seemed familiar to him, but one he couldn't immediately place.

'What that general was implying,' Raylan continued, 'was that the North Vietnamese clearly understood that my critical coverage of American army operations in Vietnam would generate a lot of negative publicity internationally. And that would certainly be the case if our troops destroyed Vietnam's most beautiful city. But was that a reason to stop doing my job as a journalist?'

He looked at the eyes that continued to stare at him from the fifth row. In ancient Buddhist and Hindu Tantric traditions this was considered something sacred. Monks used eye gazing to deepen mutual trust and intimacy. Realizing this stare was exactly the opposite, he was a bit startled when he recognized the man. The strange smile on his lips revealed he'd picked up on Raylan's reaction.

'Sometimes it's beyond your control if your journalistic work is used by others to their own advantage,' Raylan continued, seemingly unaffected. 'But it's absolutely a mortal sin, as a journalist, to consciously allow others to use you.'

He now returned the gaze of the dark eyes in the fifth row.

'Ten years ago, I was at a trial in Kabul. A young editor was about to be sentenced because he wrote an editorial for the socialist party newspaper calling for a violent coup, which included assassinating the then king, after which Afghanistan would become a communist utopia resembling the Soviet Union.'

He drank what was left of his water and waited for Sergey to translate. His throat was still dry. The two eyes glaring at him now felt like burning daggers.

'The prosecutor demanded the death penalty. But what were the facts? Very simple: a young communist student had penned and published his violent ideals. Was that a crime? After all, the country had freedom of speech, freedom of the press. So what was he guilty of?'

Raylan looked around the room. It was as if the sparks flying between the brazen man and him could now be felt by everyone.

'By wrapping a violent political message in a journalistic-style article, this editor wasn't actually guilty of abusing freedom of speech. Yet he fundamentally violated the most important rule of our profession, namely that as a journalist you must always strive to pursue an independent course.'

Raylan saw the man in the fifth row fidget in his seat and lower his eyes. It looked as if he might leave, but he changed his mind.

A young woman in the audience raised her hand.

'What was the judge's verdict?'

'Sentencing him to death would have been a repudiation of the most essential democratic freedoms in the country. However, acquittal would have meant a loss of face for the government. In the end, the editor was exiled to Russia.'

Raylan threw him another glance.

'Only when journalists consider it their highest priority to use their right to speak out in a truly independent way do they serve the truth. And with that truth, they serve democracy. Without journalism, there is no democracy, and vice versa. That brings me to the crucial question I'd like to ask all of you today: why is there a School of Journalism in a country where the state exerts constant control over what is reported? Does this mean when you finish studying and land your first job, that you're going to do the dirty work for those scoundrels in the Kremlin?'

There was a commotion in the room. Hands went up in the air.

The discussion Raylan was interested in having came to life. It soon became clear that what Sergey had told him during their walk to the university had been no exaggeration. Here, in this neoclassical lecture hall, a new generation was making itself heard. Young Russians had a vision of the future that came straight from the heart. As journalists, they would never let themselves be guided by just any political ideology. They would never describe the world from a singular perspective. Like their American role model behind the lectern, they would be guided by their fascination for the world. After his closing words – 'stay engaged, be critical' – they gave Raylan a standing ovation, and he noticed that Sergey was clapping loudest of all, with tears in his eyes.

After the last group of students had wandered off, Raylan put his arm around Sergey's shoulder. 'A journalist shouldn't really be anyone's friend, but today I'd like to make an exception for you,' he said to the blushing young man with his goatee and he took the time to write a special dedication in his book: *For my friend Sergey, with warm wishes, from Raylan.* Then he grabbed his packet of Lucky Strikes from his pocket, brought a cigarette to his lips and walked towards the man still seated in the lecture hall.

The man from the fifth row.

'Long time,' Raylan said with a grin, and he reached out his hand. 'What a surprise, Askan.'

In the old lecture theatre of Moscow State University Askan Vaziri's voice still sounded as adamant and incisive as it had ten years ago in Kabul's courtroom. This time he added a dash of cynicism.

'Thank you for the prominent role I was allowed to play in your lecture, Mr Chapelle.'

'Happy to do a friend of the revolution a favour,' Raylan replied, as he pulled out his Lucky Strikes and offered Askan one. 'And to what do I owe your attendance here?'

'I was curious to hear a lecture given by the man who once took the trouble to visit me in prison.' Askan gestured to decline the cigarette. 'I just hadn't counted on being cited as an example.'

'Sorry, but communist zeal and journalism simply don't go together,'

Raylan said as he took a seat next to Askan. 'How has life in exile treated you?'

Askan crossed his arms. 'I miss my country more than I can express. But I'm given all the resources and cooperation I need from the government to do what I wasn't allowed to do in Afghanistan.'

'Let me guess,' said Raylan, taking another puff of his cigarette. 'All those young Afghans who arrive in Moscow on scholarships, and you're here to convince them that the Soviet Union is paradise on earth and that Afghanistan should follow in its footsteps as soon as possible.'

'A revolution is the only answer for my country,' Askan said. 'Only a revolution will empower us to carry out the most necessary and far-reaching reforms and to restore respect and dignity to all Afghans.'

Askan Vaziri still sounded like he was reading from *The Communist Manifesto*. But the driven idealist with the dark curls – who'd sat opposite him ten years ago as a prisoner in Kabul – had turned into a militant activist with a crew cut, ready to storm the barricades waving the hammer-and-sickle flag and lead his country to a new earthly paradise.

'I'd like to quote you, Askan. Do I have your permission?'

'After that lecture, I wouldn't dare stand in the way of free speech,' Askan said, with an arrogant smile. 'As far as I'm concerned, you can quote me for whatever purposes you choose. It still won't stop the revolution.'

'I was in the Kremlin today at the meeting between Daoud and Brezhnev,' Raylan said. 'Daoud has had enough of all the ways Russia interferes in domestic policy. He wants to operate independently, but the Kremlin will never allow it.'

'At least we agree on that, Mr Chapelle. But you know what's so ironic?'

'I'm listening.'

'In your lecture today, you used me as an example of how a journalist can let himself be manipulated. But the same thing happened to you today. The only reason President Daoud wanted you at his meeting with Brezhnev today is because he hopes that one of these days President Carter will open *The New York Times* and read about how reliable his Afghan ally is.'

Raylan grinned. 'Touché, Askan. Still, there's a crucial difference. I don't write what Daoud or anyone else dictates me to say. I write my own articles based on my own research. I'm well aware of Daoud's motives, and they are, I can tell you, surprisingly honest. The motives of that bunch in the Kremlin, on the other hand, are founded on pure fear. They're afraid they'll have to surrender some of their power in the region. So I think Brezhnev sees Daoud's stance as tantamount to a declaration of war.'

Raylan turned to Askan and looked him directly in the eye. 'Off the record, Askan: will there be a Russian invasion of Afghanistan in response? Or will it be a domestic coup?'

Although Askan was stubbornly silent, his inscrutable smile betrayed a tinge of pride.

'Option two it is ...' Raylan said. 'And what also interests me is whether you'll be there.'

Askan stood up and extended his hand to Raylan.

'It was an enlightening discussion, Mr Chapelle.'

Raylan kept hold of Askan's hand.

'Yes or no, Askan, will you be involved?'

Askan's smile slipped from his face. With a jerk of his hand he turned around and exited the room.

Back in his lavishly furnished room at Hotel Sovietsky, overlooking the ever-busy Leningradsky Prospekt, Raylan picked up the receiver of the Bakelite telephone and dialled Edward Vallent's private number.

'It seems like you're right, amigo,' he said after Edward groggily answered the call. 'Behind the scenes, Russia is working towards overthrowing the present government in Kabul.'

'You think there's going to be an invasion?'

'I suspect the Russians have something smarter up their sleeve. They're going to make it look like an inside job. Remember the story about that young Afghan student editor ten years ago, that Askan Vaziri?'

'The one who was exiled?'

'It seems that for years, at the expense of the Russian government, he's been recruiting young Afghans who attend university in Moscow and grooming them for a communist takeover to end President Daoud's reign. Daoud's insulting antics yesterday in the Kremlin are seen by the Soviets as a blatant declaration of war. Vaziri's words lead me to believe that a coup is imminent.'

'Vaziri is your only source. How reliable is he?'

'Solid enough to publish.'

'When's your flight back to Kabul?'

'Tomorrow morning.'

'Best you wait to put anything down on paper until you're in the air. The Russian authorities won't be amused if they find your notes. You never know what they're capable of.'

'I'll write the article on the plane. After landing, I'll send it to you by telex.'

'Agreed. Good work, Ray.'

'My pleasure, boss.'

Raylan wasn't entirely sure, but he thought he'd heard an occasional clicking on the line. After he'd finished speaking to Edward, he continued to listen to the static noise. He hung the receiver back on the hook, waited thirty seconds and then picked it up again. When he heard the dial tone, the clicking and the same static noise again, he knew enough.

4
Farah

2009

She'd wanted to stay longer – so she could compile the evidence against Hafami, see to it that Sekandar's family was traced and get to know Nehal and her family better. But today was her last day. Straight after the ceremony at the Presidential Palace, she'd be driven to the airport, where her flight to Moscow was due to take off in the evening.

A few hundred metres away, traffic whizzed along the banks of the River Kabul past the Titanic bazaar. Stalls, laden with fabrics and robes, were erected well into the dry riverbed. Figures in blue burqas meandered among them. The wind blew from the east and kept the smelly exhaust fumes and the noise at bay. This spot here, the flat roof of Nehal's family home, felt like the quiet eye of a storm.

It had been thirty years since she'd last seen the city from a hill. She'd turned around and never looked back. She thought she'd left the country behind, yet all this time it had been travelling with her. 'You're a child of this land. Afghanistan is like a father to you,' Uncle Parwaiz once told her.

She ran her fingers over the puffy skin under her eyes, which was turning a purplish blue. When she touched the bridge of her broken nose, it wasn't too painful. Just a constant dull ache. She now had the same broad nose as her father. It made the contrast with her blue eyes and tight jawline all the greater.

She looked at the message that had popped up on her display fifteen minutes earlier.

Must speak urgently.

They hadn't had contact since their goodbye in the courtyard of Ashraf hospital. There'd been a time when she would have felt nervous waiting for a man like Mason. Not even all that long ago. She'd have raided her wardrobe, unsure what to wear, and frantically applied too much make-up. Now she was standing here on top of the roof, barefoot in faded jeans and a drab T-shirt, with short dishevelled hair, without a lick of make-up but with a swollen nose that was fading to purple in places. And she couldn't have cared less how she looked.

She recognized his heavy footsteps on the stairs, turned and smiled at the painful similarities between them. Mason's face was puffed up and bluish purple as well. The cut above his right eyebrow had been stitched. His swollen eye was taped shut. His gait was as laborious as his smile, and he was hiding something behind his back. When he stood in front of her he handed over a small package.

'For you.'

The parcel was light and squashy, and inside was a deep-purple *nikkah* scarf with a golden floral motif.

'Since yours was torn to shreds when you thrashed that guard, I figured . . .'

'It's gorgeous.'

She smiled in an attempt to hide her confusion. Traditionally, this type of scarf was used at wedding ceremonies. Following hymns and prayers, the Koran was held up, and the scarf draped over the heads of the bride and groom. And then a small mirror was held underneath, allowing the husband and wife to see each other for the first time.

He stared at her. She wondered if he had any idea about the symbolism of his gift.

'I handed Goldwater my medical report. I've been suspended. With immediate effect.' He looked away. His Adam's apple bobbed up and down. 'I'm flying home tonight.'

'They're not wasting any time.'

He turned to her again. 'It was my choice. It enables me to . . . I want to fix it, you know. My marriage is beyond saving, but I want to see my children. And after that . . . I'll just see what happens after that.'

Farah nodded, feeling more nervous than she'd like. She thought of the previous evening, about what they'd done, the intimacy between them.

As a beam of sunlight flashes through the water ... so the crown jewel of love penetrated through the veil of his body.

As a child, she couldn't get enough of the story of Layla and Majnun and the unattainable love that cost them their lives. Only in death were they united as lovers.

For whoever must endure suffering and bears it patiently in this world will be full of joy and bliss in paradise.

She wasn't in paradise. She was standing in the heart of sweltering, dusty, turbulent Kabul. She took Mason's banged-up face between her hands and gently pulled him towards her. Her lips touched his swollen eye, as softly as possible, and his forehead, nose and cheeks until they reached his lips.

She tenderly kissed him on the mouth. 'Good luck to you, Gunnery Sergeant Williams, wherever life takes you.'

'Home ... I hope.'

'Home is where the heart is ...'

His smile bordered on apologetic. Then he walked back to the stairs, but before he took the first step he stopped and turned. 'In that case, I should stay here ... with you.'

It would only take seconds.

All she'd have to do was take the initiative, say a few words.

She was able to stand up to a politician and tell him to change course. She thought nothing of refusing to sign a piece of paper presented to her by a US Army general. She could hang like a millstone around a guard's neck to eliminate him. But right now she decided to do nothing, to say nothing, to stand back and watch Mason walk down the stairs. He was going back to a house that would no longer feel like home, back to a life where he'd be responsible for clearing the shattered pieces all by himself. As she watched him disappear from view she thought back to that first time, when she saw him at the T-junction in his army fatigues.

He'd stood there like a pillar of strength, beckoning her over.

*

The clothes lay on the guest bed in neatly arranged piles. At the foot, her outfit for the reburial ceremony: the light-grey silk blouse, loose-fitting black trousers and black sleeveless jacket she'd worn only a few weeks earlier to Uncle Parwaiz's funeral. Her other clothes and personal items were piled up beside the unzipped Eastpak Tranverz bag at the head of the bed.

Nehal entered the room with a platter full of watermelon in her hands. 'You should eat more, *hamshera*,' she said, holding the fruit up to Farah until she'd taken at least three slices. That's when her eye fell on Sekandar's drawing. 'Who made that?'

'A boy who was found on a road outside Amsterdam a few weeks ago. I don't know where it is or what it represents; probably his home.'

Nehal shook her head. 'That's not his home. No one living there would refer to such a place as home.' She picked up the drawing and pointed to the vertical line reaching up into the sky like a long needle, the diagonal slashes that looked like roofs and the jagged rocks on the horizon that were sliced by something resembling a bird. 'It's a refugee camp.'

Just three hours before the ceremony at the Presidential Palace was due to begin, Nehal manoeuvred as fast as possible past clapped-out buses, taxis and shiny new SUVs. All the flags in the city were at half-mast. They passed construction sites where towering cranes were starkly reflected in glass façades and kept driving until eventually they saw the desolate pale-brown hills rise up in the distance.

On a map of the area, Nehal had marked the location of the refugee camp she thought she recognized from Sekandar's drawing. There were a total of thirteen on the outskirts of Kabul, but she reckoned that no other site offered that particular view of the southern mountain ridge and the phone mast.

South of Kabul they passed Bala Hissar, centuries ago a mighty fortress, now a ruin. Nehal honked repeatedly to disperse a herd of goats and parked her jeep on a hill overlooking the battered tents of Chami-Babrak camp. Most of its occupants came from Helmand, Kunduz and Nangahar provinces and had fled the Taliban. Farah and

Nehal walked down the hill. As soon as they entered the mud- and garbage-strewn alleyways they were beset by a pack of ragged children, who clung to them and begged for food.

Nehal paused, unfolded Sekandar's drawing and pointed to the red-and-white-striped phone mast sticking up into the air about a hundred metres away. Seeing the sloping contours of the tent roofs, the jagged ridges in the distance and the descending plane coming in low, like a gliding bird, Farah immediately recognized the striking resemblance with the drawing.

She showed a photo of Sekandar to the curious men and children who had flocked around them. 'This boy was kidnapped. He's supposed to be from this camp. I'm a journalist and I'm trying to find his family.'

A man broke free from the group. He had jet-black beady eyes and a thin mouth set in an emaciated, weathered face. He motioned for them to follow him. When they arrived at a threadbare canvas tent, he asked them to wait. The stream of curious onlookers had now grown into a small crowd. Minutes later, the man emerged again and introduced them to the tent's occupant, who turned out to be the camp elder. His face was creased, his hair still wet beneath a cap. He greeted them with his hand on his heart and invited them in for tea. Farah wanted to decline; there was no time for tea. But Nehal quickly accepted the invitation with an extravagant display of gratitude. These were the unwritten rules of courtesy and hospitality, Farah realized. If she wanted to get anything done here, she had to abide by them, however little time and patience she had.

The tent was barely big enough for them to stand up in. It contained a low table as well as a few small rugs. After taking off their shoes, they sat cross-legged on the floor. While his wife poured green tea from a samovar, the camp elder said he was honoured to be visited by a journalist who cared about the fate of the refugees. Meanwhile, Farah impatiently rummaged in her bag for Sekandar's photo. Nehal's hand stopped her. They had to listen to what the camp elder had to say before they could ask any questions. It was a matter of respect. The hands on her watch ticked away the already scarce time.

The camp elder's voice sounded broken. 'Being forced to move away from the place where you were born is almost like leaving your heart behind. Most of the men here are unemployed; the children can't go to school. There's next to no medication for the sick. People are starving to death.' With a trembling hand he raised his glass to his mouth and took a sip before continuing his story. 'We're Afghan citizens, but the state offers no long-term solutions. They think that if they start doing that a thousand more families will come forward tomorrow. We receive no assistance because officially we're not from an unsafe area. But there's nothing for us to go back to.' He gulped down his tea and then looked at them curiously. 'I appreciate that you've been kind enough to listen to me. But I understand you have a question for me.'

Farah took out the photo of Sekandar and showed it to him. 'I'm looking for the parents of this child. I believe he went missing from here.'

The camp elder took his time studying the photo. She saw the frown on his forehead. Then he looked up with sadness in his eyes. 'As you've seen: there are so many children here. Some die, others disappear. The ones who are left behind grow up without hope.'

He stared at the photo again, then got up with difficulty. 'Please wait for me here.' He went outside.

The woman was about to pour tea again, but Farah held her hand over her glass and checked her watch. They'd arrived in the camp ninety minutes ago. It would take them a while to get back. The idea that she might be late or even absent from her father's final farewell was unbearable to her. She wanted to get up, but again Nehal stopped her and whispered, 'Leaving would be the greatest possible insult to them.'

A helicopter flew over. The tent canvas flapped about. Excited voices could be heard outside. The camp elder stooped and squeezed through the opening with difficulty. 'Please follow me.'

They walked behind him down the narrow pathways between the tents. Outside a shabby structure of canvas and corrugated iron they stopped. A man, a woman and three small children stood in front of them, looking tense.

The camp elder's voice sounded solemn. 'Could you show him the photo?'

She handed the photo to the man.

He looked at it, seemingly emotionless. But she noticed the nervous twitching in his face. The woman snatched the photo from his hand. Her eyes widened in horror. She was about to scream, but then her legs buckled, and she collapsed.

As soon as the man began telling his story she lost all sense of time. Sekandar, it turns out, was the eldest of four children. Every day he'd go to the markets in the city and collect overripe or rotting onions, tomatoes and pumpkins from the greengrocers. He'd bring them back to the camp. His mother made curries with whatever was still edible. That was their meal for the day. His father would then go out to sell any leftovers. This is what their life in the camp was like, day in day out.

After Sekandar's disappearance, his father searched every single marketplace for his son. All he brought home were vegetables. But he refused to accept that he'd never see the boy again. He'd told Farah all this in a surprisingly gentle voice. The photo she'd shown proved him right. 'I dream about him, night after night. He'll stand in front of me, trying to tell me where he is, but his voice is too far away. I can't hear him.'

She'd explained to him where Sekandar was now. That he'd been in an accident and had needed hospital treatment. She'd skipped the rest of the story. She suspected that the man and woman might not be able to comprehend or come to terms with it. And even if they did, then shame or the perceived violation of family honour might well stop them from welcoming Sekandar back.

With the promise that she'd do her best to accelerate his return, she'd said goodbye. On the way into town, in the back seat of the jeep, with the tinted windows sparing her blushes, she changed out of her jeans and T-shirt into her outfit for the ceremony. And just as Nehal pulled up in front of the Kandahari Gate of the presidential compound, she wrapped herself in the nikkah Mason had given her.

5
Raylan

1978

During the flight from Moscow to Kabul he worked on his article about the failed meeting between President Daoud and Brezhnev. He relied on his conversation with Askan Vaziri after the lecture at Moscow State University to shed light on the consequences of the fatal summit between the two countries. Although Vaziri wasn't one of the leaders of the organization in Russia planning the coup in Afghanistan, he was ideal for elucidating how the Kremlin had worked diligently for years to instigate a communist revolution in Afghanistan.

At the top of the flight of stairs a gust of warm, dry air struck his face. The bright blue of the horizon sharply contrasted with the jagged mountain ridges surrounding the city. The terminal's sheltered roof terrace, where people once gathered in droves to catch a glimpse of arriving passengers, was now almost deserted. The murmuring of voices in the arrivals hall sounded muffled to his ears.

A broad-shouldered man saw fit to block his way to the glass exit door. Raylan had a memory like an elephant for anyone who'd ever confronted him in an aggressive way. He recognized the condor-like head as belonging to the same man who, years earlier, had brutally flung him down the outside steps of the Russian Cultural Centre. This time the man was doing his best to sound polite, but his awkward performance verged on the pathetic.

'There's a taxi waiting out front for you, Mr Chapelle.'

'How about you take that one and I'll just get the next one!'

Raylan tried to sidestep him, but the forceful flat of the man's hand against his chest made it clear that this wasn't an option on the limited menu.

'What are you going to do? Beat me to a pulp here? Do you think you'll get away with it?' Raylan asked.

A smirk appeared on the condor's lips. 'There are plenty of methods, Mr Chapelle. Ones that aren't as obvious or visible as you might think. But certainly as effective.'

His hand, painfully exerting even more pressure on Raylan's chest, was clearly meant as illustration. Raylan looked around, estimated his chances and soon reached the conclusion they were as good as zero.

A silver-grey Bentley T2 was waiting outside, its engine idling. The condor opened the rear door and gestured for Raylan to take a seat next to the man who'd just folded his newspaper closed. From the grey-green eyes in his overconfident face Raylan recognized the former director of the Russian Cultural Centre, Grigori Michailov.

'As you can see, Mr Chapelle, I still prefer *The Washington Post* to *The New York Times*.'

'For all I care, you can wipe your ass with it. What's this all about?'

'I want to set a few things straight,' Michailov replied, signalling to the chauffeur that he should go. 'Contrary to what you write, the Russian government always considers what happens in this country to be an internal matter.'

'Doesn't sound so convincing. You might want to work on your credibility.'

Raylan glanced at the obelisk in the middle of the roundabout. The driver took an unexpected turn towards a higher part of town.

'Am I making you nervous?' Michailov asked.

'Russians tend to have that effect on me,' Raylan replied.

Michailov smiled derisively. 'Not all Russians, I'm told?'

Raylan looked at him suspiciously.

'Sergey Kombromovich comes to mind,' Michailov continued. 'You took a liking to him, didn't you?'

Raylan rubbed his chin hard. 'You KGB bastards. The lowest of the low. Like sewer rats.'

'Reminds me a bit of the Western tabloid press: always digging up dirt. But that's where the comparison ends. Because we serve a higher purpose than that so-called truth of yours. We serve the state. We identify our potential enemies, keep track of their daily routines, follow them over the course of their lives. Control, Mr Chapelle, that's what matters in this world. Total control. You're at the wrong end of the spectrum. You think the truth is all powerful, what it's all about. Control is power. Truth pales in comparison.'

'Get to the point, asshole, I want to go home.'

The green-grey eyes looked at him with contempt. 'I understand we have a mutual acquaintance in Moscow ... let me put this diplomatically ... who in his enthusiasm was a bit too forthcoming.'

'You mean the man who's spent years recruiting Afghan students in Moscow as future revolutionaries? The same fellow you claimed you didn't know a decade ago?'

'I kindly advise you not to disclose the details of your conversation with Askan Vaziri,' Michailov said. He gave Raylan an oblique look.

'Do you really think I'd take your advice seriously for even a second?'

The road got steeper. The city was now far below them. Michailov let out a long sigh. 'A shame that our conversation has taken this turn.' He removed a medium-sized envelope from a briefcase and placed it on Raylan's lap. 'Perhaps what's inside will make you see things somewhat differently.'

With a sinking feeling, Raylan stared at the envelope and then tore it open. The pile of black-and-white photographs he fished out were in chronological order. In the first he saw himself walking into the lounge of the Intercontinental Hotel. In the second he was at the check-in desk with his back to the photographer. In number three he was walking the outdoor gallery to his hotel room. The photographer must have concealed himself on the other side of the gallery and taken these pictures with a telephoto lens.

Raylan already knew what he was going to see in the next photo.

With only his jeans on, he had opened the door to the room. She stood in front of him wearing a thin dress with three-quarter sleeves. Seen from the back, she could have been any Afghan woman with dark curly hair in Western clothing.

But in photo number five that likelihood significantly diminished. She'd leaned towards him to give him a kiss on the lips, revealing her face in profile. The sixth photo left no doubt about the identity of the woman who turned to close the hotel room door behind her.

Michailov broke the stifling silence in the Bentley with obvious delight in his voice. 'Of course, Mr Chapelle, write whatever you want. I won't stop you. What I find more interesting is what will happen when these pictures end up where they probably shouldn't be seen.'

Staring at the last picture, Raylan felt like a noose was slowly being tightened around his neck. He was unable to utter a word. The Bentley slowed down and stopped.

'Welcome home, Mr Chapelle,' he heard Michailov say, as the condor opened the rear door.

He didn't even notice the stench and the dreariness of his surroundings when he stepped out. All he could think about was protecting Helai. That aspect of the situation changed everything. He didn't give a damn about the *kompromat* they had on him, as long as she wasn't dragged into it. But it was too late to change that. He thought about what she'd said to him in the butterfly garden: *I don't want to raise my daughter in poverty and shame, but to give her all the opportunities life has to offer.*

He heard his luggage being tossed on the ground and only realized then that they'd driven him to a landfill. From the backseat Michailov hurled the photos at Raylan. His calm tone was chilling. 'Take good care of yourself and your loved ones, Mr Chapelle.'

The doors of the Bentley were closed. The car pulled away. Feeling almost paralysed, Raylan stared at the photos at his feet, which were swept across the ground by a gust of wind.

In the days that followed he couldn't shake that image of Helai in the doorway of his hotel room. He'd tasted the sweetness of her lips as she pressed them against his mouth. He took a step backwards to let her enter. And in those few seconds the shutter of a camera a short distance away clicked. Precisely in that futile vacuum in time the seal to their secret was broken open. The black-and-white photos he'd held in the back seat of the Bentley were irrefutable evidence of this.

*

Five days had passed since he'd left the compromising photos at the landfill on the high plateau above Kabul for what they were: easy prey for the wind. That same day he telexed a bare-bones article about the meeting between Brezhnev and Daoud to Edward, who called immediately afterwards, clearly bewildered. 'What happened to the storyline about the coup and the dirty game Russia is playing? Where the hell is your reliable source, Vaziri?'

Raylan managed to stay calm. 'Vaziri withdrew his consent at the last minute, probably under pressure from the Russians.'

A few days had passed since his guest lecture in Moscow. There he'd received a standing ovation by asserting that independent journalists only have the right to speak if they serve the truth. Now he himself had violated that truth in more ways than one. He'd concealed the fact that Daoud's reaction to Russia's demands was seen by the Kremlin as a declaration of war. He'd neglected to mention that Afghan students and cadets were recruited at Russian universities and military academies to serve as potential perpetrators of a coup. And he'd lied through his teeth to his friend Ed about the real reason that information hadn't appeared in his article.

Entangled in his own lies, he'd betrayed just about every principle he believed in: journalistic integrity, reliability and loyalty.

In the wake of that betrayal, insomnia followed. And with those sleepless nights the flashbacks returned to haunt him: the burning monk, the digging child and the begging mother with her baby. He started popping Anafranil again, whenever possible combined with an excessive amount of whiskey. Early in the morning, he drove his BMW far into the mountains, only to return home late at night. Then Isobel found him on the roof terrace, staring at the fading stars, as if the answer to his problems could be found in the heavens.

She was there for him, as always. Strong, but with a worried look. She sat next to him, just as she'd done that first time on the edge of the swimming pool at Hotel Serena. But now she was the one who rolled a joint, lit it and passed it to Raylan after a long toke.

'Tell me what's going on,' she said. 'It's time you told me.'

'It's simple,' he replied after he'd inhaled deeply, held the smoke in his lungs for a while and slowly exhaled. 'They found out. About Helai and me.'

'And who might "they" be?'

'The Russians.'

She looked at him bewildered. 'Why are the Russians interested in an affair that's been over for two years? And if they've known all along, why use it against you now?'

Raylan stared into the distance, where a column of smoke was rising into the air. The atmosphere in the city was getting grimmer by the day. The anti-government demonstrations had become bigger and, above all, more violent. There was a curfew. Patrol cars with armed police drove around at night. Everywhere in the city people suspected of communist sympathies were snatched from their beds to be taken away. From his presidential palace, Daoud seemed concerned only with consolidating his personal power.

'There's going to be a coup,' Raylan sighed. 'Maybe tomorrow, maybe next week, but it's coming. And it's being orchestrated from Moscow. A source I can trust told me. I called Edward about it. That call must've been bugged by the KGB. It looks like they've been keeping tabs on me for a very long time. They've never had a reason to use the affair with Helai against me. That is, until I found out what the Kremlin secretly has in store for Afghanistan.'

'And Edward doesn't know any of this?'

He shook his head. 'What was I supposed to tell him? That I sold my soul to the devil to protect my former mistress?'

Isobel gave him a harsh look. 'He's the first person who should know what happened. He has a right to know. He's your friend.'

Raylan kept rubbing his face in despair. '. . . I let him down.'

'No. You've done something much worse, Ray. You've let yourself down.'

There was a dull roar in the distance. It grew sharper, heavier, louder. A combat helicopter was quickly approaching in the sky. He thought of Edward's words: *I'd wager a bet that some war will find you again.*

Because of the strong downward flow of air caused by the

low-flying helicopter's rotor blades, they had to hold on to the wooden banister. Potted plants and ceramic shells flew into the air. The helicopter set course in the direction of the Abu Fazl Mosque close to the river. With panic in his sleepy eyes Paul came running up the stairs. Raylan caught him in his arms. The boy trembled with fear.

'Is it war?'

'No, sweetie. You're safe with us. Always.' Isobel ruffled Paul's messy hair, gave him a comforting kiss and lifted him out of Raylan's arms. 'We're going on a trip, honey. Will you help me pack in the morning?'

Paul nodded with teary eyes. As Isobel took the first steps down the stairs, he turned around and anxiously looked at Raylan. 'What about you, Daddy?'

'I first have a few things to arrange tomorrow.'

'Then you'll come back?'

'I always come back, you know that.'

The night brought chaos to the city. The next morning they had to act more rapidly than expected. They booked three seats on a British Airways flight departing for London-Gatwick airport in the evening. They could only take what they could carry: some clothing, documents, a few personal items, the Travel-Riter. And paintings. Raylan would go to the gallery by motorbike and remove three from their frames. Then he'd do what he'd promised Isobel.

Set things straight.

The previous night, he'd reworked the article on Daoud's failed mission to Moscow. This time as he'd originally planned. He gave it to Isobel, who put it in the bottom of her suitcase.

'I've called the interior affairs minister,' she said. 'Gailani will see you in an hour.'

'If I'm not back in time, take the jeep and wait for me at the airport.'

She held on to him tightly and kissed him as she had that very first time, but now without the peals of laughter.

As he navigated past groups of demonstrators on his BMW, he was reminded of all those years ago, when workers and students also flooded the city. A decade had passed. Ten years between protests; the first one against a possible death sentence for Askan Vaziri and now a mass revolt against the sitting government.

A decade – that's how long he'd lived in Kabul. He married here, had a child and found the calm he needed to write about the horrors of a bygone war. And perhaps this country would now become the scene of comparable horrors. He couldn't have prevented it, no matter how hard he might have tried; there were greater powers at work here. What he'd seen at the Kremlin was only a glimpse of the bigger picture, a fragment of a tragedy clandestinely planned for years and now reaching fruition.

He was approaching Zanbaq Square. The thousands who'd taken to the streets had by now grown to tens of thousands. He had no choice but to leave the BMW on the side of the road. He made his way by foot through the crowd on the square.

He stopped in the middle to listen to a familiar figure speaking through a crackling megaphone from an improvised platform. Even from a distance he saw that those dark, distrusting eyes, which had been staring at him barely a week ago during his lecture, were now on fire. His voice, which had then sounded so restrained, reverberated above the agitated crowd.

'This is the people's plaza. This is the moment of victory. This is the end of the dictatorship!' Askan Vaziri lifted his arm in the air and clenched his fist. 'Liberty or death!'

Raylan saw the triumphant eyes of a man who'd returned after ten years in exile to finally call for his revolution.

Then the first dull bang sounded. At the edges of the square the *ghund-e-zarba*, the military riot police, appeared. The tear gas cannisters they fired caused waves of panic in the crowd. People were trampled underfoot. The sound of gun salvos that followed betrayed the fact they were shooting with live ammunition.

The first casualty was the man standing on the platform with his fist still raised in the air. The back of his skull burst apart. Askan Vaziri tumbled lifeless to the ground.

Black batons were lifted all across the square: the sign of a first charge. Raylan managed to reach the other side of the square, where the crowd dispersed through the intricate network of narrow streets and alleyways. In one of these lanes was Isobel's small corner gallery, concealed by an iron gate covered by green vines.

Even though the electricity in the city had been turned off, he didn't open the shutters. Outside he heard the muted explosions of tear gas cannisters and the sharp sound of automatic rifles being fired. Inside, the narrow beam of light from his torch slid across peaceful street scenes and portraits. He first found the painting of the three of them strolling through the bazaar. Then one with Paul in front of the Blue Mosque amidst the pigeons. The third was the portrait Isobel had drawn of him when they first met. He hastily removed all the frames. He loosened the staples and dismantled the canvas stretchers, until only the painted linen was left. Then he carefully bundled the artwork all together in old newspapers and placed the roll in his army rucksack.

When he emerged outside again, the city looked like it had been transformed into a besieged fortress. Via a detour he was able to reach the location of his BMW. From there he set off to fulfil his last object- ive. Half an hour later, he announced his presence at the heavily guarded Kandahari Gate, which would give him access to the com- pound of the presidential palace.

After telephone contact back and forth between the officer on guard and a staffer from the Interior Affairs Ministry, he was taken in a military jeep from the gate to the presidential palace itself. He had to leave the rucksack with paintings in the guardhouse. Driving across the palace grounds, he saw heavily armed troops from the Presidential Guard taking up position at each building.

In front of the palace steps, other members of that same Guard were hurrying to unload two army trucks. Raylan recognized the flat crates they were carrying inside over the wide stairs. The whole oper- ation reminded him of how Isobel's paintings had been transported. So it wasn't really a surprise when Parwaiz Ahmad appeared halfway up the stairs.

'As-Salaam-Alaikum, aghaye Ahmad.'

'Wa-Alaikum-Salaam, aghaye Chapelle.' Parwaiz looked tenser than ever. 'Due to the fear of looting, the president has ordered that

416

art of national importance here in the Arg must be safeguarded,' he continued, as he wiped the sweat from his brow. 'So please forgive me.' He took the steps two at a time in the direction of the trucks.

Accompanied by a guard, Raylan raced through the long palace corridors, passing the courtyard garden, where he suddenly stopped, thunderstruck by who he saw standing there.

6
Farah

2009

Thirty years ago, she'd stood on this very same spot, alone among the butterflies. A little girl, eagerly awaiting her father. Now here she was again, lost among the hundreds around her: the president, members of Afghanistan's former royal family, surviving relatives of Daoud Khan, foreign dignitaries, ministers and generals in full dress uniform.

Barely fifty metres from her stood the secretary-general of the interior, Ahmad Shakoor. He was making polite conversation with General Goldwater, who tried his hardest to ignore her.

The voice of the man on the phone less than a week ago. *I'm talking about the Saur Revolution of 1978. Prominent victims, including the then-president, his entire family and ministerial team, have not been located until now.*

You found my father, she'd stammered.

There he was, coming towards her, preceded by a soldier holding up a life-size portrait of him. His coffin was covered in the national flag and carried by six honour guard soldiers.

The gun salute took her back to the past.

Thirty years ago.

She'd looked up in surprise and with a feeling of foreboding. The noise cut through her: the roar of swooping planes coming straight at her. For a split second she was rooted to the spot. She broke out in a cold sweat. Then she forced herself to run away, away from the approaching planes, to seek shelter inside the palace.

The first explosion was so violent she feared the whole complex might collapse. A chandelier directly above her came crashing down. But before the crystal drops burst on to the marble floor, she felt a pair of hands grab her from behind. Her feet lifted off the floor. Like a bird she flew up from under the chandelier before it had the chance to crash down on her. The hands let her float and seemed to give her the ability to bypass the falling debris. As the strikes continued, she sailed past the wounded, the dying and the dead.

Thirty years ago.

The silence around her now.

The sixteen coffins were lined up. Each one had been placed on a bier and was now draped in snow-white silk. One coffin was smaller than the others. The youngest victim had been barely eighteen months old.

An honour guard of soldiers wearing white gloves and gold epaulettes shouldered their rifles.

The guns were silent. Only her heart was pounding. She felt as if everyone could hear it. Including the imam, who seemed to be waiting for the thumping to stop before launching into his supplication. Slowly, he raised his hands to heaven: 'Oh Allah! Forgive them and have mercy on them. Take them into paradise and protect them from the punishment of the grave and from the punishment of the fire.'

The glass of her father's portrait, which had been placed on a stand in front of his coffin, reflected the bright sunlight.

The light . . . For the first time she remembered the light.

The gate through which they'd exited thirty years ago, into the blazing sun. The blasts that grew louder and louder. His hands holding on to her for one last moment. His voice. The address he called out to the driver. He knew where she lived. She turned around. He was so close. She reached out to him. She didn't want to leave him. Then the jeep shot forward.

7
Raylan

1978

She was standing with her back to him, seemingly lost in thought. As if she hadn't left the butterfly garden since the last time he'd seen her mother. 'Mr Chapelle, the minister is ready to see you.' The guardsman's prompt sounded like an order.

Raylan looked up and saw Aadel Gailani impatiently waiting for him metres away in front of his office door.

'This stronghold is impenetrable,' Gailani said, as he stoically shook Raylan's hand and glanced over his shoulder into the garden. 'My little girl is safe here for now.' With a tense expression, he looked back at Raylan. 'I'm going into a crisis meeting in five minutes. That's how long you've got.'

After closing the door, Gailani hurried to his desk to collect some documents. 'You haven't done us any favours with your article about our meeting with Brezhnev,' he said without making eye contact.

'That's why I was so insistent on seeing you,' Raylan said.

Clutching a pile of papers under his arm, Gailani stared at him incredulously.

'I assume you've been informed that Askan Vaziri was murdered today on Zanbaq Square?' Raylan continued.

Gailani had a dark look on his face. 'I'd heard rumours he'd been smuggled back into the country, but . . .'

'I have top-secret information about him and possibly others who've spent years preparing a Russian-backed coup against

President Daoud,' Raylan hastily said. 'But now the KGB . . . They've threatened to . . . It's a complicated situation . . .'

At that moment there was a loud knock at the door. The guardsman who'd escorted Raylan to Gailani stormed into the room without waiting for a response. 'Your Excellency, military units have assembled at Kabul International airport. Fighter planes have taken off. The president . . .'

Even before the guard had finished speaking, Raylan heard a rumble so deafening that he felt it in his bones before it reached his ears. His immediate response was to rush out of the room in the direction of the courtyard garden, where three Soviet SU-7s in V-formation soared overhead much too close for comfort.

He saw Farah run into a room adjacent to the courtyard and went after her. Incoming bombs shook the palace to its foundations. Part of the ceiling gave way. He was within a short distance of Farah when he noticed that one of the chandeliers was coming down. He raced in her direction, managing to grab her in the nick of time. He lifted her into his arms, pressed her firmly against his chest and took off as fast as he could. Just behind him he heard the chandelier burst apart, followed by a thunderous noise when large chunks of the ceiling crashed to the ground.

He ran with her through dense clouds of debris and rising dust, caused by the collapsing walls and ceilings. Past those in the palace who'd been badly wounded, lying half buried beneath the rubble, men and women who'd been hit by flying stones and glass. He proceeded down a long corridor, passing guardsmen approaching him from the opposite direction with their rifles ready. He held on to her as tight as he could. He descended the outside stairs, placed her in the passenger seat of his jeep, jumped behind the wheel and drove as fast as he could towards the Kandahari Gate.

Rumbling in the distance. The earth trembled, as if an earthquake were imminent.

Guardsmen, armed with rocket launchers and long-range guns, had sealed off the gate. The officer gestured for Raylan to stop. Raylan jumped out of the jeep and shouted that the interior affairs minister had given orders for his daughter to immediately be taken to safety. A soldier replaced Raylan behind the wheel. As the gate opened, he shouted out Helai's address. Farah held out her arms with a look of desperation on her face.

His eyes met hers.

Violent tremors shook his body. When he glanced around again, he saw how close the column of tanks was to the gate. A soldier in the jeep at the head of the column aimed his Kalashnikov directly at him. Raylan grabbed the press pass hanging around his neck and held it out in front of him.

When he was ordered to kneel, he protested and remained standing. The butt of a rifle knocked him to the ground.

When he regained consciousness, Raylan was lying with his hands tied behind his back among other detainees in the load space of an army lorry. They were transported across the Pul-e-Charkhi plain to a prison, where they were all crammed into large, unfinished concrete spaces. Scarcely any daylight fell through the high barred windows into the prison cells. There was no running water, nor a sewage system, just a large pail of water and in one corner a wooden crate over a hole in the ground. The men consulted with each other in hushed voices. There were so many of them, they barely had enough room to stand. The water bucket was pushed into the corner. The men huddled closer together in four groups, creating narrow paths in the shape of a cross.

Although everyone did their best to stay calm, a disturbance flared when one of the men had an epileptic seizure. The first aid skills Raylan had learned in Vietnam suddenly came in handy. He created as much space as he could around the man, cushioned his head with a jacket and placed him in a stable position on his side with his head slightly tilted, to open his airway more thoroughly. An old acquaintance stepped forward to assist him. It was the professor who'd once given him a tour of the university, Noor Qadiry. 'Small world, professor. Make sure he stays there. He might have another seizure.' Raylan got up and went over to the metal door, pounded on it and called for a doctor.

'They don't care about us,' the professor said after Raylan returned without a response. 'We are now the enemies of the revolution.'

'Is that why everyone here has been arrested?'

Qadiry nodded.

'Absurd. If there was anyone who was sympathetic to Askan Vaziri and his case, it was you.'

'I teach Anglo-Saxon languages. Apparently, for the perpetrators of the coup that suddenly translates as treason.'

At that moment the door flew open. Flanked by two armed soldiers, an officer began shouting a list of names, of which Qadiry was the last. 'You're being released!' the officer continued. 'You'll need to come with us.'

'It seems like it's time for me to go,' Qadiry said, 'but I promise, as soon as I can, I'll report your imprisonment to the International Press Agency.'

'*Khali mehraban asten*,' Raylan replied. 'Very kind of you.' After which the cell door slammed shut.

If nothing else, the departure of the group meant there was more space for those left behind to move around. And the fact that some of the detainees were being released so quickly gave the others hope. They heard the lorry with the men ride away. But within earshot it slowed down again. The engine was turned off. Orders sounded. For some reason, the men had to leave the load space. Resistance erupted. There was shouting. Soon the shouting turned into the visceral sound of frenzied pleading that continued until shots were fired.

The subsequent silence was torn apart by the engine of a bulldozer turning over.

The door of the cell was unlocked again.

Raylan heard his name called out.

They took him to a windowless room, where they tied him to a wooden chair. Through the open door, Raylan saw two men approaching him down a long corridor. The man in front, who threw him a scornful look when he reached the doorway, he recognized as Grigori Michailov. Right behind him was the man with the condor head.

'People without an appointment aren't welcome here,' Raylan growled.

'Mr Chapelle,' replied Michailov, who walked into the room as if it were his, 'you've probably noticed that today a popular uprising supported by the army put an end to President Daoud's regime. Representatives of the new government have asked me to look into your recent meeting with former minister Aadel Gailani. And by recent, I mean a few hours ago.'

From the inside pocket of his jacket Michailov removed a narrow silver cigarette case. Stunned, Raylan stared at the exotic nude woman engraved on the lid.

'This was his.'

'A gift from me. Gailani won't be needing it any more.'

Raylan shook his head, enraged. 'Popular uprising, my ass! You can kill intellectuals, professors and even ministers for their supposed sympathies with the West, but no matter how you slice it, it's still the dastardly actions of a bunch of aging Kremlin imbeciles.'

Seemingly unperturbed, Michailov lit a cigarette. 'You and I had an agreement: no reporting on so-called Russian interference in the "domestic" affairs of this country.'

'Says a sack-of-shit Russian to me in an Afghan prison. Read the fucking papers. Then you'll see I kept to the terms of your stinking deal!'

Michailov leaned towards Raylan. 'You miserable journalists always stick your noses where they don't belong. What did you and Gailani discuss?'

'That communists are resourceful halfwits, who continue to successfully mislead people everywhere and always manage to run off with the spoils in the end.'

Michailov kept shaking his head and staring at Raylan. 'I'm trying to protect you. Do you realize that?'

'How noble of you.'

'Telling me the truth would be noble. Then I'll be noble in return and let you go free. I can't think of a better alternative to being executed against a wall.'

Raylan let out a sigh. 'The death of an American journalist here . . .'

'. . . is a matter of . . . How do you journalists put it? Oh, yes, collateral damage. In the chaos of a civil uprising, deaths are bound to occur without any apparent reason ... and without major consequences. So again, what did you and Gailani discuss?'

'The truth?'

'What you crusading journalists seem to be so obsessed by ...'

'Jazz.'

'Sorry?'

'We talked about jazz, the minister and I. The art of improvisation: five-eight time signature. The mysticism of John Coltrane.'

'I don't care much for jive music. Give me the classics. Opera. *Don Giovanni* is my favourite. The womanizer who, towards the end, is confronted with an inescapable choice: *pentimento*, repentance, or *morte*, death. Our hero has doubts. He doesn't want to repent, but doesn't want to die either. What should he do? Say it.'

Raylan glanced up at Michailov. 'I have something better than repentance.'

'By all means ... tell me.'

'A transcript of my uncensored article about Vaziri and his Kremlin connections. If my editor doesn't hear from me today, it will go to press. An article about Russian involvement in an Afghan coup by a well-known journalist who happened to die under suspicious circumstances at the moment of that uprising ... that should make some alarm bells go off in the world. I suspect even those at the Kremlin won't be happy.'

'So no repentance then?'

'None at all.'

'Then you leave me no choice. Terribly sorry about this ...'

Michailov took a last drag of his cigarette, snuffed it out, nodded in Vakurov's direction and left the room.

Vakurov took up position in front of Raylan and rubbed his knuckles. The first blow pounded the bridge of Raylan's nose and was so hard he heard the crack. The next blows were at least as relentless and came from different directions, in a controlled cadence, and within no time his eyelids were swollen shut. Raylan soon lost consciousness.

A hand lifted his head. He could just make out the anxious face of a young soldier, who untied him from the chair, fastened his hands behind his back and brought him outside through the long corridor, where he shoved him onto the back seat of a jeep.

By now evening had fallen. Clouds of dust from the sandy road reflected in the headlights. They drove out on to the plain. Just outside the prison walls there was that bulldozer again. A group of men, probably soldiers, were talking to each other and laughing. He got a whiff of their cigarette smoke. When they saw the jeep approaching, they quickly got back into formation.

Oddly enough, when he got out and was led to the spot, he felt no fear, only calm. The young soldier asked if he wanted a blindfold, and he shook his head. He listened to the steps of the soldier walking back to the jeep. The crunching of his boots in the rough sand. The menacing whisper of the desert wind.

For a moment he thought he saw a flash of light. Exactly like the one in that courtyard in Murad Khane all those years ago, when he first laid eyes on her, that disarming smile, her sea-blue eyes and the Leica in her hand. Like an Alice in Wonderland about to step through the looking glass.

Where are you going, Ise?

To see the world. Get to know myself better.

She gave him a surprisingly serious look, held up her camera, pointed it at him and clicked.

The world tilted around him, just like it had ten years ago, when the riot police in Murad Khane hit him on the head with their batons. His knees gave way. Even now, he didn't feel any pain as he was knocked back against the ground. It was as if he'd fallen into a briny mixture of muck, which surrounded him like quicksand. There was only silence and darkness as he slowly sank like a heavy stone.

He was still wrapped in that same silence, but now it felt like a sheet full of hot sand scraping against his skin. In the distance he thought he heard battle hymns. Droplets of water fell on his face, cooling and reducing the feverish heat. Fingers gently prized open his eyelids. A figure bent over him. A woman's voice, old and almost impossible to understand. Hands draped a blanket over his shivering body.

Something in him said it wasn't true. What he was seeing and hearing were the last convulsions of his brain, one final hallucination before the light was extinguished forever.

Immediately after the shots his heart seemed to stop. All the energy was sucked out of his body. He hadn't felt the bullets. Was he dead before they even hit him? A heart attack, perhaps? How could you be dead and still hear the soldiers who shot you get into an army lorry and drive away?

The only possibility: they'd intentionally misfired. Followed orders and missed the target. His round of bluff-poker with Michailov had kept him alive.

However, this realization was of little comfort at the moment. He couldn't move his body. He felt like he was trapped in a cocoon of taut skin and cramped muscles. He'd lain there the entire night, on a barren sandy plain with temperatures below zero.

By the time they found him, it was morning. He could tell from the moist air and the gentle warmth of the sun's rays. From the orange light when they gently opened his eyes for a split second. They were men, and they were old. He could hear it in their muttering and feel it when their hands loosened the rope around his wrists, laid him on a large cloth and dragged him across the sand to a wooden cart.

The cart became a wooden cot, the open air a low ceiling, the sandy plain a simple room.

The battle hymns came from a radio, which was turned up louder when an enthused man read a proclamation: 'For the first time in Afghan history, power has been bestowed on the people. The reign of Daoud's dynasty, the last remnant of imperialist tyranny, has been destroyed once and for all.'

A hand gently lifted the back of his head. His lips were pressed to the edge of a teacup. Raylan managed to open his eyes. The old woman sounded worried. 'You must drink. Warm up.'

He drank greedily, choked, drank again and felt the warmth spread throughout his body. Again and again he opened his mouth, willingly gulping down spoonfuls of *kala wa pacha* to regain his strength.

In the hours that followed the trembling lessened. Early in the evening he tried to get up for the first time. Seeking support against the dingy walls, he wobbled back and forth. The dizziness then subsided, and he started to feel like himself again.

The old woman tried to persuade him to lie down again. He refused as politely as he could, unclasped his wristwatch and placed it in her hand as a gesture of thanks. He traded his jeans for wide, light-coloured trousers, a cardigan and an old *chapan*, a loose-fitting winter coat, which would keep him warm. Even though he struggled to walk, with a woollen *pakol* pulled down around his ears, he made his way back to Kabul.

Their house in Murad Khane had been plundered, the studio ravaged. Cityscapes, market scenes and portraits had been sliced to shreds with Stanley knives and hurled to the ground. As if the people portrayed no longer wanted to know anything about their former existence. The past no longer mattered. It had to be destroyed.

Raylan searched the house hoping to find a sign of life, perhaps a letter safely tucked away. Everything of value had been torn loose and taken. The house had been robbed of all life. On the roof terrace, among the wreckage of broken pots and bowls, he caught his breath and stared out over the city, where gunshots echoed. It wasn't clear if the shots being fired in the air were celebratory or if they were the result of continued fighting or even executions. Large groups of people were out on the street. They shouted, sang battle hymns and waved the red hammer and sickle flag.

He gazed in the direction of the airport. They'd be waiting for him there. He placed his hand over his heart and bowed to salute the city, which was shrouded in plumes of smoke.

8
Farah

2009

She hadn't caught much of the president's speech during the memorial ceremony in the palace courtyard. Except for his solemn hope that Daoud's reburial would provide closure to one of the bloodiest chapters in Afghan history: 'Today, at this state funeral of Afghanistan's first president, we hope to also bury our suffering, our pain and our wounds.'

Even after lying in an unmarked mass grave for thirty years, the dead were still being used for a hollow political statement.

Out of the blue he'd appeared before her, leaning on his walking cane with the silver stud: forensic specialist Professor Yusufzai. His rheumy eyes looked even more serious than during their first meeting. With the index finger of his free hand, he pushed the dark horn-rimmed glasses further up his nose and then, with a solemn gesture, he placed a small wooden box in her hand.

She hadn't waited for the coffins to be carried to the army helicopters, which would be flying them to the hills of Khoja Ghar. Nor had she boarded one of the buses that would be taking all the guests to the ceremony at the final resting place of the dead, on a hilltop overlooking the city. Instead, she got back into the vehicle and asked Nehal to take her to the place where she wanted to be alone with her father one last time, without military display, hollow rhetoric and turgid pleas.

The narrow roads of Wazir Akbar Khan were littered with white-washed speed bumps, so the minute Nehal accelerated she had to slow down again. These had once been leafy lanes with sumptuous gardens and trees casting shade on the paved walkways. Now private security guards with fully automatic weapons stood outside iron gates and high concrete walls.

Although the neighbourhood had been partially demolished, Farah recognized the gentle curve leading from 2nd Street to 3rd Street.

'Will you wait for me here?'

'Are you sure about this, *hamshera*?'

She gave her a reassuring nod and got out of the car. The tiles had disappeared. So too had the terraced rose garden in the front. What was left of the house itself was almost beyond recognition.

Dusk was falling. An elderly, unarmed guard slowly approached her. 'You can't come any further. This is private property.' However, his tone of voice gave the impression that he'd rather have a chat than send people away.

'I used to live here, *aqha*. As a child. I haven't been back in thirty years. I'd like to see it one more time.'

He looked her in the eye, asked no other questions and escorted her to where the front door had been. There he let her continue by herself. She walked through a house without doors, without glass in the windows, through bare rooms that were all smaller than she remembered.

Even the walled garden looked less spacious. This is where their clothes had rustled and their breathing had been in sync as they carried out their synchronous movements during their morning training.

She crouched down close to the apple tree holding the little wooden box. Carefully, she opened it, took out the wide ring with the greenish-black gem and slowly brought it to her lips. Then she put it back in the box and lowered the lid again. Using both hands, she started to dig in the ground by the tree. The soil that got stuck underneath her nails still held the day's warmth. The dust that whirled up tickled her nostrils. She carried on digging until the hole was deep enough for the box, put it in and carefully pushed the earth back in place.

After she got up and wiped her hands, she closed her eyes and said her prayer. 'Allah, forgive and have mercy upon him and cleanse him with water, snow and ice and purify him of sin, give him strength and admit him into the Garden.'

She stood there silently and felt his presence. Without a sound he came and stood by her side. His dark hair was shiny with brilliantine and combed back, his cheeks were clean-shaven. Dark eyes and a broad nose above a neatly coiffed moustache. He was wearing his beige linen suit, as he had on that last day.

'Did you know what I wanted to show you, *baba*, that day?'

He shook his head, sadly. 'You didn't have to show me how good you were. I knew.'

'If you knew, then why didn't you ever say anything?'

'I'm sorry, my child. I wasn't made for feelings.'

'You used to call me your "little Malalai". Why?'

'You were a brave girl.'

'You never called me your "little Farah". Not once ... Did you ever see me as I wanted to be seen?'

'How did you want to be seen?'

'As your daughter. The child you loved.'

He was silent.

'I love you, *baba*. And I still long for the child I once was. Maybe because I'm still hoping all will be well again. That you'll come to me in the butterfly garden and we'll go home. To Mum. Where the two of you are happy together. And Mum also sings when you're at home. And we're back here doing our exercises, you and me.'

She placed her hands on the tree trunk, as though hoping to feel his heartbeat.

'The old woman under the waringin tree in Jakarta, do you remember her? She wanted me to renounce what I'd learned from you. But I wouldn't do that. I want to take all the good things in life and carry them with me, and that includes what I learned from you here.'

There was no sound, not even from the wind.

'Farewell, *padare azizam*. Dear Daddy.'

She walked through the house one last time. Outside, she thanked the old guard, who'd just lit a cigarette. She was on her way back to the bend in the road where Nehal was waiting for her when she heard the soft murmuring of tree leaves. It sounded like a whisper. *Satu, dua, tiga . . .*

As night fell, the city looked peaceful. Even the traffic seemed to be taking things easy. On the large open space in front of Darul Aman Palace, dozens of boys dressed in white were lighting candles. Thousands of them. To commemorate all the victims of the Saur Revolution. Drivers passing by slowed down to get a good look at the silhouettes moving among a sea of candlelight.

If the dead could see this, they might think they hadn't died in vain on 27 April 1978. Wherever they'd been that day – her father, the president, his family and all those other desperate Kabulis – most of them hadn't stood a chance.

She thought of a quote from Raylan's book. *Dying is a very real possibility. But someone else's death improves your chances of living to see another day.*

She asked Nehal to stop, walked over to one of the boys, who was using a small candle to light a row of bigger ones, and squatted down beside him.

'*Ejaza'st?* May I?'

He handed her the burning taper, which she held to the next candle. A flame crept along the wick and became a flickering greeting to her father.

That last time she'd held his hand, in the hall of the Presidential Palace, still felt like yesterday. The moment he let go of her and walked away. She'd wanted to do what she used to do as a small child when he came home: wrap her arms around one of his legs from behind and hold on tight. When baba was in a good mood, he played along. *I can barely walk, it's like I'm dragging something around.* Then he looked down, feigned surprise and lifted her up until she was soaring high above him, crowing with pleasure.

The second candle was for her mother.

The day after the revolution, a jeep had stopped in front of their house. Soldiers had jumped out. They'd charged into the living room and had hauled her away. Her achievements as an ambitious young public prosecutor ten years earlier – trying to get a young communist

432

editor sentenced to death for sedition – now came back to haunt her. When she was released five months later, she was pale, emaciated and withdrawn. A different woman. No longer the mother who played *mancala* with her, who took her to the museum and the bookshop and who read to her every night before bed.

It is time for you to go out into the world and learn from it what you can.

She got out of the car in front of the departures hall. Nehal handed over her bag. They stood facing each other; goodbyes were always so awkward. Then Farah gave what she was holding to Nehal. She'd found it somewhere in the heart of that black-market trading network in Shahr-e Naw district. As if it were waiting for her, a key to Nehal's heart. A gift she hoped would speak where words failed.

Amazed, Nehal looked at the silver pocket mirror, with its hinged lid engraved with tigers and lions. 'For me?'

'I was thinking about what you told me. That your mother had a little mirror that she'd take out occasionally so the two of you could secretly do your make-up.'

Nehal flipped it open and glanced at the bare face of a woman with a big heart, who'd decided that if Sekandar were to return he could live in her family home, together with his parents and his brother and sisters, until other arrangements were made.

Nehal closed the mirror and looked at her seriously. Then she gave her a warm embrace. 'Do the right thing, *hamshera*.'

Abruptly she let go again, got back in the car and drove off.

PART SIX
Like a Shadow

I
Paul

2009

All those faces, all those strangers. In an endless row, stretching far beyond the funeral chapel at Novodevichy Cemetery, they came to pay their respects. Once inside, they stared at Anya's image on the enlarged photo. Standing in front of her body in the half-open coffin, they bowed their heads. Many of them kneeled, made the sign of the cross, touched the casket, blew her a kiss, let their tears flow freely, inaudibly whispered a brief prayer or some farewell words and placed their red carnation in the sea of flowers surrounding her.

Paul shook hands with complete strangers. Some shared the fact they were journalists. Others were diplomats or ambassadors. And virtually all of them uttered the same platitudes to him. The murder of a journalist was in fact an attack on freedom of speech and that 'we' – yes, he'd heard it correctly, 'we' – should 'never' tolerate this. People tended to speak in clichés.

He walked to the lectern, unfolded the piece of paper with what he'd written the previous night and gave the microphone a few taps. The dull reverberation bouncing off the tiled walls silenced the din in the crowd.

'Thank you all for coming . . .'

When he surveyed the large crowd of invited guests he was unexpectedly overwhelmed by emotion, a feeling he could barely contain. His voice faltered, and he let out a sob in the middle of his sentence.

'Anya was more than a reporter, she was a dissident. Insanely courageous. Who bears the responsibility for her untimely death? Not only the perpetrator. Not only the person who executed the order, but all those who remain silent in the face of attacks like these.'

He heard the blood rushing to his head, the pounding of his veins against his temples. The torrent of guilt was almost too much to bear.

'What we do know is that Anya was murdered because she fought the good fight, unwilling to compromise when it comes to people's right to freedom of speech.'

He could barely breathe. The silent faces watching him started to swirl together into one big shadowy blur.

He heard her voice in his head: *I knew one day you'd come knocking on my door again. Rumour has it things aren't going so well ...* Again, they were sitting opposite each other in the Tsvet Nochi Club. *You don't have a clue how you're going to go about this, right? No idea.*

He felt her touch. Without him noticing, she'd come and stood behind him. With the same intention with which she'd hugged him and touched his face earlier this afternoon in the arrivals hall of Domodedovo airport, Farah now comforted him by gently resting her hand on his shoulder.

He found the words again, without any further sobbing, faltering or melodrama. With his loving remarks he wanted to do justice to Anya. Show her as the woman she really was, not just the fighter most people were familiar with. He also spoke about how idealistic she was, but that she lived in uncertainty day in and day out, was plagued by self-doubt, but tenaciously continued to believe in justice. An idealist who understood that in today's Russian reality, there isn't a lot of room for compassion.

'Yes, Anya was a warrior. She battled the lies that unscrupulous politicians and oligarchs use every day to poison your lives and rob you of a better future. She fought despite the uncertainty, made herself vulnerable and was honest ... that's how I knew her. Here she lies, her body is dead, but for me ...' He had to stop here, take a breath. Farah's hand touched his shoulder again. He swallowed and continued. 'She lives on for me. Not only in thoughts and in words, but also in deeds. I will carry her fight forward, day in, day out. Because as long as I do that, she'll be by my side. Honour her courage and fight the good fight with me in her name.'

When he lowered his head, it was completely still in the room. His eyes were clouded by a haze of tears. Farah put her arm around his waist and escorted him over to the coffin, where, after adjusting the hoodie, he planted a last kiss on Anya's forehead.

2

Farah

2009

Farah had been with him all day. She'd walked beside him, right behind the coffin, past the bronze angel with the broken wing, the ballet dancer in her static pirouette and the infantry commander laden with medals standing proudly on top of his tank. Marble and granite silhouettes of the dead, flanking the path to Anya's grave. She put her arm around Paul's waist when he scattered a shovelful of earth over the coffin. Then, still without a word, they'd walked away together, back down the long winding path, out the gate and into the city.

Later that day, when they joined the entire *Moskva Gazeta* editorial team for bottles of vodka and plates of *pelmeni* in Club Mayak, he suddenly got up and walked to a table with an amorous couple.

'Do you have any idea what used to go on down here?' he shouted. 'This is where she stood, God damn it, on top of this table. The place was packed, but her song was meant for me alone! You hear that? For me alone!'

Then, like a crucified man, he'd spread his arms and burst into something vaguely resembling a song, but actually little more than painfully out-of-tune wailing.

'*A lyubov*' . . . *Katyushaaaaaa . . . sberezhot!*'

At that point Farah had grabbed him by his lapels and pulled him close. 'Stop it! I didn't come here to see you wallow in self-pity. We've both lost her. We have to solve this case together. We can't stop now. We have to see this through to the end.'

It took a few moments for her words to reach him.

'You want to see this through to the end? With me?'

He turned his bleary eyes on the men and women of the *Gazeta*, who'd watched the whole scene in silence. 'You hear that, you bunch of losers? I've got all the evidence I need to reveal Anya's real killer. Everything! But you've frozen me out!'

'What are you talking about?'

Paul didn't hear her. He was staring at Roman Jankovski, who'd risen to his feet and now walked towards him, gesturing he should calm down.

'There he is, the coward-in-chief, the leader of this pathetic bunch. The man who instead of backing you stabs you in the back!'

'Steady on, Paul . . . ,' Roman tried as he stood in front of him, but it was too late. Paul's right fist landed square on his right jaw.

As he fell backwards across the table, Roman took a bunch of plates, glasses and bottles down with him and then tried to scramble to his feet again in a fog of alcohol, covered in bits of food and rubbing his swelling jaw. Before anyone could react, Farah had pushed Paul out the front door.

Down a maze of narrow streets and alleyways Paul had ushered her into a courtyard near Ulitsa Arbat, where they entered the hallway of a subsided house with weathered angel statues in each corner. The worn steps of the dimly lit stairwell and a rickety front door led them into an equally rundown apartment that he'd been able to borrow from a colleague who was spending a few weeks in Johannesburg.

She let him flop down on to a colossal sofa in a cloud of swirling dust, and then brewed him the strongest coffee imaginable in a percolator in the narrow kitchen. He blew on it and drank it with a great deal of grimacing.

'Tell me what you've discovered,' she said, prompting him to recount what had happened in Moscow over the past few days. He told her how Lesha had uncovered the identity of the assailant, Kavstaskin, and about Lyov, who provided him with the proof that the attack on Anya had been orchestrated by Valentin Lavrov. About his game of bluff with the USB stick, which had saved him from the humiliations and beatings at the police station, and which had ultimately landed him in Alexander Arlazarov's crumbling castle.

'Is that why Roman doesn't want to help you?' she asked when he'd finished his story. 'Because you struck a deal with one of the FSB's top dogs?'

He nodded. 'Anya worked for Roman for years. She gave him everything she had. All those reports on the war in Chechnya. The *Gazeta* has built quite a reputation in recent years, and it owes that largely to her investigations and articles. But now that we have a chance to catch Lavrov, they're suddenly plagued by "principles" and "journalistic integrity". She's only just died and they're already dropping her like a hot brick.'

She took his face in her hands and gazed deeply into his eyes. 'Remember how you reacted when Anya came up with her plan to bring down Lavrov?'

'Lavrov's three horsemen of the Apocalypse,' he murmured.

She nodded. 'You're not dependent on Roman or anyone else for that matter. You've got me. There are still two horsemen left.'

The hard look in his eyes softened; the deep lines around his mouth disappeared. He took his mobile and showed her the text message that Alexander Arlazarov had sent him earlier that day: *Tomorrow 11.00 a.m. Burdenko Military Hospital.*

He stared at her intently. 'Do you feel up to visiting the man who's tried to kill you twice?'

She sighed. 'We'll find out ... Are you ready to confront Anya's killer?'

Paul stared into the room. 'I know I said, "Honour her courage and fight the good fight with me in her name." But nice words don't get you very far when reality knocks. When I think about facing the man who had her killed ... All I can picture is strangling him with my bare hands and enjoying it as he gasps his last breath in my face.'

Farah sat down beside him, hunched over and stared at the floor. 'I was incredibly close in Jakarta. He was so weak ... I could have eliminated him with a single kick. I'd already rotated my body, pulled back my right leg. "*Jangan!*" I heard all of a sudden. "Don't do it." It was the commander of the SWAT team that burst in. I saw the red laser beams they aimed at my body. But even those couldn't stop me.'

'Then what did?'

'A voice inside my head. The old woman who'd shown me the essence of *pencak* the day before. It was her voice I heard. *A true Pesilat is someone with a noble mind and a noble character.* I didn't extend my right leg. My foot didn't hit Lavrov between the eyes.'

'If it had ...'

'I know. Anya would still be alive. And I'd have a murder on my conscience.'

'It was self-defence.'

'No, it wasn't. Lavrov was already down. As he is now ... thanks to all the evidence you've gathered. It's our job to confront him with that. We're journalists, not killers. We must remember that and keep our emotions in check.'

He looked at her as he mulled this over and lit a cigarette. 'We're going to crack this case together. We have no choice.'

He gave her an earnest look. 'What do you mean?'

He blew out the smoke ... 'There's something else you should know.'

He got up with difficulty and left the room. When she saw the stack of envelopes he returned with, she felt a shiver down her spine.

'I did as you asked,' he said. 'I read them.' He stood in front of her and handed her the bundle. 'It's your turn now.'

'You mean *right* now?'

'Like you said: nothing should come between us, no half-truths, no lies. Tomorrow, when we confront Lavrov, we must form a united front. Without secrets from each other.'

Farah sat down at the table with the parcel, undid the two silk ribbons, removed the red velvety pieces of cardboard, unfolded all the letters one by one and then put them on a pile. Actions that helped her put off the actual reading for a while. All this time, she could hear Uncle Parwaiz's voice in her head: *I'd like to ask you,* dokhtarem, *not to jump to conclusions about what you find in here. In their quest for*

*the true meaning of life, people should be allowed to walk paths you
perhaps don't want them to go down.*

She thought of the opening sentence she'd read, which had dis-
couraged her from reading on. *The past sneaks up on us like a shadow.*
She wanted to leave those shadows behind, leave those bygone days
for what they were. With that same intention, her eyes now skimmed
the next few sentences.

> April 17, 1975
> I feel as if my love for you could end wars. I want to stand in the mid-
> dle of a square and let the fire in my heart speak to show the world
> how overwhelmingly beautiful something like loving can be.

She put the letter down. They were overblown words, but strangely
enough they moved her. She didn't understand why.

> September 9, 1975
> Getting to know you was like experiencing a reality beyond reality,
> something I'd only heard others talk about. I know it's best that we
> don't see each other any more. But I will always love you, uncondi-
> tionally, from a distance, like a man who never believed in dreams,
> but who now knows that love is a dream that can come true.

Raylan looked back at a love greater than himself. Did that explain
her reluctance to carry on reading? She wanted to remain in control.
Of everything, including her emotions. But these were the words of a
man who lost himself in his feelings as soon as he thought of his former lover.

> June 7, 1976
> I don't believe in any God, but thanks to you, love has acquired some-
> thing of the divine for me. I've become a believer who worships the
> heavenly beauty of your body, your smile and your eyes.

Farah thought of her father. Of the routine kisses he gave his wife
when he left home in the morning and came home again late in the
day. The long silences between her parents at dinner. Raylan, on
the other hand, had placed Helai on a pedestal. He adored her. With
him, she'd felt like the woman she wanted to be. In her secret

encounters with Raylan, Helai had been able to experience the passion she so sorely missed in her marriage. As this dawned on her, she pictured Raylan again. The discomfort and reluctance she'd felt earlier had all but disappeared. Now she felt mostly gratitude. Raylan had restored her mother's self-esteem and given her a chance to take pleasure in her sensuality.

> September 18, 1976
> When I think of your eyes, I feel intoxicated. The way Hafez describes draining the chalice of wine ... that's how I want to drink in your appearance.

The intensity of his feelings intrigued her. There had to be more to it than just a secret intimacy that had ended. The letter she was holding now was more revealing than the others.

> March 5, 1977
> Without me realizing it, you carried our secret inside you, a life we shared, a life in which we came together, you and me, like in a miracle.

The next part made her gasp for breath.

> A miracle that came to life. Now that I know it's her, the child you were carrying.

Her heart pounded in her throat, and she felt lightheaded. *Now that I know it's her*. She struggled for breath. *The child you were carrying*. She picked up the last letter but could barely absorb the words.

> July 22, 1977
> My darling, you once told me that you sing to her every night before bed. When you sing your song, please do it very softly, hum if necessary, because I don't want anyone else to hear. It's for her alone, and for you and for me. She's the one who connects us. Our little girl will always keep us bound together. Our child, our Farah.

Tears welled up behind her eyes. She reread the final words, over and over again: *our child, our Farah*. Keep breathing, she thought to herself. Breathe. In for four seconds. Out for six.

When she looked up, the wall clock told her nearly an hour had passed. Paul had opened the tall doors to the narrow balcony and was leaning against the railing, smoking. Farah got up and slowly walked towards him, stood behind him and hesitantly put her hand on his back. 'How long have you known?'

'She was still alive . . . Anya, I mean. I read the letters by her bedside.' He turned around. 'But I thought you should hear it from Ray himself, not from me.'

She swallowed several times before she was able to respond. 'Thank you . . . Do you know what song my mother sang to me? *Sultan-e qalbam*.'

He smiled. 'Ruler of my heart.'

She sang the chorus. 'One heart says go go. One heart says stay stay. My heart is restless without you. What would I do without you?'

She awkwardly ran her fingers over his chest.

'Does that feel different now?' he asked.

His question made her smile. 'Not really, no . . .'

'So I've always had this brotherly vibe?'

She regarded him seriously. 'The very first time I saw you . . .'

'In the butterfly garden?'

She nodded. 'I was confused, could barely string a sentence together, I . . .'

'It didn't show at all . . .'

'Oh, so you do remember that day?'

'It's etched on my memory, as if carved in stone.'

'Three nights, that's how long my mother said she watched over me afterwards.'

'Why?'

'I had a fever and I was delirious. She dabbed my face with wet washcloths and kept saying, "Not you too, my child, not you too . . ." She was acutely aware that when it came to deeper feelings I was a lot like her, even though I was still only a child. She'd seen us together, heard me go on about the blond, blue-eyed fighter, but now I realize she couldn't tell me that we . . .' She took a few deep breaths and looked up at the sky. 'I spent a lot of time there, in that garden. But the next time we met was in the bookshop, remember?'

'No idea what you're talking about.' He grinned at her. 'Just kidding . . .'

'There have been many men . . . But that confusion then, I never felt it again.' She looked at him and brought her face closer to his. 'They say the eyes are the windows to the soul . . . When I look into your eyes now . . .'

'You said I had a dark soul . . .'

'A dark soul that scared the butterflies away, yes. I was talking nonsense. Trying to make an impression, I think.'

'Maybe that's what's so confusing,' he said. 'I don't think I've ever felt as sad as I did today, or it must have been when we buried Raylan, but back then it felt a lot . . . bleaker, like there was a black hole inside my body. Heavy and hollow at the same time. But today . . .' He heaved a deep sigh. 'Today it seemed full . . . Missing her felt, strangely enough . . . no longer alone. Now I know why. It's . . .'

He looked away and peered into the darkness.

'It's what?' she whispered.

'It's because . . .' He spoke so softly she could barely hear him. '. . . because you're here. It's because of you.'

She took his face in her hands, turned it towards her, stood on tiptoe and kissed him on both eyelids.

'That calls for a drink,' he said with an awkward smile. She let go of him, and they headed to the kitchen, where he uncorked a bottle of red wine, which he took to the living room along with two glasses.

'He saved my life. Did you know that?' she said after they'd both taken their first sips in silence on the sofa.

'Raylan? When?'

'On the day of the Saur Revolution. I don't know why he was there, at the Presidential Palace. But he was the one who came after me when I ran into the main hall from the garden, away from the planes and the bombs . . . I never knew how I got out . . . it haunted my dreams. Walls cracking, grit, dust and blood everywhere, and I hear shouting and screaming and yet I'm . . . I'm flying through the marble corridors, as if I've got wings. I'm floating . . . towards the light . . .'

She took a few sips, choked and coughed, so he patted her gently on the back.

447

'At the ceremony it all came flooding back, everything that must have been buried deep inside ... His face. It was so close. For just a split second. I'm in a jeep that drives off and I'm looking back and ... he's watching me go ...'

They were silent for a while. Then Paul raised his glass. 'To Daddy. Your knight in shining armour.'

She looked at him in surprise. 'That sounds rather cynical.'

'I have my own feelings about Ray ...'

'Are you judging him for what he had with my mother?'

He took a big swig and flashed her a sardonic grin. 'It's a bit late for that.'

'Where were you on the day of the revolution?' she asked after a while.

'At the airport. It was chaos with all those foreigners trying to get out. He made it in the end ... The way we sat there on that plane, exhausted, and empty too, I'll never forget it. Isobel was crying without a sound. Raylan sat hunched over the whole time, his hands covering the bruises on his face. All I could do was stare out of the window, at nothing but darkness. When we arrived in the Netherlands, it rained non-stop for days on end. Not a single newspaper mentioned what had happened in Kabul. There was nothing on television. It was too far away, another world. And nobody was interested in the piece Raylan had written. His colleagues at the *AND* didn't even believe him. It was a domestic coup, they said. The Russians weren't capable of organizing such a thing. When, around Christmas time, Russian tanks were suddenly driving through the streets of Kabul, they knew he'd been right all along. Too bad he didn't live to see that day.'

'He said he'd never go to war again. Then why did he travel to Cambodia?'

Paul blew a bunch of smoke rings. 'You can compare it to an alcoholic who hasn't touched a drop in a while. He'll still be an alcoholic for the rest of his life. Raylan was addicted to war. He'd converted the farmhouse stables into a studio for Isobel. He'd planted his own vegetable garden. He even had plans to set up a stud farm. But when *The New York Times* called to say that the Vietnamese were about to invade Cambodia to quash Pol Pot and his murderous Khmer Rouge regime, he couldn't get to the airport fast enough. I remember us dropping him off. He crouched down in front of me and he said, *This will be the last time, kiddo.*'

Paul lowered his head and took a sip. 'He was right, too, the bastard.' He lit a new cigarette and took a few deep drags.

'One afternoon, this car pulled up. I remember it like it was yesterday, a Wednesday; I know because we didn't have school on Wednesday afternoons. I'd never seen such a strange licence plate. It belonged to the Corps Diplomatique.'

He took another long drag and held the smoke for several seconds before blowing it out in a long, thin stream.

'Isobel had a nervous breakdown when she heard they'd found his body. Edward and I thought she'd go mad ... mad with grief, with despair. Sometimes, in the middle of the night, I'd wake with a start and hear her in the distance ... She'd be wandering around the fields somewhere, half-naked. Like a feral animal, howling ... But she always let me bring her back. I'd stick her under a hot shower, put her to bed and wait for her to fall asleep.'

'How old were you at the time?'

'Ten ...'

'God ...'

'I felt really lost, you know ... I was afraid to go to school. I was always looking for a fight. I'd lash out at the drop of a hat; you wouldn't believe how many bloody noses and bruises I got ... But then Edward took me under his wing. Thanks to him, I didn't lose it completely.'

'What about Isobel?'

'One day, she was back in her studio. She realized that she could bring him back by painting him. She kept making the same portrait over and over again: Raylan, as she'd first seen him in that marketplace. She painted day and night. Obsessively. Until she'd managed to portray him exactly as she remembered him. Then she started building an entire city around him. Kabul as she'd known it for ten years. With each painting she seemed to recover herself a little.'

He got to his feet, picked up his laptop, opened it and showed her his screen saver. It was a colourful tableau. In the foreground of a busy market, two traders rolled out a bright-red carpet while fabrics in a range of soft hues hung on either side of the street. And walking among the passers-by and gesticulating traders, where the sun illuminated the scene like a spotlight, were a tanned man in jeans and a blonde woman in a blue kaftan with a little boy between them.

'Pul-e Khishti bazaar,' she exclaimed in delight.

'The Chapelle trio,' Paul replied. 'She was painting herself with Raylan and me in a world where she could be happy again. A world that no longer existed. But it helped her, it allowed her to believe in something again. Even though it was an illusion.'

Farah finished her wine and stared into space for a long time. 'They acted with the best intentions, Paul. But they were only human, our parents, each with their own flaws, just like us.'

'What do you mean?'

'That we shouldn't see ourselves as victims of their past. We're the children of people who loved each other.'

She took the empty glass from his hand. He slung an arm around her shoulder and rested his head against her chest.

3
Farah and Paul

2009

The hulking Burdenko military hospital loomed up through the last few patches of morning fog. Built more than two hundred years ago to attend to the wounded from the front lines, these days it was off-limits for ordinary soldiers, an impregnable bastion. It had been annexed by communist leaders and the military elite. Years ago, it was here that Boris Yeltsin had surgery on his spleen.

In the large marble lobby, a uniformed receptionist handed visitor's passes to Farah and Paul after first thoroughly checking their passports and press cards. Two guards were ready to escort them to the seventh and top floor of the building. Whatever these men had learned during their training, it certainly hadn't included conversational skills. Without a word they led Farah and Paul up through the glass-fronted stairwell, which, the higher they went, offered increasingly breathtaking views of neighbouring Lefortovo Park.

After one guard repeatedly pressed the bell beside the padded door on the seventh floor but got no response, the other used a plastic pass to access a space so large and luxurious it could have been a presidential suite. Classical music came from the speakers. The aroma of freshly brewed coffee filled the room. On a table stood a basket with croissants and three small plates with toppings. Next to the unread morning paper on the table was a torn-open envelope with a striking seal.

A sliding glass door opened out on to a wide terrace. There, in a purple dressing gown and with his back to them, stood Valentin

Lavrov, his posture rigid, his gaze on an aeroplane leaving a long vapour trail along the grey horizon.

One of the guards looked at his watch. 'You have fifteen minutes.' Then they left the room.

Farah's heart was racing as she walked out to the terrace. Lavrov turned around with difficulty. It had been less than two weeks since she'd faced him in Jakarta, down in the vaults among the dusty temple statues, soaked and leaning on her left leg, ready to finish him off with one last kick. Only now did she see the outcome of their fight: the neck collar, the fading bruises on his angular face, the swollen nose covered with a large skin-coloured plaster. His musky odour almost made her retch. The moment she looked into his grey-green eyes, she was transported back to that time at his villa on Lake Glubokoe. The same fear and tension she'd felt back then now resurfaced. Breathe, she told herself. Keep breathing.

'An avenging angel with the body and power of an oriental tiger.' He sounded lighthearted and condescending at the same time. 'That's how the emcee announced you in that theatre in Amsterdam, wasn't it?'

She stared at him in amazement. 'You were there?'

'I watched you from the royal box. The way you stood there, on that mat, in the spotlight ... You reminded me of a painting by Chagall, *The Struggle of Jacob and the Angel*. I began to wonder what it would be like to look deep into my black-haired angel's bright blue eyes until dawn, as I fought her over and over again, just like in the biblical story of Jacob.'

The urge. The desire to kill him. Here and now. 'I think by now you've lost that fight,' she said.

'We've reached the point where there are no more winners,' Lavrov replied. He moved his right hand to the music. 'Listen ... This is Rachmaninov's *Isle of the Dead*. The ferryman takes the deceased to an island in the middle of a lake. The oars move through the water, in five-eight time.'

Without looking at him, he addressed Paul. 'You're a smoker. You must have a cigarette for me.'

She nodded to Paul, who hesitantly took out a packet of Davidoff Classic.

Lavrov leaned forwards and inhaled deeply after Paul gave him a light with his Zippo. 'Apparently a new cosmos emerges every several hundred thousand years,' he said, as he held the burning end of the cigarette to the letter, which quickly caught fire. 'The old one simply burns up. And out of the ashes rises a new . . .'

'Bullshit,' Paul said. 'You can't undo the past.'

The remnants of the letter curled up red-hot until the black ash fell on to the terrace tiles like rain. Lavrov flicked the cigarette over the railing and raised his finger as he listened intently to the music. 'Here the boat sails into the inlet. It arrives at the shore. The deceased has reached his final resting place.'

'Why did she have to die?' Anger was palpable in every word of Paul's question.

Lavrov looked at him with an amused smile. 'The first thing a child does is ask why. It can go on forever. Every answer can trigger another "why". Besides . . . truth is a relative concept. Your father knew that.'

'We're not here to talk about my father.'

'*The Great Lie* . . . In how many countries was it published?'

'We're talking about Anya.'

'Have you ever wondered how frustrating it must have been for your father that no one believed him when he disclosed the truth behind the Saur Revolution in Kabul?'

'Why did she have to die?'

'Nothing worse for a journalist than being called a liar, right? Perhaps it was for the best that he was shot in Cambodia.'

It all happened much faster than Farah could have anticipated. She yelled at Paul, but it was too late. Lavrov's grin split in two when Paul's fist hit his chin. Lavrov swayed. He tried to grab on to Farah, but was already so unsteady that he ended up sprawled on the terrace tiles. Paul looked like a predator, ready to devour Lavrov. 'Go back inside!' she shouted, leaping between them.

'Finish it,' she heard Lavrov say.

'Please, Paul,' she begged. 'Go inside.'

Paul didn't seem to hear her at first. His eyes and contorted face betrayed the rage that burned inside him. At any moment, he might lash out again, wildly, like a man possessed.

'Finish it,' Lavrov repeated. His lips turned dark-red with the blood spurting from his mouth. 'Isn't that the real reason you're here? This is your chance. Take it.'

Abruptly, Paul turned around and walked back into the apartment.

Lavrov held out his hand to her. After a brief hesitation, she grabbed it and pulled him up. The blood had stained his snow-white neck brace.

'The hostage situation at the Seven Sisters . . .' His sputtering made him sound even more fragile than he already looked. 'Vakurov lost control. I never meant to have you . . . All you had to . . .'

'Why did you want your own father dead?' Her question sounded almost casual. 'Did you hate him because he never acknowledged your existence, even though he must've known about you all along?'

Lavrov was silent. His icy stare at Farah made her feel as if she'd ended up in the Siberian permafrost.

'The police report at the time is quite explicit,' she continued. 'Michailov lay in a pool of blood, having sustained over thirty stab wounds. All inflicted with the same knife. The perpetrator had acted in a blind rage before fleeing in a panic. Fingerprints on the knife. A trail of blood in the stairwell. For the detective on the case it was as easy as one-two-three. But he was ordered to destroy the evidence.'

She walked away from Lavrov, as if to lay claim to every square inch of the terrace, and stood by the railing, casting a dizzying glance over the edge.

'You don't have any real power over your opponent until you know their secrets,' she said before turning around and calmly observing him. 'The evidence was preserved all these years. It's in our possession now. We'll make it public soon, along with all your other dirty secrets.'

Lavrov looked at her coldly. 'All those fabrications of yours, the press and its fake news.'

She walked straight at him. 'I'm giving you the opportunity here and now to comment on the way you intimidated and blackmailed politicians from countries you did business with.'

'Fabrications.'

'The secret channels through which corporate profits were channelled to private bank accounts in foreign tax havens.'

'Falsehoods.'

'The assassinations of people like Anya, who were threatening to expose those secrets.'

'Made-up facts.'

'The plan to depose the Russian president.' She saw his face turn ashen. 'Operation Icarus.'

'An outright lie.'

'But there's a rock-solid logic behind that lie,' said Paul, standing between the sliding doors. 'Russia is facing the biggest economic crisis in its history. This, in combination with the rapid rise of foreign rivals, is fatal for an energy company like AtlasNet. Especially when you consider that the main shareholder, the Russian president, is a man who's focused on short-term results and uses his power of the veto to block any kind of innovation or big investments. That leaves only one way to safeguard your interests: overriding the main shareholder, in other words, breaking the president's power.'

'An ingenious theory,' said Lavrov, outwardly calm. 'It sounds just as implausible as that conspiracy theory about the Saur Revolution your father once invented.'

Paul held up his mobile phone in an almost triumphant gesture. Alexei Ardahev's voice came out of the small speaker: *Whatever possessed you, only God knows, but with your actions you put our entire project at risk.*

Paul paused the recording. 'Two weeks ago. Battersea Power Station.'

Lavrov's face resembled a death mask. 'I'm not surprised you're springing this on me . . .' He then turned to Farah. 'But you?' He spat blood on the tiles. 'You two aren't journalists. Merely the messengers of a frustrated FSB director.'

'Are we done here?' Paul asked.

'Absolutely,' answered Farah, staring at Lavrov.

This time the two guards walked behind Farah and Paul as they descended the flights of steps in the echoey glass-walled stairwell. She felt empty, as if she'd spent all of her energy in the short space of fifteen minutes. She couldn't believe it was finally over, any more than she could believe that the man-shaped figure was something more than just a purple dressing gown.

A gown alone would never have fallen so fast.

You'd expect it to flutter capriciously, maybe even bulge a bit, as prey for the wind. But there was a body inside that dressing gown. A body with arms flailing as if the hands desperately wanted to grab on to something.

It all happened in silence, because the falling man didn't make a sound. Or perhaps the thick glass muffled a long-drawn-out cry.

Halfway down the stairs, they stopped and stared. As if neither of them could believe what they'd just witnessed. Only when the commotion in the downstairs lobby filtered through to them did they go on their way again.

4
Paul

2009

A sharp evening wind blew fierce raindrops into Paul's face. The crumpled map of Novodevichy cemetery he was holding had all but turned into a damp rag. He stopped at a spot with freshly churned soil and looked at the metal marker hammered into the ground. That's how Anya would have liked it if she'd had a say, he thought to himself. Plain and rusty, with only her name, date of birth and the day she died engraved in it.

The sound of drops hitting an open umbrella behind him told him he was no longer alone.

'*Non omnis moriar*, that ought to be on it too. "Not all of me will die",' Alexander Arlazarov translated. He'd approached Paul without him noticing and now looked out over the surrounding graves. 'Many people find this a sinister place. Especially after dark. But I come here a lot, I like to walk among all the prominent historical figures. I'm not exactly sure where, but I know there's a poet buried here. Not all that famous, I believe. In fact, I don't even know his name. But one of his female fans apparently attempted to take her own life on top of his tomb.'

A siren sounded in the distance.

'Anya was of the same calibre as you and your Afghan colleague Hafez: fanatic, unstoppable and with the same penchant for self-destruction. Although you know that one day you'll lose the battle, you keep going until you've achieved what you set out to do.' Arlazarov gallantly held his umbrella over Paul's head. 'I can arrange an apartment for the two of you. Downtown, somewhere on Ulitsa Arbat. You'll feel at home there, I'm sure. Stay in Moscow, my dear Chapelle. You and Hafez will enjoy my protection, and I will guarantee you access to the best sources. You can be the new John Reed and Louise Bryant.'

Paul stared at the metal marker on Anya's grave. 'Of the same calibre . . .' He turned to Arlazarov. 'Anya fought men like you.'

'Anya Kozlova fought a lot of things, but most of all herself.'

'She fought for the truth.'

'How noble. But what you're forgetting, my dear fellow, is that people don't always want to hear the truth. They want to be reassured, above all else.'

'What was in the letter Lavrov had received?' Paul asked.

'What letter?'

Paul took the envelope out of the inside pocket of his jacket and pointed to the presidential seal. 'As well as co-owners of the same company, the president and Lavrov appeared to be pen pals as well. What was in it that prompted him to jump off the balcony?'

'I genuinely don't know,' Arlazarov replied, but his sardonic grin suggested otherwise.

'I guess,' Paul said, 'you should never bite the hand that feeds you. Because then it can no longer protect you. It sounds a bit morbid in light of recent developments, but his coup plans meant that Valentin Lavrov had a price on his head . . .'

'Your words, good fellow, your words. Consider my proposal. It's not every day you get an offer like this.'

'I must admit,' Paul said, 'our collaboration was unique. But also a one-off.' He gave Arlazarov a friendly nod and walked towards the gate. The two men waiting for him there remained as immobile as the statues of the dead that he'd passed.

PART SEVEN
A Chamber of Solace

I

Farah

It was as if she were looking into her own bright-blue eyes. The way he stood there in his leather jacket, his half-unbuttoned denim shirt, the scruffy jeans tucked into the cowboy boots, the rugged blond figure with the angular jawline and stubble. Not to mention that grin with which he kept staring at her. No wonder it had made Isobel weak at the knees at the time.

'The moment I saw him, after he'd ducked for cover under that stall, I fell in love with him.' Isobel had been soft-spoken when she met her at the farmhouse. A beautiful, charming woman, who looked just as eccentric as she had in her younger years, with her dark eye make-up, henna-blonde hair, dangling earrings and clinking bracelets on both wrists, in a gorgeous silk blouse and a flaring dark skirt swishing around her legs.

'Raylan is like a star to me,' she'd said. 'A star that died a long time ago, but one I can still see. And when I see him, I feel complete.'

Now her star was hanging here, in one of the largest rooms of the National Museum of Afghanistan, life-size and in vivid hues, at the heart of a retrospective full of panoramic paintings of the city that Isobel had called home for ten years. A city she returned to, like a time traveller, every single day when she stepped inside her studio.

'I don't feel the need to go there in person,' she'd said when Farah came up with the idea of exhibiting her paintings in Kabul. 'Why don't you take care of it all.' When they hugged, Farah had felt the underlying reason. Isobel's body was almost as fragile as the memories she'd captured on canvas.

As she stared at Raylan, Farah felt the fingers of the small hand in hers.

She looked into Sekandar's eyes.

'He was her *dunya*,' she told him. 'The man of her dreams. Her world.'

'I know,' the boy said. 'She told me.' Then he chuckled. 'He looks like Paul. Is he your *dunya*?'

She smiled. 'One day I'll tell you the whole story.'

Without realizing it, he wiped his lips and then looked at his hand. He did that countless times a day. And he was always amazed that his hands came away clean, that they weren't covered in greasy streaks of bright lipstick. He rubbed his eyelids at least as often, only to discover that his fingers bore no residue of black kohl.

When the Ariana Afghan Airlines plane began its descent, he'd anxiously squeezed her hand. Together they'd walked to the exit and had paused at the top of the flight stairs. Down below, his father, mother and brother and sisters were nervously waiting for him. The first thing he did was wave at the man portrayed on a huge billboard covering the terminal building's façade, welcoming him to the land of the brave.

His mother could barely stop crying when she hugged him. The father had stood there like he'd done that day in the camp when he recognized his long-lost son in the photo. His face twisted with apprehension, he could do no more than repeatedly pat the boy on the head.

In the arrivals hall, the secretary-general of the interior, Ahmad Shakoor, had addressed the assembled press. In a bombastic speech, he'd outlined how Sekandar had threatened to become a symbol of repression, but that government intervention had given him a safe and dignified passage back to his homeland so he could build a new future with his family.

Farah couldn't imagine that anyone in the crowd believed a single word of what Shakoor was saying and she thought of her article, in which she'd spoken out strongly against Afghanistan's legal system, which continued to treat child sexual abuse victims as offenders. Children weren't protected from what had happened to them but punished for it. In response to the article, the United States Department of Defense had issued a statement saying that although it was familiar with the phenomenon of 'tea boys' working as servants for Afghan military units on international army bases, it had never been aware of any sexual abuse. And if it had happened, it would have been beyond the remit of ISAF soldiers.

Exactly three days later this was refuted in no uncertain terms by a Canadian soldier, who'd contacted CNN with the story that in late 2006, at the Canadian compound just outside the southern city of Kandahar, he'd witnessed the brutal rape of a little boy by Afghan security personnel. He'd reported it at the time, but the Canadian Forces National Investigation Service had found no evidence of rape and had closed their investigation with the conclusion: 'It didn't happen.'

But the genie was out of the bottle.

On CBS, a prominent US senator lashed out at politicians and military leaders who dismissed Farah's article and the Canadian soldier's account as fake news. 'The international forces,' he said, 'would have us believe that every day brings us another victory in Afghanistan, but if only a fraction of what is now emerging about the abuse of Afghan children and the US authorities possibly turning a blind eye is true, then we are in fact suffering major defeats, which cry out for a large-scale independent inquiry.'

As if in anticipation of this, the Afghan Interior Ministry, through Secretary-General Shakoor, announced the appointment of a special commission which was to investigate reports of *bacha bazi* practices. Pending the investigation, General Hafami had been temporarily denied access to Camp Eggers and other military bases.

Perhaps what Paul had said in Moscow was true: nice words usually don't get you very far when reality knocks. Right now, though, none of this mattered. She was with Sekandar, in a building that, having been in ruins for thirty years, was now being restored to its original state. Once it had felt like her second home. As a child, her loneliness disappeared as soon as Uncle Parwaiz took her by the hand and escorted her through these rooms. He let her hold the golden crown worn centuries earlier by a young princess in Bactria, she'd greeted the sun god Surya in his celestial chariot and had blushed when she saw the river goddess and the Greek soldier together. Every room had felt like a chamber of solace to her.

'Someday this place will be just as beautiful as it once was,' she said to Sekandar. 'When I was little it was full of statues and other artifacts, and paintings as far as the eye could see.'

Fascinated, he stopped in front of a centuries-old painting of a dragon with ferocious wings and a fire-breathing human head cleaving the air. 'That's a *simurgh*,' she said. 'It lives on top of a mountain high enough to touch heaven. It knows everything, its wings are as wide as the clouds and its feathers have magical powers. One day it came across a foundling and took the boy to its nest above the clouds. The *simurgh* cared for the child, taught him the language of humans and told him all about the world. Then he brought the boy back to his father and gave him a feather. The boy was to carry it with him at all times. If he was ever in danger all he had to do was throw it into the fire, and the *simurgh* would come and help him again.'

Sekandar looked at her in surprise. Then a smile crept over his face. 'You're my *simurgh*.'

'But I can't fly,' Farah said.

'Don't worry,' he replied. 'I'll teach you.'

Flapping his arms, he ran ahead of her through the museum's large entry hall, where employees were busy placing the marble statue of King Kanisha back on its pedestal.

Ithaka

In his poem 'Ithaka', the Greek poet Cavafy describes an imaginary voyage to what Homer in the *Odyssey* describes as 'the furthest out to sea, towards the sunset'. For Cavafy the island of Ithaka symbolizes a dream destination. But it's the actual journey that really matters. It's the journey to the chosen destination that gives you the wisdom of new insights and experiences.

> As you set out for Ithaka,
> Hope your road is a long one,
> Full of adventure, full of discovery.

I consider the more than seven years I spent writing the entire Heartland Trilogy to be such a journey. And while the destination was always in my sights, many unexpected developments, twists and inspiring encounters occurred along the way. Many remarkable people have accompanied me on this voyage, each in their own unique way. They guided me through storms and windless days, helped me repair damage, steered me through shallows and past dangerous cliffs, led me in unexpected directions and to ports I would never otherwise have discovered. I have thanked most of them in the two previous books.

Thanks again to Jihane El Fahidi for her candid stories, which inspired me to create Farah as the trilogy's central character. Thanks to Lola Kawa for her translations from Dari, and Hans Scheerder for the engaging way in which he helped me to describe Paul's farewell to Anya as credibly as possible.

Thanks to Eva Reinders, who was there from the outset of the journey. Thanks to those who helpfully looked over my shoulder at the compass: editors Leo Boekraad, Baukje Brugman and Diana Sno. Publishers Steven Maat at AW Bruna, Tom Harmsen at Luitingh-Sijthoff and the always inspiring Geneviève Waldmann.

> Keep Ithaka always in your mind,
> Arriving there is what you're destined for.
> But don't hurry the journey at all,
> Better if it lasts for years.

Thanks to Marianne Schönbach, who was prepared to be my agent, travel companion and friend for the seven years of this trilogy and who gave me the confidence to continue whenever I was close to lowering the sails.

Writing *The City and the Fire* brought three new people on board whose knowledge, passion and empathy provided a wealth of new experiences and who guided me until I reached 'my' Ithaka. My thanks to Ad van Workum and Annemije Melse, and a deep bow to Donjah Hartsuijker.

And all this time there was one person who made me realize how exceptional this journey had to be: my wife and my love, Nicole.

> Ithaka gave you the marvellous journey.
> Without her you wouldn't have set out.
> She has nothing left to give you now.
> And if you find her poor, Ithaka won't have fooled you:
> Wise as you will have become, so full of experience,
> You'll have understood by then what these Ithakas mean.

C. P. Cavafy (translated by Edmund Keeley
and Philip Sherrard)

Baarn, the Netherlands
18 January 2019
Walter Lucius